It was at Michigan State I took to reading. This novel about stories comes from years of taking notes i whatd is the tasking myself important slice of I've most important whats to others to see.

Enjoy
Carl O'Donnell Knupp

Reconnections

From the Author Of . . .

A Cold War Teacher's Tale: The Challenges, Fun and Historic Moments with Our American Schools Overseas

" . . . Carol Knych tells an entertaining and informative story about the troops and supporting personnel stationed abroad during the Cold War period. Her love of family and love of country color every page." – *Terry Tanner*

" . . . Knych parallels her story with Cold War history and we are reminded of glasnost, perestroika, Gorbachev and Reagan, and how deadly serious the cold war actually was." – *Martha Zarikow*

Available on Amazon in Kindle or paperback editions:
https://www.amazon.com/dp/1502903571/

Reconnections

A Novel about a Family's Attempt to Make a Difference, and the Renewal of Love in their Lives

First Printing – 2016

ISBN-13:
978-1540493774

ISBN-10:
1540493776

Cover Design By: Cyrus Kirkpatrick (Author / Editor / Graphic Designer for Authors)

Dedicated To . . .

The memory of family beckons many to return, share, and reconnect with those forever left behind. That pull is often ignored or shaken off, to march onward. This book is dedicated to the stout souls who choose to return. Accompany three generations of a flawed but loving family returning to their roots. Experience each member's growth until, at last, their lives expand and renew. They return to America, shaken from the boredom of their daily expectations and galvanized to make sure they are present and direct in their lives. To anyone who has answered that pull, I dedicate this book.

Contents

Acknowledgments

My special thanks go to Meg Files, Ken Vorndran, Steven Salmoni, Leta Sharp and Molly McCloy—writing teachers at Pima Community College, who urged us to use new techniques and points of view. As my classmates gave me feedback and asked clarifying questions, my skills improved and I gained confidence.

Colleagues Brett Havens, Sandy Scherer-Baker, Shelly Kleeman, and Lloyd Tucker helped me begin creating this fictional story and place it in the settings we'd explored when traveling to Poland. My writing group in Tucson helped me focus those efforts. Mary Lynch, Mary Bellin, Ann Kuperberg, Carlos Alianze, Lorna Kramer, Terry Tanner, Geraldine Pietras, Brett Havens, Annie Kennedy, Sandra Lamar and Judith Petres Balogh were crucial to my evolution.

My sisters, Kate Cloud and Ellen O'Donnell, and my brothers, Tom and Pat O'Donnell, suggested revisions along the way. My Nazareth Academy classmates read my blog and urged me on. I especially thank my children, Genevieve, Michael, John, Charlie and Andrew. They were interested readers—even before it became interesting.

Military families were crucial in my writing and in our lives. Their contributions made the US presence reassuring to Europeans, and our lives richer. I thank them for seeing that 940 copies of my non-fiction book A COLD WAR TEACHER'S TALE are being read all over the world. I'm honored to be friended by so many on Facebook.

This brings me to my husband of 54 years, Bob Knych. Without Bob's shouldering cooking duties as he encouraged me to take 2 writing courses a year, this novel would never have seen daylight. Bob fostered my interest in Polish immigrants, their roots, and family members left behind. I was curious about how they're doing today.

Though my plot is pure fiction—we never ran into a Polish swindle and there was no Gienia in our lives, Bob's gutsy friendliness, curiosity, and urge to make himself helpful underlies the tale. His input colors these pages—though the plot twists are inventions and no reflection on him. He drove our family into Poland 15 times during our service to the US military. Occasionally, when asked about something he didn't know, he invented facts. I believe I've managed to weed those out.

Since my retirement I've belonged to an ever changing group of retirees who meet in Tucson's Village Bakehouse daily. They helped me maintain balance and interest. I thank Helen Fisher, Joy Jennings, Diane Winslow, Bill Neal, Steve and Marty Plevel (who kindly drew "Annie's Map"), Maxine Skelley, plus Mike Sheehan, now deceased, who enriched my plot and my life.

Finally, I owe a great debt to Cyrus Kirkpatrick, who discussed governments with my son, Andrew, as Cyrus prepared for travel to North Korea to observe life there. Since then he's toured Europe and met people from all over. Along the way, Cyrus met a professional Polish writer, Janusz Tuchowski, who proof read my tale before the last edit. He and Cyrus could sense if my fiction rang true.

Janusz informed me that absent accent marks was regarded as misspelling in Polish. I changed names affected, and I hope excluding accents in speech where they were needed won't be too distressing to Polish readers. Jan, Cyrus and Heidi Bonner helped me avoid other missteps. Cyrus has published his own material and learned from formatting my Cold War book. I am ever grateful to him. Special thanks go to my son, Andrew, who reintroduced me to Cyrus and taught me the computer skills that made this telling possible. He'd show me a procedure then insist, "Use your head, Mom. Just use your head."

When Andrew wasn't available Sebastian Perez took over. Despite the excellent help I've received I realize I've left out many who helped me along the way. You know who you are, and I thank you too. I edited the final draft, so any errors that remain are my responsibility. I pray they are few and you are free to enjoy a good read.

Major Characters

(Note: To be used as a reference. Spoilers are present!)

American Winowskis

Joe – Son of Victor, nephew of Ted and Stella, husband of Kate, father of four, he teaches accounting at Oakland Jr. College. His carpentry hobby, shared with his twin sons, is his dream. He bought space to expand the day his sons won scholarships, leaving him unable to meet his expenses. His dilemma follows him on the family trip to Poland that changes all their lives.

Uncle Ted or Tadeusz – Elderly immigrant Uncle Ted aims to use his retirement money to help extended family in Poland. He feels compelled to bring peace to his brother. Ted's insistence that Joe and his family go too throws the family into conflict. Will their values sustain them?

Kate – Joe's Irish-American wife, mother of Sarah, Brad, Andy, and Annie. Kate teaches English at Oakland. She reluctantly joins trip as a steady hand, until secrets confound her.

Brad and Andy – Twin sons of Joe & Kate who developed a carpentry business with Joe. Their abandoning Joe's dream leaves him unable to meet his expenses and begins Joe's trail of lies.

Annie – Seventeen-year-old daughter whose poor judgment indicates she's too immature to go away to college. Joe insists she accompany them on their trip to Poland with startling results.

Aunt Stella – wife of Ted, aunt to Joe and Annie and friend to Kate. She is wise and supportive.

Polish Winowskis

Dziadziu (Grandfather) – Patriarch of the Winowski clan, the father of Victor, Leszek and Ted. He insisted Joe's father, Victor, switch his brother's names on the immigration papers for the US. The results affect his family long after his death.

Leszek – Ted's brother, left behind before WWII. He's beaten by communists for Ted's rabble-rousing. Letters read in 1993 inspire him to blame his lifelong friend, Staisu, for the name switch that kept them from going to the US. Ted's gratitude and guilt toward Leszek power the story.

Staisu – Blamed for the switch. Ted's determined to restore their bond as a last gift to his brother.

Victor – Joe's father, brother of Leszek and Ted. He regretted coming to the US to work in factories and had depressions that affected Joe as a child. He switched his brother's names and never admitted his father, Dziadziu, ordered that switch.

Babcia (Grandmother) – Matriarch, widow of Dziadziu, mother of Victor, Ted, Leszek.

Piotr – Leszek's grandson, who worked in Germany for his American cousin, Fred. He and wife, Karolina, are the first relatives visited. They have ideas for business Uncle Ted aimed to help but their attitude toward repaying debt within the family stalls the plan.

Marek – Polish driver who joins the family as a guide. He introduces them to Tatyana Dorsak and later helps unravel a plot. He's worked with Piotr and they plan to help his imprisoned girlfriend, Claire.

Claire – Marek's girlfriend, jailed for stealing a jacket for Marek. Joe tries to earn her release..

K – A lonesome Detroit accountant Joe taught business Polish to before he accepted his job in Warsaw. He lends the family his Mercedes and helps Joe locate people and information.

Gienia – Joe's lost love from when he was in the army in Germany. She seems to offer relief.

Tatyana Dorsak – A stylish woman in her early forties with 3 young daughters, hired by swindlers to rope in foreign investors. Joe is determined to help her & her young daughters.

Majka-Faldo – A clever swindler trying to get Uncle Ted to invest in phony stock in Poland.

Inspector Skrzycki – A Polish detective K. contacts about swindlers after Ted's money. He is determined to disrupt criminals but he is hampered by law.

1 - HAMTRAMCK

Some people have cherished dreams they hardly admit, even to themselves. The day Joe Winowski overheard his twins, Brad and Andy, include his most cherished dream in their life plan, he backed away from the workshop door to collect himself.

Solid Brad told his slighter brother, "If we went to college here in Detroit and used Dad's little shop of horrors to engineer our own designs, we'd have our business up and going before most guys our age finish their degrees."

Andy gave his brother a playful punch, "We'd get our degree without a huge debt and take this carpentry sideline into a real business. Dad wouldn't mind our getting off to a quick start. He'd enjoy helping us take off, I know he would."

Mind? Joe had to restrain himself to keep from running in to throw his arms around them.

Brad hopped off his workbench to say, "Why should we wait for those exclusive schools to give us a nod? The

University of Detroit is respected, and our hands-on experience from working here can't be beat. Let's go for it."

Joe hadn't put the words in their mouths. They'd been talking to each other. They didn't even know he was there, but if he could improve their work space, help things go more quickly for them, well, what couldn't they do?

Inspired by hope, yet knowing their goals could shift quickly Joe called old man Pateck. "Are you ready to sell me your space yet?"

To Joe's astonishment, this time Pateck said, "Come tomorrow at six with your ten-thousand down. We'll carry the mortgage for a thousand a month. My son, Eddie, is ready to sign."

New possibilities flashed before Joe's eyes. Sure, at fifty-five he knew the negatives. He'd have to back his son's ideas, and some weren't real practical (like the couch shaped like an airplane wing), but those boys were good workers and with them on board what couldn't they do? He'd keep his job teaching accounting until they got going, but with him out of the way for hours at a time, they'd feel they were in control. Joe laughed out loud when he couldn't think of any good reason why they couldn't create their own dynasty right here in Detroit.

He'd back up, let them lead. They'd ask him for advice and he'd restrain himself. He'd be the experienced "white beard" every new business needs. He'd be there to meet rush orders and he had the life experience they lacked, he thought. They'd turn to him, and they'd cross new frontiers together.

Joe was almost as excited as when Kate agreed to marry him. Why, he thought, Kate would be stunned. She wouldn't believe he could restrain himself, but he'd prove her wrong. Overwhelmed by emotion, Joe decided to keep his plans to himself till the deed was done. He'd behave as usual, keep his head down, and savor the moment.

The next day Joe honked once as he pulled up in front of the boarded up bay-windows of Pateck's Meat Market. He imagined those windows waited for him, Joe Winowski, to rip off their blinders and bring light inside. In his mind's eye the walls hung with tools designed to transform wood into the furniture that people rushed to buy. He loved the smell of fine wood and he'd honed his skills to make sure every piece fashioned by Winowski and Sons' Carpentry shone with the craftsmanship lost to men the minute workers first walked upon a factory floor. He'd seen too many fine men burn out young, with no way to express their talents within a factory setting. But Joe and his boys, they'd create beautiful, functional furniture they'd be proud to sell.

Joe leapt out of his car and sprinted up the enclosed stairwell on the outside of the building. On the landing, old man Pateck put out his hand. "Come in, have tea with me."

Joe looked the old man over, "You're all red. Sit down and I'll pour the tea."

Pateck was thin, but the muscles he'd developed as a butcher remained. "I've been pushing those boxes over for my Eddie to take. Everything else is yours now."

One suitcase and a few boxes held Pateck's possessions. Joe guided him to the Formica-topped table. "I'll get those boxes downstairs for you. Eddie shouldn't be lifting either. He's not a kid anymore."

"I know, I know—my daughter-in-law says they can't do what they want for lookin' after me. 90 year-olds shouldn't expect 70 year-olds to worry about them, I guess." Pateck patted Joe's arm. "I'm just glad you'll put my place to good use."

Joe poured the steeped tea into clear glass cups Pateck's wife had brought from Poland as part of her dowry. He placed them beside a plate of butter cookies.

"Eddie got me into the home real quick. How'd you hear I was ready to sell?"

"I didn't. My boys said they were ready to go all out on our business so I called quick, before they changed their minds. There isn't another place in such good condition nearby. But when you said, 'Come tomorrow,' I almost fell off my chair."

The old man laughed and sat tall.

"We're pay-as-you-go people." Joe spoke matter-of-factly. "My sons applied for engineering scholarships, but no go. Without them they could run up a hundred-thousand-dollars in student debt."

"That's what it costs now days? How are working men supposed to pay that?"

"Well, that's from the best schools and nothing has come through, so yesterday my boys decided they'd work with me and go to the University of Detroit. They can live up here if they want space, but having them around, working with me—that's my dream."

"I'll bet they took notice when you told them I'm ready to sell."

"Sarah's at Michigan State and Annie's still home. I didn't dare open my mouth till I knew your Eddie signed to carry the mortgage. Banks won't touch me with our expenses." Joe paused to shake that distressing fact from his head. "After I tell the family I bought your store, could we come by? Once my boys know this place is ours I don't think I'll be able to hold them back. I'll try to keep the noise down."

"Eddie signed the papers this morning. You hand over that check, mail us your thousand dollars every month and this place is yours. I'm gone."

Joe signed over the ten-thousand-dollar check for the reclaimed wooden artifacts he'd collected from some of Detroit's fine old mansions. The check changed hands so swiftly he didn't have time for regrets.

Then Pateck passed the cookies. "Most kids can't move out of here fast enough."

"I know, I joined the army at twenty-one to get away, but after the Polish girl I fell for in Germany took off on me, this became my haven." They laughed, they sipped, and munched on cookies.

Joe said, "I feel reborn; March 18, 2004. This is my new birthday!"

On the way out he carried Pateck's boxes to the bottom of the stairs, where he used his keys and stepped inside. Tiny slits of light gave a gray hazy sheen to the room. A faint aroma of garlic remained.

He flipped the switch by the door and lights went on from back to front. There wasn't a brick or a floor board out of place. A large broom hung from hooks on the wall. Pateck must have swept up every day, Joe thought. No wonder he was in such good shape.

He imagined the room as it had been, full of hanging dried mushrooms, sausages and jars filled with powerful reminders of celebrations long past. The smells of cured wood would replace the lingering smell of spices soon enough, he thought.

Offering up a prayer of thanks, Joe walked out taller than he'd walked in, picturing a Winowski and Sons' Carpentry sign over the door. Impulsively, he ran a lap around the property, marking his territory like a puppy, then he hopped in his cherished 10-year-old Lincoln and headed across Joseph Campau Avenue, to go home.

# # # # #

Joe turned into the alley behind the house he and the kids had renovated when Kate longed to move to the suburbs. Most of the homes in Hamtramck were built between 1915 and 1925. After he'd found fault with the eighth 'perfect place' Kate found in the suburbs she'd taken a deep breath and found this fixer-upper. Joe and his sons had worked hard to turn this into Kate's dream home, and in so doing, they'd fallen in love with carpentry.

Their home looked typical on the outside, but inside Joe and the boys had installed glowing wooden floors. They'd constructed hand-crafted replicas of Stickley Mission-Style furniture, crowned by several stained glass windows Kate made herself. The house took on a startling prairie-style air, and guests stopped dead when they walked inside. The Hamtramck Citizen had published photos. Their first paying carpentry job followed Kate's showing Marius Kowalski their home.

Joe sat in his car rehearsing aloud in the rear-view mirror. "*Winowski and Sons* is a real business, guys. Old man Pateck sold us his place. There's space to work on your projects while we do commissioned work. We won't waste hours shifting projects and covering things up like now."

Could he paint a mockup sign before they got home? What a hoot'-n-holler they'd make if they spotted that when Kate turned in the alley. He sat there, pleased, joyous, contented. A thousand dollars a month of added expenses loomed large, but they'd honed their skills and were ready to produce high-end pieces that would increase house value for clients in the wealthy suburbs of Detroit. He'd increase his prices. They were a business now. He'd sell individual pieces as heirlooms. Why, they'd earn expenses and have money to spare, he thought. If he pulled this together fast, maybe Kate wouldn't have to teach summer school. Wouldn't it be great if he could give her dream of writing a chance too?

Drunk with hope and gratitude, he plotted calling his mother, Uncle Ted and Aunt Stella, plus his four brothers. Everybody, he'd tell everybody, ready or not. He looked toward the sky, "Hey Pa, when you walked home from the Dodge plant, did you ever dream your wildest boy would run his own business right down the street from where you sweated? Only in America, right?"

Joe sat in his car, talking to himself, grateful Kate and the boys rode home together late on Fridays after their last class. He'd tell the twins right up front, they'd be full partners. He knew he'd have to show restraint and respect. They teased about his being too bossy. Whenever he got repeating himself they'd stop working and chant, "STP, STP, STP" their code for "Stop That Polak"—the signal for their nearest relative to poke their head inside and save them. But they were twenty now, Joe reminded himself. He wanted this business venture to work out badly enough to back off. Oh yes, he told himself, he wanted it that badly.

As Joe stood up beside his car he glimpsed his slim, wild haired, seventeen-year-old daughter bolt out the back door. Annie pranced toward him, waving two envelopes, and threw her arms around him. "They got in, Dad! Can you believe it? Two scholarships to U of M Engineering. They both got one. Now pretend you're surprised when they tell you or they'll kill me."

Latching onto his arm, she pulled him toward the door she'd left wide open. He hid behind her wild auburn curls, grateful she couldn't see his face. The possibility he'd dismissed as a kid's dream struck him like a hammer. The

Winowski and Sons sign he'd pictured only moments before flashed, then burned before his eyes.

Joe said, "Go make tea, Honey. I'll wash up." Joe entered their small downstairs bathroom and splashed water at the disappointment he felt etching itself onto his face. As Kate's car arrived, Annie trumpeted her congratulations from the back door. She ran out to tease her broad-faced brothers, who grabbed for the offers she waved over her head.

Joe joined them as Brad and Andy verified what she'd told them. They hollered and slapped each other before they embraced their mother, Annie, and Joe, in a five way hug. In the uproar, the boys grabbed Annie and Kate to dance into the house, through the kitchen, and into the living room, stomping and twirling as they went. Joe willed their excitement to wash over him as the reality of what he'd done scalded his heart.

Brad said, "Mom, your drilling us for the SATs made this happen."

Sure, Joe knew they'd increased their scores the second time they took the SAT, but he'd thought they only wanted to show each other how smart they were. How had he deluded himself so? He should have heard them; their mother had. He'd mistaken their good-natured cooperation for commitment to his dream. They had every right to their own lives, he reminded himself, but admitting to the financial bind that his decision had put him in now would upset everybody. He'd seen fathers pin their hopes on their kids, then wonder why they fled. No, he'd brought this disaster on himself. His blood roared in his ears as he accepted that. Kate, and later these kids, had restored him after he returned to Hamtramck from his service in Germany, vulnerable and distressed. He owed them better than this mess. He would not put the worry about how he'd manage this extra mortgage on them. He'd work double-time and handle it as best he could. He shook his head as his panic rose.

Kate touched his hand, inviting him to join in this wondrous moment. He took a huge, lung filling breath. Kate had shared his every up and down. He just couldn't tell her the mess he'd created. She deserved better, and if there was anything on God's-green-earth he could do to make this right without distressing her, he'd do it.

Days later, Joe told the family Pateck had gone to a retirement home and he'd asked if they'd give his space a try. He didn't actually say it was free, but he let them think it. All summer, he and his boys worked together in their new space, leaving their free but cramped quarters in Uncle Ted's converted garage. They matched grain to make a finished product of such beauty that women from the wealthier neighborhoods ordered desks, entertainment centers, tables, and kitchen cabinets carved with the finest detail. Brad, Andy, and Joe—backed up by sanding and clean up by Annie, Uncle Ted and Aunt Stella—earned the mortgage payment and more, until the twins left for college.

Then Pateck's shop became a monument to Joe's dashed dreams. After his sons left he avoided their Saturday calls, grieving the loss that stuck in his throat like a burr.

As an accountant, Joe knew he should let the building revert to Pateck. But, the salvage he'd sold to secure the mortgage, he couldn't, he wouldn't, lose that, too, not yet anyway.

Wasn't this the land of opportunity? If there was anything a Polish-American knew, he told himself, it was how to hang on against all odds. So he agreed to any paying job and worked beyond all reason. When he looked over the tools he'd bought that had eaten up the cash he needed, he renewed his efforts. They became his call to action as he still hadn't admitted to anybody he'd bought the building.

After Ted pinned him down directly, he'd allowed the family to think he was renting the space.

Finally, Joe told Kate he wanted to hire men and he needed financial backing to cover their wages and insurance until he established a larger customer base. First People's State Bank and later, kitty-corner at Huntington Bank turned him down. His true debt-to-earning-ratio decided the bankers.

Kate was teaching late the afternoon he was turned down so, even though Uncle Ted had scolded him for forgoing the free work space inside his garage, Joe went to Aunt Stella for a dose of her world class sympathy while Ted napped. Stella and Ted had dropped by the new space often and helped, even as Ted fussed. Stella had smiled at Joe. She'd seen how much better his new set-up was.

Joe had gone to her for understanding about not being able to hire workers, but Stella said maybe they could mortgage their home to help him. Just the thought she'd consider taking on Ted's objections—and he was pretty sure she'd prevail—was something he couldn't allow. They'd worry if their home was on the line. Just the fact she'd offered brought tears to his eyes.

In desperation, he rented out Pateck's apartment upstairs to a student band that needed space to record—he was only using the downstairs. Kate had taught them to write poetry. Then she'd asked Joe, "Could you teach them to track their earnings, just in case their dreams come true?"

Joe tailored his class to those home-grown musicians, as only a junior college teacher can. Excited about "knowing their own shit," as they put it, they'd added the enthusiasm and humor accounting teachers seldom see. Those upstairs apartment walls were soon lined with recording equipment creating disks to sell whenever they played. Their rent paid the utilities and a bit more.

As Joe upped his credit card limit to cover the difference, his conscience throbbed. No fifty-five year old man should still be struggling with right and wrong, he thought. He should have been done with temptations years ago, yet there he sat with the phone in his hand, aiming to deceive Kate. Sure, it was to protect her, he told himself, but he didn't want to explain that to her any time soon. So he prayed Kate wouldn't guess what he'd done before he'd worked them out of danger. Then he begged God's pardon for trying to rope Him in on his deceit.

Kate wasn't one to carry a grudge, but never before had he deliberately deceived her. She'd forgiven his thoughtlessness, even selfishness, but deceitfulness? He was in uncharted territory and he didn't want to put their marriage to that test unless there was absolutely, without a doubt, no other way for him to hop.

2 – BETRAYAL

On Saturday, April 9, 2005, Joe had the shock of his life. He'd expected Uncle Ted and Aunt Stella to be upset at Pope John Paul's death. John Paul was a hero to many Pole's, but Joe never expected family secrets to come spilling out as they mourned. A lifetime of intrigue was dumped on him. Those dear, elderly people he'd loved and cared for his entire life suddenly thought to tell the looming backstory of their frugality.

Joe had sat at their Formica topped table in their 40's style kitchen to hear that Uncle Ted was never meant to come to the US. Ted's brother, Leszek, was supposed to come, until their father wrote to Joe's father, already in the US, demanding he switch his brother's names on the immigration papers.

That poisonous letter had surfaced during their '93 visit to Poland and caused all kinds of grief. Joe had heard the story that his father had confused his brother's names so that Ted came, but to hear that it had been no mistake, that was a jolt. Why would Joe's grandfather have done that, and why had

Victor, Joe's father, taken the blame for confusing his brother's names? Joe couldn't get it all straight.

Stella was talking, "We thought when we returned to Poland in '93 to give away our savings, all the fuss about Ted's coming to America instead of Leszek, would be forgotten. But after Leszek saw that letter he ran off to his son's and we didn't have a chance to give him our money. We came home with most of our money still in the bank in Detroit, and some in our carry-on bag, real worried—but nobody asked to open it. They were more careless then. We felt awful let down."

Joe remembered their return and how little they had to say about their trip. They'd never said clearly what happened that was so terrible—so he'd quit asking.

Ted picked up the story, "But when I saw that last picture of Pope John Paul, when he hit his head against the window, I understood Jesus wants us banging our heads before we can do what He asks of us because it isn't big-shot me that gets things done, it's Him, working through me. I'm our Lord's servant, not some Enron blow-hard."

Stella interrupted him, "Joe, in '93 your mother gave us the letters from Poland your father kept in a box in the attic to take back with us. We read one out loud every night, laughing about a drunken uncle or a lost pig. We didn't know when Leszek pulled out the letter Dziadziu wrote to Victor alone it would be so terrible. Dziadziu said, 'Switch your brother's names on the immigration papers—put Tadeusz name in place of Leszek's. Leszek would work to bring his friend, Stasiu, to America and forget us. Leszek said it, and the boy told me.'"

Ted took over, "Our father, who Leszek loved so dearly, snatched away Leszek's chance for education and a better life. Reading that letter made Leszek's life worse, much worse. We feared he would harm himself. Babcia was sick to hear it. She never knew Dziadziu wrote that letter. Now we have to make it right, we have to Joe, and we need you with us. I can't die peaceful till I do."

Joe hadn't gotten their garbled story straight yet, but he knew he had to get in front of their plan before it was unstoppable. "But Ted, I've got carpentry jobs, three kids in college, and Annie graduating in June. Besides, teachers don't take off mid-semester, and Stella's had pneumonia. What are you thinking? You can't drag her to a cold farm, so get that out of your head right now."

"You want me to put my money in a box and mail it? That's not what God expects of me. I'm goin' no matter what you say."

"You two can't go sprinkling dollars around Eastern Europe. They are doing better now. They may not even need your money. That's ridiculous."

Ted said, "Then we'll wait till you're off for summer. It's warmer then and the twins can work your shop, but we're goin' and we need you. I sat here, fat and free while my brother suffered through war and communism both. He's cared for Babcia all these years. We need to help him now, and we need you with us, Joe, we do. Please, stand beside us."

Joe threw his hands up, "Slow down, this is getting crazier by the minute."

Ted set his jaw. "Poland needs hard cash and it's not just our folks. They can hardly buy what they need, let alone buy another farm. We can help with that."

"But didn't you tell me they're sitting on rutted roads only a two hour's drive from Ukraine? Even if you doubled their 36 hectors, they couldn't compete in today's world. You'd deplete your savings only to prolong their suffering."

"I'm not Scrooge McDuck openin' his vault here," Ted banged the table and plates jumped. "But our farmers need something between them and disaster."

"So, if we give some to them now and invest the rest in Polish firms they'll have something to fall back on when we're gone." Aunt Stella said, "You teach accounting, you understand business."

Joe felt sick. He had enough worries. He didn't need them dumping this on him.

Ted threw his hands open, "We'll help Poland, too. So, what do you think?"

"I think your heart is bigger than your wallet. How much cash are we talking here?"

Ted looked away. "Well, our house is paid, we have Medicare and extra insurance. We'll keep fifty thousand here so we won't be a burden on you. We could invest say, seven-hundred-thousand."

"Zloty or dollars? You can't mean you have seven-hundred-thousand dollars?" Joe's chair nearly flew from under him. He grasped the table. "Let me see your figures."

Stella unlocked a drawer in her dresser, removed a ledger and opened it for Joe.

He pushed aside his dish to spread out and scan impossibly high numbers. Did he have to tell them they'd made a gigantic error and compounded it over the years?

Then Ted reached over and turned to cash out prices he'd gotten in 1993 and the taxes he'd paid. Joe jerked back when he saw the value of stocks in Chrysler, General Motors and Ford, listed in Ted's neat hand. The force of his reaction almost knocked him to the floor. No wonder they never wanted his help with their tax returns.

"When did you two buy these?"

"In the thirties one of the file clerk supervisors at Chrysler hired me."

Oh, how much history would they march him through to get a straight answer? His throat tightened as he studied

Ted. People smiled when they saw Ted's resemblance to Pope John Paul, but besides his angelic looks, Joe knew that John Paul's sharp intelligence was Ted's too, though Ted's could be more cagey than sacred. The question was, what else hadn't they told him?

"Stella, you tell him how we earned it. You talk better than me."

Her hazel eyes widened. "In the late twenties I waited outside the Chrysler Building for the rain to stop and a junior executive told his girl that the banks could fail, but the 'Big Three' auto-makers—they were the future. He was investing every extra penny he got in stock in those 'Big Three' auto companies," Ted said. "Pretty girls were sent upstairs to deliver files. Next time Stella went up she asked an executive how we could buy stock. He might have been pulling a joke, sending us to his broker, but he made an appointment for us and we went."

"Mr. Donovan was on Grand River. He was a real gentleman. We both took a day off work and rode the trolley downtown." Stella patted Ted's hand as she spoke.

Ted nodded at the memory. "He smiled when he met us, a file clerk and her Polak husband, all dressed up to invest our pennies, but he treated us right,"

"He told us we should buy stock in more than one company, then he said to send him a money order twice a year, regularly, and he'd buy for us."

Ted said, "We only missed in '47; the year we went to Poland and our Teddy died. The water was polluted and little Teddy—nobody should have to live—or die like that, nobody . . ."

Stella's voice called him back, "We were all dressed up, so we went to Hudson's Tearoom for lunch, remember that, Ted? It had chandeliers and linen tablecloths."

Ted cleared his throat, reminding her to get back on track.

She said, "We paid everything and invested too. Sometimes we nearly didn't make it, but helping our family through rough times made losing Teddy more bearable. He taught his cousins to care for the seeds he carried on the plane that were sewn in his clothing. He was just a little fellow with blonde curls; but he helped plant their garden while we worked making bricks to build the new house. In 1947 our Teddy ended his life helping them, so we will too."

Agitated, Joe got out of his chair behind the table and paced the room.

"Our war bonds rebuilt the farm. I signed them before we left here and Victor cashed them and sent me dollars every week, in case any got stolen. American dollars were king then, you know."

Joe's head spun, these were people whose errands he'd run and bulbs he'd changed. He'd jumped when they called, even as he juggled two jobs, four children and Kate, and now they were telling him they'd used his precious time to conserve pennies while they hid such wealth? He felt so dizzy he sat back down, hard.

Their picture of *The Sacred Heart of Jesus Crowned with Thorns* hung above the table. As a child Joe had looked at Jesus' sorrowful eyes, tiny droplets of blood dripped down his forehead and he'd always decided against a convenient lie. He'd chosen truth and Stella had said, "You're a good boy. I knew my Joey wouldn't add to Our Good Lord's suffering."

But they'd lied to him through omission. While he'd put them above himself, they'd held back. He walked in circles. Kate had wanted to move to the suburbs, creating more distance, but he figured she lacked the love that motivated the Winowski clan. How could he tell her this?

Ted's voice brought him back. "Donovan said, 'When you sell your stock, sell slow, or taxes will eat you.' We didn't want to talk foolish and then be shamed."

"Stocks grew faster than taxes by the time we cashed out to help them. But just as I opened my mouth to tell Leszek I had money for him, he said bad girls had set their sights on his grandsons. He told them there wouldn't be more dollars from the U S, so the girls left town. He said to me, 'Your help worked perfect. More would bring disaster.'" Ted shrugged, "So we've dished it out in dribbles, but what if we die or get goofy? Everything we sacrificed for would be lost. You understand?"

Stella had been watching Joe as Ted spoke. She added, "And now they must learn how capitalism works too. Should we leave them to swindlers as others have? If we buy stock in Polish companies our relatives will see how money can work for them. Then maybe life won't get so desperate, even as their country suffers its ups-and-downs."

"So, you built this up since before I was born?"

They exchanged self-conscious looks. Then it struck him. He'd bought the workshop just as the boy's scholarships came through. Then the banks turned down his loan applications so he didn't have the resources to pay his mortgage and hire men he'd have to insure privately. Ted was the first to realize Pateck hadn't given him the space for free, Joe had to admit he paid, but not that he owned the space. They knew he'd been desperate—Ted rubbed it in every time he walked by the free workshop's home in their garage. They knew, they had it, and they hadn't loaned him the money. Blood roared in his ears as Ted sped up his story, as if talking faster would make Joe miss his omission.

They expected him to go along and help them, and he had to repeat their garbled tale to Kate. He felt like there was moss growing in his brain. She'd have a million questions and what could he say?

Joe had mumbled that they should ask his brother, Fred, and took off. Ted had followed him out and put the box of cash in his back seat, "So you have money to set up the trip."

He took off like a man possessed and now he sat on his stairway trying to pull it all together.

Kate and Annie were out picking up prom shoes for Annie when Joe entered the house and plopped down on the stairway. Since the boys left for college he'd gone from school to workshop to home and back like a robot. Suddenly, that roller-coaster of activity came to a halt. He had to think.

Exhausted, he reached out and traced the banister rails he'd so carefully matched to those under their dining table and the arms of the couch. Even now, no matter what else went wrong with his day, he consoled himself, knowing that at least he'd done that right.

Since he'd begun to double-time-it Kate had protested, "You're working too hard. I hardly see you and Annie says she's grateful if you stop to fuss about her hair. I know you worry about money but we've worked together all these years and met every challenge. We aren't that hard up. This is Annie's senior year, if you work away the last real time you'll have together, it's on you."

Sitting there, Joe saw himself as a graying man who'd built his life around a disintegrating family. Sarah and the twins were gone already and Annie would be off soon. And now he knew Ted and Stella hadn't stepped forward when they could have helped him as he struggled with the mortgage. Sure, they'd helped him in other ways, but he'd jumped at their every whim and he hadn't done that for money—he hadn't known they had any. But now he knew they'd hidden the truth about their wealth from him, when they could easily have backed him—could he ever look at them the same?

Raw and edgy, he dreaded Kate's reaction to their news. He'd always blown off her protests about jumping every time they called. She loved them too but lately Kate confused him, acting fond and loving one minute and ready to go off on her own the next. Whatever her problem, he didn't dare tell her he'd taken on another mortgage. No, he'd only tell her what she needed to know, for now.

Kate's headlights flashed through their kitchen window and bounced off the hall mirror. Joe sprinted upstairs, threw on his P J's and flung himself into their big sleigh bed. He didn't need Annie's input when he told Kate about Ted and Stella.

The clear April moon shone across the feather quilt Stella had brought them from Poland on their last trip. Joe hunkered down to create a warm spot for Kate. Annie stuck her head in the bedroom door, "I'm sorry about the Pope, Dad. Tell Uncle Ted and Aunt Stella I know he was really special to them." He grunted in return as she shut the door.

When Kate climbed into bed he pulled her toward him, into his cozy space. The only thing worse than telling Kate was not telling her.

"You find what you wanted?" He tried to keep his voice casual.

"Annie picked out flats for the prom. We're lucky that Dillon boy isn't taller. They're cheaper than heels. We had ice cream and came on home. Everybody was talking about Pope John Paul. How are Uncle Ted and Aunt Stella taking his death?"

"You won't believe this. They've convinced themselves they have to return to Poland. Something about the Pope's suffering and that photo of him banging his head on the window convinced them they're obliged to go back, see Ted's mother, and rescue the family farm with their savings."

Kate tried to respond but Joe sped up his telling, "I know, I know, they went after the wall came down, but suddenly they're telling me things didn't go like they should and the Pope's death reminded them that they had it good here while Ted's brother, Leszek, suffered. It was a little garbled but I guess he was the guy coming to the US—and Ted took his place. Leszek takes care of their mother and he suffered through WWII and communism. Ted feels he owes him." Joe rubbed Kate's back so she wouldn't face him. "All of a sudden they think they won't enter the gates of heaven if they don't go now, right now." He paused dramatically, "And they want to pay my way too."

"Oh Joe, how could their little savings do much in today's world?"

"They think I can pick out Polish investments that pay dividends. I know nothing about Eastern European stock markets, but other than that, I'm their man." He felt her twisting to face him.

"Honestly," Kate said, "they think you know everything because you're a teacher. Couldn't they just leave them their money when they die?"

"They're afraid to dump all their cash on them at once. Poles are learning the pitfalls of capitalism. Ted wants to make sure they'll have more than one chance to figure out how capitalism works. He says if he invests in safe businesses they can draw on that income as they learn."

"And you're supposed to know what's safe over there? Lucky you."

Batting worries around with Kate always helped, why had he forgotten that? "They'll try to convince you this is a great idea. I wanted to prepare you."

"But how could they imagine their little savings—you'll just have to tell them I'd stab you to death with a dirty fork if you went. Make it so graphic they'll reconsider."

He spoke softly, "They bought stocks from the thirties onward, and they now have seven-hundred thousand dollars, after taxes, to spread around."

"Seven hundred? Thousand? Dollars? You're kidding—" She sat up, snapped on the bedside lamp and twisted a pillow behind her to face him.

Joe sat up too, "I thought they'd given away most of what they earned. I worried about them while they sat on gold." His voice caught but he pushed on, "They invested in the auto companies, then cashed out in the '90's. Ted shoved a shoe box full of cash in the back seat of my car to pay for tickets."

"It's bizarre, I mean, that's incredible. Did you ever think?" She laughed.

He leaned toward her but she batted him away. "Just where were those dollars when the banks refused to back you after the boys left for college?"

"They don't give family loans because Uncle Joe stiffed my parents."

"Your Uncle Joe, who your mother named you after, after he took off? That's crazy. Didn't he run out on his debts in the twenties? You're always there for them. You're not going anywhere. You have me to guide you." She'd started to joke about her scariness, but she sobered up and fixed him in her sights, "Aren't you mad? I'd be livid."

"The day the last bank turned me down for the loan I needed, you weren't home so I went to Aunt Stella. She said they'd mortgage their house for me. I mean she stood under that picture of the *Sacred Heart of Jesus Crowned with Thorns* and told me she'd talk Ted into mortgaging their home for me.

I couldn't let them do that. How could she say that when they had that cash just sitting there?"

Kate considered, "It was probably the only way she could offer to help you and not break her word to Ted. They aren't obliged to tell you their business, Joe."

He could barely swallow. "I guess women think differently."

Kate knew he'd looked for a loan but she hadn't realized his desperation. In fact, she'd seemed relieved when he didn't get it. He changed the subject. "So, how serious is Annie about Mike Dillon?"

"Oh, they joke about getting married and then he fusses over Jean. They're all three going to the Prom together. They're pals, but she's determined to have a 'glorious career' in a museum. I'll tell you when you need to worry."

Joe leaned forward to bury his face on her shoulder, "I'm not ready for that kid to grow up. I'm not ready for any of this. I'd stop time if I could."

She shrugged him off to look him in the eye. "When did anybody ask a girl's father if he was ready? Did you ask mine?"

Joe laughed, "Every day I thank God I got me a sensible woman with a forgiving heart."

# # # # #

The next evening Joe sat in his wood-lined basement office and applied for a new zero-interest credit card for himself and another for Ted and Stella—their first ever—to use on their trip. He rested his feet on his desk drawer, then he phoned his brother, Fred.

"They need somebody to drive them around Poland. You'd love it, Fred."

"Hip surgery will be my vacation, buddy. How pissed are you they had all that cash and never offered to stake you, to get that business of yours off the ground?"

Joe took a breath. "Ted said they never lent money to family after the Uncle Joe fiasco. I'm stunned they never offered, but they didn't give to anybody else, either."

"*Matko Boska*, you run every time they burp. If I had the money I'd back you."

Joe had called Fred with a lump of dread in his throat, but knowing Fred understood warmed him. Suddenly, he felt he could deal with this.

"They've helped me every step of the way—except money. Plus, my business did live in their garage for years. They helped smooth and sand, they swept up, and they fed me. How betrayed do I get to feel? And would either of us want somebody else deciding what to do with our savings?"

"But at least here they could see your business growing."

"Maybe they don't want to watch." Joe smiled, Fred's indignation consoled him.

"Go along and throw information at them until they beg you to take their money."

"Sure, they'll give up a life's dream because I say so. You've been away from Hamtramck too long if you think any old buck would change his mind about anything on their nephew's urging."

"Go and give the relatives their seed money, then bring what's left back and put it to work here. You could repay Ted's loan to you, to them. Then they'd have hard cash coming in yearly."

"But it's not Ted's dream." Fred's response made Joe feel like a cat getting scratched.

Fred suggested everything he could think of, from making horse carriages to investing in Polish plumbers. Fred dug in the back corners of his mind to help and Joe's spirits soared in gratitude.

When he ran out of ideas Fred said, "Look, just go along and try selling Ted on backing you one more time. I'll never talk to you again if you don't, that's a promise."

When Joe hung up he was breathing normally. Fred's understanding did that for him.

# # # # #

When Joe got into bed that night he hesitated to tell Kate Fred's reaction. Instead he twisted the ends of her auburn hair, the feature he noticed most often. During the day she pulled it away from her face, but at night it hung lush and free. He blinked, realizing she was speaking, and he needed to listen.

"I've been thinking about Ted's money. They're talking about a struggling economy. What if they can't sell the stock they buy later?"

"So many immigrants came to America and never looked back, at least Ted's loyal."

"But what if their economy collapses?"

"Kate, I swear to you, Poland's economy won't collapse."

"But you're the one who cares for them, Joe. If they lent money to you, you could send the family yearly payments. That's safer then investing in strangers thousands of miles away. And why should you help them out if they won't invest in you?"

Joe adjusted his pillows to support his back, "I can't demand they spend their savings on me, Kate. I can't." His voice caught.

"You don't demand of them ever. They call and you drop everything, without asking if it's necessary. But you sure can blow off Annie and me. We just don't count for as much, do we?"

"Kate, nobody means more to me than you. In my mind I know they're healthy, but they're in their eighties and after what we suffered with my dad—they were there every day—they never abandoned him, no matter what. A hospice nurse told me he was the bitterest man she'd ever seen surrounded by loving people. I didn't have you then, and I couldn't have stood it without them. I couldn't have stood it."

Kate's face softened; she seemed to make a mental leap. "Well, I always thought when the kids finished college you should go to Poland. You deserve it. Talk to them, if they'll decide on their own investments, go. They owe you that much, but tell them I absolutely won't allow you to be blamed if those investments don't work out. You help locate them, but the final decisions on what to buy has to be theirs, absolutely."

Amazed, he protested. "Honey, this trip won't be any joy ride. Ted feels he took over his brother's rightful life and he really wants to turn back time. They're all in their late eighties and I've been drafted—to do I don't know what—because he didn't tell me yet. And Stella's right there beside him nodding like if I just join them we'll make the world a better place. Does that sound like fun to you?"

Kate said, "They may be a bit off the deep end now, but the way I see it, you can sit and pout or you can take what's offered. They're upset over the Pope's death now, but they'll wake up and see what they're up against. It's up to you, but me, I'd go along to be on the spot when reality kicks in."

"So you think all I've done for them would be evened up by a free trip?"

"You didn't love them for money, but if a trip is all you're going to get for your trouble, then I say go. Bitterness is poisonous and you know from your dad it leaks all over everybody. Besides, doom and gloom never was sexy to me. Enjoy the trip and let it be enough."

Kate's green eyes had challenged him when she'd passed him a note in English class awarding him her 'Doom and Gloom Award.' He'd sat to the side as the oldest student in the class. He was required to complete the class after his CPA practicum finished, but he had no motivation to do so. Gloom had descended after he'd lost both his father and his first love, Gienia. It lingered like a dull ache until Kate passed him that note. After two years of simmering sadness Kate awakened him with her warmth and humor. He'd worked for her admiration ever since. He knew change was beckoning her now, but she loved him. He didn't want that to change.

So, if she'd respect him for going, he'd put his hurt away and go.

He steadied himself and reached out to embrace her, "I'll do it for you, Kate, but only for you. It's going to take me awhile to feel right about Ted and Stella again, but for you, I'll give it my best."

3 – ADDING ANNIE TO THE MIX

Two weeks later Joe finished up a cabinet at nearly 1:00 AM. When he pulled up behind his house he saw Kate's car was gone. He checked and Annie's bed was empty. He warned himself not to panic. Maybe her friends had a special mid-week sleep over, after all she was a senior. Kate was sound asleep. He spoke softly, "Honey, wake up. I can't find Annie. Where is she?"

The head on the pillow lifted and a hand reached out to grasp at air. She sat up slowly and squinted at him. "What? What's the matter?"

"Annie's not in her room. Where is she?"

Kate groped for the light. "Can't you look? She was working on a paper."

"She's not downstairs and your car's gone."

That got her upright. "My car's gone? What do you mean, my car's gone?"

"It's not out back and it's not in front. I checked."

Kate grabbed the emerald green velvet robe Joe had bought her for Christmas and shoved her feet into her large bunny slippers the boys got to warm her ever cold feet. "Annie was typing when I went to bed. It's dark, maybe you didn't see her." Kate rushed downstairs, into the side room they'd turned into a study. A paper sat on the keyboard. "Mom, I need Kowalski's high speed internet. They said I could use it while they're in Florida so don't worry, I'll be back soon. Your most brilliant daughter, Annie."

"I don't like this at all." Joe grabbed his jacket. Kate followed in her robe and slippers.

They sped across two streets and pulled in Kowalski's drive behind Kate's Chevy. Two other cars sat at the curb. One was the Dillon boy's. As they got near, an angry male voice sounded through the quiet night. Joe said, "I'll go around back. Give me two minutes, then knock on the front door."

Kate climbed the stairs but stood away from the door. When Joe got to the back the door stood ajar. Inside, Stan Klos, Jean's dad, swayed as he waved an antique Meissen plate over his head. Stan's daughter, Jean, had spent several nights at their house because Stan began drinking after his wife died.

Jean wasn't in sight, so why was he here?

Klos said, "Bring my Jean out or I'll break the rest of these pretty little dishes."

Annie faced him, her feet set wide amid shattered porcelain. Her lips were compressed, her chin lifted as her wild curls bobbed around her face. Joe entered and stood beside her, it appeared to Joe that only her fierce stance held Klos up.

Joe stepped between them. "What's going on? Stan, why are you here?"

"Your kid's hidin' my Jean. Tell her Jean's gotta go home with me." His twisted features and dull eyes reflected months of heavy drinking.

Joe eyeballed him. "Go home, Stan. You're trespassing and I'm calling the police. Move now."

Klos froze as Joe dialed, "We have an intruder here. Can you send police?"

When Stan didn't move Joe instinctively used his shortest kid on the block routine. He threw his hands up and let out a blood curdling Polish holler, so powerful he had to brace himself. If Stan Klos had been sober he'd have laughed, but his soft face crumpled as he staggered backwards. Just then, Kate knocked. Klos turned, opened the door and lurched past her. Kate stepped inside and Joe slammed the door behind her.

Annie's blue eyes met his, "He's been drinking, Dad."

"I can see that."

"He's been drinking and swatting at Jean, then passing out. Jean was scared so Mike and I brought her here so we could figure out how to help. When he showed up, we hid her. Mr. Klos lost his wife and his job and we thought if he was scared Jean had run away he'd agree to dry out." Breathless, Annie defied Joe to criticize that. "Jean used the house phone to tell him she'd come home if he'd go to AA, but he used caller ID and just showed up."

Mike had placed the poker he'd been brandishing against the wall and extended his hand. "Thanks for coming, sir. I'd sure hate to have to hit Jean's father."

It was hard not to like this kid Annie insisted was just a friend, Joe thought.

Kate had said, "Joe, don't worry, it's puppy love. She's young."

He'd known young love as a soldier in the 70's when his first love, Gienia, had disappeared back across the Iron Curtain, where he couldn't follow. He'd grieved so powerfully he knew 'puppy love' was a real thing. He intended to watch over his beloved daughter.

Jean emerged just as the police arrived. She described hiding when her dad came in the door.

Joe asked, "Where were the neighbors? Why didn't they come help?"

Annie looked sheepish, "I let him in so he wouldn't bother them."

Kate leaned forward and her straight amber hair mingled with Annie's red-brown curls. "You're lucky your dad's quick or we'd all be in a puddle on the floor."

The policewoman said, "Young man, you move on. We'll drive Jean home and talk to her father. Maybe we can scare some sense into him."

To Annie they said, "You'd better inform the owners about these broken plates before we do. They trusted you with their key, so you're responsible. It will be up to them to press charges or not."

Annie's freckles stood out on her pale face as she nodded acceptance.

Kate drove Annie home in her car. Joe rehearsed his scold, but as he entered the house Annie threw her arms around her mother, then around him. "Thanks for coming, both of you. And Dad, thank you for not drinking. I'm hugely grateful you spared us that." She kissed him on the cheek and before he could protest, she ran to her room.

He stood there with his scold frozen in his throat.

Kate kissed him. "Have I thanked you for sticking around all these years?"

He stepped back, "Kate, where else would I be?"

"I know you've always been there for us. Still, lots of men don't stick around and I sure wouldn't have wanted to face tonight alone. I just want you to know, you're appreciated."

# # # # #

The next day Joe couldn't concentrate. He had visions of what might have gone on in a home full of unchaperoned adolescents. He gave up on finishing a mantle and headed home. Annie and Kate were sitting head-to-head in the kitchen nook. He slid in opposite them, signaling Kate to keep still with a tight-mouthed nod, but she nudged his foot, their sign to take it easy.

He ignored that and said, "Annie, you need to tell us the rest of the story, all of it, don't leave out a thing. Just what did you kids do in that house?"

She described taking Jean to Kowalski's and inviting friends to hang out.

"And where were those kids when Jean's dad arrived?"

"They took off out the door you came in."

Then Joe rephrased it, "So you and the Dillon kid fed and hid Jean there and you talked with friends and that's all that happened in a house with no adults?"

Her lips formed a straight, firm line. "How much do you two know?"

Her mother visibly recoiled.

"Never mind what we know. Let's hear it," Joe said.

"You'll use this against me my entire life won't you?"

Kate rallied herself. Usually, she'd back off and let him handle a serious discussion, but this time she took over. "That's not the kind of response we need here. You've taken on adult responsibilities but we're your parents. We have to discuss this."

Joe cut in. "You're underage so your mother and I are legally responsible. We have to know everything." He spoke evenly but he wasn't asking.

Annie wiggled and looked around, then she straightened and faced them. Joe had to respect her stance. He tried to slow down and commit this scene to memory. Kate wore black slacks with a white blouse. Annie wore a Kelly green jogging suit, as if she'd considered running away when she dressed. Well, many a time he'd dreamt of running away when everybody looked to him for an answer. Being the father-figure meant he must step up, help figure things out, prepare to accept and move on. He knew that was a learned and practiced response and yes, he'd faltered, but Kate always stood beside him.

Joe brushed Kate's hand and said, "You handle this."

Annie pulled a throw pillow onto her lap and took a deep breath. "A few kids came over. Kids who wanted to help." She looked away when she spoke and that angered Joe, but he kept his cool.

They could lose this kid if he pushed too hard. "You've taken on an adult role here, act like a grown up now and tell us straight out."

She bit her lip then faced him. He couldn't help feeling for her. "I wouldn't allow alcohol in the house. Somebody brought beer but they kept it outside the door and nobody drank more than one."

Joe said, "They probably couldn't hold more than that."

Kate snapped, "I'm not patching things up after you two go at each other. Annie, tell Dad how you feel when he talks to you like that."

The tendons on Annie's forehead stood out. "I'm trying to tell you something and you talk to me like I'm an idiot." Her voice wavered but she went on. "I try to figure out the right thing to do, but you think I don't, so why should I even talk to you?"

Somehow, sitting eye to eye, Joe heard her. "Well, pulling stunts like hiding Jean in a house you've been entrusted with and having a party while you're at it, scares the hell out of me. How can I advise you when I don't know what's going on?"

Her eyes lids fluttered but she held his gaze.

"Was there any sexual activity?" Kate asked the burning question.

Joe studied Annie as she looked toward him.

"One couple made out but Mike said, 'We're here to figure out how to help Jean. You'll have to go somewhere else for that.' They were cool and they left."

Kate pressed on. "Is there anything we should know we haven't asked?"

"We just wanted to talk about what we're going to do with our lives. Mom, you listen, but Dad . . . ." She turned back to Joe. "You don't want me to bother you. You never have time for me anymore." Her eyes fixed on him. "Don't say you do, Dad. You know you don't."

Overwhelming her only pushed her away. It was time to level with his daughter. "I can stop that, and I'll listen if you talk to me. You used to talk to me and I miss that."

"When I got interested in boys you got all nervous and said 'talk to your mother.' but I need you to tell me how guys think. All you say is, 'Wear a clean blouse and comb that mess on your head and boys will like you.'"

"I can tell you about men. Men are pigs, keep away from them. Somebody doesn't treat you right, I'll get 'um, just tell me." He laughed at his absurdity; she didn't.

"Lord, Joe, it's your job to teach her men are approachable. I can't do that."

"You want to learn how the world works, especially the world of men, right?"

A laugh escaped Annie, "You got it, Pops. That's what I need. And Mom, I'm mad at you too. Sometimes you trust me and sometimes not."

"I saw how neat that house was, everywhere but the bedroom. The covers on the bed were mussed up. What was that about?" Kate asked.

"We sat and talked to Jean there. No sex yet, if that's what you're asking."

"Yet, what does that mean? Was that little squirt pushing you?" The words escaped Joe's mouth before he could catch them.

"It means yet, Dad. I may be thinking about it. I haven't gone that far—yet."

Joe said, "We'll trust you when you make grown-up choices, and I don't mean hopping into bed with anybody. By hiding Jean you risked everything your mother and I ever worked for. If Mike had hit Jean's father you'd both need lawyers and with Mike's dad dead and Jean's non-functional, who do you think they'd sue? I handed you the key to that house, so legally I'm responsible. I'd better protest your behavior, young lady."

"Well, I didn't think of that then." Annie's blue eyes met his. "I just didn't want you all over me like I should know what to do when I didn't. I should have brought Jean home and asked you to help, I know that now, but you've cut me out since the boys left, so I thought if enough of us got together we could figure out what to do. It just got out of hand and I'm sorry. I'm truly sorry, what more can I say?"

That hard won admission lifted Joe's spirits like a kite that found a breeze.

Kate brought the session to a close. "From now on we expect you to come to us right away. You're too old for us to tell what to do, but we can help. That's what God gave you parents for. You do that, and we'll treat the decisions you make with respect, won't we, Dad?"

"Nobody cares for you like we do. No matter how busy I am you come to me and I'll listen, I give you my word on it— just talk to me," Joe said.

Annie stood up, "All right then, I care about Mike and I don't want you putting him down because you aren't comfortable with my growing up or because he's half Japanese." Joe nodded. Better he keep his mouth shut now he'd heard they hadn't had sex, he thought.

"What is it about Mike you like?" Kate asked.

"He's honest. He sticks to what he thinks no matter what. He doesn't insult people; he just kids them so they don't go away thinking he agreed when he didn't."

Joe kept his voice light. "And you like that because?"

"Because if they say something really stupid he kids them out of it without humiliating them. Besides, Mike's thinking of joining the Peace Corps. I'd like that. Living for yourself, or getting a bigger car or a fancier house doesn't do it for me."

Joe bridled. "Is that the way you see us?"

"I see you do for others. But you act like every risk is too scary for me. It's like going into the Army killed every twinge of adventure you ever felt, so I shouldn't even think about being extraordinary. And you said public service is for morons. You did, Dad. You said that."

He leaned forward. "How many 'Skis' are heading Fortune 500 companies? Polish people have filled entire bank vaults in this country, but how many educated Poles sit on bank boards? It's a cold world out there, Honey, and I worry for you."

Kate cut in, "When you've found your own direction, do you think you'll like Mike as much?"

"We're good together, but Dad won't accept him because of his mother."

"What's wrong with his mother? She seemed like a nice woman to me."

"She's Japanese and you don't want me with anybody not Polish."

"How in hell did not wanting you paired for life at seventeen turn racial?" He hadn't even thought about that. "Annie, your mother isn't Polish."

"Sometimes you talk like marrying Mom was a mistake."

He snorted. "I may talk stupid once in a while, but if you don't know how much I care about your mother, we're not living in the same house. I have never, ever trashed Mom for being Irish. I just tell her they had it easy because they knew English."

"Then you don't care if Mike's half Japanese? If we wait till we graduate from college, marrying Mike is all right with you?"

Joe's face froze. He knew about stubborn, unreasonable devotion and Annie was as capable of fixating on Mike as he had on Gienia.

"Annie, if you commit yourself now you'll hang on like a demented bulldog, no matter what."

He used the description Kate used on him when he wouldn't back off.

"But you never had to worry you'd lose Mom. I don't want to let Mike go, then settle for some jerk just because I want kids."

If ever there was a time his talking about his first love could serve a purpose, this was it, Joe thought. He took a deep breath. "When I was in the Army I debriefed a Polish girl who'd seen troop movements as she worked her way across Eastern

Europe. I asked Gienia to marry me, but then I was sent north to debrief Poles who escaped through the border there. By the time I returned she'd vanished back behind the Iron Curtain."

"And that means I should stay home and marry some neighbor's grandson?"

He ignored that. "I applied for clearance to go behind the Iron Curtain but the military wouldn't give it a glance. Then my father got sick." Joe straightened as he remembered, "My mother asked for a compassionate transfer for me. I figured I could stick by my father and earn my discharge in Detroit. Then I'd go back for her as a civilian. But my father suffered over a year and I never heard a word from her. I'd insisted she memorize my home address, so I know she knew it, but she never sent a word."

"But you thought she loved you, right?" Annie leaned toward him.

"Gienia made me feel there was nobody for her but me." He felt Kate stiffen. "I figured as a civilian I could walk in through Austria and find her, then we'd wing it from there."

Kate blurted out, "But civilians weren't allowed in Eastern Europe then."

"I know, but I wouldn't be AWOL if I went as a civilian. Besides, I figured with my square head and talking like a Polish farmer I'd be invisible among real Poles."

"Good God, no wonder our daughter lacks good sense." Kate rolled her eyes.

"A week after my father's funeral the airlines called to confirm my ticket. They did that for overseas flights then— Fred took the call and he battered sense into me."

"What did Uncle Ted say?" Annie's blue eyes lit as she asked.

"He gave me a few smacks up the side of my head, and said even if I got over the border I'd be spotted for my arrogance—he said my walk and my jokey tone of voice would give me away and I'd disgrace the family. He said my mother had it hard enough. If Gienia hadn't sent any explanation, she didn't care enough about me for me to put my entire family at risk. So I let go, and I don't let go easy."

"Oh, so now he tells me." Kate's voice strained to sound light.

"I didn't meet your mother till I went back to finish my last English course when I'd nearly earned my CPA. I'd put it off because I couldn't write about my feelings. Then there your mother sat. If I hadn't been hurting I'd have given her more space. I told her about losing my father and Gienia, but she didn't get how bad off I was. Now she's smarter, but she's stuck." He reached across the table and squeezed Kate's hand. "You saved me."

Kate had flushed, but she pressed his hand back.

Annie said, "Well, I never heard you talk about this love of yours before. I hope you didn't tell me that to keep me from committing to Mike, because if you did it didn't work." As Annie walked away, Joe pictured a sword hanging over all their heads and he offered a quick prayer that it wouldn't fall on any one of them.

# # # # #

The next day, Joe went with Annie to the insurance agent. Later, he told Kate that the Kowalski's insurance didn't cover the replacement value of the broken antique Meissen Ware Ed Kowalski had bought Gladys in a German antique shop in '65.

Joe said, "That insurance man told Annie, 'You were courageous to take on an enraged man, but you assumed responsibility when you opened the door to him.' Courageous. That guy called our impulsive daughter courageous."

He flailed his arms and stamped around the kitchen. "This is the kid who wrote in her college admission essay, 'I can lead, I can persuade and I have a flair for the dramatic that is often useful. I operate best when I'm afraid. I may have to settle for earthly realities, but I intend to become a force for good in the world.' A force for good. You read it, Kate, and here we sit. Only God can help us now." He hadn't realized until he mimicked her that he'd memorized Annie's essay. "Good Lord, I fathered Super Girl." He pounded on the cutting board Annie had sanded when she was ten and eager to spend time with him. How he missed those days.

"If the boys had written that, you'd have burst your buttons. Relax, Joe, good sense comes with age. Just look at you, you just turned fifty-five and you're going on eighty."

He chose to ignore that.

Later that day, when Annie said she was ready to call the Kowalski's, Kate fussed with a salad and Joe stood beside her as she called from their kitchen phone. She tried to explain what happened. "I'm so sorry about your beautiful plates, Mr. Kowalski. Since Mr. Klos's wife died he's been drinking too much. He lost his job and he has no money, but he loves Jean and we thought if we hid her he'd wake up and get help before we'd have to call the police. I used poor judgment taking Jean to your house and letting him in. I'll work all summer to replace your Meissen Ware. I'm just worried it won't be enough."

Kowalski said he'd call back. Ten minutes later he called to say they'd accept whatever Annie couldn't replace with her summer earnings as their loss. Joe knew they'd been more generous than she had any right to hope for, but Annie was stunned.

"They'll take my entire summer wages to replace those little plates." Tears swam in her eyes, but she straightened up as she absorbed the blow.

His heart ached for her, "I'm sorry, Honey, but you've entered the adult world."

She turned back to him, her regal chin held high. "Will you look over my papers for Kalamazoo College?" She thrust a manila envelope at him. "My eighteen-thousand dollar package includes my scholarship, student loan, work-study and my Pell Grant. I figured I could pay room and board with the three thousand I've saved plus my summer earnings, but paying for those plates will leave me short."

Room and board ran over ten thousand dollars. Losing the shop wafted before Joe's eyes like a poisonous cloud. He'd make it to summer using credit cards, but when they hit summer break and his and Kate's regular checks stopped, even with the twins helping, he couldn't meet his expenses and hand Annie the ten thousand dollars she needed on top of everything else. He couldn't.

"Is there any way you can help me? I'll pay you back as soon as I can." Her eyes pleaded.

Kate's hand went to her throat. They both looked to him.

Joe's chest hurt as he tried to stall, "I'm proud you're sharp enough to earn an offer like that, but I'll have to look over those numbers."

"Dad, they only accept one out of every three applicants."

He gulped his coffee. He had to deflate her and there was no point in putting it off. He scrambled to think of a gentle way to let her down.

"Can't you look over my papers now?"

Joe pulled out his pen and the incriminating numbers appeared as if from another hand. "Annie, I know how hard you worked for this, but our mortgage and living expenses are only the beginning for your mother and me. We've put nearly a thousand dollars a month on credit cards since the twins and Sarah all wound up in college at once. I owe on the equipment I bought when I thought the boys would be working with me all year long. We live as well as we do because your mother works and we've never run up credit cards before this, but things piled up once the boys left. We can't take on another ten thousand, or eight thousand, or five. We're struggling. We can't do more now."

Annie's freckles stood out on her face, "There's nothing left for me?"

"Sarah and the boys went to Oakland before they asked for our help. Tuition for four kids in college at once would choke a millionaire. If you see how we can take on more, let me know."

There it was, minus only the fact he'd bought the workshop.

"So, I say 'Sorry,' after I worked my way into a top midwestern college?"

"Maybe they'll hold the package." Joe handed the papers back to her.

Kate's voice stuck. "We're strapped now, but maybe by next year . . . ."

Joe cut her off, "Annie, I'm one generation off the factory floor. I used the G.I. Bill and I worked your mother through her Master's degree. We've come further than my father's wildest dreams. We'll help, but you need to start out at Oakland like the others." She rolled her eyes as Joe pressed on, "My parents didn't pay for my schooling but we intend to help you, within reason. It's the within reason we're discussing now."

But Annie held on like a bull dog. "You couldn't do more taxes?"

"Taxes take time and if I cut back any more on my cabinet-making, people will stop calling. I can't start over in five years, and if I quit teaching to be an accountant I'd come in on the bottom rung. I'm too old for that kind of big change, but your life is ahead of you."

Kate appeared to be biting her cheek to keep still. Annie's eyes narrowed, "You don't need that workshop. You could move back to Uncle Ted's garage. You said working in his garage rent free was our ace in the hole. We've all sacrificed so you could work in Pateck's place. You could save by not paying rent there."

"And when the boys come home for summer our earnings would be down because we'd be tripping over projects again. They need every penny they can earn for next year's expenses. I've scrambled all year to hold on to that place so we can make the most of it when we're together. Would you really take that from your brothers?"

Annie softened, "I'm just saying, we all contributed, not just you."

"I need the boys to earn real money, without them the bank of dad is closed."

"But Dad, I need a superior education to get hired by a museum."

Joe wanted this to end. "Did I lose your summer earnings or did you?"

Kate tried to soften his tone, "You start at Oakland and after Sarah gets her Master's at the end of next year, we'll help you."

Defiance set Annie's face; "If I can't work in a museum I'll join the Peace Corp. I need to make my own mistakes, not you." She jumped up, but turned back, seeming to remind herself this was an adult conversation. She sat back down.

Her tone scalded, but Joe stood firm. "Wanting that college and needing it are two different things. I may want more money, but I need to pay my bills. No responsible adult would consider a higher debt level than the one we carry. Your mother and I are doing our best every day and I can't tell you how sorry I am it isn't enough."

Annie took a quick breath, "I'll auction my carousel horse over the Internet. I could get a couple of thousand easy and I've saved three. I'll figure out something if you won't." Chin-up, she tossed the greatest expression of love he'd ever made at him. They'd spent 500 hours carving that horse together.

Shocked, Joe said, "You sell that horse and you won't get a penny for school from me, ever."

"You're a mean man, Dad. A mean, mean man . . . ." This time she jumped up, threw the pillow out of her way and stomped upstairs, slamming her door.

Joe slumped, relieved that the conversation was over.

Kate had stood when Annie did, but she sat back down. "Your warnings about credit cards didn't prepare me for this. The boys haven't asked for much yet and we use the card sparingly. How can this be? Explain it to me, Joe."

"I paid the boys more than me to keep them from working with their buddies. Then there was the roof and the Roto-Rooter, car repairs and the numbers got away from me. I double-timed it so I wouldn't burden you, but without the guys—reality caught up with me." This was the conversation he didn't want to have. "Anyway, Annie's not ready to leave home and this fiasco with Jean just proves it. Even if we could scrape the money together we have no business letting her go yet."

Kate faced him. "So, if she'd come to you about Jean you'd have done what?"

"I'd have talked straight with Stan, then I'd have Jean stay with us until he pulled himself together. I'd only have called police if he lifted his hand to one of us."

"You're so crabby lately I hardly know you. Is your snarl about money?"

"We've worked hard, and we're worse off than ten years ago."

Kate said, "What about your salvage? It's our emergency fund, right?"

Why did everything have to come out at once? Hadn't he answered enough? "It's gone. I sold it when I couldn't cover our bills without the boys. I wanted to tell you, 'If it's only money I can take care of it.' Well, I can't. I'm sick about it, but I can't."

Her hand went to her throat, "My God Joe, that salvage was what stood between us and disaster. Should we sell this house?"

"We've never lived with debt, but anybody else might not feel this is too much." He looked around the kitchen he'd hand crafted, hiding modern appliances behind wooden facades and he willed himself not to shudder.

"Anybody else doesn't live on a teacher's pay while putting four kids through college. If our debt increases a thousand dollars a month, when will it stop?" She was gasping for breath. "That salvage was supposed to be our retirement. My God, Joe, where are we?"

"Don't worry. I'll work it out. I give you my word, I'll work it out."

"Do you think I can't count? You gave up accounting before it got so lucrative and you're a wonderful teacher but this is beyond a teacher's pay—you need help here. What are we doing?"

"I'll work harder. I just wanted people to say, 'There goes Winowski, he's kept his family together no matter what came his way. He's some guy.' Dope that I am!"

"You are 'some guy' to us. You've just had too much on your back. I'll take over the household bills. We'll cut back. This won't happen to us again, ever."

He thanked God for the new credit cards that wouldn't show how he'd covered Pateck's place. She was too upset to tell her he'd obligated them for another mortgage now. He'd use the cash from the box Ted shoved into the back of his car to pay for the trip until he figured out plan B.

4 – SEEKING PEACE

Days later, Joe was sanding a cabinet door when Ted and Stella arrived at his workshop, their gray heads close together. From their exchange of nods he realized that Kate had told his mother about Annie's trouble and his mother had filled them in—nothing surprising about that, but he kept his head down. He wasn't anxious to hear what they'd have to say about Annie taking Jean to Kowalski's home.

After an uncomfortable moment of little gestures between them, Stella said, "We talked it over and we want Annie and Kate in Poland with us. We'll pay the Kowalskis what Annie would earn for the days she's gone, but your grandfather, our Dziadziu, saw things. After Annie wrote him to ask for our family story, he asked her to visit his grave. He knew she'd see the world different after she visits our farm. She's a good girl, but the world around her is real confusing and she needs to see what a different world her cousins live in."

Ted added, "In Poland kids learn real quick they can't run the show. Annie doesn't understand what being born in America gets her and she needs to see that. And Kate's been good to us, we want 'em both along. We're payin' and we won't take no for an answer."

Their invitation hung in the dusty air. Joe nodded as he worked the fragrant pine.

That evening Annie was at the library doing a class project when Joe got home for supper. He brought up their invitation to Kate after she'd placed their dinner on the table.

She sat up straighter, "You'd have to hog-tie that kid to get her on a plane with us right now. She's upset and she's nearly out the door, whether you're ready or not, Joe."

"But she doesn't realize what a privileged life she leads. We may not be rich, but she's had everything she's ever needed. She's always been protected. Ted and Stella think she needs to see how her cousins respond to hardships. I want her to meet people limited by their birthplace. It might help her face whatever life hands her later."

"Even if she went, Joe, she wouldn't come home with your vision."

"Should I give up because she might not get it all? She needs to meet people who've accepted disappointments to sustain her when we're gone. Good Lord, I've swallowed my pride and accepted Ted's offer and I want that little dreamer to get a taste of reality." He steadied himself before he added, "Please, Kate, don't stand against me on this."

Kate played with the fish on her plate and seemed to soften. "It may be the last real time she'll have with Ted and Stella, but that doesn't mean she'll want to go."

He took her hands in his. "And how about you? Will you come?"

She shook her head, "No, you'd tell me what to do in Polish, then get mad when I didn't respond. Besides, this credit card debt, how could it get this out of hand before I started hearing about it? I thought we were a team." She put her hand up to quiet him. "I need some time alone to deal with this without you telling me what I think."

He couldn't discuss this now, he just couldn't. "Kate, I want you there with us."

"You want? Well, I want too, and don't give me your 'uga, uga' line about sparing me. I'm struggling to hold myself together here and you're saying, 'Oops, I'm too busy to share the facts of our lives with you, Honey, but I sure like you picking up the slack for me.' Let me tell you now—when there is nobody here I'm not aiming to upset--that doesn't do it for me. It doesn't do it, and nothing you could say now would." The anger he'd expected earlier reverberated off the wall.

"You say I don't make time for you, that I don't listen and I work too much. We could share this. We'd be together and I swear I'll treat you right. I promise, I'll treat you right. I will." Joe reached across the table.

She backed away, "Excuse me if I don't want to be where I'd have no escape."

"I don't know what to say. I thought you'd want to go."

"You're skating on thin ice here. I've contained myself because Annie is home. I don't want her memories of her last year home to be of us fighting, but I'm choking on this, Joe, I'm choking."

"I know I crossed the line, but it won't happen again. You're my best friend, Kate. I want you there." He needed her to keep his bearings. How could she not know that?

"My being your best friend doesn't seem to make you mine."

She wouldn't go if he didn't promise something she really wanted. Desperate, he said, "'I want things right between us. I'll go to that marriage counselor you suggested after the boys left. I'll go, but I guarantee we won't have anything to talk about."

Her mouth set. "Sure, say that now, then when we're back you'll tell me to get counseling alone because I'm the one hurting. How stupid do you think I am?"

"When the boys left, I obsessed trying to hang onto the progress we'd made. I figured if I just worked harder we'd be alright. I couldn't have done any of this without you and I took you for granted, I know."

She turned away from him but he saw tears on her cheeks.

"I wanted to make things work so bad I groused at you. I'm sorry, Kate. I am."

"We're in trouble and you've fixated on Annie's growing up—a simple fact of nature. Are you harping on her to distract me?"

"You know that kid isn't ready to turn loose on the world. She thinks she's up to life's challenges without input from us. That makes me crazy."

"Do you really think locking her in a car full of old people will help? I can just picture it. Ted will say, 'Where does she get the words from?' Then you'll snap and Annie will pout while he stares moodily into space. I may love you both but I wouldn't sentence myself to ten days locked up in a car with you two for anything on God's-green-earth."

"Look, I'll struggle to pay down that damn debt, but I need you with me. I don't know how I could drive and handle Ted, Stella, and Annie without you. You make things right. I need you, Kate." She wouldn't look at him. "Look, I'll tell Ted if our talking bothers him he should take out his hearing aid. You can take over paying the bills and you'll know where we stand before I do. We'll work this out together."

She wouldn't meet his eyes—she wasn't buying. "Just because I'm not screeching doesn't make your telling me about our debt after the bills are due all right. I'm screaming on the inside."

"I know. I know. I'm—"

"No, you don't know. You think of me as some kind of tool, always handy when needed and oh so easy to use—like a shovel or a stapler, or maybe even an eraser that disintegrates with use. Now there's a happy thought." When she looked him in the eye he saw she was more than 'mad at' him.

"No, no, you've never been a stapler or an eraser to me. Maybe a Swiss Army Knife, but never a stapler." His lame stab at humor didn't earn a smile.

"We were partners. What let you think you were the only adult here?"

"You can set me straight at the counselor's as soon as we're back, but Annie won't participate if you aren't there, she'll pout. Kate, it won't be a family trip without you."

Desperate, he said, "Besides, what kind of mother would you be if you abandoned Annie to going along with us, without you?"

Kate looked like he'd hit her. "Are you threatening to be mean to her if I don't go?"

"No, I just want her to enjoy this trip and Ted thinks twice about his nags when you're around. When I'm driving I can't tune in like you do. You keep us sane, you know you do." He was begging,

"Please, Kate, we'll never have a chance to be together like this again, not with Annie and Ted and Stella. And she'll see her heritage. I may be hurt about their not financing me, but they've been a positive force in all our lives. I won't let my hurt block the good I know they'll do for our wild child."

Kate's face was set but he sensed she was rethinking. She blinked and shifted. The muscle on the side of her cheek moved. "I'll walk to the airport barefoot if Ted starts one of his nags. I won't have him carry on about Annie's shoes, her hair, or her silly remarks. She can't be older then she is. And I'm not a child. Don't you boss me, either."

She'd go. She said she'd go. He could hardly believe it.

"We'll be so charming you won't know it's us. Ted wants you along and he'll behave. I promise you, I won't let him get a nag going, I won't."

"And you'll stop grumping around and watch your mouth, right?"

"I won't even complain if you pump those Gregorian Chants of yours through the whole house, I swear you'll think I'm one of those fellows from Franklin."

Her laugh was almost a hiccup but it was genuine. He kissed the tears off her cheeks and that night he loved her with a passion he'd almost forgotten.

# # # # #

The next day, Joe pulled in the driveway just as Kate got out of her car. He threw his arm around her as they entered the house.

Kate said, "I figured Ted would get all frustrated calling around so I did the research on my computer. Air Lot has the best deal—Detroit to Warsaw—June 10-21. I printed it out. If Ted's serious after he sees the cost for five people he can call and secure the reservations."

"Great. And I called and made an appointment with the counselor for after we return. We're all set. I'm more excited about Annie seeing Poland with Ted and Stella than I am about going myself, and I've wanted to go my entire life."

Their voices traveled up the stairway to where Annie stood. She descended on them, "What are you saying? I'm not going anywhere with you. I'm going to Toronto the day after graduation."

Joe said, "It's early enough to get your deposit back for a school trip. You can always get to Toronto. This is the trip of a lifetime."

"When you carried on so much about money we got our deposits back. Jean, Mike, and I are driving up and we'll go to museums and all the places we want to see and not pay for things we aren't interested in. But Dad, if you don't have money for my tuition, how can you pay for a trip like that?"

Joe's mouth gaped at the announcement of the changed plans. Before he could respond Kate silenced him with a look and took over, "Ted and Stella insist on paying. They want you to see Poland before the things they remember change forever."

"I wouldn't use Ted and Stella's money, ever."

"Don't worry, they made big money on stocks," Joe said. "They can afford it."

"Whatever, but I'm going to Toronto. You two have a good time." She turned and her unruly curls followed her movement.

"Wait a minute, young lady." Joe stepped forward, "I never agreed to any unchaperoned trip for a seventeen year-old and I never will. That was not an option, ever."

Her blue eyes, the exact shade of his own, flashed. "I'm not a little kid anymore, Dad."

Kate touched her arm. "We're talking about a week of living history with Uncle Ted's family. You'll never have an opportunity like this again."

Annie said, "Did I beg Grandma Conlon to take me to Ireland when she went last year?"

"Stella and Ted did for you before your friends ever knew you existed. Our connections will break apart if your cousins don't get to know each other. Who deserves more, your friends or the people who wore out their rosaries praying for you every time you had a runny nose?"

"Connections? Dad, you might as well visit Eskimos as your Polish relatives. Your father never went back but I'm supposed to drop everything and hop on a plane. You haven't made time for me since the boys left. You work, eat, sleep, and nag, yet I'm supposed to be thrilled to do what you say? Well, I'm not. I'm really not."

"My father was homesick his whole life, going back would have made it worse. He gave up his position as oldest son and heir to the farm to come to the US. The best he could do here was work in a factory. He became a bitter man. Now, I'm telling you, if you want help getting to that expensive college ever, you'd better remember whose pockets have to open up for you." She flinched. Her stricken face turned away.

He said. "I'm your father and I'm telling you, you're going with us, like it or not."

Tears sparkled in her eyes as she stamped her way up stairs. At the top she turned. "How can I go anywhere with you? You're so bossy I can hardly stand you."

Joe stepped forward, but Kate tugged him towards the kitchen. "Let her call Jean and have a good cry. Don't push, she'll go."

"No kid is going to talk to me like that."

"She'll come around. You're the adult. Please, don't make this worse."

In the kitchen, he stared out at their lone pine tree as Kate prepared the low-cal chicken salad that had replaced his beloved fried meat and potatoes after Dr Gawley recommended changes for him. Suddenly, Annie entered the kitchen. Averting her eyes, she grabbed the keys to Kate's Chevy from the rack beside the door and dashed outside.

Joe hollered after her, "I didn't say you could take that car."

But she pulled out fast. He banged back inside, only to look up a few minutes later and spot her shuffling back up the alley. He grabbed <u>The Detroit News</u> and waited.

She opened the door and came inside batting away tears. "I slid over the curb at the corner and I stopped against the stop sign. I can't get the car unstuck by myself."

He took two steps, enveloped her in his arms and rocked back and forth. He restrained himself from whispering, "My baby, my baby," into her untamed hair.

# # # # #

The next time Jean and Mike came by for Annie, Joe invited them in for a banana-split. He lavished them with nuts and syrup while Annie pouted. Joe explained how much it meant to him that she participate in their "back-to-our-roots tour." He spoke directly to Mike. "If Annie doesn't get to know her cousins, all our connections will break when Ted dies."

Annie spoke up, "I don't want to go on your old people's tour."

Joe's heart lurched. She'd never used that snappy tone on him before, especially in public.

Mike answered for him, "That's the chance of a lifetime, Annie. Poland has got to be exciting now. I'd give anything to meet my relatives in Ireland or Japan with both my mom and dad. I blew up a picture of Dad and me sailing on Lake Michigan and put it on my door after I started to forget what he looked like."

Joe knew that through their combined effort, Annie wouldn't have a rational premise anymore to not go; he'd save his most persuasive argument for last. "Annie, Babcia, is still with us. She's my grandmother, your great-grandmother. She's ancient now, but she's still here. You will never have another chance to meet her. This is your only opportunity, or you'll regret it for the rest of your days." Joe watched as Annie's teeth clenched, but she nodded in defeat.

# # # # #

Mike looked up information on Poland on the CIA web site. He used the site to learn that 977 is the Polish emergency number and he located fine art exhibits in Warsaw and Krakow. And he figured out the time difference from Warsaw to Detroit, so she'd know when to expect his e-mails.

Kate told Joe, "If she wasn't upset that Mike's not insisting she go to Toronto with him, she and Jean would laugh their heads off over his teaching her about Poland. I like that kid more every day, but she's still mad at you. Beware, Pops."

So, why hadn't he listened? In his agitated state, critical remarks seemed to fly unbidden from his tongue, always just loud enough to be heard. The next Saturday Annie appeared at the top of the stairs just as he left to work on his carpentry.

He said to Kate, "Tell Medusa if she wants to impress that guy, she'd better do something about that mop on her head."

Kate's shocked look made him hope Annie hadn't heard that one.

When he returned Annie was sitting in the kitchen nook, looking like a newly shorn sheep, her blue eyes defiant.

Tufts of curly auburn hair jutted out at him as they had when she was a tiny critter, unable even to walk. Her natural beauty was so startling he blurted out, "Good lord, how will I keep the boys away now?"

Her head jerked back and she stomped out of the room. She'd taken control of herself, father-be-damned. Oh, how he regretted indulging his mouth at that moment.

After that, he didn't comment on her fashion statements, even though tiny beads appeared in tufts of her hair and mismatched socks peeked from atop laced boots. She seemed nourished by the attention her newly-revealed cheekbones and fine features earned her, especially the discomfort it gave her father. Joe watched as her confidence increased. All was well with her, except him it seemed.

# # # # #

Joe rubbed his chest as an outlet for nervous tension. His heart ached and his throat hurt as he realized no matter how hard he tried he was falling hopelessly behind. Kate called Dr. Gawley and made an appointment. Joe was glad she did because he was beginning to worry himself.

Sitting on Dr. Bruce Gawley's examining table, he felt the good sense and counsel Gawley had provided in Germany, when he'd been Joe's captain. Gawley's hair was gray now but his rumbling voice recalled years spent in the military.

Gawley's presence calmed Joe once again as they looked over his test results. "That diet paid off. You're in better shape than most men your age. You're good for another couple of decades at least, my friend." His wave dismissed Joe.

"Then why does my heart hurt? Is it all in my head?"

"I can only tell you your heart's healthy, Joe."

"But nobody understands the mind-body connection?" He sighed.

Gawley punched his arm lightly. "You're asking me are you crazy? I thought so when you said you'd follow that girl you'd fallen for into Poland, remember? You've got more sense now, but nobody can juggle life like you do and not ache somewhere."

"Hell, I figured I at least had a hair ball. Medical science disappoints me."

"When I was in medical school I thought I had one of those sci-fi ailments. You know, a worm exits your navel to take over the world. I took stress management to keep from cracking up. Do your family a favor, if you need help, go get it. You can't control it all. Do what you have to, then let God do His thing."

That was it, if he wanted to feel better he'd have to let go. Driving home he adjusted the dial to a classical music station. Kate irritated him, talking about "maintaining her peace," yet he relied on her calm. Well, he could calm himself if she could, it couldn't be all that hard.

# # # # #

On Saturday Joe went to his workshop to finish a bookcase. Ted and Stella showed up in the early afternoon. They pitched in and then, as wood and wax and stain filled the air, Ted said, "I want you to make hotel reservations for us in Warsaw, Krakow and Zakopane. We won't visit the farm until the day before we're headed home; and we'll go to the hotel near the airport that night."

Shocked, Joe said, "What about Babcia? What will she say if you don't stay on the farm?"

Stella looked at Ted and stroked her flowered apron. "Near the end of our stay in '93, Ted's sister read the letter your father got from Poland."

"Yes, you told me that." Joe wondered if they'd forgotten telling him all that.

"We couldn't believe what she read. Ted took it from her to see for himself." Stella's hazel eyes filled. "Usually the letters made us laugh."

Ted began quoting his father's letter as if it was burned into his memory word by word. "He said, 'The boy told it. Leszek would send his friend Stasiu money to come to America to work him through school. He would forget us. You must replace Leszek's name with Tadeusz—but never say I ask this. It is better my sons believe you confused your brother's names than that they hate their father for changing their lives. Tadeusz is Mommy's boy. He will not forget us.'" Ted gasped for air. "Pa said 'destroy this letter,' but it lay like a snake to strike us."

Stella said, "Leszek believed only his friend, Stasiu, knew his plan, so only he could reveal it. After a lifetime of friendship Leszek, ordered Stasiu out of his house. Out!"

Ted stared as he spoke. "I can still see the day the immigration papers came. Pa handed Leszek the packet to open, like it was his. When Leszek read my name, the cry he made was terrible, terrible. Mommy said Leszek must go, not me; we could exchange our names, forever. But our father said no, I was just 14, Leszek was 16. He looked a man, me a child. People would talk, and the authorities would arrive—he couldn't trick the police. Oh no, he couldn't trick authorities, he could only trick his sons. "Father said I must go the next day to avoid more pain. He stuffed the clothing and food they'd gathered for Leszek in a large box he tied with rope made of horse-hair and dragged me across dirt roads, onto carts, and onto a train north to a ship headed for the US."

Ted sat a moment before he could go on. "Pa tricked us all. It was him, not Victor who switched us. It was him, but to my shame, I blamed your father," Ted told Joe. "Now don't I know how wrong grudges are? Now I know when both Victor and Dziadziu are gone, only Leszek remains. To make this right I must return his friend, Stasiu, to him. For the end of his life, I must."

Joe listened—how many more twists and turns could there be?

Stella said, "The city clothes prepared for Leszek were so big they swallowed Ted. Where Victor roomed, men tripped over Ted in the night and laughed when he cried out. My mother was a widow running a boarding house next door. Ted asked, could he work for food and sleep under our table? Matka couldn't say no to the boy whose clothes ate him."

No wonder they hadn't talked about this before, Joe thought.

Ted's voice thickened, "Leaving home was terrible—but hearing Pa's trick was worse. I was angry at Victor when he'd sacrificed for me. He hid that letter and remained kind to me, letting you, his youngest son, stand by me even when I bad-mouthed him. He saved my love for our father. Joe, your father was a great-hearted man and I called him an ignorant peasant. The shame is on me—on me."

Stella put her hand on Ted's arm, "When Leszek read that terrible letter he cursed Stasiu. Ted begged him to remember Stasiu was his friend from birth but Leszek drenched Ted in his poison too. Then Leszek stomped away to his son's home, refusing to speak. Babcia feared he'd do himself harm so we had to leave without ever speaking to him again.

Those were dreadful days as we waited to return home, dreadful."

Joe struggled to follow, "Leszek planned to forget your family to bring over his buddy, right? You'd been helping him, then you found out he intended to abandon your entire family. No wonder he couldn't face you. Once you knew that, why did you keep worrying about him?"

"In agony I went to our priest. He said it's our duty to bring peace wherever we can. I must not drop one grudge to pick up another. Besides, we were many and Pa refused Leszek's schooling. He was our smartest boy." Ted's face reddened. "I would be a speck in God's eye if I used his angry words to dismiss the harm Pa did him. He would be an engineer. Instead, he accepted his place and used his talents to forge parts for broken-down machinery to make life tolerable for others. He is my brother and he suffered, truly he suffered. The Good Lord tested us both. What would I be saying to My Lord if I treated Leszek badly now?"

Stella said, "We've prayed Leszek will forgive Stasiu. Stasiu's wife died, and his children left when he drank as his father before him."

Ted stood. "Leszek has respect and his children, but Stasiu walks like a ghost. He is innocent, that I know. I must do what I can to make this right for this scalds my heart. While this wound remains open I cannot sleep in Leszek's home, please don't ask it of me."

# # # # #

That night, as moonlight streamed across their bed, Joe described the letter fiasco to Kate. "Can you imagine my father died without telling anybody that his father demanded he switch his brothers?"

"Dziadziu? That's their father, your grandfather, right? Lord, what a mess."

Joe said, "What Dziadziu did was dirty, that's for sure."

"No father does a thing like that for fun, Joe. In a crisis his duty is to look out for the family, individual dreams be dammed." The moonlight illuminated Kate's earnest face. "Your grandfather had to send the son who'd remember the family, and Leszek let it be known he wasn't that guy. No father who cared for many could indulge one selfish kid."

"What are you saying?"

"I'm saying this heroic figure turned into a self-centered crumb-bum in front of everybody. If you got caught out like that, you'd turn on somebody too."

The pressure on Joe's chest eased. Kate's name-calling soothed him.

Kate frowned, "But I don't get why Stasiu would tell. It robbed him of escaping a cruel father by going to America, didn't it? But that switch-a-roo accounts for your dad catering to Ted. In most Polish families, the oldest brother doesn't listen to a younger sibling like he did to Ted, do they? Your dad must have felt terrible about that lie. To me, your dad's the hero of that story."

Joe had never thought of his dad as heroic. As a defiant six-year-old he'd run to Uncle Ted, refusing to obey his father. Ted had walked him home and guided him into the parlor where they'd sat like guests. Joe's mother had stood there, pinched and pale while his brothers listened through the vent.

Only Uncle Ted had stood between Joey and his father's strap. Everybody knew that.

His father had peeked from under his bushy eyebrows at him. "So," he'd said, "I feed you. I make a home. What did I do so terrible that my son won't mind me?"

Uncle Ted had said, "Tell him, Joey. Tell your father why you won't mind."

He'd glanced at his mother, then at his feet. Head down, he said, "You don't want me. You won't say my name. You never say my name."

His father didn't get it. Finally, Ted told him in Polish. Joe noticed he didn't use his name, ever. Only Dzikus (the wild one), *Number Three*, or *The Pest*. Joe's mother moaned. The silence went on and on till his father spoke in bursts; "It's not you. You're okay. It's that name. Mommy was sick. The priest, he baptized you, in this room. That one," he pointed at Joe's mother, "she gave you her brother's name. We signed a bank note for him . . . and he ran off and never sent a penny. The bank came to us. Many nights we ate sugar bread. Mommy named you for him and I curse Joseph every day of my life. We could not prosper. Why is his name on my beloved son?" He looked down. "I think you don't notice."

Joe caught his breath and choked. Pa yanked him up and pounded his back.

"Don't die, Son. Please, please, don't die."

Joe had coughed, then he'd snorted. They all laughed together. And he'd slept in his own bed that night. After that, his father occasionally called him Joe, just to show he'd let the grudge go, or at least didn't extend it to everyone named Joseph any more.

Still, he'd loved Ted more than his father. Now, Kate said Pa was noble just when he had to face the fact that Ted didn't love him like a son. Joe needed to deal with the fact he'd been disloyal to a good and decent man, his own father.

# # # # #

Pamphlets from the Polish Economic Consul in Chicago provided information on the Polish stock market. The smorgasbord of possibilities: trucking firms, importers and sausage firms, might overwhelm Ted and Stella, Joe thought. As things stood, Joe risked losing his business space but maybe, if he ran this trip well and they got confused by the number of possibilities, Ted might throw up his hands and he, Joe, would be there to relieve the burden of choice.

Besides, he'd always thought of himself as a worker bee, not a lying manipulator. He wasn't comfortable with the demands of that new mantle at all. He didn't dare disappoint Kate again. He had to win her sympathy and respect back before she learned about his buying Pateck's store.

Joe's mind raced back to when he'd lost Gienia so many years before. If she'd returned to Poland and he located her, would she tell him why she'd run off? Maybe if he understood that, he could prevent losing everything he valued this time around.

He thought about Adam Kaczynski, the Detroit accountant everybody called K. When K applied for the position of running his firm's Warsaw office, a fellow Joe had worked with at the firm recommended he help K with his Polish. K paid well, so Joe tutored the young CPA in business Polish each Thursday evening in the dining room at home. They'd worked for six months, and though K was ten years Joe's junior, they'd become friends.

When the twins came so close after Sarah, Kate had fallen apart. If more than one baby cried, Kate cried. At first he'd been concerned, but then he'd allowed impatience and disrespect to creep into his voice. He'd honestly thought he only needed to take on enough work to support them. He'd told Kate, "You only have to keep them quiet so I can get some sleep. After all Mommy and Aunt Stella drop by and they take the babies once in a while. Why is this so hard for you? Is a night's sleep too much for me to ask when I'm supporting this circus?"

The shocked blank look that came over Kate's face should have warned him that when her feelings resurfaced they'd be strong, but he'd been so full of himself he hadn't even seen it coming. She jumped up with a baby on each arm, which normally she couldn't do, and plunked them in his lap.

"We'll see how easy this is Mr. Smart-Mouth, after you've cared for them alone all weekend. I'm driving to my sisters so I can have two of those good nights of sleep you're talking about." She turned at the door, "I don't want to come home to a mess either, so good luck to you."

He'd thought she was joking and he opened his mouth to kid her but she cut him off. "See if you can manage without conning the old ladies into taking over. Show me how easy this is. You manage this weekend, then we'll talk about how we're going to survive this together."

She didn't pack or say goodbye to Sarah and she didn't stick around for him to protest; she slammed out the door. He heard her pull away. At first he thought she'd drive around the block and come back laughing so he got up, placed a baby at each end of the crib and started restoring order. He worked quickly so she could see how it should be done when she returned.

But then Sarah started whining. He fixed bottles for the twins and propped them so they could hold them. He'd suspected Kate just wanted to hold them—she didn't want time to clean up while they ate—but the bottles kept falling out of their mouths no matter how carefully he placed them. He was sitting in her big chair with a baby on each arm and Sarah on his knee before he realized Kate had really left him to go it alone.

When his mother called, he told her Kate had gone to her sister's like it was a joke. His mother said, "Well as long as you think managing three little ones is fun, you'll be fine," and hung up.

He'd made a few demeaning remarks about Kate's management skills in front of his mother and she'd said, "Joseph, Kate's a loving, educated young woman. She'll be fine once she can read to them, but right now it's hard and you have to help her." He'd helped, but they were two months old. She'd had time to recover from their delivery. Why wasn't she coping like every Polish woman he'd ever known?

Joe's mom and Aunt Stella let him struggle. They called to make sure nobody was choking, but they let him know where their sympathies lay.

By the time Kate walked in on Sunday afternoon he was an older and a wiser man. "You don't have to say a word. I hope you got some sleep. They're okay, I think. I listened to every gurgle in the night to make sure they were breathing. Those noises they make are scary. And Sarah, I thought I could get her to help out but she's really little and she just wants to poke their eye balls. She needs more attention than I thought. Every time a car went by I was praying it was you."

Kate scooped a squealing Sarah onto her hip and she was smiling, her rested, beautiful smile.

"We have to figure out a way to handle this so neither of us goes crazy."

"I was thinking, maybe one of us could go to my mother's for a nap while the other holds the fort. I know what you're talking about now. I've never been so tired."

Kate looked around, "You did a good job with the apartment—it doesn't look half as bad as I expected. Go to your mother's and lie down but don't stay forever, I'll need help later." He kissed Kate and walked to his mother's—he was so tired he was afraid to drive. Kate called ahead so his mother had a quick dinner ready for him. Then he slept.

By the time he went back home his mother had called Kate to suggest they leave their tiny apartment and move in with her. His mother and Aunt Stella would care for the children on Monday and Friday and Kate's mom committed to take over on Wednesdays. Kate applied for and was hired to teach freshman English at Oakland Junior College part time, which was all she could manage. When Kate mentioned her husband was a CPA, the woman suggested he apply for a teaching job, too.

Kate's teaching revived her spirits. Joe went into teaching to gain more time with the family. Accountants didn't make a fortune then and, though he was good at numbers, he soon realized he liked people better. He did take a pay cut, but Kate's earnings made up the difference. By the time Annie arrived they'd mastered life with everybody helping. Elderly Polish ladies visited, held a baby and taught their young Polish. It was a hectic but happy time.

Joe's side job of tutoring K in business Polish was a pleasure. It was a tie with his old career and he'd enjoyed retaining that connection. After K got the job in Warsaw, he called Joe whenever the accountant he'd dated hadn't been home to take his call on a Saturday night. Joe enjoyed receiving a trans-Atlantic call and K always shared a joke or new accounting jargon.

Now, dialing K's number in Warsaw, Joe smiled as he anticipated the familiar bear-like voice. K answered on the third ring and they chatted before Joe brought up Ted's wanting to invest his life savings in Poland. "Could you come by our hotel in Warsaw and tell a few scare stories? We'd love to see you and Uncle Ted wants to invest there. That's fine with me, but if Ted holds onto a portion to invest in my carpentry shop life would be easier all around."

K said, "I'd love to see your family again and I've got stories, no problem."

"And I was wondering. Can you help locate a woman I knew while I was in Germany? She returned to Poland in the early seventies. I'd like to locate her."

"She's Polish? If you know her town I'll call the local priest."

Two days later K called back. Gienia was in Poland. She was married and she and her husband ran shops in several cities. He faxed the address of each.

Joe couldn't remember how he'd gotten the nerve to ask Gienia to go with him to that little pension in Heidelberg. He'd never had the nerve to ask another girl, though he'd dated several. Yet somehow it had seemed like the most natural thing in the world to do. They'd gone up, rung the bell and asked for a room with a double bed. The woman asked for their papers, read them, and nodded toward the stairs. Gienia led Joe past the purse-lipped woman who very obviously objected to their not being married. Joe remembered how the woman's sour expression had made it more fun.

Gienia had tossed her head and floated upstairs as he'd gathered the huge key to their stout wooden door. She smelled fresh and wholesome, like raw apples. He turned the key and groped for the light cord. Her firm curves were illuminated by the light on the street seeping in through the filigreed curtain. She carefully laid her skirt and sweater over a chair and turned toward him. Her white slip shimmered as his breath quickened. He approached, but hardly dared reach out for her. She closed the space between them and slid her hand down his leg. He eased her onto the bed and his initiation propelled them through the night.

In the morning they lay pressed together as light struck a painting hung at the foot of their bed. *The Sacred Heart of Jesus Crowned with Thorns* looked down in agony on them. It was the same image Joe's Aunt Stella had stood him before and said. "Our Dear Lord Jesus suffered for our sins. You wouldn't want to press those thorns into Sweet Jesus' head deeper, would you, Joey?"

With Jesus looking down at him with sorrowful eyes, tiny droplets of blood dripping down His sad face, Joe had always fessed up. He didn't want to be the fellow adding the weight of a lie to the sins pressing the thorns ever harder into Sweet Jesus' head. Oh no, not him.

That memory had jerked Joe onto his knees under the painting. He'd said, "Don't worry, Lord. Gienia and I will marry and we'll raise our family in Your name. Don't shed an extra drop of blood for us. We'll dedicate our family life to You."

He'd leapt back beside Gienia, thinking she'd be pleased with his inspired proposal, but she jumped out of bed. "That witch wants us to remember this night with guilt forever. I'm leaving here as soon as we get the breakfast she owes us."

Gienia had stalked into the breakfast room and stuffed her pockets with bread and cheese. Joe faced the sour proprietress to pay and reclaim their papers. Stumbling over each other, they laughed their way up the street. Those days with Gienia flooded back over him like a charge through water.

Joe loved Kate dearly, he told himself, but she hadn't known the movements or gestures that came so naturally to Gienia. All the things he'd had to teach Kate sprang from Gienia spontaneously. Of course, Gienia probably had a batch of kids of her own by now and maybe she wouldn't like him seeing her, care-worn and aged. But he needed to find her, to settle that part of his life in his mind. Idealizing her had gone too far. He'd used her image as a distraction and escape for years. It was time to face reality and get Gienia off his mind. So he wrote short friendly notes, each one different, to the addresses K had faxed him, inserting his itinerary in each.

From the moment he posted those notes, thoughts of Gienia surfaced like bubbling gas. The more he resisted, the more persistently they rose. What harm could that small indulgence do, when worries howled at him like a monster that had caught his scent? Thoughts of her offered relief from those muddled thoughts. He knew, he knew, he was going out on thin ice but it was such a relief to his cluttered sense of responsibility he couldn't let it go. Not yet anyway.

5 – WARSAW

Joe reached across the aisle of the Boeing 747 and gripped his uncle's arm; "We're circling Warsaw to land, Ted."

Ted nodded. "In '93 I came by ship. I had time to get my head straight, but today I woke up in Detroit and I'll sleep in Warsaw. This is a big day for me."

Joe understood. He'd gone to Germany on a military transport and flown home on emergency leave because of Pa's cancer. He'd been so distressed about Pa and his lost Gienia that that flight was a blur in his mind. And here he was, for the first time ever, about to land in Poland. Joe laughed aloud, excited. Why not? He'd be a cynic not to savor the moment. He squeezed Kate's hand as she strapped in for the landing.

"Thank you for coming. I'm so glad you're here with me." His childhood dream of villages surrounded by fields, said to be home to ancient bison, came to mind.

Annie leaned forward as their day in Warsaw dawned. Joe watched her unwrap herself from a light fleece-throw Mike had given her just before they went through the gate. Sure, she'd put up resistance to coming but when that boy was long forgotten, she'd still have these memories.

Light filtered through the window onto Stella's fine white hair. Her unlined face took on an unearthly glow. She caught Joe's eye. "Now don't get nervous. You're supposed to be the calm one." Joe smiled; she knew him well.

Ted leaned over both women to say, "You know why Poles recover from bad times? Because they keep the faith and they're not afraid of work. You can trust 'em."

This was the man who normally preached caution and distrust, declaring an entire population virtuous. Joe shook his head, just last week Ted insisted, "People got to earn what they get, or money goes foolish."

If Ted was more open than usual, maybe, just maybe, he'd change his mind about staking him, if he played this right, Joe thought. Leszek was too old to need Ted's money, though the younger Winowskis could certainly use a safety net. Most of all, Joe wanted peace in his family, on both sides of the ocean. And yes, he wanted to see Gienia again, no matter how she'd changed. Maybe then he'd stop diminishing Kate in ways he knew were unfair. He prayed he'd have the good judgment to handle himself well and help work things to a positive conclusion, God willing. It was the God willing part that cautioned him now.

Joe took heart from the Poles exiting the plane. They appeared prosperous, stepping lightly as they neared home. Normally, Ted stood bent and weathered, but as the Polish stewardesses gave them a warm goodbye, the weariness of the flight seemed to slide off his shoulders. He'd looked uncomfortable in his new navy cardigan and white shirt in Detroit but here, as he straightened himself and gave his crown of gray hair a pat, he resembled a retired millionaire. Well, why not, he'd earned this moment.

Through the sparkling-modern Okecie Airport they walked alongside hordes of bustling people and a bevy of alert guards. Large windows displayed low clouds hanging damp and heavy. Annie poked Joe, "Look at the guards, Dad. Do Poles have terrorists too?" He assured her there weren't many places in the world that didn't.

Stella looked tired. "I'd forgotten how dreary the weather can be here." Anticipation seemed to invigorate Ted, but it visibly deflated Stella. If things didn't go well, the burden of dealing with Ted fell on her. Joe squeezed her elbow.

Annie said, "If the sun shone, Uncle Ted would think Disney had taken over."

Kate said, "Ted's like Ulysses returning with booty after years of struggle."

Annie picked up on her mother's vision, "And he found his wife's suitors eating his flock of sheep. Ulysses beat them all bloody before dropping his disguise."

Joe winced, "Why do you say things like that? You sound like phonies."

"Oops, I forgot I must ask permission to speak. Forgive me Great White Father," Annie laughed as she said it, but Joe heard her and took note. Annie hoisted her bag and moved on. She wore a light weight red jacket and Kate had on her navy pea-coat. They both had on navy slacks, fresh white blouses and ankle high boots. They couldn't have looked more American if they'd plastered themselves with stars-and-stripes, but Joe knew better than to say so.

After handing their bags to each family member as they came round the turnstile, Joe herded them into line. As Ted flung his suitcase open for customs the Ulysses image intruded and Joe pictured Ted, throwing back his head with an exultant cry: "It is I, Tadeusz, home at last, triumphant!" Joe smiled and glanced to his right.

Annie flashed him an "I caught you" smile and his heart lifted. Oh, how he'd missed sharing her vision of life. A man staring at Annie smashed into the counter. By cutting her annoying mat of hair she'd accentuated her high-cheek-boned beauty. Now he worried about every man who saw her.

"Beware what you wish for," wasn't that the saying?

The young man at the car rental counter reached for a key separate from the rest and handed Joe a note. K had made their arrangements and he'd swapped his car for a rental so they could have more room. His note said he'd meet them at the hotel later.

K's brand new, four-door, white, Mercedes stood out. The smell of leathery, wood-trimmed luxury tweaked Joe's feeling of well-being as he drove over to pick up the family. He braced himself for Ted's reaction. The average age of Joe's cars was 13 years, though Kate's had to be under six or she refused to drive it. Nonetheless, this shinning automobile spoke to men from an automobile town.

Ted bent his head and inspected the car as Joe loaded the trunk. Finally, he said, "This is a sturdy car but what's he doin' bringing a German car here?"

Stella spoke up, "Ted, that's enough. Joe doesn't know that young man's thinking so don't badger him. I think it's wonderful that young man thinks enough of Joe to share his car with us. Look at how roomy this is. We could fit another adult in here, easy. Annie, hop in the middle and we're off." They all breathed a breath of relief. Stella had cut off Ted's first opportunity to rant.

Ted nodded and eased into the front seat. He opened the glove compartment. Joe pulled ahead and they looked over the booklet till they'd figured out all the gizmos. Ted strapped himself in and waved Joe on. The Winowskis official tour of Poland began.

A wide tree lined boulevard led into Warsaw. Joe had pictured it so often he felt he was on a familiar street. "Don't anybody chirp at me. I've studied the maps."

The fifteen kilometers into town revealed green fields hemmed in by thick, neatly sectioned woods, in remarkably good order. This Saturday morning awakening of Warsaw was, for Joe, a spiritual moment.

Ted rolled down his window. "Breathe in a Polish day. Where you see American stores turn away. We came to see Poland, not McDonald's, or Coke, or Marlboro's."

Annie jerked her head in exaggerated turns, after Ted's directive and Kate laughed. Joe drove by the tall state-built apartments with blue or green balconies, he presumed a feeble attempt to make them less drab.

"Look, the Pilot's Monument," Ted said. "Heroes hid this fine statue so the Nazis could not steal Polish pride." Ted insisted Joe circle it twice.

Stella tapped Joe's arm. "Copernicus' statue is near our hotel. No fancy computers for him. Of him you can be proud."

Ted reached back to tap Annie's knee; "Now, now you see what was destroyed is restored. The world beat us down, but never bow your head to ignorance. You come from a proud culture that knows how to rise again, even after insult and injury."

Joe stole quick glimpses around. He'd love to walk this route with Kate and Annie, but he was driving and the plan was to rest now and drive south in the morning.

Ted said, "Look, we're here. It's the ancient Saski Palace with the Tomb of the Unknown Soldier. Sunday at twelve they change guard. From this hotel we'll see it before we leave town." The Hotel Victoria parking attendant waved Joe into an open spot.

Kate said, "I was all set for a farm. This hotel is impressive."

"I came to spread my money, so why not? Besides, Joe needs good sleep to drive. Farmers don't understand about hotels. I told Leszek we stay with Detroit friends so don't anybody say different."

Inside, Kate looked around, "This is elegantly modern. Look at that huge flower arrangement with exotic flowers." Kate, Annie, and Stella staggered about, silly with fatigue while Joe turned in their passports and signed in. They looked at displays of amber jewelry and admired a carved-wood flower lady placed besides another carving of an old fellow sitting on a beer barrel.

When they reached Ted and Stella's spacious room Ted took off his slacks and crawled into bed, peeking elf-like from under the comforter. Stella had insisted Annie stay with them. She said, "We'll call Annie's friend, Mike, and thank him for driving us to the airport." She didn't mention the kiss he'd planted on Annie or the manila envelope containing cards Mike had given Annie for each day she'd be gone, as she reached security.

Annie plopped down—she'd make that call after her father left the room.

Joe and Kate went to their room and put on the hotel's terry cloth robes. He wrapped his arms around her and they slept until Annie rapped on their door at about six PM. Kate opened the door for her.

"Get up, get up, you lazy bums. I didn't come to watch you two hibernate."

Joe threw a pillow at her. Her call to Mike had obviously erased her pout, but whether that made her father-friendly for long, he'd have to see.

Annie imitated Ted's reaction to the PAY-TV sexy, multinational programs he'd glimpsed, then outlawed. "Uncle Ted thought he'd have to explain the birds and bees to me before he figured out that clicker." She threw back her head and laughed.

Annie and Ted had gone exploring and Ted had an immense grin on his angelic face when he came to their room. "You eat here and you know you've been someplace. It costs plenty, but it's time Poles got a share of what people are spending on travel these days."

Ted was prepared to spread money wherever they went. What a relief Ted wouldn't be complaining about every penny, Joe thought.

The family had slept away the day and when they reached the dining room, the sparkling lights of the evening shone in through the hotel's immense windows. Their table was surrounded by a bright red semi-circular booth.

Ted had taken over as tour guide, telling them, "There are Jews from all over the world at this hotel. Annie talked to cousins who came here from Brazil and Israel. Lucky I reserved early; it's busy."

"Dad, the girls from Brazil—their father hired a guide to take them to a nightclub tonight and they invited me. They speak four languages and they all play instruments."

Joe started, "That's crazy, you're not running off with people we don't know."

Ted waved off his protest, handing Annie a wad of Polish money. "Jews don't send their kids off with just anybody, you know that. Stay near the guide, then tip him."

Good Lord, it seemed that anything was all right with Ted once he touched down on Polish soil. Maybe those fathers did look out for their daughters, but Joe went to the desk to ask about the guide hired for the girls from Brazil, anyway. Yes, he was told, Marek Zielinski was recommended by them. Often he escorted young people around Warsaw. He spoke English, Russian, and French. He was from a known family. Never did they hear he was unable to handle a situation.

Reassured, Joe returned to the table.

They ordered *koltety wiepizowe z rusztu* (pork cutlets grilled with sauerkraut and mashed potatoes). The homey fragrance wafted across the table as a pretty waitress with an elaborate hairdo served them. Ted breathed deeply, "The smell of Polish food reaches out to me like a hand from home. I feel not so much an orphan."

"Now Ted, since when were you an orphan?" Kate asked.

"You smile? I wish nobody ever felt like me. Yes, my parents lived, but what use were they when I was torn from their side to go to America? Oh, children with living parents can be orphaned, that I know. Just you thank God you had a youth without wishing to disappear." He glowered at her from under his bushy white eyebrows.

Kate patted his hand until he began pointing out hotel guests to Annie. "This is a hotel for foreigners." They could see a man practicing his Polish on the bartender. "True Poles won't come here, unless they're out to swindle tourists." Joe doubted that was true anymore but he wasn't about to challenge Ted's every pronouncement.

Annie perked up. "Could that guy be criminal? Will the police grab him while we watch?" Her talent for inopportune comments had traveled well, Joe thought.

A voice out of nowhere interrupted. "Is Hamtramck functional without the Winowskis?" A man with the coloring of a blond, rosy-cheeked boy grinned down at them. K wasn't yet forty, but in the time since Joe had seen him, he'd gone nearly bald.

He extended his hand to Ted. "I am Adam Kaczynski, but please, call me K. Your nephew made possible my present job. I offer the Mercedes you drive as a small thank you. You have had no problems, I hope?"

Joe smiled as he noted K's good suit was topped off with a jarring red-and-green patterned tie. He pulled over a chair for him.

Ted ordered wine, then asked, "You like working in the land of your fathers?"

"Poland is moving forward. Exporters invest heavily in getting local products up to standard. 90% of the new building is with foreign money; more than 3 billion dollar's worth. It's exciting for me to watch others gamble."

Kate said, "We saw the building as we drove in. Warsaw looks prosperous,"

"Some farmers sold their land to speculators. Others sold their horses to the French gourmet market and bought tractors so they are more efficient."

Joe sat back to watch his family, transfixed. K had that awkward air of someone living between cultures, too involved with both to separate them completely. His Polish grandparents had come to Hamtramck to raise him while his parents worked. His English was a tad odd and his Polish had been childlike before Joe tutored him. Kate's insistence their children speak English with them and Polish with the ancients had insured their fluency in both, and seeing K in action assured him Kate was right.

"The French eat horse meat?" Annie wiggled her nose, "Disgusting."

K smiled, "Exports are necessary to prevent a drain on Polish resources when Poles buy kiwis and bananas. Paying for imports depletes the national treasury, but who can tell a working man he can't taste what others have if he has earned his money?"

Ted muttered, "Shame on the hooligans who seduce Poles with fresh fruit." Even Ted had to join in when that earned a hearty laugh.

"I read that pyramid-schemes work here too," Joe said "They pay small dividends with the last guy's money, then when anybody tries to cash out, they stall."

"There are definitely losses to such schemes," K said and accepted more wine.

Ted scowled at him as if he had perpetrated the frauds. "They should be ashamed to treat hardworking people like that. They hadn't better try a fast one on me."

"Police react quickly," K said, "but who calls police when they believe they make money? I tell you, investing here isn't for the faint of heart."

"They haven't developed all the checks and balances we take for granted and even for us they don't always work," Joe said. "Investing in stocks is relatively new to most people here."

"Remember we're not in Disney World—and 'buyer beware', is that it?" Annie asked.

K nodded. "Exactly, Poles won't tolerate the lawlessness that parades as government in Russia, still their inexperience makes them vulnerable."

"Polish hams are famous," Ted said. "Why must all be the same for the EU?"

"When a country joins the European Union, farmers can no longer sell fresh meat and cheese from tables at a market," K said. "Only rich farmers have refrigerated stands. Lives will be saved, but a thousand years of tradition will now disappear."

"The World Trade Organization is behind that," Ted accused.

K didn't flinch. "Foreign-based companies must follow international rules. Investors are wary of creative bookkeeping and for good reason. But I see it. If domestic butter lies beside Dutch butter, with only a small difference in price, the foreign product sells first. Men wonder what others have." Ted's blue eyes brightened, his bald forehead wrinkled in concentration. "My family raises apples, tomatoes, currants and ducks. They must go through an expensive middleman. What do firms you work for do?"

"Some export to German and French stores," K said.

Ted stiffened. There was a long history of Germany's shoddy treatment of Poles.

K. said, "Germans now behave more kindly toward Poles. One said to me, 'Our fathers ran before the Russian Army and many reached home due only to the kindness of Polish farmers who allowed them shelter and eggs. We remember, and we behave more civilized toward them.'"

Joe interrupted quickly. "Do you think Poles can function in a free market?"

"This country is the size of New Mexico and it has 38 million people. They had 1000 years of free trade before the last 45 of socialism. Poles know how to barter. Sure, roads are poor but trucks bring economic activity. They also create potholes and accidents. So it is."

Ted's chin came out. "We want to help here, not exploit people."

K nodded, "Then start your own bank and charge low interest. Short-term loans at 25-60% don't help ordinary people. If they got reasonable rates—."

Good Lord, all Joe needed was for Ted to start a bank. He interrupted, "I read that in 1992 there were more than eight thousand villages without phones."

K said, "That's improved now. AT&T is prominent and other companies also have ventured into that market."

Kate said, "Eight thousand? That can't be. You must have misread the zeroes."

"Numbers are my business, Kate." Joe winced; he'd promised he wouldn't snap. "Besides, I couldn't believe it either. I checked them three times."

Ted looked thoughtful, "So, Mr. K, have you invested your money here?"

"No, I sweat when my clients lose money. Investing is not for me."

Joe's spirits soared. K worked here and if investing was too risky for him, Ted had to hear that. Besides, who could pick the number of investments Ted wanted in ten days? Joe visualized a rowboat full of Ted's money drifting back toward America.

Then K turned to Annie. "You wish to connect with your friends? I believe the young all use MySpace here. My card will give you access to the hotel system, without a business card you must use an Internet café."

Annie accepted K's card with a huge smile. "Thank you so much. I can keep my friends up-to-date with what we're doing every day with this. Thank you, thank you."

Turning to Ted, K said, "If your family imported fertilizers, they'd have a business that guarantees 100% profit. I'm no farmer, but I'm told good fertilizers can't be beat." He wrote on a napkin and handed it to Ted.

Ted announced it was their bed time. Stella said good night, and K stood to leave too.

K said, "My girl won't return until we marry, so I'm a lonely guy. Joe, take this telephone card. It's needed for pay phones in hotel lobbies. It's less expensive than your room phone or any cell phone. I'm giving you a pre-paid cell phone for your safety outside the city. My number is inside. I would like to hear your impressions as you travel. I'll see you again when you return to fly home."

Joe accepted K's phone card, picked up Annie's camera from where she'd left it, settled the bill, and walked into the lobby. Annie's acquaintances had gathered. Joe stepped forward to meet the guide

The guide's lean face reflected a quiet wariness. He was slim but sturdy looking. His boots were shined. A button down shirt protruded from under his frayed jeans jacket. He looked clean and tidy but if he was working for foreigners why hadn't he bought better? Was he angling for a better tip? Probably, but he was the kind of young Pole Ted wanted to meet.

"Marek Zielinski, these are my parents, Kate and Joe Winowski," Annie said.

Marek's face lit up as he shook hands. Strength radiated through his work-toughened hands. "I would enjoy guiding your daughter."

Joe watched as Marek made sure each girl had enough cash for a taxi and a card with the hotel address in her pocket, "Emergency plans we have to have, but you are safe with me."

Almost before the thought had time to clear his mind, Joe said, "We're going to Krakow and on to Zakopane. I'm the only one with an International Drivers' License. Do you drive and do you work outside Warsaw?"

"I drive very well and I know that part of the country. I can be helpful to you. You'll save money if you hire me."

His thoughtful English projected shy confidence, Joe thought as they negotiated.

"You pay me daily, plus food, plus my room. I'll make your visit easier and safer."

Joe stifled a laugh, the kid probably could make himself useful. "Be here at 7 tomorrow morning ready for a weeks work. We need someone who knows his way around."

They shook hands, then Annie, plus three Brazilian girls in designer jeans and brightly patched, expensive-looking, jeans-jackets followed Marek to a taxi.

Kate turned away. "I can't watch. Those taxi drivers cut into traffic like crazy." She squeezed his arm. "You think Ted will accept your hiring a guide?"

"I'll tell him I can't drive, find toilets, and research businesses too. We'll see."

"Having that young man along might cut down on Annie's fussing. I'm all for that."

Joe nodded. He felt wound up. As they entered the elevator he said to Kate, "I want to talk Polish for a while. You go on to bed; I'll be up soon."

He went into the lobby bathroom and washed his face. Just being here was a dream come true. He'd recommend one of the investment groups he'd read about in May's *Financial Times* for investment. Just as long as part of Ted's wad was left to fund his carpentry, that's all he asked.

Joe tapped his smiling reflection for luck and reentered Hotel Victoria's elegant lobby. It was windy and it smelled damp. With his tweed jacket on, he walked through the gigantic doors and jogged downhill until he slid to a startled stop. *Stare Miasto*, the old town, appeared before him. He recognized *Plac Zamkowy*, or Castle Square, where a Corinthian column stood bathed in light, crowned by the massive bronze statue of King Zygmunt Wasa III, who lost the throne of Sweden for championing Poland. Standing on his toes to see one of the grand monuments in Europe, he tried to read the inscription placed there by Zygmunt's son in 1633.

The ancient, oddly-shaped buildings had been rebuilt after World War II. Joe remembered sitting beside his father to view photos of workmen puzzling rubble back into place. His father marveled at how they'd consulted old plans, then encased shreds of the old within the new. And here it was, restored and lined with trees, looking as if it had stood there, just so, for centuries. He sent up a prayer of gratitude that he'd seen that site.

The red tiles of the old city walls shimmered under the spotlights, creating a medieval glow. Tears of wonder and gratitude blurred his eyes. He wished Kate was beside him as he photographed the jewel-like, rain-soaked square with Annie's forgotten camera. He aimed and clicked several times before drizzle forced him under overhanging branches. He inspected the Royal Castle, an impressive stone structure where parliament met. He knew this square's history. The sword, scepter and chain of the Order of the White Eagle rested there along with the ashes of Tadeusz Kosciusko, who'd fought in the American Revolution. Through a courtyard in the south side of the royal he saw the imposing Tin-Roofed Palace and to the north, Merlin's Royal Library, the part not destroyed by Nazis.

As he jogged back toward the hotel, pretty women and Gypsies beckoned him. He waved back and by the time he rapped on his hotel room door he was soaked.

A disheveled Kate opened the door. "Good Lord, what happened to you?"

"I jogged to Old Town. You'd have loved those ancient buildings."

Her mouth flapped before she said, "I looked everywhere, even the men's room. What were you thinking, running off jingling with dollars strapped to you?"

"It's early here. Lots of people are walking around out there." He turned to the bathroom and grabbed a towel. "I wasn't in danger. I thought you'd feel that."

"I thought you'd been mugged. I didn't want to scare Ted so I prayed."

Her tone didn't sound very reverent to him but he decided it was best not to say so. "I've been in the Army, Kate. I can handle myself." He pulled on his pajamas.

"But I can't speak enough Polish to ask about you. You walked off with your pockets stuffed with cash but my psychic powers should tell me you're okay?"

Irritation took over. "Do I have to account for every second? Are we fused?"

"Fused? You sold me on time together and you throw fused at me?" She slammed the bathroom door.

He fell asleep and dreamed her fear. He'd been kidnapped and tied up and she was there too.

Suddenly, Kate cried out and the light went on.

"Joe, you're hitting me, wake up." She shook him as he struggled to wake.

Jumping out of bed, he fumbled in his pockets for zloty and shoved the Polish bills at her. "I dreamed somebody tied me up and they had you too. Here, keep this money for emergencies." His hands were clammy. "I had an Annie moment and I'm sorry."

"You both think you're invincible."

He pulled out K's card. "If anything ever does happen to me call K, he'd know who to contact." Satisfied he'd done his duty, he turned out the light again.

"You big dope. What would I do if I lost you?"

Her renewed warmth made him reach over and turn the light back on. "I had to make sure I didn't get in bed with the neighbor lady by mistake."

She batted at him with her pillow as he reached for her.

6 – FIRST IMPRESSIONS (THE FUN BEGINS)

By seven AM Sunday morning the Winowskis were up and ready for their first full day in Poland. As Joe and Kate walked into Ted and Stella's room he saw both beds were made, "So those nice ladies won't have to work so hard," Stella offered. A tip sat on the table.

Annie perched on the big bed talking at whoever would listen. "You won't believe last night." Suddenly Annie turned to Joe. "Dutch and French students and an English girl invited us to sit by them and a German guy joined us. Everybody was speaking English. The girls from Brazil were dancing but the German recognized my accent. He said, 'Don't worry; we don't hold Bush against you. I didn't vote for Schroeder either.' I didn't want to say, 'I'm only 17. I can't vote yet,' so I listened." Ted squinted and his bushy eyebrows met.

Annie said, "The German guy said Europeans know what war does to innocent people. Both the French guy and the German said they thought Americans don't insist our news people give it to us straight—that we get our news through a dirty oil filter. They think we listen to too many opinions. I didn't know what to say so I said we listen to Canadian news sometimes. They said that was smart."

Joe turned to Kate, "I find our parenting methods showing up as useful strangely disturbing."

"Oh, be still and let her tell us," Kate snapped. "Go ahead, we're listening."

She repeated, line by line, her conversation with those young people. She learned that the English Prime Minister has to go before their Parliament once every week, where "politicians yell all kinds of abuse at him for 30 minutes—then they return to being polite till the next week." And she quoted the German who said they vote on Sunday so nobody has to lose a day's pay to function as a citizen. He said, "Anybody who'd change laws to prevent working people from voting by us would be drummed out of the country in shame."

"Mom," she continued, "they wanted a real American to hear what real Europeans think. The U.S. is such a powerful nation and they're worried that our voters don't get news straight. You and Dad and Uncle Ted talk politics, but I leave the room when you get into it. I won't do that anymore."

Joe had tried to get her interested in the workings of government for years, and one hour with a group of foreign students did the trick. He shook his head and bit his tongue. He was grateful Annie was speaking to him again about politics or anything else. Would wonders never cease?

Annie grabbed her mother's arm. "We talked about music and literature, too. Thank God I play violin and I read the Russians you pushed at me or I'd have sat with a sock in my mouth. The girl from Brazil said the door-knobs in Tolstoy's books all represent sex. I sure didn't get that."

"Yes, in Polish it's the same," Ted laughed. "You ask me, I'll tell you."

"It was great. I can't remember what I said, but Marek, the guy you paid to take us, said I did a good job. I didn't want to sound like an ignoramus, so I listened mostly, but I stood up for America."

Stella put her arm around Annie. "You're a good girl and America thanks you."

They'd reached the elevator when Joe said to Ted, "Marek, the Polish guide the girls used last night, drives and he charges by the day. I can't arrange everything and look into investments too. The car's big enough for one more. Why don't we take Marek along and see if he can earn his keep?" Ted didn't acknowledge he'd heard, but Joe knew he was thinking. He hadn't said, "No."

Marek stepped forward as they entered the lobby. Joe shook his hand, "Marek, let me introduce the rest of my family."

The young man bowed to the women. When Ted stepped forward to shake his hand Annie's fingers flew to her hair. His shy polite manner spoke to them all.

Stella said, "It's good if somebody who knows his way around travels with us."

As they entered the huge dining room full of linen-covered tables busy with tourists, Marek stopped. Flushing, he said, "I'll wait outside."

"Come, they feed us too much, don't waste good food." Ted grabbed hold of Marek's arm and propelled him to a table. The family gathered ham and cheese, boiled eggs and rolls from the buffet and passed their choices to each other, including Marek.

"Mass is at eleven. Where would you like to go? You wish to take tourist pictures?" Marek's English earned a smile from Ted. His thin face, muscular arms and leathery hands spoke of hard physical labor and Joe could see by the cock of Ted's head Marek had passed some test.

Joe said, "We'll drive to Krakow. Our cousins begin a new business. Help us find them. We want to see how they're doing." He felt silly as he realized he was speaking very simply, too.

"But Dad, Warsaw has must-see museums. Are we going to drive on by?"

"Ted and Stella are tired. I don't want to push them. You can see those later."

She bristled, "You'll dump us on that farm and say, 'Sorry Annie,' won't you?"

"No, no, I'll make sure you see your treasures. Don't start something now." Joe was stressed enough already, he didn't need Annie in protest mode.

Annie scowled, then she brightened, "Can't Marek take me? Don't we have the rooms till noon? You guys hang out, we'll be back for Mass, see the change of the guards, and take off right after."

Stella rushed in. "That's a fine idea. We can take it easy this morning."

Ted handed money to Marek to cover costs. Annie fished in her mini-backpack for her camera. Joe handed it over without scolding her for forgetting it the night before. "I shot some pictures in old town last night. Please, don't erase them."

As they left, Joe turned to Kate, "Annie's all excited about antiquities and that kid's English is minimal. He won't understand what she's talking about."

"She'll speak Polish if you aren't around and his English is more fluent than it sounds. He's a little nervous with us yet. They'll do fine." Kate directed Joe's attention towards the entrance where Marek stood speaking to a blond woman in a navy blue suit with a flared skirt and a purple scarf. They glanced towards the Winowskis.

Marek worked his way back through the linen covered tables. "Pani Dorsak knows about Polish businesses, if you're interested. Would you like to speak with her?"

Ted waved to Annie to bring the woman over. Joe watched her approach, slim and petite, her head tipped up as she listened to Annie.

Marek said, "Pani Dorsak, I want to introduce you to the American Winowskis."

Extending her hand, she said, "Tatyana Dorsak. I am most happy to meet you." Joe pulled out a chair for her as Annie and Marek turned to leave.

Ted asked, "What firm do you represent?" He knew how to talk business when he wanted to; a fact he usually hid behind his simple, immigrant uncle routine. Since he'd revealed his hidden wealth, his persona had undergone subtle changes that Joe watched, fascinated. Ted's head was up, his eyes were attentive.

"I work for a broker who represents companies eager to contact foreign investments. For example, both real estate developed by venture capitalists, telephone services and mobile or at-home internet are very popular."

Ted responded, "I saw people using cell phones as we drove in. I've read about your tele-com company, Tridium. I saw nothing of that when I was here in '93."

Dorsak recited facts about the next big move being to connect people to the net. Joe had read about a telecommunications company in The New York Times and he'd shown Ted that article.

Ted said, "Aren't their control centers in the US and Italy?" Dorsak charmed, and Ted preened. The woman couldn't be thirty and Ted was flirting. Stella looked amused.

"For some months now I travel my country speaking to business people who realize the impressive future for investments in Poland. AT&T first committed to our modernization and many others join them. There is a future of growth."

Ted said, "Isn't MCI available too?" He was teasing her.

"Oh yes, their future is bright also because our citizens are so new to service. It is similar when no Americans had automobiles, yet they were becoming available. We have cell coverage everywhere now. Internet availability will be the next necessity. Those who invest will do well."

She spoke to them in English and Joe enjoyed foreign-speakers. They were surprising, inventive and they used words in startlingly fresh ways that held his interest when he might otherwise have been reduced to counting ceiling tiles.

Ted sat erect on the edge of his seat. "What do you do, exactly?"

"I connect investors with a broker who obtains stock for them." She set her briefcase on her lap and carefully removed pamphlets, handing each to Ted.

"These are many, I know, but our business offerings become stronger each day. When an investor is prepared to sign documents, I will arrange the investment—without charge to you. The broker pays me. I recommend the new regional cable Internet services most emphatically."

"My family lives on a farm. They waited years for a home phone and now you're saying they need e-mail and the web?"

"We can now guarantee hooking them up for service quickly. For every $5,000 invested a line can be laid. People who invest receive low service charges too. Many buy stock for a low rate, then they are pleased with the profit statements and they invest more."

Was Ted envisioning a solution to his investment problem through a woman working out of a hotel? Keep your head, Joe told himself, Ted might be caught up in the moment, but he'd never buy stock out of a hotel dining room.

"So people check into the hotel and you invest their money for them, as simple as that." Sarcasm dripped off Joe's tongue, but nobody noticed.

"The broker purchases stock. I dispense information and facilitate the transfer of funds only."

Joe bet she did. No office, nothing traceable. What a deal for a sucker. Well, finding out this gal's pitch was ridiculous might shock Ted into rethinking investing his entire savings in stock here, he thought.

Stella spoke up. "And is it normal that the broker pays you?"

"Yes, for many would invest if they had access to accurate information." Stella's attentive posture told Joe the stock appealed to her too.

Ted said. "You'd think quick availability would be a priority. They'll regain their costs through neighbors signing up once the connections are available."

"The workload is overwhelming. The company installs state-of-the-art equipment. It took several weeks for me to learn it." Her English was practiced. She gestured as she spoke; a charming woman armed with a spiel, Joe thought.

"What didn't you know?" Kate asked.

"Our policy is to make high-speed cable Internet connections with reduced rates available to investors. I would not have imagined how quickly profits build. I'll place additional facts in your box, if you like."

Ted looked smitten; she was reeling him and Stella in, Joe thought as he watched Ted jot an address and hand it to Tatyana Dorsak. "We're leaving after the changing of the guards. You can send your information to us at our relatives, near Krakow." Ted wrote down the address for the family farm.

"I also go on to Krakow and then to Zakopane in the next days—they wish me among tourists. Read this information and choose your preference for when we meet again." She handed Ted a printed copy of her itinerary and closed her elegant briefcase.

"What a good idea, to give internet service anywhere— at a good rate, and earn money from owning it too," Stella said.

A young woman from the front desk approached Tatyana Dorsak.

"Forgive me, I have visitors, but do please ask for me in Krakow." Dorsak shook hands all round; then she was gone.

Joe pocketed her card as Ted and Stella began to wade through the print outs. Some they rejected. Some they checked. When they were done they headed upstairs.

Kate picked up a <u>Herald Tribune</u> Joe said to her, "I want to see who I can talk to in Polish, okay? I'll be up soon."

"Fine, just don't disappear. I don't want to get frantic again today."

Joe walked around to the phones. After what he'd just witnessed, he was relieved he had access to a man with genuine business contacts. "K, my uncle is determined to invest his savings in Polish companies. Can I run some ideas by you? He worked too hard to risk it all now."

"I can check if a firm is legally registered, I can't tell if they'll make money."

"We met a woman who claims she works with a brokerage firm that sells stock out of hotels. She says if Ted invests $5,000 in Internet service-provider stock he'll get a free hook up with the least expensive rates available for a designated relative, is this possible?"

"It sounds like an imitation of an American come-on they didn't get quite right," K's voice rumbled. "I heard about a firm building a bridge from Poland to Sweden your uncle might want to invest in." They both laughed.

"Ted's talking big bucks here. Want to trade jobs with me?" The booth seemed stifling. Joe propped the door open with his foot.

"Oh no, I know a barrel of herring when I smell it, but I'll ask around. Besides, seeing your family together made me wish I'd gone home and married my girl."

Joe had met the young accountant K referred to. She was a big boned girl with a hearty laugh and brains, but she hadn't bothered to stay home to take K's Saturday evening calls if she had somewhere else to go. Maybe she threw out the marriage ultimatum as a way to let K down gently.

"Don't Polish girls appeal to you? Those I've seen so far look pretty good."

"They are, but I don't want another generation stretched between two worlds."

Joe nodded, forgetting K couldn't see him. Had it been the fact he'd been away from home for the first time that made him fall for Gienia? He'd dug out his only photo of her and carried it in his wallet. Once inside Poland he looked for her in the faces of every women he saw. His heart pounded when he glimpsed a familiar gesture, only to find the woman didn't resemble Gienia at all. Later, he imagined that he smelled *Replique*, the perfume he'd bought her in the PX. He laughed realizing he'd traveled back in time.

Joe said to K, "Maybe we should trade jobs next summer so you can go marry that girl." Kate's face appeared in the phone booth window. Joe hung up quickly.

"Who were you talking to?"

"I thought you were resting."

"I want to see a few things too. Who are you offering to trade jobs with, Joe?"

"I was joking with K. He said he's thinking about marrying his girl in Detroit. I said I'd cover for him next summer if he did. He also said you could call him if you get worried and I'm not on the spot. He said he'd check on stocks for me, and the girl I lost track of years ago. He'll ask her priest if she's still around."

Kate paused for a moment, puzzled by Genia's intrusion on their discussion. Then she shrugged and said, "It would probably be good to contact her and see she's doing okay. And if you took over his job awhile I could write travel articles, how about that?"

"Kate, you're in a hotel. If you lived like real people do here, you'd be shocked."

"Perfection is your hang up, my friend. I could adjust, don't think I couldn't." She spoke lightly but her tone told him she was serious.

"Are you crazy? Will you listen to yourself?"

"Oh, I forgot, you're the only one with dreams, I'm just back-up to the "I get to choose for everybody guy," silly me."

"If I suggested we live here you'd flip out. What's got into you?" Joe wondered aloud.

"Oh, be still. We can bicker at home. I'm going to check out the Warsaw Ghetto Museum. It's not far and I want to see their photos of the sewers where people hid to fight the Nazis. I'll be back in time for Mass."

Joe ordered a cab. He was so relieved he'd been able to mention trying to get in touch with Gienia without getting a reaction, he gently placed his hand over hers as he gave the driver directions.

Kate was a bit of a historian. Sometimes that was annoying, but in this place it was perfect. She went off happy, and Joe had time to mull over what he was doing.

# # # # #

The Winowskis sat in overstuffed chairs in the lobby as a taxi pulled up. Ted held his pocket watch to his ear, as if he was telling time by sound. "Three minutes to spare, not bad for a kid who thought there was nothing she wanted to see here."

"You two don't embarrass Annie in front of that nice boy," Stella said.

"They won't." Kate swung her foot, pretending she'd kick them if they dared.

Joe watched his daughter leap out of the cab and come around to where Marek counted out *zlotys* (Polish coins). She bounced on her toes, her mouth moving the moment he turned toward her.

She walked backwards, talking at Marek as he guided her inside.

"We could do it, Marek. Anybody could. It's just sitting there like fruit, waiting to be picked." She darted around the couch to hug Ted, then Stella, "You should see that museum. There's great art just sitting there with antiquated protection."

"You didn't swipe something to prove it?" Joe indicated the seat next to him.

Annie plopped down. Her face was flushed; she looked so young Joe had to restrain himself from taking her head in his hands and kissing her forehead.

"I didn't, but I could have. I was just saying how easy it'd be." She threw back her head and gave her hearty, full-throated laugh. "I scared Marek, Dad. He gave me a huge lecture on Polish law. He says nobody robs museums, not even Mafia."

"Take his word for it, Honey. He should know."

Kate said, "I wouldn't appreciate visiting you in jail."

"In Poland you go to jail to think, and you think good," Ted warned.

"What talk is this about jail?" Stella asked, "Why are you talking crazy?"

"I didn't do anything, much. I just clicked pictures of pieces they wouldn't have on posters." Annie pointed her finger. "I shot a page of Gregorian chant they had on loan from Holland. Somebody had sewn up the parchment with sheep tendon. There weren't any posters of that, Marek. I looked."

Marek interrupted her, "I say to her, no pictures. Police take pictures."

"I'd fool them with this camera."

Kate said, "That digital camera is so high-tech they'd know you were up to no good. Marek lives here. You listen to him."

"Oh, Mother." Annie threw herself back against the chair, breathless.

Marek moved away to write a note. Joe watched as he slipped some money into an envelope. He pressed it and a phone card into one a waiter's hand, then turned back to the conversation.

"And Uncle Ted, I saw the biggest sign in the entire world. It weighs 11 tons and it took 13 Alpine mountain climbers to hang it on the side of this huge building. It says 'Coca Cola.' It made me proud to be American." She laughed at her own zinger.

Ted shook his head but didn't respond to her tease.

Kate pulled out a brush, "Enough, brush up or we'll be late for Mass."

Annie raked her fingers through her stubby curls and said, "Well, come on you lazy bums. Uncle Ted used to walk five miles to church and was never late till he got involved with crazy Americans." She tugged on his arm. "Right, Uncle Ted?"

Saint Joseph's Church was huge, crowded, and chilly. They stood in back. Stella seldom wore slacks, but she had on a trim navy pantsuit under her beige rain jacket. Music swelled into ornate crevices where the voices resounded. Tears stood in Ted's eyes as Stella rested her hand on his arm.

Linking his arm with Kate and Annie's, Joe offered up a prayer of gratitude. He felt privileged and guilty and appreciative.

Marek worked his way back outside. Concerned by the look on his face, Joe followed as he went around a side altar and out a small door. Joe followed Marek into a light rain. Men stood smoking under umbrellas as the sermon, piped through speakers mounted above the doors, descended around them loud and clear.

Marek stood near the street, talking to a large, bluff-faced Pole. Why wouldn't he spot a friend in church? Joe did it all the time he told himself, yet, how much did he know about Marek? It didn't hurt to keep an eye on him—after all, he'd introduced them to Tatyana Dorsak and what she was selling didn't seem real. He might be happy to have Marek around, but trusting him blindly could be a huge mistake, so he wouldn't.

Stella turned to Kate, who couldn't follow the sermon; "The priest said freedom is more difficult than oppression because each person must take responsibility out of love rather than fear."

Ted went on, "He said the young carry civilization's burden on their backs." He waggled a finger at Annie.

Annie shrugged, "Oh sure, pile it on me, I'm young, strong, and Polish."

Ted said, "It was hard on the church that people didn't back Walesa longer. He brought them through hard times."

Walesa's name roused Marek. "Walesa is good man, but he says, 'Remember, only remember.' Poles need educated smart guys who can be with other smart guys. He was a workman, the Pope must tell him what to do and we need a political, smart guy."

Joe said, "The priest said people came late so they could stay outside and smoke and there I stood, caught with my first cigarette in ten years, handed to me by some fellow I'll never see again. I felt just like when my father caught me lighting a cigarette in the garage when I was ten."

"I expect better of you, Pops. We're setting an example here," Annie mimicked him.

Ted said, "Practicing Catholics couldn't be a member of the communist party. Leszek's grandson, the one we're going to see, stole away from his army post for Christmas Mass. He was thrown into solitary and couldn't go home for months. Poles don't look for comfort. They look for heaven."

"Forget the fact the kid was AWOL," Joe added.

Kate took Annie's arm, "In grade school we prayed for the conversion of Russia, and today I witnessed the answer to those prayers. These people held on to their faith against all odds. Now I understand what *'The Communion of Saints'* means."

Annie turned toward Marek, "You were singing your head off, then you left."

"My friend brings news. He needs money." Marek hung his head.

Stella asked, "Was it bad news?"

"A friend is jailed. Polish jail is bad . . . very bad."

"What did your friend do?" Annie asked. Kate threw her a reproving look.

"A stolen jacket . . . the shopkeeper," Marek coughed, "was very angry." The lines beside Marek's mouth deepened.

"It was for me. I did not ask it." His little revelation caused tiny involuntary gasps to escape them all.

Soon, they rounded the corner to their hotel and the Saski Palace, with only its colonnade standing. It served as the soldiers' monument and garden.

Embarrassed they'd asked, they all concentrated on the precise slap dash of the military display in the changing of the guard. Blooming plants lined the pruned grass. Soldiers marched by, dressed in drab gray uniforms. People placed fresh flowers, then sat on benches talking as runners wound around the paths.

Joe parked and they got out to inspect the colonnades— a remainder of a grand old building. A biting wind assaulted them as they stood in respectful silence. Finally, Joe asked Marek to drive so he could see Warsaw as they left.

Annie pulled a card from her backpack and set it on her lap. Mike Dillon had given her a manila folder at the airport— a card a day for the duration of their trip. Joe could see the drawing of a Mexican struggling to get his donkey moving. Underneath it read, "THE HARDER THE TRIP, THE MORE REWARDING THE ADVENTURE. TAKE NOTES, MIKE."

Joe relaxed when he realized it didn't say "Love."

Annie wrote her reply on an over-sized card saying, "'Next to our hotel there is a great ruin with only enough left to imagine. I see a giant saying, 'I'll have a good time ripping this apart,' but he got distracted and left enough to hint at how special it was. Poles keep an honor-guard there 24/7.' More later, Annie, Professor of Adventure."

Well, she saw it and that's what counts, Joe thought as he looked away.

Tiny buds peeked through ground that was otherwise gray and bare. Soot clung to the ground. They followed street car tracks out of Warsaw and proceeded through scattered villages. People walked, heads bent to the wind. Mud stuck to car fenders. They took in the neat, gray stucco trimmed homes and though prosperity had touched some, others looked as if grim determination held them together.

Kate remarked that the stucco looked neat and well cared for. Ted waved his hand in disgust. "Asbestos! Poison for Poles," he said.

The tree-line reminded Joe of northern Michigan. There were the squared off homes he'd expected, but also those built to another taste, obviously earned by years in exile. Those were set back, sparkling with self-importance. Ted laughed aloud when he spotted a house with timbered details on A-frame wings.

Piotr, Leszek's grandson, lived fifteen miles from downtown Krakow. Piotr had gone to Germany to stay with Joe's nephew, Fred Winowski, when Fred was stationed there with the American army. Fred lent Piotr a thousand dollars for a car, then got transferred back to the US before he could collect. Fred Jr. asked Ted if he could ask when they intended to repay the money.

Leszek had written Ted that Piotr had opened a laundromat near Krakow, far from their farm. He'd sent Ted directions Ted read aloud from Leszek's letter. "Piotr has a large place about fifteen miles east of Krakow where we can all stay. It's in a village of clustered houses with farms out back. We'll see a tiny brown shed whose wooden flap will be up, if it's open for business. We can ask for Piotr there." There was a pause as Ted considered. "Let's go tomorrow. I'm too old for more excitement today, and maybe if we stay where that little girl selling stock stays, we can meet up with her again."

Joe's spirits had soared thinking he'd have another day before being drawn into the family drama. But here was Ted, looking for Tatyana Dorsak so he could invest with her shady company. With a deep sigh, Joe turned the car toward Krakow's city center.

7 – KRAKOW'S RINK

It was getting late, but Ted wanted to see the countryside, so Joe navigated the pothole-speckled side roads. They spotted several older cars but couldn't decide what make they were. People walked along the roadside in dark clothing and as dusk descended, Joe used the warning flash of white socks to avoid them. He entered Krakow alongside huge buses loaded with summer tourists as lights came on.

Joe wound his way into the heart of the city where bus stops were abuzz with square-headed men talking to women with wonderful cheekbones and straight noses. They were small boned, attractive people, neat and well dressed. Not one was fat.

Ted said, "Marek, point Joe toward Hotel Orbis where that Dorsak woman stays. I want to learn more about that Internet business she told me about."

Okay, Joe thought, let's see how long it takes Ted to wake up. If he's that eager to suspend his usual cynicism, maybe getting sucked was necessary.

Krakow's elegant Hotel Orbis had two rooms available. Marek insisted he knew a cheap hotel so Ted gave him money, and told him to "keep the change."

Joe registered the family, canceled the reservations he'd made for another hotel with the cell phone K had given him, then Annie led them all into the dining room. Her father watched heads turn as she walked before her elders to a lovely, large table.

Ted ordered six Zywiec Porters, the dark Polish beer. Kate protested Annie's but Ted said, "Children should learn to drink with family, so if they misjudge how it affects them there's somebody who loves them to look out for them."

"You're going to get me drunk?" Annie asked.

Laughing, they settled in for one of those family meals that stick in the memory as typical, simply because they aren't.

Annie said, "You know, Uncle Ted, if you want to help your family you could build a little factory. Then they could boss their neighbors around."

"Should I turn my people into exploiters of others? Have I learned nothing?"

Stella said, "We want the farm to be their spiritual home, not their curse."

"But farm life isn't for everybody, you know that," Joe said.

"I know God's not in my wallet, but money can buy a second chance. That farm is the hub of the wheel that unites all Winowskis. A man with a hub can take a chance. Sure, he might embarrass himself, but he's not a slave. I'm not here to make 'em rich, I'm here to keep 'em free. That's why I'm keeping my eye opened for that Dorsak women who handles stock. I want to hear what else she has to say."

Ted continued, "In the States a man can bounce back. Look at all the poor cars Detroit's survived. Money changed the molds and kept the business going. It takes back-up money and experience to get capitalism to work for you. Americans get a chance to practice without starvin' their family. I want that for my people."

Joe shrugged. "It's up to you. If you want to play Scrooge McDuck leaving his vault open, go ahead."

"But how can they chase opportunities without your money disappearing before they learn?" Kate asked.

Ted didn't acknowledge she'd spoken, "We don't want to bankroll fights and divorces. We see what happens to people who get rich quick back home."

Annie said, "You don't want them ordering take-out, or buying hundred-dollar shoes with money the family gave them, right, Uncle Ted?" she teased about the time she had to return a pair of shoes because the price had upset him so badly, and his general disdain of take-out.

"Families fall apart because nobody's countin' and nobody's cookin.' Loving times come over food, even food that's not so good," Ted said.

"Like the time you said 'anybody who drops her mother's lasagna on the floor by accident should eat with the chickens for a week'. You said that, Uncle Ted, you know you did."

"Sometimes I got a big mouth, but with take-out, you don't need to remember you love the cook. Take-out doesn't even smell like love."

Joe said, "So, explain to me how a man I've seen rage against outsourcing jobs, takes dollars he's earned in the US to invest it all here."

"Americans aren't hungry enough and they aren't following Christ's word. If they were they'd demand any firm making goods outside the US to improve their standards. If they'd done that so many factories wouldn't have found taking off so attractive, and workers all over the world wouldn't be facing slave conditions. They didn't look out for others and now they're scared, but did they say this isn't right? No, they turned on their TV's and drank beer. They might as well be in a Roman colosseum for all they did to save the American working man."

Kate tried to calm him, "It takes more than intent to insist people treat each other with respect, Ted."

"Poles need a fair chance—I don't want 'em robbed by greedy folks searching for suckers. My bringing my dollars here says I see it, and I don't go along with it. My money is coming to help working men and women. That's it!"

When Ted paused for breath Joe said, "Is there some logic missing here?"

Stella broke in, "This cabbage with mushrooms smells like love to me. So let's enjoy our meal and stop talking crabby, all of us."

But Ted was stung. "When you do your carving, we work together and you're proud of what you do. Why hire other men to do what you love? Why do you hand over your best skill to workmen and get stuck managing? Managing isn't your love." Ted had never said that before. Thousands of miles from home he'd croaked out what the withholding was really about.

"Yes, I'm a good carpenter, but I'm a better teacher. I want to give men in Hamtramck work they're proud of and I'd hoped my boys would join me. It's about keeping pride in our community. If I could employ men I paid well and who came to work, proud to be there, I'd think carpentry did me a huge favor."

Ted snapped, "Never mind that. You'll see how Poles keep house no matter how little they got. You think they got clean the day they jumped off the boat?"

Stella and Annie threw their hands up to stifle their giggles, but when Ted fixed the evil eye on them, they all laughed so hard they swiped at their tears with the backs of their hands. The ladies were too tired to pretend they weren't hearing silly talk. Ted shooed them off to their rooms.

Joe stayed to pay. When he reached his room, Kate and Annie sat on the bed. Their sheepish expressions told him they'd been laughing at him, too. Annie giggled at him when she left to sleep in the other room. He touched her hand as she passed; it had been too long since they'd teased and laughed at each other.

Kate said, "Aren't we blessed to share all this with our feisty daughter? What is it about a dopey conversation that reminds you, you love your own?"

Still stung by Ted's remarks, Joe warmed himself against his beloved Kate.

# # # # #

The next morning Joe roused the others early. Monday, their third day in Poland, remained gray. Ted pressed Joe about investing and Joe promised he'd call a broker after he toured Krakow.

Marek joined them at the table as they worked their way around the buffet.

Kate told Joe, "Mike's card to Annie has a mouse holding binoculars to his eyes and it says, 'I WANT TO SEE THE WORLD WITH YOU. KEEP YOUR EYES OPENED. MIKE.'"

Thinking it best to keep his mouth shut on that topic, Joe only nodded in response.

Annie must have told Kate it was alright to share because she joined their conversation saying, "Mike never said anything like that to me back home. Can I use the business card K. gave me to use Myspace from the hotel, Dad?"

Oh, she's back to consulting me, Joe thought. He nodded and proceeded to pick out his breakfast. He'd nearly forgotten where he was. However, he mused how it would be hard to forget for long—when he was surrounded by men in business suits and most women in the room, except his, wore a skirt and heels. Even Ted wore dark slacks, a white shirt and a black sweater. Joe loved the contrast in fashion to his everyday life.

Three little girls sat by a huge window, the overcast city framed behind them, hands on their laps, as they waited. Wanting diversion, Joe chose a table near theirs. When Annie pantomimed greetings with her feet together and a little bow, they clasped their hands to their mouths, suppressing their giggles.

Joe pulled out a brochure, tore it at the crease and unfolded it with elaborate slowness, growling as he put the hole up to his eye. One child hid her face in her fingers, stealing peeks at him.

Annie dug in her backpack and pulled out three Hershey Bars. "I'll offer them these, Dad."

Ted said, "I'm not comin' after you when they jail you for foolin' around with strange kids. You two should just sit still." He turned away to drink his tea.

"Go ahead," Joe said, "offer them. They'll enjoy them."

Pointing to the candy bars she held out, Annie beckoned the little girls. They approached slowly in their colorful dresses. Annie handed each child a chocolate. They looked from one to the other in confusion. The eight year-old, whose dress had a fabric llama stitched up the left hand side, took her candy, broke it into three portions and handed one to her middle sister. The smallest stood, wide-eyed, then she stood on her tiptoes and tugged at her sister's sleeve. "Dorotka," she said quietly. Her sister smiled and handed the candy over. They hurried back to their seats when a gentle voice summoned them. The voice belonged to Tatyana Dorsak, who arranged cereal, orange juice and rolls by each child. They showed her their Hershey's and pointed to the Winowskis.

Dorsak was probably in her mid-40's—but with her blonde hair worn loose she appeared softer and younger. She approached them smiling, "You have met my girls." She extended her hand, giving a special nod to Marek.

Flustered, Joe jumped up, "I hope we didn't frighten you. My daughter had some small candies she thought your children might enjoy. We've never seen better behaved little girls." He felt silly.

Dorsak introduced the children and they nodded politely—mischief reflected in their eyes. "They are the meaning to my life. I should not bring them here, I know. But I released my home when I began this work. My director does not know I fetch my babies as I drive into Krakow to spend the night. I must return them to their school now."

"You go on, go on, they can't be late for school," Uncle Ted said.

The children finished their breakfast then came by, saying a hardly audible, "*Dziekujemy bardzo*" thanking them, in unison.

As they stood with their mother, Kate nodded towards their elaborate dresses. "Babcia must be sewing night and day to dress these children so beautifully."

"Not Babcia. Mama. My mother was Russian, my name is from her. My father had some small influence and he arranged for me to go to Germany and work for a woman with the clothing firm 'Siggi Kind.' She wished her children to learn English so I studied your language and the clothing her children wore. I dreamed to be Poland's answer to children's fashion. With my earnings I bought a wonderful sewing machine that rides in the trunk of my car. Evenings, when I miss my babies, I sew."

"That's a different life than selling stock, I think," Ted said.

"Yes, in these times all dreams are not possible. I inherited my parent's small home where I began a tiny shop. When Poland opened to the West, people rushed to buy foreign goods, not handmade clothing like mine. I tried to make them inexpensively, but my seamstress used child workers like my daughters. I could not continue so."

Kate nodded, "Americans worry about child labor too."

What a story, Joe thought. Ted, Kate and Stella hung on every word.

Stella asked, "How did you go from designing clothing to selling stock?"

"I lost my home when times became too difficult. My husband found he must travel to earn his living and that is not a life for children."

Annie asked, "But how did you start selling stocks?"

"I never dreamed it. An old friend knew Pani Majka, a businessman, who taught me. The pay is generous and my children live a healthy life on a farm. Mr. Winowski, I must return to my room for the children's things. If you would accompany us, I have gathered additional information for you."

Surprised, Joe was about to decline, but Ted said, "Follow her, she might have a different slant then what you got reading newspapers in Detroit. We'll wait here."

Duck-like, Dorsak led her daughters through the dining room. Joe came from the rear. Upstairs, the girls exploded into their room. "The pamphlets are on the desk for you, Mr. Winowski." Dorsak headed into the bathroom to comb her girl's hair.

"I'll find it.   You take care of the children." Joe inspected the room. He saw pages of information and brochures stamped with Tatyana Dorsak's firm's address and phone number. Joe gathered the packet and looked around. Beds were made and computer boxes peeked from the closet. Having their printed material could save time tracing the extended tendril of this swindle, he thought. Photographs of the girls in several different outfits lay spread out on the desk. A neat farmyard appeared in the background.

Joe spotted nearly identical photos of two men standing in front of a hotel. They weren't looking at the photographer, but their profiles were clear and distinctive. Could these men be her backers? He stuck one of the photos into his pocket. How could an obviously devoted mother involve herself in fraud? K had told him the girls he'd noticed along roads and parking areas were prostitutes waiting for truck drivers. Could swindling tourists seem a lesser evil? It sickened him to think it.

The oldest child came for her coat. Joe helped, brushing away a tiny smudge of current-jam on her mouth with his handkerchief. Her lashes fluttered her thanks.

Back in the lobby Annie stood with Marek. She handed him her camera. "Take a picture of us with the family." He lined them up outside as Ted, Stella and Kate came forward to say goodbye. The youngest child ran and threw her arms wide, hugging Ted's legs. Startled, Ted swung her up and hugged her. She hugged both Kate and Stella, then ran back to pile into the smallest car in the lot.

Impulsively, Joe stepped forward as Tatyana Dorsak pulled out. Her window was down. "You're an intelligent woman. You can earn an honest living. Break all ties with these people and stay with your children." Dorsak's face froze, then flushed. She pulled out without a backward glance.

The Winowskis watched until she turned and disappeared. As Joe turned away he met Ted's eye. "Let them use someone else, not a woman with children."

Kate took his arm as they entered the lobby. "My good old chauvinist hit the nail on the head today." He squeezed her in reply.

Joe asked Marek to pack up. He headed for a pay phone. He repeated Dorsak's claims to K.

"That woman could well be an innocent dupe. Anyway, I warned her off," Joe said.

"I hope you're right. If not, she'll be back under another name. I'll notify an inspector I know. It's hard to spot a new scam. People will swallow a loss if it makes them feel foolish, that's why stopping them is so hard. I'll sound an alert, at least."

"I hoped a scam would frighten my uncle out of investing everything he has here, but that young mother could wind up in jail. I doubt she realizes her danger."

K said, "Police would like to trace her contacts, though."

"I'm sure she wouldn't have brought her little girls along if she knew."

To keep his word to Ted, Joe called the broker whose number K provided. The man spoke excellent English and sounded knowledgeable as he discussed throwing Ted's funds in with one of several savvy venture capitalists. That wouldn't appeal to Ted, so they discussed a sausage maker, a soap manufacturer and even the American firm, Alpha Graphics, which had opened several outlets there. Land O'Lakes and Nestles were producing domestically too, he said. When the broker began to repeat Dorsak's spiel, Joe asked him if buying in would earn an investor reduced service charges.

The broker laughed, "Mr. Winowski, we are not rich Americans. We give away nothing. But I promise you most Poles can afford our services. A client called to say he had difficulty passing a gypsy caravan because the driver wasn't minding his horse. He was on a cell phone. High-speed Internet is the next in line."

Joe had figured as much.

Kate came up. "We're all ready to go. Who are you calling now?"

"I spoke to a broker and I called K. He appreciates hearing from a friend."

"Doesn't his company treat him well?"

If he didn't have to explain the broker's suggestions to her, so much the better. He said, "They treat him well, that's the trouble. People bring him little gifts, then they watch him. If he says he thinks their business is doing good they go all out. If he acts reserved they pull back. The responsibility is daunting. It's a relief to talk to somebody without an agenda."

Kate kissed his cheek. "You're a good man to help a homesick accountant." They entered the lobby together.

Ted looked glum, "So what are we going to do now? How do I invest my money if you got that woman to quit?"

Joe muttered, "I'm calling around. I'm trying."

"How are we going to help if we don't buy somethin'?"

Joe gritted his teeth, "I don't know, Ted. What do you think?"

"The people who hired that Dorsak woman must have somebody to take her place. They have a business to run, don't they?" Ted scowled and fingered the bill.

"I doubt they have a trained replacement. K said he'd find you a broker."

Ted nodded. "Okay, we want to do the right thing. We're here to do good."

Stella squeezed Ted's arm, "You'll do good, Ted. You'll do it with Joe's help."

Joe walked to the counter to complete checking out. When he turned back, Stella had disappeared behind the couch.

Ted's voice rumbled with disgust, "What are you even lookin' for? I told you to leave it. Now the best thing I ever got you is ruined."

Joe placed himself in front of Ted. "What's going on here?"

"That watch I bought her, they don't make them like it anymore. I told her, the stem is loose, leave it home, but she had to show off and now it's ruined for sure."

Stella was on her knees, feeling the floor between the couch and the table. Kate looked too. The multicolored throw rug didn't yield the tiny stem.

"Ted, stop chirping and back up. If you can't help, get out of the way. We'll remember how you're carrying on at Stella the next time you make a mistake."

Ted's basset hound expression appeared as Marek helped Joe move the heavy wooden table.

Annie came over and when Stella described the watch stem; she turned and ran toward the dining room. She came back with the tiny stem in her hand.

Grinning, she said, "This was on the table but I didn't recognize it." She elbowed Joe, "You don't know the breadth of my powers do you? I said I'd be a hero one day, but did you listen, oh no."

Joe bowed and took Annie's hand, which he kissed in an old world gesture of respect all Poles recognized. She looked pleased. Joe watched through the display windows as Stella had a jeweler deftly secure the stem, then graciously refuse payment. When she showed Ted, he began his bickering, "I told you . . . why don't you listen . . . how many times?"

If Ted got his teeth into this, Joe knew there would be no end to his nag. He had to gain control quick. "Marek, you drive. My uncle will tell you where he wants to go. I'll rent another car for us. We'll meet you back here the day before we leave."

Joe handed Stella her and Ted's passports, then took off his money belt and set it next to Ted, ignoring his protests. He asked Marek to carry his family's cases back inside. Joe asked the girl on the desk to please reserve a car rental for him. He led Kate and Annie back into the dining room for tea.

Kate leaned forward on her chair, "What are we supposed to be doing?"

"Ted will carry on at Stella every time he gets a little anxious if I don't end this now. Don't either of you look sympathetic no matter what. I know how to handle this."

Stella approached them, her eyes anxious, "Joe, aren't you coming?"

"I won't subject my wife and daughter to a baying hound. When Ted accidentally swallowed Sarah's contact lenses nobody carried on like this. We'll visit the relatives a couple of days before he goes there. You can come with us. It's up to you."

Joe turned away, but he felt Ted recoil as Stella walked past him and settled herself regally in a chair away from Ted. Fifteen minutes later Stella and Ted approached the table. Clearing his throat, Ted said, "Okay it's finished. I won't say another word. If she wants to act stupid, that's her business."

Obviously it wasn't over. Joe held Ted's gaze. Mouth down, Ted bowed his head. "All right, I won't grump anymore.

If I forget you say, 'That's enough' and I'll stop. I tell you; I'll stop."

Stella added, "We want you with us. It won't be the same if you aren't there."

Tension, the kind that makes you dream up ways to flee while it rivets you to your chair hung in the air. Then the girl from the desk said, "Mr. Winowski, I have a rental car for you."

He handed the young woman a dollar bill. "I'm sorry, could you please cancel the car for me? Our plans have changed. The fighting Winowskis roll again."

8 – THE PAST AWAKENS

After Marek took over driving, Joe's thoughts turned to Gienia. Had she gotten his note? Would she be in her Krakow shop on Monday? Would she tell him why she ran back east when he'd offered her safety and marriage? Hell, she could say anything, how could he tell if it was true or not?

Maybe Gienia would turn out to be somebody he wouldn't like much, maybe he should prepare himself. Still, he needed to know she was all right. He'd tucked away a hundred dollar bill in case she needed it. No matter how big his worries, Gienia's could be far greater. With a guilty shrug he turned toward the window. He felt like a kid waiting for a pony and Kate read him too well to face her.

The cloud over Ted's head seemed to have lifted. "Krakow's Wawel Castle, burial place of kings and Rynek Glowny." He said to Marek, "You take me to those and I can die happy."

"What's that talk?" Stella said, "We came for a reunion, not a funeral,"

"I'm just sayin' I never thought I'd live so long to see this. Don't worry, you can't get rid of me so easy." He smiled and touched Stella's hand, his idea of an apology.

Marek drove them to the far-side of the winding Vistula River, through the inner city, dominated by ancient shops of stone, built to service a king's retinue. Signs for Coca-Cola and Marlboro cigarettes whizzed by. Joe liked to think of his fellow Americans as the industrious, family-centered, honest people, working to make this a better world. Who were these people using America's hard-earned reputation to pollute the world in the name of freedom, he wondered?

Then suddenly, the sun shone through. Marek parked behind a giant tour bus below the castle. The family got out and followed English tourists uphill, Kate grabbed Joe's arm, "These are the oddest buildings I've ever seen. I can't look and walk too." Her face glowed. It had been a long time since she'd pressed against him like that and he'd missed it.

Annie pointed at the top of the castle. "Those half-rounded towers, I'll bet a Disney ancestor worked on them. Why is each roof so different?"

Ted answered, "They began this in the fifteenth century. It took a hundred years from one tower to the other. They used what was handy. Poles get a job done."

"For centuries Krakow was the center for European politics," Marek said. "Poles invited Swedish kings to rule here to prevent family fights. Their artisans and women of elegance enjoyed this land. Later, to be nearer their home-land they moved our capitol north, to Warsaw."

Annie, fresh and sassy in her blue jeans and black boots, teased Joe. "Not too shabby, Dad."

Ted pointed at the immense walls that isolated and protected the inner structures. "This was built just after Columbus sailed. Not many walled cities were built then. Since school days I've read about this. I never thought I'd live so long to see it."

When they were well within the castle walls, Kate threw her arms out and twirled on the cobblestone courtyard. "If I close my eyes I'm a lady of the court. I'm stepping from my carriage in a curled wig and layers of petticoats under my magnificent dress." Bowing, she indicated her dress as she created an illusion of finery.

Ted looked embarrassed that she'd act silly in the midst of other tourists but then he shrugged, probably realizing they didn't know him, so why not?

Annie bowed to her mother. Picking up on Kate's elaborate gestures, first she stamped her feet on the stones, imitating horse's hooves; then mother and daughter became grand ladies, dancing in another era. Extending one leg as if it held up yards of gown, Annie squatted—which unbalanced her as her tail-bone slowly met the cobblestones. Tears of laughter came to Joe's eyes as he stamped his feet, bowed low and advanced to where she perched with one knee bent and one leg extended. He offered his hand. Accepting it, she jumped up, flushed but triumphant. He nuzzled her head, then released her.

Ted turned away, pretending he didn't know them.

Kate's cheeks were red. "This place is wonderful. Can't we hire an English-speaking guide? Marek said he's only read pamphlets. I want to hear it all."

Joe whispered, "For a woman of Irish heritage, you seem unduly interested. Are you a spy?"

"No, I'm thrilled this is part of my children's heritage. Besides, you're doing all the work. I could easily get used to you carrying the load." Joe realized Kate's enthusiasm had resurfaced, how could he have overlooked what energy caring for all of them took from Kate?

"I'll ask if we can get an official guide," he said, "but you know Ted."

Just then an elderly man approached wearing a shabby jacket and fingerless gloves. His fingernails were meticulously clean. "You wish an English tour? I know this shrine. I will tell all." Marek started to protest that he was the guide.

"Ted, I'll pay him. I want all the details of this place." Kate dug in her purse.

Ted signaled her to put away her wallet. "Marek, let this expert take over. Next time you come you'll know all the facts."

The old man led them across the courtyard. "The Dragon's Cave is a cavern deep in the side of Wawel Hill. A vicious dragon lived here. Prince Krak vanquished him, so the city was named Krakow after him. See there, the iron sculpture of the dragon?"

They approached the glittering gold dome of the Sigismund Chapel, a startling example of Italian Renaissance built in the 16th century. Kings of Poland, who were imposing men with beards of stone, were placed in separate burial chapels, each with its own style.

"Here we bury Paderewski, who governed in our independence between World Wars and Sobieski and Kosciuszko." The old man challenged Annie; "You know these names?"

"They helped win the American Revolution, then returned to fight for Polish independence and lost, right?"

Pleased, the old man jerked her hand up in a victory salute. "This American girl knows history." Annie graciously curtsied, acknowledging his compliment.

Whenever the old man had difficulty translating, Marek helped him. Joe bit his lip to keep from blurting out the words they sought. Ted was so thrilled to hear it all, his angelic face made him look like a happy baby.

"Many times this sacred place came near ruin. Hans Frank, the Nazi Governor General of Poland, made headquarters here. Frank believed the royal drawing rooms looked too Polish so he would not use them. The Gothic chambers became a beer hall. He used our stables and kitchens, and so accidentally, his presence saved our treasures. This sacred place was never bombed by Germany."

When Ted asked to see Frank's quarters the old man refused, as if the humiliation of Frank's presence remained. Marek showed Annie a tomb with a carving of a young woman with a stone dog at her feet. "Queen Jadwiga gave her jewels to found Jagiellonian University, the oldest university in all of Europe. She was so loved the people called her King, and Pope John Paul called her a Saint."

Marek spoke quietly with the old man as they walked, halting their discussion only when they stopped to relate a fact. Joe caught snatches of them discussing Marek's imprisoned friend.

The Arras Tapestries and the 16th century gold and sapphire reliquary holding the head of St. Stanislaus amazed Joe. Annie stared at the lavish silk tapestry tents that King Sobieski took from Turkish invaders in 1683 when he stopped Ottoman hordes from penetrating Europe.

"These tents are older than America," Annie said.

In an upper level room, their guide showed them a painting depicting the election of an early king as he stood on a rise, surrounded by nobles on one side and common people on the other. The painting covered two walls of the large upstairs room. The family read the picture's story like the ultimate type of comic book, from one end of the room to the other. Its golden tones recorded a summer day in a red-gold wheat field.

Kate asked, "Is this the same land we've been seeing? It looked drab to me."

"This is the Poland of freedom," the old man said. "When the land was free, colors were bright, fields grew full. You see this peasant on the sidelines? Even he is fat. Poland was magnificent then." His face glowed with pride.

Kate said, "You're free now. Later this summer, will it look like that again?"

The old man's eyebrows knit and his voice snapped. "For me, Poland will never be free. When I questioned communism I lost my place to be an engineer. Now I am free only to suffer." Agitated, he advanced on Kate. She backed away. "Look at me. Think what I eat. Evil men buried our magnificent land in soot. Never will there be such a summer again and never will I overcome my poverty." Surely he meant Kate no harm, but Joe stepped between them.

Rocking from foot to foot, clearing throats, staring at the painting, they stood, each at a loss for words. No pat American fix-it would restore this man to the position communism denied him. And as far as Joe could tell, nothing he might say would help. The moment must pass. He took Kate's arm.

Then Marek pulled a guidebook out of his pocket. The introduction was by Pope John Paul, when he was Cardinal of Krakow. He read aloud, " . . . and so he who enters this Cathedral, even as a chance pilgrim, must linger before this grandeur. The whole of our great thousand years-old tradition emerges as reality in Wawel Castle." Their moment of awkwardness was over.

Ted nodded yes, it was so. "I thank you for showing us this sacred place."

Annie pointed to a nobleman painted in vibrant colors. "That man looks like you, Marek. Maybe you're of royal blood."

"I cannot claim it. I can only claim to be an honest Polish man."

Honest? Joe wondered about Dorsak, as he was the one who introduced them. Marek seemed decent. Joe hoped he was honest too.

By the time they reached the place where "Szczerbiec," the 12th-century Piast coronation sword was hung, Joe was caught up in the nobility of the men who had flourished there. He'd always been proud to be Polish, but even the intelligence and canniness of Hamtramck's Poles hadn't prepared him for this.

As a kid he'd yearned for a sign he had a noble heritage and this magnificent castle smoothed off the sharp edges of self-doubt, filling him with pride in the valiant people who kept their sense of self, despite insurmountable odds. He thought of his father, homesick in America, keeping his memories of home alive by reciting this history to his sons. Joe felt his heritage as never before.

Kate nudged him, "I see it now. You are a Polish Prince." He laughed and strutted for her.

They prepared to leave and Joe slipped two twenty-dollar bills in the old man's pocket. He was rewarded by a Polish bear hug. Certainty, the man could use the money, but the fact he'd found a sympathetic audience seemed to matter more. As they descended, the old man called out in Polish;

"Never go outside the law or all will abandon you as they abandoned me. Look out for yourself."

Joe pretended he hadn't heard, but if Marek had discussed his troubles with this old man, he had a conscience. Joe couldn't ask much more of a young man he'd known so short a time.

Centuries old cobblestones gripped at their feet as they worked their way back toward the car. After her third stumble

Ted said, "Hold on to me, Stella. You can't die on Krakow's streets, you gotta stay around for what's comin'."

Joe looked at them. They'd shared so much. Thinking of Gienia was innocent enough, he told himself, but he linked Kate's arm in his. Her laugh made heads turn. When had she last sounded this care free? He couldn't remember. He said to her, "I should apologize to your father for snapping you up so young. I appreciate his feelings more every time I see men looking at our beautiful daughter."

"My dad cursed you. You know the one, 'Someday you'll have a child.'"

# # # # #

It wasn't a long walk from their hotel to Old Town, so Joe parked by the hotel. The clouds had lifted and it had warmed up. Marek put their jackets in the trunk and they walked from the hotel, crossing streets where mad taxis and foreign buses dropped tourists off like ants defoliating a forest.

Rynek Glowny sounded like the English word ring, so they called it The Ring. A medieval looking building that sat on a large square surrounded by shops with brightly-colored flowers stacked on tables under colorful umbrellas. Exotic, with its immense arches and Moorish details, it bustled with people dressed neatly in layered sweaters; some few wore narrow-legged jeans while others had expensive looking leather coats.

A tiny, hunch-backed, black-robed nun appeared. Ted followed her across the square to press wadded dollars into her hand. Startled, she laughed and squeezed his arm before shuffling away. Ted swayed with satisfaction.

People-friendly pigeons fluttered above, taking flight each time the sharp crack of the market pump's wooden handle gushed water for the stall keepers. The Ring sat like a cathedral in the middle of the open square, beckoning tourists with its pale yellow walls.

An ornate cafe' sat tucked into one wall, its outside tables covered by bright red and white Marlboro umbrellas. Joe braced himself for Ted's fit about those ads, but he didn't seem to notice. Waitresses stood in the doorway in colorful costumes. He saw they served tea and tiny sandwiches with their crusts cut off—and luscious looking poppy seed cakes that rotated in a showcase.

Joe remembered Gienia saying he had never tasted cake until she fed him poppy seed cake with her fingers. That had never happened, but her shop had to be nearby. He looked around. Many women were small and dark—a tilt of the head, a profile—could she be here? He froze, his heart pounding, as he wiped his sweaty palms on his pants.

Kate gestured to him, pretending to put a slice of cake in her mouth then sipping a cup of tea. He mouthed the word, "Later." She smiled, bringing her hands together, as if in prayer. She'd done that when he first met her. She'd replaced Gienia and his shattered dreams. With her, life was real. He pushed back the intruding fantasies.

"This once was a center for weavers," Marek said. Ted looked over the building's interior, full of dark little booth-like shops manned by Poles selling treasures of hand blown glass, amber jewelry, blouses, tablecloths and dolls.

A trumpet sounded from the taller of two towers at the end of the square. Marek pointed. "From the Tartar siege in 124, The Trumpeter of Krakow, his blast tells—no Huns come." They stood a moment, caught up in that famous story.

Ted saw a brightly costumed folk music group. He told Joe and Annie to go on inside with Stella. He'd found what he enjoyed, musicians.

As Kate proceeded inside, Joe scanned the periphery. He spotted Gienia's shop across the street. If she wasn't there he didn't want to know it yet. He wanted to savor the moment, disappointment could come soon enough. His fantasy included his sweeping down like a Tartar raider. He shook his head to knock that picture from his mind and followed Kate through wooden doors, designed for a carriage to enter with its horses abreast.

From the far side of the aisle he watched as Stella flashed her credit card. Buying without Ted's input was possible with plastic. Ted's largess today might well be gone tomorrow, Joe thought. By nature Ted was tight, tight, tight. And though Joe knew Stella had the last word in all things, he'd also seen Ted's scowl stop her cold.

Marek consulted Joe. Watching dollars go for non-essential items worried him. Joe made up a story to ease his discomfort. "Stella buys for her niece's store. She'll earn dollars when she sells these items in America." Stretching the truth even further he rubbed his fingers together, in the international sign for money so Marek could relax about the cash they were spending—and they were spending. Polish prices were not cheap since they joined the European Union, but Ted had told them to spread his dollars around and they were taking him literally.

Joe had dreaded telling Ted prices were comparable to those in the US, but when he did—Ted said, "It's time Poles get a good price from the rest of the world. Don't be cheap. Money we spend will trickle down. I'm going to tip everybody I come across double. These people don't have it easy yet."

Oh boy, Joe thought, this will be something to see. He said, "You know, everybody is better off than the last time you were here. Poles are proud people. We don't want to mow over their dignity."

Ted's eyes widened and he sat up straighter, "I may be a country boy but I know something about showing respect to a working man. I know how to hand it out respectful. Don't you baby sit me."

So, Stella bought amber jewelry set in silver without attempting to barter. Young girls displayed the jewelry until the owner saw how much Stella had set aside, then he took over. Stella waved for Marek. She wanted to shop without people knowing she understood Polish, so she said to Marek in English, "Tell this man loudly, so the people in those booths hear, those girls must be paid the commission for my entire purchase or I will not buy from him."

Marek looked startled, then he grinned. He flirted with the girls, who blushed and bowed their heads before he voiced Stella's request. The shopkeeper frowned, but he agreed they'd keep the commission.

Marek said, "I say to him 'Pretty girls sell' so he pays them and he keeps them."

As they walked the length of the building Annie gave her father a quick run-down of the treasures she'd found in the museum upstairs, then steered him toward a doll-filled booth. "They have authentic Old World costumes and natural hair." She held a doll dressed like an elderly Jewish lady.

He saw the price. "You want a replica of a Jewish doll from the 1800s?"

"It's the workmanship, Dad. They're museum pieces. Detroit can't touch these, guaranteed. These are top quality. You could put this . . . " She picked up a wax faced boy in a knitted green sweater, a red hat and scarf, with red and green checkered knickers and red knit stockings with jet-black shoes. " . . . on our fireplace."

"Should I want a doll on my mantle?"

"The certificate says he was hand-formed in *Guy Luy I Hubert.* If you don't want him, I do. Buy him as my souvenir of Poland." Her blue eyes met his.

"I could, but you might want to see what else we find."

"Why should I choose something I'd treasure when you're set to pick my boyfriends, my blouses, and my souvenirs? What was I thinking?" Annie walked away.

How did he get to be the bad guy again? Joe bought the doll and shoved it on top of Stella's purchases. Suddenly, the building was too crowded for him. He exited through the far door only to see Ted peel off ten dollar bills he handed to the folk singers, along with a list of songs he'd written on a napkin, so they would play songs he knew.

Joe looked across at the shop where he'd spotted the name he'd gotten from K. The window displayed carved pine furnishings and hand-loomed wall hangings. The tapestries were not the symmetrical offerings shown in The Ring, but flowing designs of wildflowers executed with great craftsmanship. People stood inside but only one clerk was visible, a man. Joe steeled himself and walked in the door.

He began at the front right counter and worked his way around, taking his time, pretending he was engrossed with each display. Hand-carved tables and chairs of pine sat draped with scarves and rugs of exceptional color and workmanship. He paused to examine the details on a table. If he could have carried it home, he'd have bought it on the spot. Maybe he could recreate the design. He asked the young clerk for a booklet.

Was Gienia here? A door in the back of the shop might conceal her. Joe's heart threatened to leave his body. He decided he'd look at every display before he'd ask. Halfway around, he sensed someone watching him. His hand rose to his racing heart as he caught sight of her.

There was an attractive stripe of gray at Gienia's temple and tiny lines around her mouth—but her eyes, her figure, remained as he remembered. Joe's throat constricted. He stood exposed, dreading discovery. Would she recognize him? He'd kept fit and didn't put on a lot of weight, but his hair was salt and pepper now and of course he didn't wear a uniform. What would she think of this older man who stood before her with the heart and memories of a boy?

Joe pretended to inspect a small tapestry, then he caught a whiff of the light flowery smell of *Replique,* the perfume he'd so carefully picked out for her in the PX. He'd hunted down and bought a bottle for Kate, but she'd put hers away somewhere to save it because they didn't make it anymore. He hadn't smelled it for years. Gienia must have worn it for him. She also wore a large diamond ring.

He had discovered her once before, when he was interrogating refugees. She had traveled from the far side of Poland, across Czechoslovakia, and by some clever trick of attaching herself to a German who came in and out legally, she'd reached the West. She had noted several troop movements as she traveled and she was able to pin-point where they were. The Captain told him to interview her repeatedly to get every morsel of information she might have noticed on her trek and he did.

Even tired and frightened, she'd appeared like a jewel in a heap of glass, and now he'd found her again. When Joe could speak he said, "I'll take this." He fumbled for his credit card, then searched her face for acknowledgment. Obviously, he was the one who'd changed.

Only after she saw his signature did she break into her marvelous eye-creasing smile. "And so, Joseph, finally you come. You are not disappointed, I hope?" Her voice, husky and intimate, just as he remembered it, thrilled and soothed him at the same time.

"Gienia, you haven't changed since the day you dropped out of my life." *Matka Bosko*, that was the last thing he wanted to say. Her hand brushed his.

"I was a foolish girl. What more can I say?"

"Nobody went back behind the Iron Curtain in those days, nobody."

"But you see, I did."

"But you had a future," *with me*—he kept himself from saying. "What made you go back?"

"You were gone when I was told if I performed a service for your government, I may enter America freely. My stupidity I can barely think of, even today."

"I was only gone two weeks. I promised I'd come back. I gave you my word."

"I had no faith in myself. How could I believe in you?" Her hands opened.

He had to understand how this tragedy had befallen him once and for all.

"How could you imagine you'd reach America by going east?"

Her voice was a whisper. "I did not know I was to go east. An MP came among us displaced persons. Whoever helps him locate stolen US cigarettes earns a visa, he said. I passed word that I had a generous buyer and I arranged to meet the thieves. As you might imagine, the MP took the stolen goods, put me in a van with the thieves and drove us to the East Germans border. We were returned as undesirables. I could not admit I had betrayed them. They bought their freedom back, but I suffered badly before police released me to find my way home."

Stricken, Joe wanted to protest. He'd linked her loss and his father's illness as signs from God he should stay home and forget his dreams. He'd never dreamed this. "But why?"

Gienia sighed, "I wished to enter freely, so your choice would remain also."

"Did you think I'd marry you simply to gain a passport for you?" He nearly said, "I loved you," but pride held his tongue. He couldn't swallow.

"Joseph, some things are not meant to be." Her voice thickened.

"I paid a smuggler to look for you, but he found nothing."

Her face softened. "I believed all chance for me in the West was gone. I realize now that the M P was a thief also. He could record nothing, but then I only saw that East Germans did not live better, so I returned to Poland." Her words struck him. "You said to me no matter how bad things get, Poles find strength to go on, you remember?"

Joe remembered. He remembered every minute that he'd been with her. What could he say? He couldn't just walk away. "And now, are you happy? Are you married?" His voice rasped. He'd expected to have a profound insight, and he heard himself blabbing.

Gienia said, "Just as you, I made a new life. I was fortunate. Do you recall the clothing you gave me, from the officer's wife; the red sweater, the plaid skirt and the tennis shoes?"

He smiled, "You looked like an American girl."

"I wore the loden cape you bought me and her clothing to appear rich enough to buy the cigarettes. Those clothes and a few dollars I hid in my sock was all I carried. When they released me I walked east, mile after mile. I crawled into a farm wagon to cross into Poland. When I sat on a rock to repair my shoe, my husband saw me and stopped. He said I looked like a modern woman who could work in his shop—so here I am." She indicated her store. "Joseph, do you have time for me?"

"I'd like to visit with you and have you meet my family. They are shopping there," he indicated The Ring. "I'll have time tonight. Tomorrow we go to relatives, then on to Zakopane." He couldn't abandon her now that he'd found her, he couldn't.

"Tonight is not possible but I will be in Zakopane early next week. Take my card. After all these years we must find time together."

As he walked out, Joe caught his reflection in the window. He noticed his short, curly salt-and-pepper hair; and even though he had more muscle than fat he wasn't a skinny kid anymore. He straightened up, hoping she was watching. How long had it been since he'd felt such stirrings?

Gienia was well off. That answered his prayers, yet somehow it shocked him. She'd done well without him. He was unprepared for that.

Across the plaza, Ted clapped and beamed as a crowd gathered to sing with the folk group. Marek approached with Kate and Stella. Each of them carried a single rose and bulging satchels. Marek handed Annie his remaining rose. "For you, beautiful."

Was Marek saying that Annie or the rose was beautiful? Oh, for the days she'd hidden behind that wild hair, he thought.

She blushed, and thanked Marek in Polish.

Kate came and said to Joe, "If the locals had cameras they'd snap us for when they wanted a good laugh." She spotted Joe's bag. "I didn't see Stella buy that doll."

"Annie asked for it and then she took off. Give it to her, will you?"

"She asked you for this doll and you made it an object lesson, right? One of these days you'll learn." She leaned over, kissed his cheek, and said, "I'm forever hopeful." She left him with the doll.

Joe turned to his daughter, nodded at the red rose she held and said, "You'll get the chance to sponsor Marek to America yet." That didn't sound like he meant it.

Annie wiggled her nose at him, "Uncle Ted, will you dance with me?"

This elderly uncle, who claimed he disliked all forms of show, put out his arms, and turning his head from side to side, spun her in ever-widening circles, whooping as they whirled. Marek offered Kate his arm and Joe caught hold of Stella. They all joined in. The circle was complete. Joe twisted and turned, hollering and stamping as he asked himself if he would ever learn. Breathless after their dance, Stella said, "Joe, you promised us lunch."

"At the café' with the pretty cakes? My mouth's watering," Annie said.

Shaken by Gienia, Joe turned to lead the way. Eating offered distraction.

Marek interrupted, "My friend's restaurant is not so far away. I'll show you the way."

Marek had introduced them to the woman perpetrating a swindle and their belts were lumped taut with cash. Joe was sticking to the beaten path. "Stella can't walk far. We'll eat at the café here." Joe flushed, embarrassed to use Stella as an excuse. She was active and trim; her hazel eyes were lively. She wore orthopedic shoes, but it was the ring of white hair that Claire she'd aged.

Stella overheard his comment and threw a sharp look at him as he offered his arm. "You're helping your aged aunt now are you?"

Joe whispered, "It's safer if we stay near other tourists but I don't want to hurt Marek's feelings. Do you mind?"

She patted him. "You're a thoughtful man, Joseph. Use me whenever you need."

The small rooms opened, one into another. Elegant brocade-like wallpaper and small chandeliers gave them a look of royal patronage. As they walked into the ornate restaurant Joe realized that Ted and Stella were both sagging with fatigue. He needed to seat them quickly.

The waitress waved the gaggle of hungry Americans inside behind a nearly toothless babcia, whose intricately-wound braid reflected the colors of her lifetime, from white at her temple, to dark brown on the inside coil. Her hands shook, but she greeted them with the Polish equivalent of "Welcome to my happy home." She had probably taken a break from her work at one of the stalls outside, Joe thought.

She had on a frayed shawl and what Joe's mother called her "house dress." It was faded by washing but spotlessly clean. She lifted a small girl with large roses on the skirt onto her lap and patted the chair beside her for Stella to sit. Several old fellows rose and freed the table beside them for Kate and Joe.

Their long thin menu listed elegant sandwiches cut in wedges and fancy cakes covered with poppy seeds or glazed fruit on top. Joe ordered tea while they considered their orders.

Annie took the wilting roses and placed them with the table's flower. The child slid off her babcia's lap and onto hers. When the tea and glasses of water arrived, Annie gathered teaspoons and tapped them together as Joe had when she was small.

The child followed Annie, who tapped her glass and sang, "My father killed a kanger-oo-oo, gave me the grizz-l-ey part to chew. Now wasn't that a heck of a thing to do, to give me to chew the grizz-l-ey part of dead kanger-oo?" She ended with a flourish.

The child grinned as Marek clapped for Annie, who flushed at his response. Joe sighed; she was seventeen. How many crushes could she handle simultaneously?

An elegant variety of sandwiches with their crust cut off arrived. They looked delicate, but they passed Ted's stringent taste test with murmurs of approval. The babcia beamed as Joe placed tea cups and a sandwich before both her and her granddaughter.

Ted said to Kate. "You write about this. I'll read it back home."

Kate said, "I brought an extra journal. Want to give it a try?"

"No, Leszek says they can picture what Stella writes, but my letters read like a shopping list. He said he wouldn't read them if Babcia didn't make him."

Kate said, "Sometimes the way you tell a story matters more than the story you tell. I'm Irish, don't forget. I could give you tips on story telling."

While they spoke, Gienia invaded Joe's senses. He felt her presence, he smelled her scent. Had she truly thought helping that M P would ensure their marriage wouldn't be burdened with her need to escape? Or had she wanted into the US with no ties to him? Engrossed in thought, Kate and Ted's conversation swirled around him in sound bites.

"Ted, when you talk to Leszek about his friend Stasiu, if you give him details about the day you heard him plotting it might help him remember better."

Ted threw open his hands. "I wrote. I said it was me who told Father. I said it, but Leszed says I confessed only so he could keep his life's friend." He gulped for air. "He said God gave him both curses and blessings. He'd accepted staying in Poland and God rewarded him with Zosia and eight wonderful children—and me. He said my remembering them, all the years when others forgot, meant the world to him." Ted's voice caught, "He said only Stasiu knew his plan and he couldn't forgive because he'd have sacrificed the love of our family to bring Stasiu to the US. He wouldn't hear it was me who told."

Ted had told? Was that why Ted needed to repair the old men's friendship so urgently?

Kate patted Ted's hand; "To take in a hard truth, people need details. You know, you say he was standing in this place, doing that. You walked in because . . . ."

"I forgot my hoe, I did, I went to dig carrots and I forgot my hoe."

"And he didn't see you because . . . ."

"Father cut the door in half to let in fresh air. The bottom was closed, but the top was opened for air. I ducked down to hear why they laughed. They never told me their jokes and I wanted to laugh too. Leszek was rolling in the hay laughing. Leszek said, 'Tadeusz thinks we're good guys, doing the hard jobs. He'll have the rest of his life to think how nice we are.'

Staisu said, "I will continue to help your family while you earn my fare.'

Leszek said, 'And I will tell them bad guys robbed me. When I send your visa and ticket to join me in the US you must be sure they think you ran away from your drunken father.'

Stasiu said, 'I will take your job and work so you can learn. Maybe when you are educated and rich you can send something for them, if they haven't put a curse on you.'"

Ted took a deep breath before he could continue, "They were roaring, laughing their heads off at stupid Tadeusz."

Kate interrupted his story. "There isn't a 14-year-old kid on earth who wouldn't have told on him, Ted."

"My father stood over a barrel of smoking sausage. I ran to him and said, 'Leszek won't send money for us. He'll send for

Stasiu who will work him through his studies. They'll fool us all. He laughed and said we were all stupid. I heard him. But Father waved me away, like a rat. I ran to the river and stuck my head in the cold water to wash it from my mind, but weeks after Leszek read that letter out loud, God showed me that day in a dream. I didn't know the truth when he read the letter, but later, I saw it was me who told in a dream, and now I must make this right for Stasiu."

Joe was startled. He thought he'd heard the entire story but it had more twists and turns than he could take in. It was unbelievable, but he did believe it. And he knew he'd have to help clear this up if he wanted peace in the family. A feud among the elderly could trickle down. Joe understood that he'd better think up a way to help Ted figure this out, if he wanted his own plans to work out.

Kate smacked Ted's hand lightly, "Leszek caused his own problems. Forget him." She smacked him again, absolving all guilt, as if she'd been empowered to do so.

Stella said, "But Kate, Stasiu lived with a drunken father who crippled him. His friendship with Leszek got him through and now, again he has nothing. Making it right for Stasiu, that's what we must do."

Kate stroked Ted's hand. "You describe that scene like you did for me, and Leszek will see it—whether he wants to or not. If I spoke Polish I'd tell him. I'd make him see."

Ted nodded to Kate and then he changed the subject. "I wonder what this restaurant's lease costs? Wouldn't this be a beautiful place to work?"

What could it cost to buy the concession to a famous landmark? To Joe, Ted seemed crazed—open to anything now that he'd opened his wallet.

Kate picked up on Ted's thoughts. "You couldn't lose with a place like this."

Had she lost her mind? Desperate to keep Ted looking at his own business Joe said, "Look Ted, if you'd bring cousins to Detroit on a three month visitors-visa we could put them up and I'd teach them how to carve on my state of the art equipment. I'd show them how to track their business and order supplies. You supply them and they could return to that farm ready to run a business you'd be proud of. You throw in a good truck and their limits disappear." There, he'd said it, he'd put his last cards on the table.

Instead of reacting to his proposal, which Joe was braced for, Ted burst into song. He belted out

"Hoopi-Shoopi-Donna."

For a quiet guy, Ted was going against habit, but he was home and maybe the dynamic was different on home soil, Joe thought. He joined in, then Annie and Stella and Marek sang too, filling the room with their voices. When they were through, Ted meticulously counted out zloty for their meal. He tipped the waitress in dollars saying, "For your retirement."

The child crawled back on her grandmother's lap, blowing kisses. Ted kissed the child's cheek and pressed something into her pocket. Well, that was Ted, Joe thought—the good uncle.

As they walked outside Ted said, "If nothing else happens, Wawel Castle and The Ring made this trip for me."

Marek took Annie's arm. "You sing very well. So, do you enjoy the land of your fathers?"

Annie beamed at him. "I like everything so far."

What the hell, Joe thought, as they walked into the cool damp afternoon, at least he'd thrown the idea of training cousins in the U S out there so it wasn't still sitting on his stomach like a suppressed belch. He linked his arms with Stella and Kate and they walked out arm-in-arm, not just family, but comrades—at least for the moment.

They waited as Marek secured two cabs. Ted looked from under his bushy eyebrows at Joe, "Where do you get all the words?" Ted asked.

Joe knew Ted didn't expect an answer. He squeezed Kate's elbow. She bumped him with her hip, turning away so Ted wouldn't see their smiles. A reproof from Ted wasn't total dismissal. Encouragement often lies in what wasn't said, and Ted's revelation to Kate about his brother's betrayal and Ted betraying Saszek in return—well it clarified a lot. No wonder Ted was hell bent to help Stasiu.

His tale telling had cost both Leszek and Stasiu their chance to come to America. Ted's plan to buy off Leszek didn't look so crazy now. At least Joe understood this whole, complicated, quest better.

Marek located two cabs. He appeared to know both drivers. The first looked a lot like Ted, only he had a full head of hair. Ted asked him to return them to the hotel. The driver initiated an impressive roar and off they went to rest and wait. Marek and Annie took the second cab to a museum.

9 – PIOTR'S PLACE (CASH FOR COUSINS)

Touched by all they'd experienced, the elders returned to the hotel in silence. Joe secured Ted and Stella's hotel room for an extra half day and he and Ted lay down on Ted's bed while Kate and Stella repacked. When Stella Claire the doll Joe had bought for Annie a treasure, Joe smiled. The events of the day kept him from napping so finally, he ducked downstairs to call K in the privacy of the hotel phone booth. He wound up telling more of his family dynamics then he intended.

K said, "I consider marriage more seriously every day. I miss the give and take of a good argument." He laughed, then he seemed to remember, "I contacted Inspector Skrzycki. He'll check other hotels for the scam you described. He'd like to speak with Pani Dorsak. I'll tell him you have the fellow who introduced her to you."

"I couldn't put Tatyana Dorsak and her children at risk, I just couldn't."

"If she appears again he'll want to speak to her. But enough about that. I spoke to an American engineer from Food Pro. His firm designs and restores processing units as simple as fruit drying racks, selling for about thirty-thousand dollars, combined with packaging equipment that can be imported from twelve-thousand up. A farmer could charge his neighbors for using his services. It's beautiful because it adds value to what already exists very simply."

Joe was nodding and jotting notes on a small pad he'd packed to keep Ted's business ideas together. "That's good, that's good. I'll tell Ted about that. Anything else?"

"There is a trucking business up for sale with state-of-the-art equipment, everything necessary's here. It'd take all of your uncle's money for a down payment. It's massive and your people would need management skills they might not have yet."

"Well keep asking, at least there's something out there a good farmer could use besides getting caught up in risky stock. I appreciate your help, K."

When he exited the booth Kate stepped out of the elevator. She stopped short, "Joe, you have to be honest with me. What is it that's bothering you about Marek?"

"A green card could make our little girl more than attractive. Maybe the two of them shouldn't be alone much, that's all."

"Why didn't you just say that? Am I this child's mother?"

"Oh come on. Don't blow this up." People were glancing their way.

"You didn't tell me you were concerned, but that's okay because Kate doesn't need to know everything, is that it? Well,

I can pick and choose what you need to know too. If that's our deal, tell me now. It would sure simplify my life."

Oh boy, he thought, she's been fine the whole trip and now she's going to blow—in the hotel lobby.

He ignored her point. "I doubt K will make it through his contract. When I call he begs me to apply for his job. Did you want to hear that?" Hearing himself, Joe took a more reassuring tone. "Look, I get goofy about Annie I know. I thought I should keep that to myself. I grant you it's probably irrational." He wore his most sincere expression.

Kate held his gaze a moment, then shrugged and walked into the gift shop.

When Annie returned, their cases were already in the car. Kate acted like nothing had happened but Joe knew he'd have to watch himself; her antenna was up.

The drive out of Krakow distracted everybody. An old-fashioned hardware store with tin cups in the window nestled adjacent to a color-filled Benetton shop. Kate scribbled in her journal as they saw poverty alongside prosperity. She'd told Joe she'd try to write an article on the Poland of today for Poles in the Detroit area and she was hard at it. He'd have to be careful about what he told her when she asked about areas he didn't know. If he made up anything too far-fetched he might see it in print.

They headed towards Nowa Huta, the industrial complex placed outside Krakow to punish dissenting intellectuals with their unscreened smokestacks. Nowa Huta's high rise apartments stood, monster like, covered with a fungi of soot. A few older women, whose dark clothing blended into the background, walked small children and waved at them as rain drops splattered on the windshield. Nova Huta had been given new life, but the fresh smell that normally accompanies rain was missing.

Annie pointed at a balcony high up on a gray building, "What's that woman pulling inside?"

"She hung out a skinned rabbit she bought at the market. They're too big for apartment refrigerators," Ted said. "I never had a Detroit rabbit that tasted so good. But forget rabbits and look around." He waved his arm to take in the entire area. "This is the town built without God. Communists allowed no churches. Poles found an empty field and they put up a cross. Soldiers tore it down. They put up a bigger cross, a bulldozer ripped it out. Every day a cross, and every week a Mass. Pope John Paul was Bishop of Krakow then. He made sure Mass was held in that field every Sunday. In all weather hundreds—no—thousands came to this Godless city to celebrate the risen Christ."

Stella patted Annie's hand as she took up his story, "Finally, after twenty years, they allowed a church here. They say people carried a million stones from river beds to cover the outside of the church. John Paul and people of faith brought Jesus here."

Joe spotted the curve of a dome. He turned and came upon the massive curved structure whose bells were rung in joy when John Paul became Pope. They walked around it gaping at giant stones, stacked like Lifesavers, up the walls of the church.

Ted said, "Sometimes I wondered if Poles didn't have a lesser God to give them such troubles after all their prayers. During the war I put tape on the mouth of our Madonna to punish her when Poland suffered. Stella told on me. Our priest came to our house. He asked me what life would be for Poles without their faith. He said if Babcia kept her faith here, why was I, sitting in my cozy home in America, scolding the Mother of God? He said Poles have credit in the bank of love. After that

I offered up my agony for those who know no God. Offering up my doubt restored my faith."

Annie giggled about tape placed on the mouth of the Madonna as Joe steered her back toward the car. He congratulated himself that the family was getting along so well in the close quarters Kate had dreaded. What more could he ask?

Ted pulled out Leszek's directions and Joe turned K's Mercedes toward his cousin's farm. Suddenly, Uncle Ted turned around and asked, "Annie, you still thinking you want to work for a museum or have you thought up something else yet?"

"Uncle Ted, I said that when I was twelve and for the last five years I've done everything I could to qualify myself to work in a museum. Why would you even ask?"

She had always coped with Ted's twenty-question routine well. Why would she take exception now? Joe turned toward her, "It's no insult to be asked, Annie. I'd appreciate it if somebody asked me what I want out of life once in a while."

Stung, Kate jumped to the edge of her seat. "You wish somebody would ask what you want out of life? Joe, you're fifty-five years-old. You have a home you picked, four wonderful kids you wanted and a wife who's supported your every whim. If you aren't getting what you want out of life, do me a favor and keep it to yourself."

"*Matka Bosko*, I just said it would be nice to be asked, that's all I said."

"No, it isn't all you said. You said, 'Nobody asks me.' You meant me. You meant I don't care enough about you to ask what else you might possibly want. Don't you dare dream up one more scheme that, if I asked, I'd have to work on. It's my turn to set a goal, not yours. I will jump out of this car and disappear over the next hill if you dump one more of your consuming little wishes, on me."

"Are you crazy? How did you get into this conversation? Ted was talking to our daughter. How did an innocent question turn into a battle cry for women's liberation?"

"You pointed that remark at me and I'm telling you, it's not your turn. Ask me what I want before you slip 'just one more little thing you'd like' by me, why don't you?"

"Say what you want any time of the day or night. Who said you couldn't?"

"I'm saying it now because you think you're entitled. If I don't elbow you out, I obviously don't want anything. Well, I'm informing you now—the next turn is mine."

"You don't even know what I was going to say." He'd change what he was going to say to something she'd like if she'd just hold on.

Annie spoke up, "If you two don't stop, I'm the one going over that hill. I didn't come along to be trapped in a car while you two bicker."

Kate turned on her "And Miss Difficult, you're so sensitive I can't protest Dad's pulling his take-over routine on me? After what you've put me through? Oh no!"

Joe cut her off. "Annie, ask your mother nicely to put her grenades away. If she does, I promise I'll store mine." He caught Kate's eye in the rear view mirror.

Kate laughed, "That's the beauty of marriage. I'll get you later, Buddy."

Ted sighed, closed his eyes and mumbled, "Forget I asked. From now on I'll keep my questions to myself."

Stella touched his arm. "Oh Tadeusz, you take everything so personal."

They rode in silence until they reached the village where Leszek's grandson, Piotr, lived. They spotted the shed.

The lady sold Annie lemonade and pointed downhill, signaling someone was home.

Joe said to Marek. "Don't tell anybody we're asking about making investments here, okay?"

Marek said he understood, then he jumped out to direct Joe's drive down the muddy ruts. There was no sign of life as they approached the padlocked gate except the yapping dog and free-ranging chickens that were smart enough to jump out of the way.

"I see a motor bike by the vegetable garden." Ted got out and pushed the bell.

The basement door flew open and a young man whose feet were jammed into his boots, burst from the bottom level of the house, hollering welcome. He threw the gate open, motioning Joe onto a short driveway extending out from the closed garage door.

Annie reached for her camera. "This is 'a Kodak moment,' Pops. I'll snap it."

This moment, arriving at a family home in Poland, was straight out of his father's fairy tales, Joe thought. He wondered whether he should hug a chicken, pat the yapping dog or kiss the ground. He longed to use every Polish word he ever knew. Ancient memories surfaced as he embraced the smiling stranger he'd known only in a previous life.

A young woman appeared at the side door of the basement level. Piotr introduced himself and waved to his wife, Karolina, to join them. She flushed as Joe kissed her cheeks in the traditional three-sided kiss, right, left, then right again. Ted kissed the girl's hand in a courtly, old world gesture.

Annie said, "I always thought they overdid the kissing bit, but it seems about right after the trouble we went through to get here."

"You behave yourself," Joe warned, but he realized he was grinning at her.

Piotr's broad shoulders and blunt features contrasted with Marek's slim muscular build, Joe noticed. Marek stood back, frozen in wonder as Piotr mimicked his movement, looking him over more closely. A howl of recognition went up and they fell upon each other in an immense bear hug. They drew Karolina in as they turned into mad men, thumping and laughing and stamping the ground, hardly able to speak.

It was Joe's turn to stare. Words flew and he caught something about Warsaw and selling a car. Piotr tugged at Marek's sleeve, ribbing him about losing his jacket to close a sale. Joe gathered they had shared much, but somehow lost track of each other. To find each other at Piotr's home because American cousins had hired Marek was a coincidence beyond compare, they all agreed to that.

Startled, Joe stood back while the friends' wonder played itself out. He caught the mention of a name, Claire. Marek's answer had been an open hand and a down-turned mouth. *Matka Bosko (Mother of God.)* Joe wondered, was the kid married? That would explain a few things.

Piotr threw his arms around Joe in thanks and the sharp wind of a damp afternoon blew a chill up their backs. Piotr ushered them into the cozy quarters behind the garage where Karolina turned on her stove to make tea.

Red and gold-trimmed plates filled with sliced kielbasa and potato salad stood ready. Ted had called saying they were on their way. The narrow room had a couch squeezed behind the extended table. Books and treasures were on display. They appeared well off by anybody's standards.

The women oohed and aahed over a shiny veneer cupboard containing glass cups in ornate handled holders. Karolina ceremoniously removed one for each guest.

While she prepared tea, Piotr guided them upstairs. They inspected the unfinished rooms on the top floor. The second floor revealed a series of well-furnished rooms. Fold out couches waited with sheets and feather quilts ready, though it was probably too warm to use them, Joe thought. Somebody must have told them that Americans are always cold.

At the top of the pine staircase landing stood a couch, a fireplace and a pine wooden bar with stools. Piotr explained that occasionally travelers who had known his American cousin, Fred, in Germany showed up and paid to spend a night, but Fred had been gone a long time. He said he couldn't hang out a sign to attract strangers for fear his landlord, now living in Chicago, would hear and increase his rent. "Not much of a business," Ted mumbled.

Piotr lit the fire to remove the chill upstairs before bedtime. The house was thick and it was cool. Maybe they would use those quilts. Annie asked for the couch-bed by the fire; nobody protested.

They trooped back to the basement apartment where Stella helped Karolina pour tea. The house was far more luxurious than Joe expected. When they were eating, Piotr explained, "The owner built this for his retirement before his permit to stay in America came. When he found no buyer I offered to pay a hundred-fifty dollars a month for five years. Next year I must pay more or others will take it. I must make business pay."

Ted said, "But you brought cash home from Germany, right?"

"The Wall opened in '89, our American cousin, Fred Winowski, lived in Germany by your Army. I called him and I said that I could reach his town by bus, but that I had no money for hotels. He said, 'You can come stay with my family.'" Piotr struggled to tell his story. "He found for me work cleaning, painting and a little gardening."

"A priest sent me also—but I didn't speak English yet. The people he sent me to called Fred. He said 'Marek, you work with Piotr and stay with us.' We worked together, slept on sleeping bags in his boy's room, and we stand as friends."

Young Fred had told Joe about cousins who traveled back and forth from Poland to Germany by bus the last two years he was stationed there. Fred's friends hired them at a low rate, then tipped them with good American castaways the Poles resold back home.

"We earned dollars there and we sold our gifts in Poland," Piotr said. "We bought used cars we repaired to sell after we pulled each across two borders. We were rich guys." They laughed together.

Marek said, "We paid fifteen hundred dollars tax for every car we brought into Poland. Bad men brought wrecks they could not fix. People cried 'swindlers.' Then no one would buy from us. We lost."

Piotr said, "We earned much money. We lost much money. Cars sold only in cities. Our last car we took to Warsaw. We lost most of our money and Marek's jacket."

"We wait for days," Marek said. "We sleep in our car nights so it will not get stolen." His English faltered as his excitement increased. They spoke English to include Kate, then the one not speaking translated for Karolina, who appeared painfully shy. She not only didn't speak English, she only nodded when spoken to in Polish.

Piotr said, "Fred returned to the US, I married, and Marek went to work for a German circus." Marek threw his hands open indicating how that didn't turn out to be much of a job.

As they spoke, Joe savored the farm-cured kielbasa, sauerkraut, brown bread and poppy-seed frosted cake, served on their large dining room table.

Drunk with good will, Joe accepted coffee from Karolina, though the others drank tea. He was so relieved she'd spoken that he'd have accepted crank case oil. However, he caught Ted's look of warning too late. What she brought him was boiled coffee, like American cowboys made on the range. The loose grounds, supposed to settle on the bottom of the pot it's boiled in, were lurking in Joe's glass cup. Struggling to avoid swallowing a mouthful of grounds, he pursed his lips and sipped slowly, experiencing an instant cure to his hankering for coffee. After a prolonged battle, Kate reached over and switched cups with him. She emptied his remainder into a plant behind her. He tapped the top of her hand in gratitude.

Then Piotr opened the back door and urged them into a large two-car garage. Joe caught his breath. Had he walked into an appliance store?

Behind him, Annie made a quick count, "Fifteen washers and five dryers—all American. And their stove and fridge are American too. Isn't that something, Uncle Ted?"

"Matko Boska, where did you get these?" Ted's tone implied he thought they'd hijacked a truck. The young men stood, chests out, full of their accomplishment. "Your Army sells off such things. We are mechanics. For us they work."

Joe said, "How on earth did you get them here? Was this legal?"

"Your Army doesn't want old machines when they closed bases in Germany. We bought these for five dollars each. When friends drove horses to France for the horse meat market, they bought gas in Germany. Fred rented a truck for us to reach an Autobahn gas station. We drove from there, here."

Joe pictured young Fred transferring appliances from one truck to another in an Autobahn parking lot. No wonder he hadn't described that to his father, Joe thought.

"We had to wait twelve hours at the border. Our drivers wished to go home. I gave them a washer and dryer. Their wives love me better than them," Piotr laughed like a kid telling a prank. "German Border guards thought I stole them and would not allow us to exit. I went from man to man. All refused me. When the next shift came I place five hundred German marks on a washer and I pray very hard. A guard hides my marks in his pockets and waves us over. The Poles waved us in, no problem."

Karolina slipped Joe a stack of tissue-thin Army receipts for used appliances—sold for ten dollars each. They rested in his hand like feathers. He passed them to Ted who puzzled over them. Joe said, "I've seen these receipts. They're genuine and good as gold, but how could those customs men have known these flimsy receipts were real? "

Annie's thick eyebrows shot up. "Remember in Warsaw? K talked about selling horses to eat in France? These machines got here on one of those trucks."

"Smart use of an empty truck," Ted said. "Real smart."

Piotr said, "We'll make business in this house. When the land warms I'll dig another water line. Karolina's papa knows electric and gas. We need a small car, then . . . ." Their struggle for words left them wide eyed, looking for confirmation from their American cousins, their hope and pride shone in their eyes.

"But you've had these for years. Why are you beginning now?" Ted asked.

"In Krakow we made a laundry. We put a paper to sign up on the wall of college. Eighty signed that they wished for us to wash."

Joe leaned forward as Piotr's voice trailed off. "What happened?"

"Hot water. We could not get as much as we needed." Piotr said, "My sisters use machines till now. For five hundred American dollars I bought an old water heater." He pointed to an immense heater lying on its side on the floor. It had known long, hard use. "Marek and me, we'll clean and repair it. We'll have a second chance and we'll work this business together."

Marek grinned, "I work for American dollars. Also, Pani Dorsak's boss pays me each time I call to say Americans invest with no other. After I earn money for my friend in jail, I'll return here." He spoke as if he had made an acceptable arrangement.

"Wait. Are you saying somebody pays you to tell our business?" Joe asked.

"I say only you buy from no one else. You say to me what you wish and I'll say it to him. No problem." Marek's thin, bony face reflected hope Joe hadn't seen signs of before. His eyes lit with enthusiasm as he pulled out a card he handed to Joe.

Stunned, Joe read it and realized it matched Dorsak's contact number. Unbelievable, Joe thought, this was unbelievable. Marek was straightforward and up front but now he'd have to ask him about Dorsak's boss later, out of Ted's range. Maybe the police could use Marek if he had contact with Dorsak's boss, and leave her out of it.

Ted returned to the house where Karolina prepared more tea. Joe brought up his cabinet business but Ted changed the subject. Piotr and Marek had plans, but if he planted his idea with them, he figured their cousins would hear about his business from them. He'd talk to them later.

Finally, Ted went back to their business. "Let me get this clear. You had cars. You need a car to run this business, but you don't have one now. Is that right?"

They nodded and the enormity of it silenced the room. Piotr said, "Car prices went bad. Fred paid for our parts. We make a laundry to pay Fred back, but with no hot water, we have no business."

"And how long did it take you to repay Fred?" Ted asked, knowing they hadn't. Joe had grilled young Fred, who admitted the army's reduction of forces happened so fast, he'd left Germany with the Polish cousins owing him two thousand dollars for parts he'd bought to repair cars. He'd insisted Joe not tell his father the entire story because he'd hear about it forever.

Fred had said, "I know Americans must seem rich to those guys, but we opened our doors and helped them earn more than they ever saw before. My wife cooked and drummed up jobs for them and her friends cleaned out their closets. I'd seem like less of a man in her eyes if I never went after what we lent our cousins."

Uncle Ted had promised Fred he'd square things up for him in Poland. "I don't want anybody thinking they don't need to repay an honest debt, especially in the family. A family that helps each other and can count on being repaid is the cornerstone of our connections."

"You'll help us to get dollars to Fred," Piotr said. "You'll carry our dollars to America!"

Kate reacted, "Ted, we're all carrying cash. We can't have dollars spilling out of our pockets."

Joe began to describe how international money orders work until he saw their eyes were glazing over. Their expressions said, "It goes with you or it doesn't go."

Finally, Annie interrupted, "How many dollars do you want us to carry?"

A heated discussion followed. Karolina actually spoke, reminding them that if they ran out of cash they had nowhere to turn. Finally, Piotr said, "Five hundred dollars now. We remember the rest to the third generation."

Joe played it over in his head . . . remember to the third generation? He meant they would forget it until their grandchildren could make it right? No wonder the World Bank charges high interest rates when they get into poor countries, he thought. The look on Ted's face was thunderous. That would not be the end of the story if Ted had anything to do with it, Joe knew. Those boys didn't know the risk they were taking—just saying they'd pay a little regularly would have helped, but remembering to the third generation? Oh no, that was not acceptable.

Annie said, "If we all carry $100 extra we can do it."

Annie had a hundred dollars on her already—gifts from the extended family. That was a lot for her too, but it wouldn't change her life, or it wouldn't have until now. Joe'd watch so she didn't empty her pockets at the first sad story. He knew there'd be enough sad stories to clean them all out. He'd have to stay tough-minded. Suddenly, exhaustion set in and voices enveloped him like a warm blanket.

Kate leaned over, "Joe. Go to bed before you fall on your nose. The bed is made upstairs, and I put your pajamas on the fireplace."

He roused himself and found his PJ's warm and waiting. He got into bed quickly. When Kate eased in beside him she said, "You should see Annie. She just opened today's message from Mike. It's a drawing of a bear being lifted by a heart shaped balloon. He printed, 'DON'T FORGET WHAT EVERY WELL BROUGHT UP WOMAN MUST KNOW UPON REACHING HER ROOTS: TABLE, TABLE, CHAIR, CHAIR! LOVE MIKE!!!'"

Joe reached over and patted her. "Ummm," he answered.

# # # # #

When Joe awoke he drew warmth from a sleeping Kate. He missed the rooster, but he heard chickens and the dog. This was his fourth day in Poland, but somehow it seemed like his first. He eased out of his nest and tucked the feather bed that was snug around Kate. He dashed over the cold floor and offered up thanks that he was inside as he sat on a chilly toilet. Ted had warned him: Poland is often cold, even in summer. They'd all brought sweaters and jackets. Still, it surprised him.

Ted sat at the coffee table, spreading out the dollars they'd carry, sorting them into stacks of ones, fives and tens. He'd built a roaring fire.

Annie sat up. "If you'd told me I'd get rich here, I wouldn't have fussed about coming."

Ted said, "We'll look like Mrs. Bluchi who carried two purses, remember?"

"If anyone tries to rob us act cool—like it's counterfeit," Annie stood beside Ted in her pink nightgown, her hair twisted in all directions.

Stella stepped forward and hugged her great-niece, "Go run water in the tub and wash your hair, then sit by their heater downstairs to dry. You can't go out in this damp weather with a wet head; I don't care how hot it gets later."

Joe suppressed a grin, Annie's hair was so short it wouldn't take long to dry. Why, when he was young he'd worn his curly hair that length, but when a girl told him he looked like Simon Garfunkle he cut it. He looked up as Marek appeared in the bathroom door stripped to the waist. A small gasp went up from Annie. Marek excused himself as he brushed by her. Joe forced himself to look away. Some things a father shouldn't witness, he thought.

Ted and Stella busied themselves locating places to stash their dollars. When Marek walked through to help with breakfast, Ted showed him all the clever places to hide money. Marek grinned, shook his head and proceeded downstairs.

Kate protested, "If one of us showed where we'd hidden money you'd holler your head off. We're all in this together, Ted. I'm asking you to stop flashing your cash."

"Marek knew we had money, he handed it to us."

"That doesn't mean we have to show off every hidden zipper, does it?"

"Don't worry about these guys," Ted reassured her. "They're family."

"But our hiding places might seem goofy enough to mention to somebody else and I'm not chasing anybody who runs off with your glasses case stuffed with bills."

"Who's asking you to chase anybody? Are you crazy?"

Stella interrupted, "Dollars affect lives here. Kate's saying we mustn't tempt anybody and she's right." When Stella spoke, Ted listened. She was small, but she was mighty.

Ted pouted, "I know I don't carry God in my wallet."

Annie laughed, "No, you just act like you do."

Joe made a short cutting gesture signaling them to drop it.

Kate shrugged, "If Annie's washing her hair I'm going back to bed. I'm still tired."

10 – MAY YOUR PIGS NEVER HAVE PIGLETS

Joe leapt back into bed. "Did you see Marek gawk at your daughter?"

"No, I heard her gasp at the sight of him. Besides, she has on a long nightgown and Marek has been noble about ignoring her nonsense. I don't think you could have picked a safer companion she'd enjoy being with, Joe. Consider yourself lucky."

"He wasn't ignoring her in there."

"Girls test their powers and she feels safe with him. Besides, it irritates you. Why do you fall for it? Lighten up; you used to be a fun guy." She rubbed his back.

"I don't want her pining after anybody, that's all." He turned over. "I could take care of you now, come to think of it."

He'd had his mind on Gienia, but he knew he belonged with Kate.

"As long as our daughter doesn't suspect we fool around."

Thirty minutes later an invigorated Joe hustled down the drafty stairwell. Ted and Stella were in the cozy living room already. Annie's auburn wisps feathered the arm of the couch where she lay. By the time Kate came down, Marek and Piotr had entered from the back room. Annie fluffed her hair with her fingers.

Breakfast turned out to be more of what they'd eaten the night before, plus fresh hard-boiled eggs. As they finished Piotr announced, "Tomorrow family comes to Babcia's farm from all over Poland to see you."

Heads spun. They'd planned to hit the farm just before they flew home. Startled, they rearranged their itinerary. Ted said, "We'll go to Auschwitz, but we'll have to skip the salt mines and the Black Madonna."

Annie protested, "Everybody knows about Auschwitz, but what about miners who carved chapels out of salt during their work breaks, praying they wouldn't cave in?"

Kate spoke up. "Honey, Stella's grandparents and uncle died in Auschwitz because they tried to hide a Jewish girl. We're going to pay our respects."

"Oops, somebody forgot to tell me." She threw Joe an accusing look. How had she lived in his home and not known? Joe shrugged.

"My father came to Detroit from Zakopane. He was walking home from work and was struck by an uninsured driver," Stella said. "Matka wanted me to stay in school. Running a boarding house for Polish workers seemed a good way, but she couldn't read or write English. Banks wouldn't lend to women, so she went to a Jewish lady who lent money to men."

Ted said, "Mary said her name was X for the mortgage. The woman liked her spunk. She loaned Mary $1,200 for a house big enough for boarders. For years she could pay only the interest."

"Father's family offered to bring us over to their farm in Poland right after my mother got that loan. Matka paid a man going back to tell them that a Jewish lady made staying in America possible for us. She thought that was why they agreed to hide that girl years later."

"After the war a displaced person from their village came and told Stella their story," Ted said.

"My father's family hid a girl the priest brought to them. Money my father sent to his family bought a piano for his young brother. The girl played that piano beautifully. The music carried through the air, sweet and true. People stood outside in the snow to listen," Stella said.

"After a while the Germans noticed," Ted added. "They caught the girl with her hands raised over the keys. Stella's entire family died at Auschwitz with her."

"I'm sorry, Stella. I'll go to Auschwitz and stay as long as you want."

Stella patted Annie's hand; "I don't want to go to the gas chambers, the mass graves, or see that horrid film. I only wish to pay my respects."

Ted sat frowning. Joe asked, "What's wrong, Ted? What do you need?"

Ted's tone betrayed him. "I held anger for Leszek's selfish plan but Leszek longed to live in a city and go to school. He nursed anger that I never wrote of cultural things. I wrote only of work and worries, maybe of hearing a polka band, never of a symphony or theater, even when Stella got me to go. I didn't wish to make him sadder, you understand?"

Ted took Annie's hand, "Leszek said I have a peasant's soul, that I did not deserve freedom because I didn't tell of cultural things. And this he said before I wrote him I was the boy who told Pa his plan." Ted steadied his voice. "Annie, I am old enough to forgive such things, I know now it was God's plan for us to change places, but if you say to your cousins you don't only hear Polkas, that you know music and art, and you will vote when you can, I'll be proud."

"Don't worry, Uncle Ted, I'll polish off crabby old Uncle Leszek. Your father was right to leave that old poop there." Ted smiled at her irreverence as they headed out.

Marek brushed against Annie's hair as she bent to enter the car; he looked at his hand as if he'd touched a delicate flower. Joe decided that Marek should drive and he took his place in back with Annie leaning against him. It reminded him of when he'd corrected papers and she'd rested on his chest like a warm kitten. Joe snoozed until Marek pulled off the road into a neat, sparsely-filled parking lot.

Auschwitz was a series of orderly barracks. It had an eerie symmetrical orderliness. An elderly couple exited their car with German plates and entered through the wrought iron gate that had cut off all hope for escape. The family followed them inside the complex. Scores of wooden buildings, perfectly aligned, lay before them. There were people around, yet the silence of the place assaulted his senses.

The woman dropped her cane and up went her hands. "*Meine Gott, das ver Deutsche!*" as if she had never acknowledged Germans did this until she saw it for herself. A vision of Doubting Thomas when he realized he'd denied the resurrected Jesus flashed across Joe's mind.

Annie swooped and returned the cane to the woman's fumbling hand.

"You see this." Marek hurried them into a building on the right. The walls held larger-than-life photos of starving, confused looking people whose dark eyes stared as they stood before the camera, awkward in their state-issued prison uniforms.

Gasps escaped each of them as they huddled together in rooms, holding wooden bins built out from the walls, about waist high. Window glass extended from the top of the wood to the ceiling, creating large storage spaces. The bins in one room held brushes, terribly worn, with long strands of hair forever clinging to them. Another bin held hundreds of belts and suspenders. There were tattered suitcases with the names of their owners painted on the lids. A bin of braids, cut off at the nape of the neck of women before they were gassed, sat ready to stuff mattresses.

Annie took Stella's arm as they walked into the next room. Bins filled with patched high-top shoes, so worn they must have conformed to every peculiarity of their owners' toes, were tied together by shoestrings. Ted stood a step behind Stella and Annie. They approached the bin where the children's shoes tumbled over each other, appearing even more worn than those of the adults.

Shaking her head, Annie turned to Marek, "Look, children's shoes."

"Not one child. For such shoes, many children."

"You mean as one was gassed, their shoes were passed on to others?"

"The best shoes arriving on small feet were sold."

Annie lurched towards the stairs as Ted took Stella's arm and headed outside.

Joe gulped at damp air as he hit the door. "I'll make our donation. Marek, go start the car." He knew that the chill that came with this place was one that no heater could dispel. He hurried towards the entrance where he shoved twenty-dollar bills in the box. As he approached the car Annie, Kate, Ted and Stella climbed inside. The car was running but Marek wasn't inside.

Scanning the lot, Joe spotted him speaking to a taxi driver. It was the Ted look-alike from Krakow. Marek smiled and pointed, "Taxi man." The man nodded to Joe.

Was Marek setting them up? Was this cab driver connected to the guy Marek telephoned about their plans? Were they being followed? He weighed leaving Marek in the parking lot, but if it was a set up he'd better not let them know he'd caught on. He barked, "Come on, we're out of here." He got in the driver's seat and Marek got in back next to Stella. As he turned onto the road the cab driver waved. Joe didn't wave back.

They hadn't gone far when Kate touched his shoulder. "Joe, did you take your blood pressure pill? You're all red. You look ready to explode."

"A place like that upsets everybody. We shouldn't have come." Stella patted his shoulder, "Oh no, Joey, I'm thankful you brought me."

"We both thank you for this," Ted said.

"Many don't know Christians died here too," Stella began. "Most for standing for justice or protecting a Jew. This ground sanctified Christian and Jew alike. Here I see the Holy Spirit saying, 'I have room for all who suffer. I speak in many tongues and he who hears Me will not be lost.'" She sighed, "You saw this with me. Now I can die happy."

Glancing at Marek, Joe caught his faraway look. Was he seeing the light? Could his accomplices have him under surveillance? Possible, Joe thought as he turned back toward Piotr's home.

The silence in the car was so complete they might each been alone. Relieved he didn't have to put on an act, Joe rehearsed asking K to check out the taxi's license plate number. That driver might lead them to the man who hired Tatyana Dorsak to swindle people out of the hotel. He needed a private place to call from where Marek wouldn't hear him. He had to get away from the car.

Joe was thinking so hard he thought he could hear the wheels turning in his head. As if in answer to his effort, he caught sight of a rest stop. He jerked the wheel to turn in. Two men stood beside a narrow wooden building with a high sliding window and an overhang like a carport with three pine picnic tables underneath. A sandwich board listed prices. Joe figured he could get a moment to himself there.

Ted sat up. "I smell homemade kielbasa. We need comfort food after that place. Let's walk around."

He spoke with the men grilling sausage as Joe pulled out the cell phone K had given him. He rehearsed a quick message asking K to call his friend in the police department. He could check out the taxi driver. The idea that Marek might have criminal connections was making him jumpy. Joe liked the kid fine, but he was still uncomfortable enough to check him out.

The Poles sprang into action and bottled lemonade appeared from boxes wedged behind the building. They handed a drink to Marek; who handed it to Annie without meeting her eyes. Then he passed on hard rolls with an immense kielbasa sticking out the end. Ted peeled off a handful of dollar bills, insisting the men eat a serving themselves and join them at the table. Suddenly Ted had a party going and the pall of Auschwitz lifted.

Annie busied herself taking pictures of them while maneuvering to photograph Marek alone. While eyes focused on her, Joe slid into the back seat of the Mercedes, as if he was looking for something. He pulled out K's cell phone, dialed and blurted out the cab's number, not giving K a chance to comment. Nobody seemed to notice his activity. He exited to pick up his food and eat.

Marek offered to drive and Joe pushed in beside Annie. As they left Ted said, "I'll bet that's the first time anybody paid those fellows to eat their own kielbasa."

"Can't we drive through a village before we head back to Piotr's?" Kate asked.

Marek turned off on a country road. The village they drove through was built around a town square with small shops lining the streets and an immense church stood at its heart. Ted pointed to a side street. Marek eased the car around and nearly came up against the back of a horse-drawn wagon.

He slammed on his brakes and the horse reared. The farmer raised his fist, yelling a lengthy curse.

Joe jumped up through the open sun roof and hollered a reply. People on the street laughed and cheered. Joe gave a little bow before he sat back down.

"Honestly Joe, you're something," Stella laughed. "He said, 'May your pigs never have piglets,'" Stella translated for Kate.

"My father said that if he was mad and Mommy wasn't nearby. It came to me in a vision." There were better curses, but right off the top of his head, Joe thought, it wasn't bad. They were off the beaten path experiencing Poland and he intended to enjoy those moments. "May your animals not know their master." Joe offered in Polish.

Annie scolded him in Polish, "Watch it, Dad, or I'm telling."

Joe put his finger to his lips. What fun to share mischief with his youngest.

At the edge of the village, fields were marked off for a country market. There was a small section for horse and wagons and another for cars. A farmer in high boots waved them into a parking place behind weathered, wooden stands, covered with goods.

Fred had lent them a video camera and Ted placed it to his eye as they walked into the market, Stella grabbed one elbow and Kate the other to guide him safely. The ground was muddy where people had walked. Green fields surrounded the stalls packed with bright-patterned aprons and work dresses. Kitchen implements and imported fruit crowded other stalls. Stella steered Ted to a stall with tablecloths and paused by those with patterned stitched cutouts.

Ted helped Stella select colorful patterns, and Joe took Kate's arm and they walked side-by-side, nodding to shopkeepers. Annie walked ahead, happy she was wearing her red rubber boots. Joe's chest swelled with love for her. At the end of the market a large rosy-cheeked woman stood by a plank displaying Jockey shorts knock-offs. A boy, about eight, stopped to barter, pointing to the smallest pair.

The woman held it up, pulling at the elastic band, showing how it sprang back. The boy pulled out money and the woman shook her head. He dug deeper. She spoke to him. His head was down as he took his final dive for zlotys—he didn't dare return home empty handed. Finally, when his money was handed over she folded the shorts, handing them to the boy. He nodded, pushed them into his pocket, then headed towards the fields.

Joe's sharp whistle froze the boy mid-step. Joe waved him over. The boy stood at a wary distance. Joe spoke in Polish. "I am an American uncle. I like the way you trade. You try to hold your money, yet you act like a Cavalier. I wish to reward your trading skills." Joe reached over and pushed five one-dollar bills into the boy's pocket.

The boy's gaze stayed on Joe's face a moment. He nodded and mumbled "Thank you," in English, then turned and raced toward home.

Kate squeezed his arm, "Have I told you I love you lately?"

"Hey, if five bucks will do it, what have I been so tight for?"

Annie appeared, "Dad, Marek argued with that guy selling shoes, then walked away. I spoke to the seller. He was trying to buy a pair of patent leather shoes for a little girl's First Communion but Marek said they cost too much. If he's married why didn't he say so?"

Kate said, "No, no—he has a Godchild. He told me about her the other day."

"I feel stupid," Annie paused, "Dad, haven't you paid him anything yet?"

"Ted gave him some pocket money. We'll pay him at the end of the trip."

"Oh Joe, it must be awful for him being out with us with no money," Kate said. "Why don't you pay him by the day? You can save his tip till last."

Annie said, "The man said he wouldn't find a better buy anywhere."

"Are you sure about the price?"

"He wrote it to be sure I had the correct number of zeros."

Joe looked, "Actually that's cheap. Go ask if dollars will cut the price any."

Annie reappeared with the shoes wrapped in paper; "It worked. I got them."

Marek stood on one foot and then the other when Annie presented them to him. He insisted on counting out the exact zlotys into her hand. He emptied several pockets in his thin jacket to get the money, just as the boy had. Maybe he'd only been asking and they'd put him in an embarrassing position. Joe thought about how he'd told Ted to be careful about people's feelings and now he'd been the one to presume. He'd talk to Ted about paying Marek daily.

"I like Marek," Kate said. "Annie could do worse, you know."

"You want to restart this immigrant process when she's second generation? Are you crazy?"

As they bundled into the car Ted rolled the window down and rested the video camera on the door. Annie leaned forward and said, "Remind me to give Uncle Ted a lesson on using that camera. Right now it's zoom, there goes the market. Zoom, zoom, there goes town. Zoom, zoom, zoom there goes Poland."

Ted said, "You laugh but that tractor the farmer cranks, who would believe me if I tell it? Here is proof." He pointed to the right where an ancient tractor stood with a handle sticking out front. Men in overalls stood scowling while one stepped forward and cranked away. After several tries it caught and a cheer rose.

Ted laughed, "I got it. That tractor will run in my home forever."

"But Uncle Ted, you don't own a computer, a DVD player, or even a VCR."

"I'll come to you. You're smart. You can figure out how to show it to me."

"There's the couple with the rearing horse," Kate said. "They bought a new couch, set it behind the wagon's seat and they're sitting on it for the drive home. Look he's driving and holding a cell phone. He's probably bragging to his buddy."

"I'll drive slow, Ted. You film. Everybody in Hamtramck needs to see that."

They waved and checked their horse for Joe to pull out, all curses forgotten.

Stella said, "Isn't it the same the world over? A man is angry when his wife insists he goes shopping, then he gets something and the world must see his buy."

Ted said, "He's entitled. It takes a lot of sugar beets to buy a couch."

# # # # #

Back at Piotr's home Karolina breaded fish as her potatoes boiled. She pantomimed how she'd scooped out the largest fish the lady in the shack kept in her rain barrel. They needed to cook longer.

Kate asked her to show Joe and Ted photos of their large country wedding. Stella pointed to a refrigerated truck whose shelves held cooked meat, baked chickens and cakes. "Look Ted, our gift paid for the refrigeration needed for their wedding feast."

Annie announced; "I count forty single-layer cakes on those racks."

Kate said, "We aren't renting a refrigerated car or baking forty cakes for you. Forget that." Joe patted Annie's hand. "If that's what my baby wants, that's what she gets." Kate made a face at them.

Ted smiled as Joe slid the album to him and said, "Tell us who is who."

"Here's my brother, Leszek and his wife, Zosia. There's my joking sister."

Joe tried to fix the images in his mind so he'd recognize them when they met.

Annie whispered to Ted about Marek suffering through buying the shoes. Ted went out back to settle up with him. Joe thought the laundry business would give Marek a chance to hide away from any criminal connections he might have. He could work here and let Piotr do the deliveries, freeing himself—that is if he was really involved with the criminals pushing fake stock.

Later, as they sat by the upstairs fireplace, Annie asked, "Dad, who's Claire?"

"I'm not sure, but I've heard the name a couple of times, why?"

"This morning when Marek went out for bread he made a call. I heard him tell Piotr some girl named Claire was going to a very bad place. Piotr said he'd help if he could. Who is she? Is she sick?"

"I didn't hear it so I can't just ask, but I'll keep my ears opened."

Progress comes in unexpected places, Joe thought. Claire might be key. People connected with criminals were often charming and believable, but Marek's odd behavior made Joe think he was resisting whatever they wanted of him. If he understood about Claire he'd know how strong a grip they had on Marek and whether he could be trusted.

11 – ON REACHING THE FAMILY FARM

Before The Winowskis bedded down at Piotr's, Uncle Ted announced, "I'll say we can't stay at the farm tomorrow because Stella is expected at her uncle's home near Zakopane early. We'll try to stop on our return, but no promises. I must see how it goes with Leszek and Stasiu before I say it."

Stella spoke up. "Ted, this is the last time you'll ever see Babcia, and Joe's waited a lifetime to meet his family. Do we have to run in and out so fast?"

"I've slept in that house with my heart broken too many times—too many times. When my heart's torn, I can't swallow. Then they push food at me and watch, oh, how they watch. I can't suffer that again—not for my mother, not for Joe, not for you. I can't."

Stella turned to Joe. "After Leszek threw Stasiu out and ran off himself, we had a week before we could return home. Leszek resented Ted all those years and that letter loosened his tongue. Once his resentment spilled out nobody could take back his words. The days before we could return to America were terrible, terrible."

"Americans, they can walk away and never look back, but in Poland, where could we go? Babcia was upset already. If I'd left in anger she'd never stop cryin'."

Stella patted Ted. "We acted like we dismissed Leszek's words and what his father did we forgave, but we worked in Babcia's garden to hide the pain on our faces."

"I choke when I think of Babcia feeding us again and again." Ted rubbed his stunted finger. "When I mourn, I want a sheet over my head, but there was no place to hide. If we're set to leave before I talk with Leszek, I can face him better because if I fail, we can go. I'm too old to come again. I know God is on my side, but He's given me a task I must perform. It's up to me; with the help of Jesus."

Joe sighed. Babcia might be deaf enough to miss the action but what shape was Leszek in, or Stasiu? Attempting to reconcile these crusty old men had heart-attack written all over it. Ted's exit plan sounded better all the time. Besides, Gienia waited in Zakopane and he'd kept that to himself. She'd said they'd have time together. If things went sour on the farm he had that to look forward to. Beyond that, he dared not think.

Joe squeezed Ted's shoulder, "We'll leave the farm by four o'clock tomorrow. I'll rattle the change in my pocket and we're gone. You can count on me."

As they prepared to repack the car, Kate said, "We can't paw through suitcases at the farm. Let's separate the presents now."

Stella produced fabric, buttons, buckles, packets of thread and high-quality needles while Kate brought out hand cream, colored pens and barrettes. Ted fetched disposable shavers and Joe donated several of his small but prized wood working tools. Finally, Annie lugged in an old Samsonite suitcase and opened it slowly. She revealed the mesh Christmas stockings full of marvelous junk that Mike had sent along. By the time she'd pointed out their mysteries, circus barker style, even Ted was laughing. Joe shook his head—these might have been prized gifts in 1993, but in 2005 Poles had traveled and worked all over the world. They were in better shape than most of Europe because so many of the new homes in Poland were paid for, in cash, from foreign earnings. They'd have to be very good sports to respond with warmth about the gifts displayed in his trunk, Joe thought.

"They'll think this is all they're getting. Wait till I tell them about the hook up I'll get them."

Cholora, Ted still thought he could get them high-speed Internet at discount rates. Joe said, "Wouldn't it be better to talk about that after the deal is complete?"

Ted scowled, his bushy eyebrows meeting, "Why?"

"Well, I'm thinking they might wonder how long you've had that money. The fact that you've been generous won't disguise the fact you held out on them," Joe's own feelings, exactly.

"They might think you've been poor-mouthing them," Kate said.

"The home I built Leszek to care for *Babcia* is better than our house. Look around this place. Are these kids hurting? Why, they don't use half what they've got."

"But Ted, don't you see?" Stella said, "We own our own home and we have Social Security. They have a farm in the path of centuries of turmoil. If they guess wrong about crops or their government changes, they could still be destroyed. We show up with all this money and we look like we've lied to them."

"No one better call me a liar, that's all I got to say." Ted's bald head flushed.

"But if Dorsak's firm sends a notice you arranged Internet hook ups for them later they'd never know the details," Joe said. "They'd be thrilled and you'd be an even greater hero."

Ted's mouth puckered. "I want them to know Stella and me, we're sharing everything we got with them. Besides, how can I press Leszek to forgive Stasiu if I don't say it? I'm not just braggin'."

"I know, Ted. That's exactly why I thought you might want to hold back."

"Leszek knows I never wanted his place in America but I did tell my father. He's got to know it wasn't Stasiu. How can I make him hear me without that high-tech hook up to get his attention, tell me that?"

"Whose selfishness caused his problems? Leszek would have turned his back on you forever. Don't bribe him. Give him a chance; let him step up and be a man."

Ted didn't respond but Joe knew he had his attention.

"Did Stella sacrifice so Leszek's stubborn-ass behavior could put you down?"

"Nobody does without for others like Stella." Ted patted her hand.

Joe rejoiced, Ted was thinking. "Don't stun them with what you're giving, that's all. This laundromat project needs help. The plumbing isn't there and their rent could triple if the owner gets wind of the investment they'll make in his property to get going. They could set up in town on five thousand-dollars and not be hostage to that landlord."

Ted bristled, "Not with my money, they won't. Piotr didn't aim to repay Fred till I shamed him. Let him see how bankers treat him when he says his grand-children will pay in the third generation. Let bankers put their boot up his ass."

Ted was alive and well. If Joe wasn't up against it himself, he wouldn't have sympathized with Piotr and Marek, but he was, and he did.

Annie joined in, "Just think, Uncle Ted, Leszek will think they have everything you'll ever give them, then—ta-ta-ta-ta—internet is installed and they'll be the first in their area to have it. They could earn money for just having it. He'll feel like he got kissed on the head by an angel."

Ted shook his head, "I got to tell what we're doing for them. Don't say another word. You make me dizzy you talk so much. I'm going to bed." He stomped off.

Joe's stomach jumped. Sure, he could buy stock legitimately, but that wouldn't get inexpensive internet out there. Years ago Kate had said that Ted was addicted to playing hero (even in small ways.) Joe had been so offended he'd hardly spoken to her for days. Had she pegged him? If Ted insisted on announcing his gift, Joe couldn't stop him. He'd cope with it later. Sometimes Kate saw through walls, he thought.

# # # # #

Ted had given Piotr and Karolina the zloty to rent a neighbor's car so they could join them on the farm and remain a few days. The car was small and slow so they had started out early. Marek offered to drive to the farm so Joe could take in the scenery. The Winowskis rode in silence as each strove to commit the day to memory.

New homes and renovated buildings interspersed alongside the occasional tumbled-down, straw-roofed hut on the verge of collapse that flashed by. Neon signs and flashy cars contrasted prosperity with poverty, especially as they drew nearer the Polish-Ukrainian border. Joe had expected to go back in time a hundred-years, but progress hadn't waited for him. Some few men in shabby pants and thin jackets roamed back roads, but the countryside looked well-tended by people who maintained order and pride despite war, devastation, invasion and communism. Many had worked out of the country and done well. People they saw on streets and in cars as they passed looked as if they would welcome the next great challenge.

Poles had paid a high price to remain on their land and suddenly, Joe's own striving to make his family and community proud made sense to him. A group's honor and dignity were important; but who was he to get disheartened or frustrated? Was he worthy of all the privileges he'd had so far? In the grand scheme of things Joe knew he'd been blessed. Poles rose and went about maintaining order despite the blows history had dealt them. Joe sent up a prayer of thanks that he'd seen this. He felt both gratitude and guilt. He'd immigrated in his father's genes while others were left behind, did that supreme good fortune entitle him to squeeze others out? He'd never thought so. His father, Uncle Ted, and now he, tried their best to encourage and support the people around them. It was their mission, their duty, their joy.

After more than an hour and a half on the road, Marek slowed to read a sign. Ted pulled himself forward to direct the last few turns that took them into a neat farmyard. The buildings were set back from the road. A two-story red brick house stood in front of a cluster of buildings. A log cabin defined one side, a small, low-roofed house rested behind it and an immense cement block barn rose above and squared off the rear. Marek eased the car into the central courtyard.

"There," Ted pointed to a scruffy house tucked behind the rest. "Your father was born there. We lived in front; the animals in back. There I heard Leszek's plan that changed our lives forever."

Stella said, "Ted and I brought our Teddy here in 1947 to build this house and barn after the old one was burned by retreating troops. Times were hard. People couldn't buy necessities. Joe, for weeks before we traveled, your mother and I sewed seeds in small packets inside our clothing. They were more valuable than gold. People were starving. All crops and husbandry had to begin again. Leszek traded some of the seeds for chickens to begin his flocks. And our Teddy, while we rebuilt the house, he and the other children carried buckets of water. They hoed and got tomatoes and potatoes and some berries growing, just like I'd taught him. He was only a child, but he was excited to help. He was a happy, kind, proud boy."

Ted couldn't go there. "See those cement blocks we used to rebuild? We made them by hand, every one, with 3 forms only. Cement blocks don't burn. They'll never be burned out again."

Joe turned to Kate and Annie, "This farm was in every fairy tale my father ever told. I used to sit under the table and fall asleep listening to him and Ted talk. For me, this is the end of the rainbow."

Annie patted his shoulder; "No Disney stories for you, huh Dad?"

As Marek switched off the motor, men in high rubber boots put aside their tools and walked in from the surrounding fields full of ripening crops, lush and green. Joe looked to the back of the barn and spotted the manure pile covered with fresh straw. He smiled at memories of the two men most central in his life weeping with laughter, arguing about who had chased who into that dung. That steaming manure assured Joe he was, for sure, on his father's farm.

Several young women and alert children stood on the outside stairway going up the back of the house, elbowing each other as they caught sight of their American cousins. An old man took a broom made of twigs from a girl sweeping the packed courtyard ground and placed it against the wall.

Ted opened the car door and stepped into the damp wind.

Annie jumped to his side, "Did every neighbor they ever met come to meet us?"

"They're all Winowskis." Ted's voice wavered as he turned to Joe. "Keep Leszek away from me. I need time with Babcia before I talk to him."

Joe stepped forward and reached out for Uncle Leszek. Leszek returned Joe's hug with tears of joy. Ted embraced his brother, then he stepped back to holler in Polish to those approaching, "I brought you Victor's son, Joseph, his wife, Kate, and their daughter, Annie."

Relatives swarmed them with welcoming smiles and three-sided kisses.

Joe turned to check on Kate, who seemed to be doing fine. Wind whipped at Annie's beaded head just as Leszek reached her and put his weathered cheek to Annie's, smacking a kiss on each cheek and back again. She laughed and smacked him in return.

Chickens pecked around them, undeterred by the commotion. A watchdog yapped, pulling its chain. Joe relaxed amid the smells and sounds of his ancestral home, this was a moment he'd cherish.

Suddenly the great barn door swung open. Everybody froze, then turned to see a fine, muscular young man wearing a ribbed under-shirt, leading a workhorse outside.

Kate muttered, "Good Lord, its Poland's answer to Jean-Claude Van Damme bringing his horse to say hello."

Giggles escaped from behind Annie's fingers. "It's Mr. Under Shirt, himself."

Joe administered a parental pinch as he said, "*Ania ma jet laga!*" He translated for Kate, "I told them Annie has jet lag, more or less."

She nodded, Leszek's wife, Zosia, waved to Kate to come upstairs from the top step. She placed her hands around Annie's waist and directed her towards the steps, "Come on, Sport, we're going in."

They trooped upstairs, touching the hands extended by cousins as they passed. Stella had prepared them to pause and remove their boots. They'd worn heavy socks for inside. Annie and Kate's bright red cut off galoshes glittered like glass as they placed them alongside drab farm boots.

Joe stood back to survey the farm from the top of the stairs. Four well-kept greenhouses, covered with heavy-duty plastic rose from behind the barn. He'd seen photos of them because Ted had sent the money for their construction, helping the family raise seeds to sell and barter.

Zosia, ushered them into the kitchen where flowered curtains stretched flat across the window. The aroma of beets and sauerkraut cooking on the stove made his mouth water. He'd waited a lifetime for this meal, in this home.

Three young women helped Zosia tend the food. Because their names slid by him in the cacophony of greetings, Joe gave them nicknames. The one with skin as fair as a china figurine he dubbed "Dresden." The second, who bustled among the simmering buckets of food on the stove, he called "Peppy." The third gave the orders, so he called her, "The Chef."

Joe said, "Annie, say hello, then lend your cousins a hand and get to know them."

She nodded with understanding as they looked over the treasured tile oven in that kitchen. The dish cloths hung from the chimney of the huge stove while giant pots sat firmly bubbling on its even surface. Zosia beamed as the Americans slowed to appreciate her efforts, but Leszek tried to hurry them on, away from the simmering onions and steaming borscht.

Joe stopped mid-stride, "Leszek, wait, let me smell the food in my father's kitchen."

Leszek halted the procession and Ted went ahead, entering his mother's room alone. Kate pointed to boxes peeking over the top of the wooden cupboards, Cheeze-it, Nestles and Ritz Crackers. Leszek whispered in hesitant English, "Empty, all gone, pretty boxes."

"American pop art in Poland, isn't that great?" Annie shook her head.

They stood admiring everything until Zosia needed to check the stove, then they moved on to greet Babcia. "She's got to be fragile," Joe said, "so let's not get everybody all worked up."

"Oh Joe, do you think we won't behave?" Kate objected.

Babcia sat propped up in bed under a white cover wearing a fresh long sleeved night gown. Her white curls popped out from under a small flower-print kerchief.

Annie whispered, "Dad, look, she's wearing a scarf in bed."

Joe slid his arm around Annie and felt her laughter rising. "Don't you dare laugh. This woman suffered through two wars, the death of loved ones, and communism. Don't you dare."

"I know, I know, but that just makes it worse." She drew a deep breath, then Babcia motioned and Joe pushed. Annie knelt before her great-grandmother, threw her arms out and they hugged. She took Babcia's work-gnarled hand in hers as Babcia greeted her in Polish. "Dziadziu wished to meet our

Annie. He had many things to say to you, but you must only look and you will see. You will see your family who loves you and wishes to keep you in our hearts as you will hold us." Annie was nodding and affirming that she would hold them in her heart, forever.

Then Babcia patted her own curly hair, took hold of one of Annie's beaded strands and pointed to her own head. Ted had told them Babcia was upset—she'd had to cut her hair when she was in bed so much that winter. Now, she laughed as she pointed at Annie's curly hair that matched her own, and the silly hair decorations that irritated Joe so.

Annie slid onto the edge of the bed and gently removed Babcia's scarf. Digging in her pocket she produced first a pick she used to get Babcia's hair poofed out. Then she pulled out colored beads and braided several into Babcia's white hair.

"Perky" appeared with a hand mirror. Babcia tried to hold it but her tremor shook the mirror. Annie held it steady and placed her own head close. Their reflection shone side-by-side. Their close-cropped, curly hair and their identical, dancing, blue eyes, reflected their genetic links. A roar went up as Kate took a picture of them together.

Babcia said in Polish, "You're almost as pretty as me."

Ted nodded at his siblings, "For them, it's like seeing Babcia young again."

Leszek had loomed so powerful in Ted's stories, Joe hadn't realized he was so slight. His blue eyes shone bright over weathered cheeks. Joe wondered how much Ted had put on this brother when he hadn't been there to defend himself?

Leszek waved Joe to the space beside him and tugged at Joe's short, tightly curled hair. He gestured towards his sisters and their children. A full third of the people in the room, including Ted, had Babcia's eyes. But only Joe and Annie had both blue eyes and the thick, wild, bothersome hair.

Babcia's three living daughters smelled like apple blossoms. They were in their seventies, sweet-faced and well-scrubbed. Joe held his aunt's work-worn hands in his. They greeted him with stories of his father, Victor, as a boy. Their oldest brother had both teased and helped them, teaching the first to milk the cow, the second to weed the garden, and the third to break the branches off felled wood so their father, Victor, Leszek and Ted, could load it on the wagon and pull it home.

Joe tried to imagine his father and these wizened ladies as young, but it was beyond him until they giggled and began correcting each other's memories. Their impish characters peeked through, and Joe began to understand what his father had missed so dearly. After they'd elbowed and wagged their fingers at each other, the ancient aunts assumed a lady like demeanor. They each turned to Kate and greeted her with a few well-rehearsed words in English. "Dresden" offered to show Annie around and she disappeared to parts unknown. The meal wasn't ready, plus relatives were gathering from afar.

When Piotr and Karolina arrived, Babcia gave out a joyful cry. The elderly aunts and uncles moved into the connecting rooms and Piotr knelt beside his great-grand-mother to answer her questions. He told her he'd start a business with his friend, Marek. Babcia called for Marek and grilled him about his faith and work habits. He answered her patiently and she released him, satisfied.

Babcia asked for a special album. She opened its dog-eared pages and pointed out a photo of Zosia slicing into a giant 10 lb. Hershey Bar Aunt Stella mailed to them as a special Christmas treat twenty years earlier. Babcia described how for months she'd used those shavings to convince their gaggle of children to play quietly and allow the mothers to visit. Each time they received chocolate shavings as their reward.

Piotr stood up to announce that on one occasion he had been so good they'd given him six, yes six, (he held up six fingers) slivers of chocolate. His laughing mother stepped forward to hug him, reasserting her pride in him.

Stella reached over to playfully swat Ted on his shoulder. "I told you it was worth mailing that Hershey Bar. I told you." Speaking in Polish, she turned dramatically, "He talked mean to me when the stamps cost me more than the candy bar!"

The family hollered and stamped their feet in mock protest on Stella's behalf.

As relatives entered and greeted them all, Babcia beckoned Joe and Kate to come to her side. She held up dog-eared envelopes from the back of the album and Joe recognized his printing, done on graft paper so they could read it. He'd taken lessons in writing Polish script, so he could write some Polish but he'd ignored all the markings that made the word read correctly. He'd written to Dziadziu and Babcia when he hadn't realized how unthinkable it was for an American soldier to cross the Iron Curtain into Eastern Europe, even after his discharge. He'd written again, after he was long back in Detroit and his dream of seeing his father's home seemed a boy's fantasy.

Zosia called Annie back from cutting fresh noodles for their soup so she could hear too. Babcia directed Joe to read his letter aloud, in English, for Kate.

He unfolded the yellowed paper and a picture fell out, the kind couples take in a booth at a train station. A very young Kate, looking more like Annie than he'd remembered, smiled back at him.

Kate gasped, "I remember that night, but was I ever that young?"

The room grew still as Joe deciphered his own script and mentally translated it back from Polish to English for Kate. Ted paraphrased it in Polish about ½ a line behind Joe so everybody could follow.

Joe began by saying he'd come home from Europe to be at his father's side during his fight with cancer. He described how Ted had sat with Victor, telling tales of home to cheer him as he weakened. Then he'd written; "But the reason I'm writing now is to tell you I've given up my dream of visiting Poland because politics did not allow me behind the Iron Curtain and now I've found the girl for me in my own back yard. She's not Polish, but she is Catholic and her people treat me great. My dream of visiting Poland must be abandoned to begin my family. I can't chance some Irish guy snatching my girl away from me. Only someone so special could inspire me to not come to you. I ask you to remember Joseph, your grandson, in your prayers."

He got a cheer and Stella nudged him. "You were always a good boy, Joey."

Kate kissed his cheek, "Annie, take a photo of this. I'd like a copy, even if I can't read it."

Annie did, then she turned to her father. "Dad, Piotr said Babcia's children and grand-children have never been photographed all together, not even at his wedding. They'd like that better than money. Can you get them lined up so I can snap them?"

Joe clustered Babcia's children, then her grandchildren, then the great-grandchildren around her. They attempted to waste no film. When Joe announced that Annie's camera had a disk that could record over ninety photos, a great "Ahhh" resounded.

The sleeper couch hemmed Annie in. "Can I stand on the couch in my stocking feet?" Waving hands encouraged her. She climbed up and braced herself on the back of the sofa with her bent knee. She started snapping, one after the other, until she shifted her weight.

Whoosh, the hide-a-bed opened, smashing Annie into the wall. She slid slowly down onto the flattened couch and lay motionless. A shocked silence filled the room. Marek reached over from the end of the couch and lifted her as young men stepped forward and pushed the bed back into a couch.

They moved concerned relatives out of the way as Zosia grabbed a clean towel off the stove and wet it to place on her head. Kate slid into Marek's place, and when Annie smiled faintly to reassure them, Kate laughed.

Annie reared up, "You're a bad mother, making fun of me." Then they both collapsed into tears of laughter and pain.

12 – SURPRISES ABOUND

While Ted visited with Babcia, Annie went back to hanging out with her cousins, preparing the feast for the gathering of their clan. Relatives arrived every few minutes. Joe joined the engineer, Piotr, the newspaper man, and several young cousins who straddled chairs around the small table where Uncle Leszek sat. If Leszek blessed his proposal, Joe knew that Ted would back his business.

Joe asked for permission to speak. When Leszek gave his nod he said in Polish, "In America, small businesses provide hope for proud, hard working men. If I offer fine products I can charge more than cheap imports because I guarantee my work."

When he had them nodding, he described his carving equipment, demonstrating the rotor with his fingers. He drew them in as he might a group of students.

The engineer said, "What you say is interesting, yes, but custom carpentry our grandfather and our father did also. In the country, men come from far away for great skill, but they trade services without the payment of cash, most normally."

In desperation Joe pulled out his machine's booklet. The engineer took it from him and the young men gathered around. The excited buzz he'd anticipated began when they saw he could carve four chair legs simultaneously. Pencils appeared.

Joe gave his all. "I have equipment. If two or even three of you work under my direction for six months, I will teach you all you need to run a business. Then we could ship the equipment necessary here, to create a shop of your own." He didn't dare say Ted would pick up all costs, but he implied it.

They nodded. It sounded good, but no—after a few minutes of quiet discussion the engineer announced that not one man there was prepared to go.

Joe's throat constricted. Of all the obstacles he'd imagined, disinterest in living in the US hadn't been one. What were they thinking? He asked, "But why?"

"It is acceptable for us to say it to you? Yes, I think we must." Leszek glanced around for confirming nods before he went on. "For generations our youth contributed their strength and intelligence to make foreigners rich; now the European Union promotes opportunity here, in our beloved home country. This chance comes only in one hundred years. To leave now would say to God, 'We sleep in despair as the Apostles did when they did not understand they could follow Jesus.' Who of us, who prayed so faithfully, can turn his back on all God's won for us? We cannot go in this hope-filled moment, for if things went badly here while our backs were turned we would grieve badly. Poles must discuss and work out their future. There will be much distention. We must have our say."

The engineer said, "Why must intelligent men leave their beloved home to appear ignorant in a foreign land? Does the America of today offer more than we, working together in a free land, can create? We have done much for others. This moment in history belongs to us."

The newsman said, "Too many jobs go away for even American workers to flourish. What place would there be for us?"

They spoke thoughtfully, in turn, like a ball passing from one to the other.

A thoughtful young man spoke up, "Christ says look for the poor, for peace, and social justice."

Shocked by their position Joe said, "But that's not the whole story."

"We hear German, English and Ukraine news. Each presents world events another way. We see trouble for you and we are sorry," Leszek said.

Piotr said, "We Winowskis stay in our beloved land as long as hope lives."

They looked down, as though embarrassed to see his shock.

The engineer said, "We inside small countries must be wary to survive. Russia will not stay small if she sees weakness in any of her old satellites."

Leszek said, "We have grieved too many lost children. We will fight to keep our family ties. When Winowskis do well, Poland will flourish. We've seen our cherished land through every indignity, not this government or that one, but we . . . the people . . . we are Poland."

A bowed old uncle said, "We Poles were unfortunates, adrift is other men's power too often. You have made a kind offer, but at this time in history we must stay and build our government.

Matka Bosko, Joe's chest hurt. He sat open-mouthed, rallying his thoughts. An uncle who hadn't spoken took pity on him and asked if he saw what ventures might do well for them in Poland.

Relieved to change the subject, Joe scrambled to share what he'd noticed in his travels so far. He knew that Poles think Americans get a business idea a minute. He pulled at his observations for an intelligent reply.

"Well, I think Piotr should establish his laundry in the city where people walk to him. He'd need no truck and he wouldn't be trapped in a lease that comes due shortly." He took a moment and scratched his head. "Good post cards seem scarce. You might think about printing some. We could send over a digital camera, a computer and paper to print them, if you're interested."

He squirmed in his seat, "In Krakow I saw a stainless push-cart that spat out doughnut middles. It was made in Minneapolis. Ted could arrange for you to get a couple of those, too."

They watched attentively as he spoke. He searched the recesses of his mind for ideas. He suggested they comb the countryside for old implements; wagon wheels and butter churns might decorate their restaurants and hotels. And he said, "Kate likes your brooms made of bound sticks, maybe you could sell those?"

An uncle said, "Yes, these things we've seen."

Silent, they waited. Desperate, he threw in what K had said about preserving fruit and importing fertilizer to sell neighbors. "I'm told that could earn 100% profits."

100% profits? Could it be? They told him they grew organically, but maybe . . . .

Ted had helped enough to give the family confidence and they gave him their honest thoughts. Joe realized in a flash of self-awareness he'd played the "Ugly American" when he'd pushed his needs and ignored theirs. Embarrassed, his self-respect was shaken.

He promised he'd give their question serious thought as he continued his travels. They nodded, careful not to look at each other. He glanced around, feeling hemmed in. How could he escape?

He looked out the bedroom window and spotted people approaching from the main road, arm-in-arm, singing. The young men scattered to greet more cousins. The school supply man came from Szczucin, another family had hitchhiked from Tarnow. Two girls approached across the fields carrying their nylons so as not to run them. They received deafening greetings among the covered picnic tables that had sprung from some mysterious place to accommodate the guests who came carrying food to share with the gathering. Joe watched as Annie was absorbed by the young crowd.

Aunt Stella picked a place out of the way for Babcia in the dining area. Ted propped her pillow against the flower-stenciled wall then Piotr carried her in and set her down. Ensconced as queen, she introduced Joe to the cousins who'd arrived after three. The rooms filled, then dissipated to other rooms or the courtyard outside where they gathered, as if for a wedding.

Amid all the excitement, a middle-aged uncle arrived by motor-bike. He asked for vodka to quench his thirst. Perky presented him with a shot of tea she'd poured from a vodka bottle. The handsome, graying man threw his head back twice before realizing he felt no accompanying glow from the tea his niece had placed in the whiskey bottle. Babcia enjoyed the joke, then brought out the genuine whiskey. After he put away two shots, she confiscated the bottle.

Young women bustled in to fill the soup bowls, then Uncle Ted tapped his teacup and quiet settled over the room.

All attention focused on Poland's favorite icon, *The Black Madonna,* a silverbacked painting of Christ's mother, discolored to a distinctive black, brought to Poland in 1382 by the Pauline order and copied to hang in the homes of faithful Poles. Legend has it that where she stayed armies did not triumph against Poles. Visions and miracles were attributed to her and John Paul venerated her, so Ted had purchased this fine example for his mother in '93. It now presided over their family meals.

Karolina plugged in Christmas tree lights that adorned the icon and a sigh went up. Everyone bowed their heads and Leszek blessed them.

"Zycze wam zdrowia, szczescia, wszystkiego dobrego."

Joe told Kate, "They pray for health, happiness and good things for all."

Only the Americans sat to eat. An occasional noodle's uneven length spoke of Annie helping her cousins. First they had soup, then mashed potatoes with mushroom gravy, and finally, duck and chicken and farm-smoked kielbasa with marvelous fresh vegetables—peas, carrots and even tomatoes grown in the greenhouses out back, giving them fresh produce for the entire family. It was a small farm, yet there was little need for shopping in cash only stores.

"I am proud," Ted said, "my family does beautiful by us."

Kate said, "Ted, they told me about your Care Package Underground Railroad. You and Stella mailed them seeds and those small things they could not buy so they could carry on. This family didn't have to leave home because of you. I'm proud to say I know you."

Ted's bald head flushed red. At home he was unassuming, but here he was a monk and elder statesman combined.

Joe bit his lip as Kate caught his eye. She'd seen his distress. He plastered a lopsided smile on his face for her. How could he eat now that his invitation had been rejected? He'd played his last card. After the twins went back to school in August he couldn't hire men without the means to pay insurance and social security for them. He'd lose his work space, no doubt about it. He ached all over. If they'd stomped him he couldn't feel worse. Ted had said on a farm everybody watches your heartache. It was true, Joe realized, there was no place to hide in this crowd.

Kate said, "You know, if we could produce a 'scratch and sniff' book of Polish cooking, we could sell it all over Hamtramck and in every Polish community in the US."

Joe clutched at her silly remark, "Every kid who came from a Polish neighborhood would pay big bucks for that."

"Dad, only Leszek, Babcia and Marek are eating. Why aren't the others?" Annie asked.

Joe glanced around. Annie was right, the relatives didn't have a crumb or a cup among them, though they urged the Americans on.

Ted answered, "They'll eat outside so they don't crowd us. Eat slow and save room for desert. Say you appreciate every morsel, that's what counts."

They ate slowly, praising each course. Leszek asked how Joe's American wife liked their food.

Kate answered, "I think the best Polish chef works for you."

There was scuffling behind them, then a chef's diploma was handed over heads to be deposited in Ted's lap. "Where is she?" Ted hollered, "Where is our chef?"

Leszek's granddaughter appeared, pretty and shy, still wearing the flowered scarf she'd cooked in. Ted tucked three twenties in her pocket-for her and her helpers.

He waved away Leszek's protests, "If you don't let these magnificent cooks keep my dollars, I'll tell the neighbors Leszek won't feed me."

"Oh, Tadeusz," Babcia swatted at Ted as the poppy-seed cake appeared.

After the plates were cleared, Annie said, "I feel sick after all that food and the fall I took. I'll walk outside awhile, then carry in the Christmas stockings for the kids."

"Hide them." Kate said. "Babcia can pass them out later. We didn't bring nearly enough for all these children."

Marek walked into the entrance hall with Annie and she tried to slip her foot into her cut-offs without bending. Marek knelt down and pulled her socks up, then he eased her boots on. She leaned against the wall as he lifted each foot.

A young man wound his way past Joe to make sure baby geese weren't suffocating each other. If they weren't watched and separated they would trip over each other, so they took a lot of tending.

Kate pulled out photos taken at Ted's eighty-second birthday party. They revealed a crowded living room and a group gathered on the front porch of his small, wooden, well-kept home. Apparently, she'd provided the first peek at their benefactor's simple life style the Poles had ever seen. Eyebrows shot up when the photo was passed around. Finally, the engineer approached Kate. He'd noticed she was taking notes. She told him she was interested in details that spoke of daily life—like the stenciled walls, the hand-made brooms etc. She was recording her impressions so those at home could see it too.

The engineer asked her to send him a copy. "I read English for mental exercise and I would enjoy very much seeing how our American cousins see us."

Joe saw her preen at the prospect of sharing her writing, however small her audience.

Ted worried aloud that Poles were too successful as saboteurs.

"Yes," the engineer said, "but we who remain work together. It is complainers we sacrificed to America who return with directions for us." Everyone laughed.

"We nearly cannot believe France and Germany can work together now." Piotr said, "If they cooperate for the common good, we Poles can work together, easy."

"Our hope centers on this farm," Leszek said. "It draws all travelers home. We cannot hope to hold all here, but because of Babcia's prayers and Ted's aid, we hold this as a great refuge."

As Joe listened, he pictured a man with an annoying rash spending a day with a fellow convinced his chemotherapy would work. If his cousins didn't read defeat in their lives, why should he grieve over a business failure, regretful though it was. He could still feed his family. He wasn't going to die. What was a dose of humiliation in the grand scheme of things? Who was he that all his efforts must bear fruit? His misplaced ambition and pride had taken over his mind, convinced him that lying to Kate was for the greater good. He was not proud of that. He'd make things right quickly, he thought.

In that instant Joe willed himself to turn away from his grief. He didn't know what he'd do, he knew only that opening up was better than giving up and just sitting there, among his extended family. He saw that life didn't depend on this dream or that one, it depended on the ability to take hope and hold it no matter how life beat you down.

Joe was finishing his meal with renewed appetite when he caught sight of Marek sneaking in a back room with his jacket wrapped around the Christmas stockings. Dresden,

Perky and Annie followed him, while a gaggle of children, one a tough looking eight-year-old who'd managed to rip the knee of his pants, waited outside.

Eventually, the bedroom door opened and Dresden and Perky appeared, carrying a thick red rope hung with bags of red and green tissue paper tied to the rope at even intervals. Perky whispered to Babcia as she handed her a box of numbers. Piotr and Mr. Under Shirt tied each end of the rope on the curtain rod so it hung like a decoration. The youngest children were gathered to stand before Babcia.

Marek handed Ted the Santa puppet as Piotr tapped a glass for quiet. Relatives jockeyed into doorways and small children gathered in front of Babcia. Joe watched the children's faces as Ted lifted the puppet and spoke through it in Polish.

"The American Winowskis came across an ocean to visit children who pray loudly and help their mothers."

The children's eyes widened. Ted asked for them to tell him their hopes and dreams. One wanted to raise his own rabbits, another ducks, and a little girl wanted to make a doll dress from scraps of her mother's wedding dress.

Ted put the puppet down. "After eighty years my strength fades," he raised his glass, "but new energy surged in me when Babcia said, 'Our family needs you.' She sent me to America wrapped in the mantle of her love. I stand here today because I was protected by the cloak of her prayers. Now, for the first time in many years, Poles must not push their children over the sea for a better life. I see that hope lights your faces and gladdens your hearts. Your American uncle stands between you and destruction like a gorilla. I will help you flourish in this changing world. On that I give you my word."

The family clapped politely, not realizing the breadth of his promise.

"Babcia reached across the ocean to summon her son—that's me, and her grandson"—he pointed to Joe—"and her great-grand-daughter"—Annie gave a bow—"to join you today. We stand together to remember those with us no more: Dziadziu, Joseph's father, Victor, and our son, Teddy, who we left in your care so long ago. We pray that our being here today brings blessings to all Winowskis for years to come. Amen."

The youngest baby squealed, and everyone clapped and hollered.

Ted handed his handkerchief to Babcia, who dabbed at her eyes.

"I felt like yelling 'Amen!' Didn't you, Dad?" Annie whispered in Joe's ear

Just then, the engineer brought out a violin he placed under his chin. Little children squealed and older children danced as he played a gypsy tune. By the time he finished off with Chopin the room had hushed, with even the youngest held enthrall. Then he bowed and presented the violin to Annie.

She flushed and backed up. She'd had half-hour lessons once a week for five years. Joe couldn't remember her ever playing an entire selection. But now, as the engineer held out the bow, Ted's stricken face told the story. He'd bragged on her.

Annie looked to her father, wide-eyed, begging.

Joe stepped between them. "My daughter played for Ted as a child only." The engineer bowed and put the violin on the table, excusing himself.

Then Joe caught sight of Leszek's look of triumph aimed at Uncle Ted.

Annie saw it too. Before he could stop her, she scooped up the violin, made *The Sign of the Cross* and poised the bow just as Ted had taught her.

Matko Boska, Joe thought, how could she even think it?

She faced Leszek and spoke in Polish, "You see before you an amateur whose uncle, missing one finger and humming loudly, taught her to play. I do my best."

Standing erect, her fingers raised, her chin firm, she played. The notes rose, almost true. First she played a snippet of Chopin, then Tchaikovsky, then a bit of The Last Chord plus some of Be Not Amazed. Finally, when the entire room strained with each note, wishing her well, she broke into the Polish National Anthem. Her cousins stood.

Not every note reverberated as intended and the most difficult passages she skipped. But she played with flourish. When she finished she lifted her shoulders as if to say, "That's the best you'll get from me." The room resounded in cheers.

The engineer hugged her, shaking with laughter, as Joe squeezed Kate's hand.

The room resonated with applause. Leszek began a loud rhythmic pounding on the table and stamped his feet. The others joined in. Then Leszek rose to kiss Annie's hand. "Who could believe an American girl would bring our culture back to us?"

Annie threw her arms wide and hugged the old man.

Ted beamed and when the noise subsided, Perky scooped up the youngest child and told Babcia to pick a number. She picked out the first card. Marek cut the prize off the rope, handing it to the baby's parents. The father, Mr. Under Shirt, who had donned a Hawaiian shirt sent to him from Detroit, held his chubby baby while his wife unwrapped the gift, a candy pacifier. When the knot was untied, it plunked onto the mother's lap. Annie sat very still. She must have realized she'd overdone it with those cheap gifts. Joe patted her hand as the relatives greeted those silly items as the best fun imaginable.

The cards Babcia picked miraculously produced the proper gift for each child. The girl with crossed eyes got a number that gave her glasses with a funny nose.

Kate laughed, "They gave gum to a child with rotten teeth."

Ted heard her. "Who cares? That kid's thrilled. I'll give her mother money for a dentist."

The last prize, the harmonica, was for Mr. Tough, the boy with the ripped pants. Joe plucked it gently from his hands and coached out a tune. Pointing to his own mouth he showed the boy how to pucker. Soon, the boy had it, and he waved his arm like the Pied Piper. Everyone able scrambled into their boots and followed him toward a log cabin next-door. It was the home of the widowed aunt who allowed her nephews to raise geese in the front half of her sanctuary.

Ted walked behind the boy. Leszek took Joe's arm. They trailed the group, crossing the farmyard together.

Suddenly, a disheveled man lurched around the corner, stepping in front of Leszek. What he said was unintelligible to Joe but Leszek's head snapped back, his face reddened and his voice came out harsh and abrupt. Guttural words flew. Leszek stamped his foot, calling the skeletal beggar a drunken dog. He hollered at him to get off his land, moving forward to enforce his word with an upraised fist.

Joe stepped between them just as Piotr appeared and gently led the old man away.

Leszek and Joe stood together, both breathless. Piotr had called the strange man Stasiu. Ahhh, the moment to settle things had come and gone and he'd missed it. He'd just stood there stunned. Now, Stasiu was gone and Leszek was too upset to be rational. What had he been thinking to imagine he could unite two crabby old men with one of them drunk? It was hopeless. Joe knew he'd have to face down Ted and tell him it couldn't be done.

Not knowing what else to do, Joe guided Leszek toward the cabin.

One of the young men appeared and took Leszek from him. A friendly arm guided Joe past relatives and into the cabin where the boy stood in a pen full of baby geese that walked awkwardly every which way. Triangular frames with three bulbs attached to each hung from the ceiling, heating the room. The boy played and the geese righted themselves, waddled into a crude formation, and followed him. Tiny balls of fur strutted in a circle as ancient uncles laughed and offered suggestions.

Annie stood back, snapping pictures. After a few minutes Joe signaled her and they backed out, so those excluded could squeeze inside to see too. He walked her towards the house, intending to have a private talk, but when they reached the house Annie opened the basement door and slid inside.

Joe followed, to scold her for intruding, but she flipped a switch, "Ta-da-da-da! Look, Dad, they never need to go to the store. They haven't harvested all their crops yet, either. Some of this is even left from last year. They're rich!"

An immense tile stove, spotlessly clean, sat against a wall of shelves filled with jars of tomatoes, carrots and jams. He could see where goods had been removed but there remained links of sausage and giant hams that hung from the rafters. Flour and sugar were tucked on shelves in burlap bags. Obviously Annie had been given the tour. Heavy-lidded barrels revealed sauerkraut and pickles that Annie pried open to show him. Joe's father had stored food too, but always with a worried, "Ai, yi, yi, yi, y."

No matter how much he accumulated, Joe's father had never felt he'd accomplished enough. Joe had imagined that by becoming a businessman he might pile up money, hung like these hams swinging from the ceiling, to fulfill his father's dream. But if his father's vision of this larder was his standard, it was little wonder he's cried out in frustration.

Joe marveled, "This is better than a bank account."

Though Father described this room to him many times, Joe had never understood how a farmer might feel, opening the door to this irrefutable testament to his labor. No wonder nothing his father accomplished as a factory worker lifted the dark frustration that clouded his life.

Taking Annie's hand in his, Joe bowed his head, "Thank you, Lord, for allowing us to view Your bounty to those who survived. And may we never lose faith You will replenish what's been lost to those who hold You within their hearts. Amen."

Annie echoed his amen as they walked outside. That moment brought Joe an overwhelming sense of peace. He thought of the years this family had so little to show for their labor. What an accomplishment this room displayed, the variety of food was remarkable. His great-grand-mother nurtured many plants through hard times and Ted and Stella had brought more, still. There they were, in all their forms, dried or preserved. His mind cleared and he was able to think of things other than his own dashed hopes.

Joe didn't want to lose track of what was going on with his daughter. He asked, "What's with Marek? Why did you look upset when you came out of Babcia's room?"

"Oh Dad, you know the friend he told us about, the one in jail for stealing?"

"I remember. Why would he take responsibility for a thief like that?"

"It's not a guy. It's his girl, Claire. A man demanded his jacket to complete the car sale but then they owed so much he couldn't replace it. He kept sending Piotr money to repay Fred—they owe him a lot, I guess. Anyway, Claire saw he was cold and she swiped a jacket. The police arrested her."

Well, that didn't sound like the criminal connections Joe had imagined.

"Dad, how can Marek build a life with her? If she'd steal for him now, what might she do if they had children and she wanted things for them he couldn't afford?"

"Every girl who is ever tempted to shoplift should give that thought, Honey."

"Isn't there anything you could do to help him, Dad?" Annie's blue eyes met his. "He's saving what you give him, and the guy Dorsak works for pays him to report if you're still interested in her stock suggestions. Anyway, he'll have some money, so could you ask K to ask the inspector he knows if Marek pays a fine, he could get Claire out quick?" She stopped, breathless and squeezed his arm, "Please ask, Dad. If you do I'll be your friend."

She still seemed to think he controlled the world. Oh, that he did. But he could tell Inspector Skrzycki that Marek had access to Dorsak's boss and he'd cooperate if they'd help get Claire released.

"I'll run it by K, but don't say a word. I don't know how they operate and I don't want his hopes up."

13 – CHALLENGES

Kate walked up behind Joe and linked her arm through his. "Ted sent one of the boys across the road with a note for Stasiu. The moment of truth may be upon us."

"Staisu came and Leszek ran him off. Leszek's shaken and I feel sick—it was absolutely impossible from day one. How did I let Ted talk me into even trying? There wasn't a thing I could do, now or later." Thank God he had Kate to talk to.

"We're dealing with elderly people here, Joe. Somebody could have a stroke." She patted his arm. "Why don't you suggest to Ted he'd get a better response if we double back when Leszek is rested and the relatives are gone? Why ruin today for everybody?"

It seemed obvious, once she said it. "Yes, it's crazy to push them now." He drew her into a giant bear hug, "You may have saved the day. I'll talk to Ted."

Marek stopped to tell Joe that Piotr had taken Ted and Stella and Annie over the fields, to the family cemetery. "They snuck off without me?" Joe could barely believe it. When Annie was 13 and wrote asking for family history Dziadziu had asked that when she finally came she should visit his grave.

Annie was prepared. But why was he left out, Joe asked himself?

Kate offered, "Maybe they felt you being so close to them was somehow disloyal to their son Teddy."

Well, he could live without the cemetery. More power to them, he thought. A moment's respite seemed like a huge gift at the moment.

Joe sent Kate inside and he talked to the young men as they approached him, fishing for a business idea that Ted could finance for them. But their dreams were small, backing everything they mentioned could be done for under fifty thousand dollars, easy.

Mr. Under Shirt spoke of financing a high tech chicken coop to raise 30,000 chickens at a time for Krakow restaurants. When Joe asked about European Union regulations he was told, "They say only we must deliver chickens live to guarantee they die healthy. And they provide the chickens."

But to raise 30,000 chickens over and over and over? Would Ted finance such an honest yet miserable career? Chickens and pigs—raising them for large firms was risky. Once a farmer sunk his cash into all the equipment the company made their demands. He'd seen a program on how that worked. It sounded worse to him than handling fertilizer.

Another cousin said they'd leased a building to stage a disco, using a boom box and strobe lights Piotr had brought from Germany. They'd earned a couple hundred dollars on drinks and tapes they'd sold at a huge mark-up. But they'd donated much of the profits for a statue for the new church. Piotr said, "We young men dragged our bodies into early Mass the next day to prove we could party and pray too." Several young men had gathered round during his telling, jostling and laughing as each acted out his role. Obviously, these boys knew enough to grab fun when they could, but he'd let them figure out that path themselves.

"Does anybody have an idea that could employ more people?"

"How big can dreams grow when disaster loves us?" They laughed and shrugged.

An uncle had joined them and he spoke up. "We cannot see how life will flow. Will we be overrun once more? Will our work be for nothing? Foreigners plow our cities for money as we plow our soil for crops. But foreigners have other money, other homes, and other dreams. We have only God and each other. Our necks grow stiff from watching out for this and that. Ted has protected us from evil forces. When he is gone and crisis comes, we must stand united."

The engineer joined them. "We build a bridge to the future. You Americans have 200 years of peace behind you and oceans and mountains protect you. It is not so with us. We must use our wits and our strength to flourish without arousing envy from our most aggressive neighbors."

Joe wondered, did his problems compare to theirs? Taking deep breaths of sweet farm air, he realized that his disappointments weren't even in their league. If they faced the future with hope and faith, who was he to wallow in defeat? Their realistic stance reached out to strengthen both his resolve and his acceptance.

He refused their urging to go inside; Joe paced in the courtyard. The farm smells and the yapping dog comforted him as he stalked around the barn. It was twenty minutes before Piotr, Ted, Stella, Annie and an elderly aunt reappeared. Ted's face had a nervous tick.

"Everything is done now but my talk with Leszek. Stand by me, Joseph."

Joe put his hand on the old man's shoulder. "Let's not spoil this day. Everyone is tired. When all guests are gone I promise we'll return and I'll help you do this right."

Relief registered on Ted's face. "Yes, yes, why didn't I think of that? We'll hold today sacred."

Joe nodded to himself, "All right, let's get goin' then."

They went inside to say goodbye. Annie knelt by her great-grandmother's bed and Babcia extracted a promise that she'd return. "If I'm in my box. Bring me a rose, a red one. Put it on my grave and I'll know you've been to see me."

"I'll bring red and yellow and white roses. I'll bring some for you and some for Dziadziu. I'll pile on so many you'll have to swoop down from heaven to share them with people who got none."

Joe led Annie from the room backwards, blowing kisses. They waved goodbye to uncles who sat, toothlessly smacking soup-soaked brown bread. The emotion of the day fell away and relief invigorated Joe. He sprang ahead, to get them moving before any more emotional grenades exploded.

Kate tugged on his sleeve and whispered, "How do I get out of here?"

"Say *'Dziekuje Bardzo,'* nod your thanks and head for the car." He propelled Kate and redirected a reluctant Annie to the car as Ted and Stella helped each other down the staircase outside the house. The wind ruffled the beads and butterflies that now accented the heads of Annie's cousins.

Dresden appeared with *oplateki*, wafers received from the church and carefully set aside after Christmas dinner. They occasionally shared them again on Easter day, but seeing them in June, now that was special. The engineer stepped forward and broke off a small piece to give to a cousin, offering a touching wish for health and happiness in the coming year. That cousin broke off a piece and turned to another with a lighthearted wish.

The jolly elderly aunt blessed Joe. He responded with a heartfelt wish for health and happiness. They formed a circle around Ted and Stella, blessing each other and then blessing them. Joe was grateful to see this self-sacrificing couple treated with such love and respect.

He got in the car just as Mr. Under Shirt appeared with the family treasure, the Black Madonna, wrapped in a protective blue cloth, as a gift for Kate.

"We can't drive off with the heart of their home in my lap. What should I do?"

Joe threw up his hands. "I don't know how to refuse it, Kate. I don't."

The Chef reached into her pocket and pulled out a neatly folded, rose-bud patterned scarf, identical to the one she wore and placed it over Annie's thick hair, touching a red-brown curl as if it was spun gold. Annie hugged her.

Marek said, "Annie comes from the land of rich hair. Now she must go."

Annie bowed and clowned, patting her scarf as she got in the car.

Kate reached out and tugged on the engineer's sleeve. She asked him to please return the picture to Zosia, "Our oldest children must come to see this Madonna on her wall where it belongs."

He turned and spoke. Zosia nodded that she understood and accepted her treasure's return.

Just then, Mr. Under Shirt broke off a tiny shred of wafer and challenged Annie to bless him. The crowd hushed as she teased him in Polish, "I wish you a happy life and I pray that you will find a shirt with sleeves for Poland's many cool days."

Cousins near enough to hear laughed and slapped him on his back as all car doors closed. Joe began to inch his way up the farm road. The windows were down, and their arms hung out. Someone began singing, *"Sto lat, Sto lat, niech zyje, zyje, nam."* (May you be allowed to live one hundred years for us.) Everybody joined in. Joe slowed the car. Even though he intended to return, this was a moment to cherish.

Several young men walking ahead of the advancing car stepped into the field to let the car pass.

Ted stuck his head out the window and hollered instructions. "They'll spill out Stasiu's vodka. When he looks for a sip, it's gone. He'll sober up before we come back and our young men will clean him up. Oh, he'll curse me." Head thrown back, Ted laughed like a boy performing mischief. His delight with himself infected them all and the car shook with their laughter as Joe turned onto the country road.

Kate asked, "Honey, could you roll up your window?"

"Kate, I need air. If we'd stayed another minute we'd have drowned in syrup."

Ted said, "I know, I know, they pour it on. But some folks don't even turn off their TV when you visit. The youngest child here will tell about today his entire life."

"I'll tell about today my entire life." Annie sighed and echoed Ted. "Now, I can die happy." Ted accepted her ribbing with a deep-throated laugh.

Annie said, "I got the names and addresses of the entire family. I organized them to know who's trying to do business and who has an elderly relative living with them, in case you want to prioritize for that Internet hook up, but I have to tell you they know how to use a computer, and if there is a place in the next town, like Tarnow where they can go online, they'll do that. They don't really need to get ahead of their neighbors unless you want them able to charge customers for using their connection. They told me they don't need it a lot yet. They use the net sparingly." Annie handed her list over the seat to Ted.

Stella said, "If there's no need to buy these connections, couldn't we sponsor a low-interest bank? People don't get jealous about money they must pay back."

Joe sighed. Stella had a good and generous heart, but starting a bank? She had no idea how complicated and costly that was, and he didn't have enough energy to explain it to her.

Ted said, "I never opened my mouth about the hook up and I gave only normal money; still it went perfect. Perfect. I prayed to John Paul and he stuck by me. He helped bring peace to this day. I felt his presence." Ted turned in his seat.

"Today you are my hero," Ted said to Annie. "The money you need for that college . . . Stella and me, we're givin' the part you owe, and your parents' part too. You earned the best there is today."

Shocked, Joe looked in the rear view mirror. Annie's smile lit up the darkening car. Okay, he could accept having his money plans kicked out from under him, but he wouldn't lose his daughter too. He'd have to think hard to keep Annie from taking that offer. And he'd thought his worries were over.

Annie opened her mouth to thank him but Ted interrupted "Now let me rest, then I'll see what I can manage."

Joe drove while the others slept, emitting irregular little bursts, forming an odd rhythm that kept him awake. The night sky was clear. Stars lit the mountains toward Zakopane. Suddenly, he realized he'd wandered toward the left side of the road and he cracked his window. Kate scooted up and began describing interactions he'd missed to him.

"The girls who cooked our dinner, they plan to start a restaurant. They'll sell take out and handicrafts too. Like a Polish Cracker Barrel. They're excited."

"How do they intend to pull that off?"

Kate ignored his tone. "A neighbor owns an orchard on 1 1/2 hectares of land on the road to Tarnow, I think. Anyway, Leszek said he'd trade land he has near here for them. They'd start with a lean-to, like the one where we stopped near Auschwitz."

How could Kate go on prattling about nothing when Ted had just provided Annie the means to leave home? She wasn't ready to leave home. Didn't that upset Kate? Joe said, "Not one guy mentioned any restaurant to me and I pressed them for ideas. Those girls are deluding themselves. Forget it. It won't happen."

"You think they shouldn't try because the men haven't taken it on as their own? The women have ability and passion. With a little help they can make it happen."

"Did ability and passion get my business going? Am I a woman?"

"Maybe this once, it isn't about you, Joe. The US isn't the only place in the world to make money and those women have a right to dreams too."

Stung, he said, "Nobody's coming to Detroit and I can't make it alone. You're right once again, congratulations." He hadn't wanted to talk about it, but she'd started it.

"Oh? And I thought we'd worked for your business together, silly me."

"Kate, I can't get my boat in the water. I'm not blaming you. I've failed."

She punched his arm. "Joe Winowski, you've done more of value then people who have triple your income, yet you act like you'll hit some worthless list if you don't earn more by Wednesday at noon. Don't you try to sucker me into that craziness again, please."

She flopped back and didn't say another word, though she bumped the back of his seat with her foot and her breath heated up the air around him. Kate wasn't one to lash out. In fact, her cherry, "Oh aren't we lucky," attitude, irritated him. So why did he react to good fortune as if it didn't quite measure up? Was it a habit of mind, unworthy of the blessings he enjoyed, a childish trick to ward off bad luck? Was he self-centered and morose? He couldn't go there now, he turned his mind away.

Tatyana Dorsak, had she heeded his warning? If she'd been replaced . . . Joe couldn't think about that, either. Everything seemed unreal. It was only nine when they signed into Zakopane's Hotel Orbis. Ted ordered sandwiches sent to their rooms and they staggered upstairs, exhausted. Joe would see Gienia to assure himself that losing her had turned out for the best. Then, maybe he could accept the loss of Pateck's workplace and Annie's going away to college. What would he do if he lost Kate too— or at least her sympathy—if he couldn't confide in her anymore? How could he bear that?

14 – ZAKOPANE

Zakopane's Orbis Hotel, room 352, caught the reflected sunlight off the Tatra Mountains. Joe threw himself into bed without pulling the curtains and he woke to the glow of morning light in Poland's cherished ski resort.

In the privacy of early morning quiet he tried to accept that none of his cousins would come to Detroit. His dream that Ted would invest in him was over, finished, dead. The financial worries he'd relegated to the back corners of his mind bubbled up like bile from his belly. He focused on memories of Gienia to ease his mind.

Kate woke and curled up against him. She spoke into the curve of his back. "Joseph, you were outstanding yesterday. It reminded me of why I married you."

Lord, she was determined to be cheerful. He was about to cross the loyalty line and that realization made her joyousness weigh on him even more. "Well, nobody dropped over dead, yet." His dismissive tone resounded in his ears.

"You lived to tell the story. That's what counts." Her hand caressed his back and he stiffened. "In my mind you're a bull. I mean, what's a little cholesterol if you lived through yesterday? You've been playing up your aching heart to get me to wait on you but I see through you now."

"Right, forget chest pains and check-ups. I'm a bull you thought was a lamb. Poor, poor Kate."

She laughed, seeming to find herself particularly funny. "If you describe the last few days to Gawley he can write you up in a medical journal, because you're so genetically remarkable."

"I'm always remarkable. But why is my blood pressure and cholesterol high? Did I invent that?

"Ahh—but you survived yesterday so I'm not babying you anymore." She ran her finger down his thigh. She was giving him a chance to get a grip without rubbing it in. Her generosity incensed him.

He had to escape or he'd do real damage. He jumped up "You stay there while I make some calls. You rest."

Hurt registered in her voice, "Rest? We're in a world class ski resort. You've done your best for everybody. Why can't we enjoy being together for five minutes?"

He turned on her, "Can't you see I've got things on my mind?"

"Do you pull that dark cloud behind you for the fun of it? I didn't contract to live with habitual suffering. If that's necessary for you, tell me now so I can jump aside." She gathered the covers around her knees, braced to argue.

"I don't need you shooting your mouth off about buying internet access. I figured if I exposed that fraud, Ted would realize how risky investing here is and turn to me. I could use your help here."

She shrugged, "You warned Tatyana Dorsak off, not me."

"Her children's welfare came before justice, but Ted didn't understand that. He asked me if her boss sent a replacement to complete his transaction."

"And you expect him to spot a scam when you act like you believe it?"

"He jumped to conclusions all by himself."

"That doesn't make you a Boy Scout to anybody but yourself."

He couldn't discuss honesty with her now. "Let me handle this. I'm looking out for you every step of the way. Just don't operate behind my back, that's all." He couldn't believe he'd let the words he dreaded hearing from her out of his own mouth.

"Joe, Ted's single-minded and you don't fit into his plan. Give it up. If he picks up Annie's college costs, we can cut down our expenses and you can give carpentry your all. I'd like to try writing. I've put off that dream, but I can write while you build. Without the kids around we'll have more time than we've ever had before."

She'd opened herself up and he pounced. "So you'll look for glory once the kids are gone, is that what you're itching to get rid of Annie for?"

"Don't you use that scum of the earth tone on me. Annie is gone whether you like it or not. I used my time with her well, and I warned you your time with her was limited—if you're just seeing the light now, it's on you. But that's another issue. I need to know right now, will you let Ted get taken? And will I be branded the resident liar when the truth comes out?"

"I'll shoulder the blame for letting him think Dorsak is for real along with everything else. Why not? I've been carrying this family on my back for years anyway." With his whine echoing in his ears. He changed tone. "You have a right to dream too. I know I ask a lot of you; it's just I can't handle all this alone."

She got up. "I'm here, just don't think I read your mind. I deserve better than your crabbing at me. So, should I hurry them along or not?"

"No, Lord no. Slow Ted and Annie down. I need some space."

"You need space? Well, go, you phony-baloney; go and snarl at somebody else." She slammed the bathroom door.

Her anger lanced the boil of his frustration. He walked downstairs feeling better. He began to rethink the scam. If they replaced Tatyana Dorsak, Ted might go after the deal again. He reached the marble-floored lobby figuring it was time to talk to K's police contact. Hell, he thought, it was past time.

Joe called K, who told him Inspector Skrzycki had checked and the taxi driver was clean. Marek had no criminal ties beyond Claire. "No one wants to tie up the courts with a once-in-a-life-time offender, but there has to be a fine. He'll look into it. Everyone he checked with spoke of Marek's decency. The kid has even had some university. He dropped out when he went to work in Germany."

"I'm glad you got my message straight. I didn't have time to talk."

K laughed, "You were quick to make your point."

"Could someone with a legitimate company be behind this scheme? Or the Mafia?" If the scam smacked of organized crime Joe'd grab his family and run. Police have their own agenda, he knew that.

"Poland hasn't let criminals take over though, of course, they're here also. I doubt you've stumbled into a Mafia scam, but I'll tell Skrzycki you're concerned."

When K hung up, Joe called Inspector Skrzycki himself and told him that Tatyana Dorsak was registered at the Orbis Hotel.

To Skrzycki he said, "I realize this scam has to be stopped but we just learned our family has ways to get Internet access for the little they need, so I can't guarantee my uncle will be in the frame of mind to help you catch swindlers."

"We must try every way possible."

"Our Polish guide, Marek, said Dorsak's boss offered him money to report on tourists interested in her spiel. He's agreed to tell the guy what I want him to say."

"Did he get his name?"

"He called himself Majka." Joe recited his phone number.

Skrzycki's excitement resounded over the wire. "The man he calls Majka we know as Alex Faldo. Majka-Faldo operates out of Warsaw. We watch him. He is not Mafia. My informer says he pays them to operate freely."

"He isn't Mafia," Joe's relief made him weak-kneed.

"Majka-Faldo is young. He imagines he wins Mafia respect through cleverness. No killings are connected to him, only cunning and greed." Joe was amazed Skrzycki was so forthcoming with him, but of course, he wanted him to participate.

He pressed, "But if his backing was Mafia and I helped bring him down, I wouldn't be safe anywhere. I might as well put my family on a butcher's block."

"I will not allow that. Your involvement will never be known, trust me."

"I don't trust anyone I've never met. I know we can't meet at this hotel but I plan to drive into the mountains alone this afternoon. Is there someplace we can meet?"

Skrzycki called back five minutes later. He would leave an unmarked car for Joe, with directions. Had his questions about Mafia connections made him nervous,too?

They were finalizing the plan when Kate tapped on the phone booth he'd taken over for privacy. "Joe, leave K alone. Ted wants to eat in a restaurant somebody recommended to him in town. Come on, we're starving."

Joe cut Skrzycki off, relieved that Kate presumed he spoke to K.

# # # # #

On a street above the restaurant, a man at a kiosk stepped out and waved them into a parking space. Marek said tipping a local to park was helpful, so Joe tipped him. The family started down the steep walker's street, past an array of small wooden shops, many resembling log cabins with large, slick windows displaying luxury goods. Joe's annoyance with his delayed breakfast chewed at him. The cold wind tingled his nose and brought tantalizing whiffs from restaurants rejected only because they weren't the one Ted was looking for. Joe needed coffee badly.

He snarled at Kate, "Why are we passing all these restaurants? I'm hungry."

Kate said, "Will you stop? Look at those mountains. Where's your sense of reverence? Stop snarling. You're missing all this."

"I have a happiness hangover from yesterday. Go walk with Annie."

She looked him over, shrugged and sped up to join her daughter.

Wooden exteriors resembled scenes from the Old West. Shops with enclosed porches housed slick boutiques, filled with clothing and ski equipment.

As Kate tripped over an uneven walk, Ted said, "Careful, you're stepping on a national treasure. I never thought I'd see anything this wonderful in Poland, beautiful." His face glowed.

Joe had a headache. Try as he might to accept the inevitable, it was closing in on him. At home Kate could read signs, use the telephone, or even order his food while he thought things through. Not so now. She was irritatingly oblivious here.

Ted had told him long ago. "A wife is like shoes, if the fit is good you can forget you're wearing them. If it's bad, you'll hurt every step of the way."

Kate had been a good, if bouncy, fit. Joe tried to push back his growing surliness. He yearned for time to think about Gienia, his Gienia—here—in Zakopane. Wasn't her shop on this street? He searched for her number on buildings they passed.

Kate and Annie followed Marek downhill. Ted and Stella came next and Joe brought up the rear as a trail rider. Suddenly, Kate called out, "I'm in here." She stepped into a shop with wall hangings and pine furniture in the window.

*Lord in Heaven, i*t was Gienia's shop. Joe rubbed his face with the back of his glove. His heart thumped as he entered. There was no sign of Gienia behind the counter, but she could be there. Kate stood at a side counter staring at a tapestry. He had to get her out of there fast. All he needed was for the two most important women in his life to meet now.

Annie said to Kate, "Look at the way these colors weave together. They're impressionist painting in wool. The colors flow from the poppies to the daisies."

A clerk waited for Kate's gaze to shift. He mentioned a number. Joe converted it to dollars quickly—Kate never bought expensive decorative items, yet there she stood, looking at the pale blue tapestry, brightened by a field of woven wild flowers, as if she meant to buy it. The clerk explained that none of this artist's creations were alike. He pointed to smaller versions with the same, blended technique. Marek stood nearby.

As Joe stepped forward he smelled Gienia's perfume. Goaded, he turned on Kate. "Are you crazy? That costs over a hundred dollars. You can't throw money around here like that. Grow up." He stomped towards the door. Kate recoiled, apologized to the clerk and followed, gaining speed as she caught up.

Joe realized his harsh tone had poured over Kate like unbottled gas, but he couldn't let her head back into that store. She maneuvered around him and sped up as she headed downhill. He stayed on her heels, carrying on so loudly people turned. He didn't notice a man whose clothing and haircut identified him as an American soldier on leave until Kate stopped short.

He spit out a last, "Grow up, woman." And the young man's head shot up.

Kate said, "Can you restrain this unpleasant man? He's bothering me."

The guy clamped onto Joe's arm as she took off. Joe sputtered, "That's my wife. Let go of me. That's my wife."

"That's no way to talk to any woman, Sir, especially as a guest in a foreign country." Calm, yet firm, the kid looked like he might be straight out of Hamtramck.

"Let me go. That's my wife." Joe couldn't think of another thing to say.

The soldier held on. "If she wants you, she'll find you, Sir."

Annie stood behind him, wide-eyed.

"Annie, tell this guy I'm your father."

"I don't know where this man came from but I think he's disturbed. Hold on and I'll get away too." She took off after her mother.

The American and Joe stood frozen in dance, until Ted demanded, "What's going on here? What's going on?" This prompted the man to finally release Joe.

Joe attempted to reassure the young rescuer to ease the situation, and then he hurried onward. He looked in doorways and shops, but there was no sight of Kate or Annie. When he reached the restaurant they'd been headed for at the foot of the hill he opened the door and saw Annie's red jacket hanging beside Kate's navy pea coat.

Relieved, he turned to Marek, who'd come up behind him, "Please, give me five minutes with my wife." Marek turned back to divert Ted and Stella.

The seating area held huge log booths. Kate and Annie sat side by side. He slid in opposite them. Annie carried on as if he wasn't there, "What's the matter with him, Mom? He didn't have to attack you."

Kate stared him down. "The train station is down the street. I can get to Warsaw and fly on home. That was not my idea of fun."

"I'll go with you, Mom. I don't want to be with him, either."

"Ted and Stella want you here. It's important to them that you're here." He paused for a quick breath, then reached for her hand, "Kate, please. I know I shouldn't have gone off like that, but Marek doesn't see that kind of disposable money in a year. You can have what you want, I just didn't want to play the Ugly American."

"But you jumped right into The Ugly Husband without a blink, didn't you? Just tell me, what kept you from telling me quietly that Marek was your concern?"

"My brains fell out, what can I say? I'm sorry, but it'll ruin the trip for Ted and Stella if you go. Please Kate, I need you here. I won't crab at you anymore."

"I won't to be your punching bag. Don't imagine I'm trapped here. I'm not."

"I know you can get along without me. It's me, I can't get along without you."

"You won't talk to me like that again, ever." Her face looked pinched.

Annie took her hand. "Mom, I know you're mad at him. But if you leave they'll boss me off the face of the earth. Don't leave me alone with them, please."

"That wall-hanging wasn't the problem. Dad needed to holler and that tapestry was handy, but you won't carry on at me again, will you, Joe?" She wasn't asking.

"When we get back home make him stay at Grandma's, Mom."

"Now, just you wait a minute, young lady . . . ," Joe began.

Kate touched Annie's wrist. "Dad cares more about things than I do."

Was she going to psychoanalyze him? He cut her off. "Your mother will see that I get what's coming to me, one way or the other. That's what keeps our marriage alive, she tells me."

Kate laughed, but Annie's flinty-eyed expression told him she was still upset.

He tapped the table. "So my daughter doesn't know me. I'll remember that, kid. I'll remember that." He laughed as he said it so she'd know it wasn't a true Polish curse—a grudge that can go on and on. "I tried to invite that young fellow your mother sicked on me to join us, but he wouldn't, can you believe that?"

"Who'd want to join crazies? He was cute, too." Then she laughed.

Gienia didn't need the cash he'd brought for her and the tapestry was a perfect excuse to return to her shop. He could see her with Kate's blessings if he bought her the rug. It couldn't get much better than that. Joe ordered fluffy omelets and coffee just as Marek arrived with Ted and Stella for breakfast.

When they finished, they walked across the street to Zakopane's market, crossing the planked bridge over the icy stream. Women seated on three legged-stools extended their work worn hands, offering yellow goat's cheese shaped like miniature footballs. The snow may have melted around them, but it still appeared on the mountains above them and cold bit through their jackets.

Marek bought a cheese and pulled out his pocketknife, handing each Winowski a slice. Ted ate his with great pleasure, but the strong, salty taste stopped Annie. Her wide eyes begged Joe to save her. He smiled and nodded to her to keep munching. If she dreamt of ripping Marek's attention away from Claire, she'd better choke it down.

Kate reached over and took the offending cheese, wrapped it in Kleenex and slipped it into her purse when Marek was turned away. It was all babble to her, but her antenna was working fine and concealing things from her was not his best plan, Joe reminded himself.

Usually these market experiences would be grist for Kate's story telling. For years he'd thought she couldn't carry on a conversation without a story, but suddenly they had dried up, disappeared. He'd noticed she wasn't entertaining him with her funny little takes on life a couple of weeks before they left home—after the boys came to say goodbye, actually. Well, he thought, this market should give her a story worth telling.

"We'll meet mountain people here," Marek said as he took Annie by her elbow.

Joe took Kate's arm, Ted took Stella's, and they negotiated the walk beside a stream that cut through thin, slivered ice.

Painted lacquer boxes, with folk scenes on their lids, attracted Stella. Ted spotted a Russian Army uniform with a hand drawn, crudely sewn label reading KGB, tacked above the front pocket.

People paused and laughed, then walked on.

Ted tried to hide his grin. "I want this. Nobody will believe me if I just say it."

Joe said; "They probably doubled the price when they sewed that silly insignia on. If you want to get robbed, don't tell me about it."

"It's like our putting 'CIA' on a private's uniform to sell to Russian tourists."

Joe shrugged and wandered away to where the market forked. People without the luxury of a wooden shop set their goods out on blankets. Their shelter from the weather was the cement roadway overhead. The road was their roof and protector.

When Ted returned, he held the KGB suit. He was ready to return to the hotel.

15 – GIENIA

As The Winowskis walked toward their car, Joe's conscience bubbled up like gas in his belly. He'd mentioned Gienia to Kate but it had flown on by her, and he'd let it. Keeping Gienia secret wasn't what Kate expected of him. He'd always condemned teachers who encouraged flirtatious students so he was pretty sure Kate would be offended by the idea he'd arranged to meet Gienia without a word to her.

Normally, Kate took life in stride. She kept a kind of sloppy order, claiming untidiness as her God-given right, refusing to peel potatoes or match socks. When he'd chided her she said, "Some chores are unworthy energy burners. I won't allow you to disturb my peace for the nag of minor details. If those things bother you, you do them."

And she wasn't kidding. She refused to let his fussing about how the wash "should" be hung on a line or how the girls' hair "should" be curled, control her. She stood up to him and she stood up to the old ladies—nicely, but they knew better than to push her, too. He overheard them discussing Kate's insistence on disorder years ago.

His mother had said, "I think we'd better let little things go. We didn't raise her, and she has a college education. She could manage without us and she knows it."

Stella had ended the discussion, "Besides, she's only messy. Her house is clean, she reads to the children, and she treats everybody right. We don't want a fight for nothing."

Grudgingly, he'd taken on some of the tasks that bothered him, because "people will talk in back of my behind," as one of their elderly neighbors put it. After a while he'd silently dropped one after the other and she'd had the good grace not to throw it at him.

For her part, she was so accepting of him he'd been lulled into thinking anything went. Then, just when he relaxed, she'd blow. She always had a point, he had to admit. She'd dig in her heels when he piled on tasks without noticing what she'd already done.

Kate might not even bat an eye about Gienia. Why complicate life by trying to explain to her what he couldn't explain to himself? He loved Kate. Still, wasn't he entitled to one fantasy? He'd loved Gienia before he met Kate. One had nothing to do with the other, he thought, and he'd make things right with Kate later: one more responsibility notched on his already perforated belt. How much more could he handle, he wondered.

Joe maneuvered Marek beside him as they worked their way up the street. "Marek, what will we do about my daughter's crush on you?"

"You need not worry. Annie is a family girl, smart and clean and very kind. American boy will love her. She is a good friend to me. She plays with Papa."

That I can live with, Joe thought, as he decided to enlist Marek's aid. "I need some time by myself. Could you drive my family to Stella's family village tomorrow?"

He'd drop by Gienia's shop for Kate's tapestry, if Gienia was there—what a coincidence. How could Kate object if he discovered Gienia while shopping for an item she herself had picked? That's when he'd tell Kate, after their next meeting. Everything would be above board.

Marek nodded, he understood; it was an arrangement between men.

"Let them see the homes built with slotted timbers. Take your time and keep this between us."

"I'll care for your family—my mouth is shut. You don't need to worry."

"And don't mention I'm not with you to anybody else, understand?"

"I won't say this to Pan Majka who asks me many questions each time."

"You talked to Majka, again?" *Matko Boska*, the kid said it with a smile.

"This morning, is that not okay? I said only you make no other plans."

Joe gulped. He had to talk to Inspector Skrzycki. "That's fine, no problem."

"I said your interest in the Internet investment remains. I said you see only family and tourist things. I do not say Pani Dorsak leaves. Is that not correct?"

"Yes, yes, nothing about Mrs. Dorsak. You got it right." Joe breathed easier.

"He sends five dollars at the desk each time." Marek flushed as he said it.

Joe laughed at the guy thinking Marek was a cheap spy. "Say we're talking about buying more stock. Maybe he'll give you a bigger tip. And I'll pay you extra for tomorrow."

"No, you pay each need for me. Pan Majka tips." Marek's desire to play it straight played across his anxious face, reassuring Joe.

"I'll tell the family I don't feel good. You care for them and you'll get extra. Don't say no. That's worth more than I can say." Marek grinned at the compliment.

Later, Joe called Skrzycki who suggested, "We'll meet outside Zakopane so eyes don't follow. I leave directions and keys for the car in your box."

That sounded overly dramatic. They could have met in the ski café behind the hotel, but the guy probably figured he had to keep the suspense up for him to hold his interest, Joe thought.

Kate had reminded him of his "heart problems." He called Gawley just to rub it in that he was traveling. When he was about to hang up Gawley said, "I mentioned your being in Poland to Sue. I reminded her she helped Gienia when she'd arrived with only the clothes on her back. Sue said that when she went to register our car, Gienia was waiting to talk to an MP and she was very nervous. She said he'd promised her he'd get her papers to enter the States if she got info about stolen cigarettes from refugees."

Joe said, "No MP had that authority. Asking about stolen goods was dangerous."

"Sue said Gienia was suspicious enough to ask her to run the story by me, but our boy fell and had to have stitches and Sue didn't remember to tell me till the next day. By the time I followed up, Gienia had disappeared. I cornered that MP. He said they'd recovered some cigarettes but he denied knowing her. One refugee thought she'd gone back into Eastern Europe and I figured she'd been threatened for helping police and ran home."

"You never told me that." Joe turned and placed his head on the booth's glass.

"I didn't because you'd have hopped that border and wound up in jail."

"That bastard! One woman told me Gienia helped an MP, but the guy had shipped out. Being short probably gave him the nerve to pull that stunt. Mother of God!"

Joe had to restrain himself from slamming down the phone. The tale Gienia told him when he found her in Krakow and Susan Gawley's matched, puzzle perfect. She didn't just dream up a dramatic story to cover her disappearance. She'd been the victim of a scheming thief. He stood there wrestling his surging emotions.

# # # # #

The next morning Joe said he felt sick and sent a sympathetic Kate to breakfast without him. By the time she returned with a tray, Marek had volunteered as guide for the day. As soon as the family was safely out of sight Joe called Gienia's shop. The clerk said she would arrive after 2:00.

He located the car Skrzycki had provided for him and headed into the mountains, imagining Gienia, reliving their days together. When it came to their weekend in Bopard on the Rhine, he realized continuing the daydream constituted disloyalty to Kate, Nevertheless he had to see her. For years he'd fought back visions of what life would have been with her, and now that her story had filled in the gap of her mysterious disappearance that fantasy filled his mind and touched his heart. He rolled down his window and cold mountain air shocked him back to the moment.

Skrzycki had instructed him to drive to the parking area of Tatra Mountain National Park and catch a horse-drawn carriage to the restaurant beside the immense lake called Morskie Oko. In Polish it sounded like Eye of the Sea. It was a magnificent lake. Hikers and climbers skirted it now, on a pilgrimage of endurance.

A light summer snow sat puffy on the trails and crystallized branches stood out like sculptures. Magical snow banks surrounded Joe. The scene cheered him as he fought to calm himself. He was usually critical of adults who got all worked up over nature, but he was excited to be here, about to partake in an out-of-a-novel police adventure.

He turned into a biting wind, blowing so hard he had to hold onto the fur-lined cap Ted had forced on him to ensure a market woman sold her quota. One carriage waited to traverse the path through the mountains. As he climbed on, the driver offered him the blanket he removed from the horse. Imagining the fleas in it, Joe declined that hopping treat, with what he hoped was a hearty smile.

He spotted a young family: father, mother, a boy about six, and a small child the father carried. The mother's hooded coat exposed only her face. From the steady stream of people along the path it was obvious that most walked the distance. He asked the driver to stop and offered the family a lift. They accepted with a rush of "*Dziekuje's.*" The father sat beside Joe. The red-cheeked mother wrapped her boys snugly under the horse's blanket as they turned to wave to the hikers they joyfully passed.

A powerful wind coursed through a break in the mountains as they pulled before the rustic restaurant. He breathlessly doubled the price of the fare, asking the bear-like driver to return in an hour.

The driver grinned, "I wait. No problem." His English earned a double take.

The father again placed the youngest child on his shoulders but the older child was so buffeted by the wind he couldn't move ahead alone. Joe swooped up the boy and tucked him under his arm like a leggy football. The mother held the door open as a leather-trimmed flannel curtain, fastened to a half-circular iron rod designed to protect the people inside from the wind, blew up and into the room. Joe set the child down and slammed the door. The family took a table on the enclosed porch. Joe walked to the darkened bar, not far from the river-stone fireplace.

A powerfully built, large shouldered man with a trim, gray beard turned on his stool,

"Winowski, here."

A waitress, wearing a huge green apron over a brightly flowered dress, set down plates of sliced beef, potato balls, and cooked beets. Inspector Skrzycki said, "I ordered a Polish treat for you."

Skrzycki had a full head of graying, tightly curled hair. While Joe's own hair was clipped short and retained some black, they were remarkably similar. Joe realized he was looking into eyes of the same, intense blue he saw in the mirror each morning. He had the uncanny feeling he was looking at his cousin. No wonder he'd felt a connection with the rumbling voice on the phone. Joe greeted him in Polish.

Skrzycki's smile crinkled his eyes. "So the resemblance strikes you too. My people were startled, also."

"Do you think we share an ancestor?" Joe laughed.

"I come from an area two days' walk from your people. Many woodsheds held foreign soldiers on their long walk toward home. Perhaps one was unusually active."

When they got down to business Skrzycki suggested they speak only English.

Joe said, "More is beginning to make sense to me. Marek told me Majka-Faldo pays him five dollars each time he reports on us. Faldo uses innocents, so if anybody asks, they'll question a misinformed witness, giving him time to disappear."

"Innocents cost little—they know not their risk."

"I hope you can put that bastard away for a long time."

"He is clever, but like a bee I circle before I sting. Your military trained you to observe and I enjoyed hearing from you. You help our innocents free themselves from criminals. I thank you."

"You have a difficult job." Skrzycki spoke better English than Joe had expected

"I work for my people through many changes. I was a pioneer with these emerging criminals. I continue to have the best experience. Now, because of you, we see the next wave. My man is a cook for Majka-Faldo. We listen at his sauna and his phone. I will use your information also." Skrzycki said.

"I thought I'd been civilian too long, but I'm happy to help if I can."

"Men leave the military watchful. Many insights come from men such as you. The photo from Pani Dorsak helps my investigation. Majka feels clever, but we will foil him."

Joe appreciated the affirmation. "I'll pray you stay lucky."

"I make criminals look foolish, and who follows a fool?" He grinned.

How many times could lawmen rejoice in their jobs, Joe wondered, as he observed Skrzycki. He loved being part of this. It felt like salve to his wounded soul.

"We'll swoop in to confirm Dorsak is not the criminal. If they watch, ha!"

Joe had to make sure he was getting the plan straight. "If we frustrate their set up, we return home safe. If you pursued the true criminals, my family and I would be in danger, right?"

Skrzycki's face lit up. "I pit myself against crime. Poland has this chance for the next hundred years. John Paul helped us achieve this gift. Evil surrounds our fragile democracy, but crime will not defeat us. If we lose ourselves to others again, no one will save us."

"I could return the photo I gave you and ask Dorsak who the second man is."

Skrzycki reached into his pocket. "Yes, I'll return this photo to you—my men know him."

Touched by his sincerity Joe said, "Naming the second man would help you and for me it would be a positive among negatives."

Skrzycki looked at him full on. "Winowski; we have suffered, but we are up to this task. We look to the young. They will rebuild our beloved land with our aid."

Yes, Joe thought, the young Winowski's were right to work for Poland. He'd proceed with an open heart. He begrudged them nothing. When Skrzycki left, Joe picked up the family, boarded the sleigh and headed towards Gienia's shop.

16 – ON THE EDGE

Nerved up and jumpy, Joe watched the kiosk owner shoo away a truck. The thought of Gienia inspired him to sprint to the walker's street, then stop in front of her shop. Taking a deep breath he pushed the door open. As he entered he saw that the tapestry Kate had admired was missing from its place on the wall.

Gienia sat with her back to him at a wooden desk in back. As he approached, she turned, caught his eye and rose. Joe tried to memorize her animated face, her clothing, her every move. Her puff-sleeved red sweater, worn over a blouse decorated with tiny flowers and silver buttons sported a heart design of the blouse fabric on the pocket of the sweater. How could he have forgotten her style?

It was past one; he should think about his family returning, he thought, but he stood there dazzled. Out of his memory a dark-haired, brown-eyed young woman appeared. The two overlapped as if he'd seen her from a distance and suddenly focused his binoculars. A few lines appeared at the corner of her eyes and lips but this was the woman who taught him to love and he loved her. His racing heart confirmed that.

He sputtered, "You, you had a large tapestry on that wall."

Gienia said, "That is gone. These are what remain." Her smile blinded him. He had to resist reaching across the counter to touch her.

She waved toward four other tapestries. "Would any of these do? They are the same artist."

He felt exposed, alive, yet somehow, dreading a more personal conversation. Everything shifted to slow motion as he pulled out the cash he'd brought in case she needed it. "I'd like the wild poppy standing alone in the field."

Gienia turned to take it down and when she looked at him, her immense dark eyes held his. Her presence awakened memories of intimate moments. Did she cherish those memories, too?

"And so, Joseph, you have come to me?"

He swallowed hard. What did she mean by that? "Gienia, I prayed you were well and look at you. You're timeless." He was never good at compliments." And now, are you happy?" He felt young and bumbling all over again as his color rose.

"Just as you, I made a new life. My husband is older, but good to me. My life is comfortable, but I have missed my Joseph." She brushed his hand with hers.

The heat from her touch nearly scorched his hand. He didn't pull away.

"Tomorrow your family attends church?"

He nodded his reply.

"Come take me for coffee. We'll dissolve these many lost years."

Lost? Did she consider the years without him lost?

Then, as if having an after-thought she said, "Will you come to me tonight? Say you must walk the mountains at night, and come to me. I understand that teachers in America have times they may travel, is that not so? So you are here. We must use our precious time well." She handed him a map she'd drawn.

Yes, he'd come. Yes, he'd be there. Yes, yes, yes.

Joe stumbled out the door. He'd entered a different man. He'd been trapped among people who knew his every fault and failure. They each, in their own way expected he'd give his all for them and accept their right to criticize and sigh in disappointment no matter how hard he tried.

Then suddenly he'd stood before a woman who lit up in his presence and whose only demand was that he meet her. Well, he could do that, he would do that. He owed it to himself, he told himself.

Tourists entered as Joe walked out, his belief in himself muddled, yet somehow restored.

Twenty minutes later, as Joe entered the hotel elevator, he glimpsed his family's return. He stepped back into the elevator and as the doors closed he saw Tatyana Dorsak approach Kate.

When the family finally came upstairs Joe was truly asleep. Kate used her key and they descended upon him with their tales of Stella's father's village. He fought to rouse himself but he felt like he was surfacing from underwater. Reality was the dream.

Kate had ordered and brought up a tray with tea and a sandwich of Polish ham for him. He was full, but he sipped and munched so he wouldn't have to talk.

Stella sat on the chair at the side of his bed while the others stood in attendance. She said, "Chocholow's farmsteads are like museums. We drove around before we saw the village restaurant. Ted told the woman who ran it my family name."

Ted laughed, "That lady took off running."

"Her mother was a child when my father's family lived there. Her grandfather was the mayor. He'd confiscated my uncle's piano for the city so the Germans wouldn't take it."

Ted touched Stella's shoulder.   "It was nextdoor to where we sat. They hold meetings and receptions there and play it still. She brought her mother to visit with us."

Annie cut them off, "Marek played the piano and he's good, really good."

"He doesn't play kid stuff. He's almost as good as Annie." Ted was serious, as if she had set some high mark for musical performance, which in his mind she did.

Kate told him they'd spoken with Tatyana Dorsak while they waited for his sandwich. Dorsak wanted them to understand that if she sacrificed being with her children for two more months she could begin business again. She'd thanked Kate for Joe's interest.

Ted said Dorsak would arrange his stock purchase. He'd made an appointment to transfer his money at the hotel bank at ten on Monday. Then, he said, they could drive to the farm for the afternoon, reckon with Leszek, and drive on to Warsaw in time to fly home the next day. Ted asked whether Joe was up to going out or if they should all nap. Joe realized that avoiding naps now meant he could get them to bed early, then visit Gienia. He whisked them to the marketplace.

Nestled under the overpass at the foot of the snow-covered mountains, shopkeeper's stalls appeared to grow snow from their roofs. Graying piles nestled against their sides. People in traditional mountain costumes lined the wooden bridge leading to the area teeming with carved plates, lacquered boxes and knit sweaters.

"If you bought a wide brimmed hat, pants with silver buttons and a leather belt with those tiny buckles, people would pay to have their picture taken with you, Dad."

He smiled and kept walking. Ted bartered for fur-lined suede mittens. Market women wore large fringed scarves, wrapped around their heads.

Kate said, "Tatyana says those scarves are made in Chicago as table cloths."

Everywhere Joe looked, Poles wore dark layered clothing. Tourists stood out. Dressed as they were, he couldn't lose his family. Ted, Stella and Marek could blend into a Polish scene, but Annie's red coat and Kate's red white and blue ensemble didn't blend. If the scam blew up and he needed to spirit them out of harm's way, then he'd have to throw a blanket over their heads and even that wouldn't do it, because today they both wore their bright red cut-off rubber boots.

Joe shrugged and let Gienia take over his thoughts, becoming so preoccupied Kate nudged him to ask where Annie was. Scanning the crowd, he spotted her in the area where the poor sell ticky-tacky things dug out of their lives in desperation. What did this child of American malls know about circumstances that drove people to sell old knobs and faded blankets? He moved to get her out of there.

Marek and Annie stopped by an ancient woman balanced on a wobbly, three-legged stool in a lumpy gray coat. A threadbare blanket at her feet displayed miss-matched spoons, two forks, a little box of matches and a small black knob. It was as if she'd gone through drawers in her kitchen asking, "What can I part with so we can eat?"

As Joe approached, the woman noticed Annie and rallied. She wore fingerless gloves and she waved them over her goods as she stood up, ready to do business. People around the woman paused to see what in that pathetic pile interested the American.

A voice taunted the woman, "*Memo, Amerykankai,* (Mama, she's American.) The babcia rubbed her fingers together, the international sign for a deal.

Annie said, "*Moja Babcia wyjechata do Ameryki.*" (My grandmother went to America,) pointing to the most ornate, sadly bent spoon on display, as if her dear old grandma—born in Detroit, Michigan—had brought that very pattern with her on the boat. Annie pulled out a twenty-dollar bill she squeezed into the woman's hand, stooped, picked up the spoon, and pressed it to her heart as if it had great value. The woman turned to ask for change.

Annie closed the woman's work reddened fingers over the bill. The flurry to make change stopped. Observers froze in place. Marek began to move forward but Annie's left hand held him back. With elaborate care she wrapped the spoon in the embroidered handkerchief Stella had given her. When she was done, she leaned over and hugged the woman.

Joe turned and ducked between kiosks as she walked back towards him. Marek looked stunned. With a sudden spurt he caught up, grabbed Annie's elbow, bringing her to an abrupt stop. "Why did you waste Papa's dollars? Why?"

She shook free. "I work. I save. I give my dollars. Not Papa's dollars. Mine."

Marek stood firm, "That spoon is no good. It's an old, bent, bad spoon. No dollars should go for such a bad spoon. Papa will say, 'Marek why do you let my daughter waste dollars on a bad spoon?'"

Joe stepped between them. "Marek, it's all right. That babcia will eat for a week on Annie's hard earned dollars. I'm proud to be her father." He resisted the urge to kiss her forehead, but he put his arm around her and they walked back to where the others waited together.

Marek trailed until the family was gathered, then he spoke up. "Nearby is the Tatra Museum with history from this area, it's open until four. I could show you it."

Annie brightened and Ted insisted Stella must see the history of her father's area. He'd read that the museum had displays of the flora and fauna. They all seemed ready to follow Marek when Kate put out her hand to stop their progress.

"Joe and I will see you later. We're going for a walk together." She tugged Joe in the opposite direction.

Startled, he tossed Marek his keys. "You drive them to the museum and we'll see you at four at our usual parking place."

Maybe Kate wanted him to buy her something she'd seen. Anything, as long as it wasn't in Gienia's shop, he thought. They meandered away from the pedestrian street and he tried to focus on Kate. She must have noticed he'd been avoiding her.

"My family can be overwhelming. Thanks for coming along."

"What's going on, Joe? What aren't you telling me this time?"

"What do you mean? We've been together almost every moment since we left home. What do you think I'm not telling you?"

"I know when things aren't right. Don't make me play 'What's wrong with good old Joe' again. That's tiresome and it's affecting me. I'm asking a straight question. I deserve a straight answer."

She couldn't know about Gienia. She was guessing. Things hadn't played themselves out yet. If he snapped at her maybe she'd let it go. "I'm worried about how to get this troop around the next corner. Do I need more?"

Her eyes were luminous and her clamped-mouth expression startled him. At the corner a mountain man waited to cross the intersection with his horse and wagon. Joe waved him across. He never should have let her get him alone.

"Joe, you're not in this alone. I prayed this trip would lift your gloom and we'd come out the other side together. But how many times am I supposed to go along? You may have decided secrecy is the best for you, but it's not good for me. How stupid am I supposed to be?" She turned away from him and crossed over to the right.

Before he could react, a truck blocked his vision. Then she was gone. Didn't he have enough on his mind without her being childish? Good Lord, would she go to Gienia's shop for the wall hanging? Unnerved, he scanned the area. The street bustled with tourists, but Kate was gone. He looked in the closest shops, nothing.

Beyond where he stood was a park with people walking past snow covered benches. No telltale hair heralded her presence but as he turned her familiar profile caught at the edge of his vision. She sat slumped on a bench, her suede mittened hands tucked under her arms. She'd jammed her hair into the wool ski cap he'd bought her. It struck him as silly for a grown woman to appear so overwhelmed.

The cold had reddened her nose, the wind blew chilly puffs up her slacks. She didn't look up when he stood beside her. Finally, he touched her shoulder. Her hands shot out, palms up, gesturing him away. She might as well have seen a snake.

"Kate, what's the matter with you?"

"Get away. I don't want you near me." She shooed him away.

"What's going on? What's the matter with you?"

Her eyes challenged him. "You thought I'd never figure it out, didn't you?"

She knew. "Kate, I know what we have. I wouldn't hurt you."

"Don't you dare talk at me if you won't say what has to be said. I will not be excluded from our life again, ever."

"Kate, I'd never jeopardize our family. No woman can compare to you."

"Ha! Another woman can see how she'd like to be the one you sacrificed for, the woman who stopped all adventure in your life, forcing you to hole up in your workshop, pushing all of us away. Oh, poor, poor Joey." Her tone was unknown to him.

"Is that what this is about? Of course I had to give up some things, you did too. Four babies in six years were overwhelming, but we did it, you and me and the old girls. And you'll have more time when Annie's gone than you'll know what to do with. You did more than your share. I don't tell you that much and I should," he babbled.

Her eyes narrowed, "I deserve the booby prize. I pushed myself to grow up quick, while you threw yourself into 'getting control.' Every choice made you more remote and the more you withdrew the harder I tried. I never knew which way to hop."

"Of course I aged. I accepted responsibility and I provided."

"Ah, but if you hadn't married me . . . I was your out. Finally I understand."

He gestured toward the empty park, "Anybody listening to you would think you're crazy. I wanted to marry you. I can't think of one adventure I might have had without you that I regret. Does that satisfy you?"

She was way off and if he could get her inside somewhere she'd talk herself out of this. He took her arm, attempting to pull her up, but she batted him away, as if he'd stolen from the collection plate. Well, he'd done the best he could. "Look, I'm tired and I'm worried about how I'll manage when we get home. Does that mean I don't love you?"

"I was twenty years-old. I hadn't lived yet. You used me to avoid doing what you bragged you'd do before you went in the Army."

Thank God, she was off. "Pa's illness brought me home. I didn't meet you till years later."

She tucked a strand of hair behind her ear. "And just when your mother could do without you, you conveniently fell for me. My hero." Chin high, she challenged him.

Lightening his tone, he touched her hair. "Was loving you so terrible?"

"Everybody expected you'd take off again. You used me to close that window of opportunity. I never realized how perfect I was till now."

She wouldn't budge if he didn't shake her. "Is something not right here? One day you tell me you don't want to hear my dream and the next you're mad because I didn't ask you to follow one. What can I say when you get like this? Let's order tea and you take the rest of today for yourself. All this togetherness would get to anybody."

If he gave her control now she might hold until he figured a way to appease her. She allowed him to lead her to the elegant downtown hotel on the next corner. Few people ate in the wood paneled room at three in the afternoon so he guided her up the carpeted stairway, seated her and ordered one tea and a piece of cake.

She picked up on that. "You didn't order for yourself?"

"No, you need time for yourself. You warned me being cooped up together was too much. Here, take a taxi to the hotel." He wadded zlotys up and pushed them into her pocket. "We'll eat at the restaurant Dorsak described at six. Please, join us." As she opened her mouth he said, "We'll talk when we get home, Kate. I can't handle this now."

His stern tone echoed. A few diners paused, forks in mid-air, then turned away. A man alone at the next table met his eye. Joe nodded and turned back to Kate, lowering his voice, "Believe me, I know I don't tell you how much I appreciate you, but I do."

She jerked back like he'd slapped her. "Believe you? Believe you? You bought that grocery store months ago without a word to me and I should believe you?"

Her words struck him breathless and he sat down hard. "What did you say?"

"When the twins came home a couple of weeks ago they went to a party in the old grocery store you've been working in."

Joe's heart sank. He knew where this was going.

"The guys showed our boys how they'd fixed up 'your folks' place. I told them you had probably planned a surprise for me, so not to say a word. I've given you every opportunity to tell me. Oh, I know you admitted the salvage was gone, but that was only one part of the puzzle, wasn't it, Joe? So stop playing games. Stop it now." Her face had blotched and she almost choked out the last words.

"Without the boys I couldn't earn enough. I didn't want to worry you."

"We've talked about buying that space. I'd have helped you figure it out. Why protect me from that? When did I become your child?"

Kate knew and the boys knew? No wonder they'd all looked at him funny. Trapped, he attacked, "And you're so scared of me you couldn't ask?"

"You never want to talk when you're down, and I figured you were more than down so I shut up and did everything I could to get you through it, like you helped me when the kids overwhelmed me. I thought this trip might shock you out of it so I tried to wait it out . . . but I'm sinking, Joe. This down isn't just yours anymore. I'm sinking."

"We could have doubled our output if the boys stayed, but they abandoned me. You knew I couldn't make it alone and you didn't look out for me."

"They told you. And you dismissed them. You said, 'Don't bother with that damn test, it will just make you feel bad about yourself.' As if they weren't smart enough. You disrespected your sons' dreams like your grandfather mowed over Ted and Leszek. Blame me all you want, but take a good look in the mirror first."

Her words hit him like a sucker punch.

"With more space and the three of us working together we'd have been efficient. I could have insured additional workers and maybe even quit teaching. I sold my salvage so our business could take off before I saw I had a dream they didn't share."

Her hand flew up, stopping him. "Your salvage? Your business? Everything I ever earned went into helping you. We worked together until suddenly your sons' dreams didn't count and good ol' Kate was just one of your tools. How did you stretch your head-of-the-family position into playing God?" Her voice was low, but so fierce it sounded like shouting.

"I came to tell you right after I signed, but the boys' scholarships came through that day. If I said I'd bought it, they'd know I couldn't handle that mortgage alone. I'd steal their joy and not help anybody. So I swallowed it. I didn't want my foolishness—"

"Foolishness? This isn't about foolishness. It's about trust. It's about control. It's about us." Her hands shook. "The old Kate pitched in, trusted and prayed." She gulped for breath. "But suddenly I'm outside, not worthy of being informed. Tell me, was it when I asked for my turn? Was that too much for you?" Tears filled her eyes.

He glanced around. People studiously ignored them. "That's not what I was thinking. I didn't think that, Kate." After all he'd done for her, she had to hear him, "Salvage or property, they're yours and mine, but I couldn't earn enough to insure workers going at it alone. I couldn't take that leap with those expenses on my back."

"What day did you carry that load alone? Did I disappear after I donated every penny I ever earned and spent my precious free time running your errands?"

"I didn't mean it like that."

"I thought we were a team, but I guess you showed me."

"I wasn't dismissing you. I just wanted to hold on till I could figure out what to do. I wanted you to be proud of me." He caught hold of her left hand and held it.

"I was proud of you, you worked your heart out for us and you stuck by me when the kids came so fast I almost fell apart . . . and I stuck with you when accounting turned into a disaster. So how did we get to this, tell me, how?"

She was gasping for air as she spoke and people were beginning to look up again.

"I wanted to spare you. That's not an excuse, it's just what happened. I got so I couldn't think straight anymore. Do you want a divorce?"

Her left hand went to her throat. "Did you do this to get me to leave you?"

"No, I just thought our marriage was worth more than the price of a mortgage, Kate."

She blinked and straightened up. "There's nothing left for me to leave with, is there? So it's like it or lump it time, isn't it? So much for being a team, so much for love and respect. It's done, so it's 'live with it Kate time', isn't it?"

He stood and released her hand as the waiter appeared to replenish her tea.

She looked up at him as she sat with her hand on her throat. "My God, you've changed our lives. Things will never be the same, will they?"

"I'll make it right, I will. I just can't deal with this now. You can't ask me to deal with this now. We'll work this out as soon as we get home, I promise."

He kissed her forehead and walked away. If she knew, why had he suffered through so much of this alone, he wondered? What would he do if she left him?

He didn't dare tell her about Gienia now. The truth sounded like a bigger lie. If he reconnected with Gienia, how would she feel then? She'd said it herself, life wouldn't ever be the same for them. The rush that thought brought fueled his anger. He nursed that feeling as he stomped around till his family returned from the museum. He told them Kate hadn't felt well and she'd meet them later. He suggested he'd drive them around to see houses built outside the city. He hadn't driven far when he went around a curve and saw an immense church. Marek jumped. "Pope's Church, Pope's Church."

A larger-than-life statue of Pope John Paul stood with arms outstretched, part way up the steps toward the church entrance. Stella reached out and gripped Ted's arm.

Annie pulled out her camera and started to click, "Can we go in, Dad? Babcia will be so happy to see my photos when we go back."

Visiting a *church* in his state of mind? But he couldn't think of why not, so he pulled in and they climbed the majestic stairs, past the fresh flowers at the foot of the statue of John Paul, hero, brother, friend and Pope

Marek said to Annie, "Pray for help to do right. God tells you how."

Inside, master wood carvers had created an immense open interior. The walls' light wood gave the church an earthy yet cheerful effect. A man stood on a ladder dusting the Stations of the Cross with a feather duster.

Stella said to Annie, "Ted was fussy already, but now he's seen this fellow dusting off God, there'll be no living with him."

Annie said, "File for divorce as soon as you get home, Aunt Stella."

Ted turned on them, "You two better get on your knees. This is God's house."

Stella and Annie giggled so they had to stagger outside to collect themselves.

Faith permeated the workmanship. Craftsmen had created this expression of their faith and Joe forced himself to admire each facet. He resisted putting his dilemma in God's hand. How could he ask for help when he knew his interest in Gienia bordered on sacrilege? Instead, he thanked God for protecting his family, avoiding the examination of conscience that must come.

When Ted rose, Marek removed his hands from his face. Joe wondered if his own turmoil shone on his face as it did on Marek's.

It had grown dark; branches shimmered and stars shone so clear and bright they took on a glow. Lights came on in homes and newly lit torches fastened to carriages wound their way down the mountain. The peace of the church had rested Joe's mind. He hadn't intended to play God, but if his marriage crumbled it wasn't because Kate had broken faith with him. She'd protected their young when he'd gone his own way. Sure, he intended to include them all in his largess, but his grand plan had taken on a life of its own. It was up to him to make this right. How in hell he'd created such a muddle he didn't know.

17 – IT'S A LONG WAY TO TURN AROUND

Taking another route, The Winowskis passed two-story mountain homes, where elaborately carved balconies protruded. The homes rested on stone-faced basements, their steep pitched roofs let snow slide to their sides. The homes looked hand-wrought.

Ted said, "That's where I'd like to stay."

"My room is in such a place," Marek said. "I found it by asking the information house." The family looked at him with envy. The hotel had high ceilings, multi-colored hand woven rugs and Polish art work on display.

"They're awesome, Dad. I'd love to stay in one of these."

"The Polish price is not so much and they give tea," Marek offered.

Joe wished they had stayed in a house like this. Not only were they attractive houses, he felt they'd be safer if there was any danger from Dorsak's backers, because he couldn't deny that possibility loomed. But he couldn't lose his focus; he had to square things with Kate. She'd stood by him always, only insisting on change when he'd been immobilized by his own self-criticism. She'd questioned him relentlessly, but after he answered her concerns. she helped him accomplish his goals, always.

For a moment, when Gienia had touched him, Joe would have thrown everything away to rescue her—and she didn't need rescuing. He shook himself; he had to be up to the tasks that remained and for the first time in the nearly twenty-seven years since he'd first met Kate he stood alone. Kate wasn't there because he'd tried to hide what he was doing and, to his shame, he'd pushed her away.

# # # # #

When they reached the hotel, Joe asked Marek to come read for a while in his room. He wasn't ready to face Kate alone, if she was there, but she wasn't. She'd left a note saying she was taking a carriage ride up the mountain. At least she hadn't caught a train to the airport, he thought. Stella must have told Ted to keep his remarks to himself, because he went into his own room without starting his twenty questions routine.

Marek turned to Joe, "You wish for me to call Pan Majka to say all is well?"

"Yes, I'd like to hear his voice, if you don't mind. Call from my room here."

Marek dialed and pushed the speaker button. He grinned at Joe as if they were playing a joke on a friend. A secretary answered, then Majka-Faldo picked up the phone.

Joe heard a man carrying on a business conversation in formal Polish. Marek told him the Americans were sightseeing while they waited anxiously to invest with him. Majka-Faldo said the usual envelope would await Marek at the desk. He signed off with, "*Dziekuje bardzo*." His distinctive tone made his "thank you" memorable.

The conversation had been short and to the point, exactly as Marek had described it. Joe thanked Marek for allowing him to hear Majka. Somehow, the voice validated the man. He felt he could pick him out of a crowd. Joe stretched out on the bed. Marek settled into the chair by the desk and picked up Kate's copy of Suzanne Strempek Shea's *Hoopi Shoopi Donna*, about a Polish-American community in the US Kate had discovered that Marek read English well and she'd told him he could read from her book whenever he had to wait for them. She enjoyed hearing him emit little bursts of laughter as he read about and recognized the idiosyncrasies of Polish-Americans.

Joe longed to sleep but he decided to go back to the lobby to call Skrzycki out of Marek's hearing. Anxiety tightened his throat. Was he in over his head, he wondered? Could he count on Inspector Skrzycki? Would Kate follow his lead if he needed her to? Where was she? She sure had picked a poor time to take off in a fit, he thought

In the lobby Tatyana Dorsak cornered him. "Mr. Winowski, I thank you for your concern but I believe I must complete my duties." She wrung her hands.

He eyed her coolly. "You must do what you think best, Pani Dorsak. It was not for me to speak to you as I did. I'm sorry if I worried you. Have you seen my wife?"

"We spoke. She wished me to accompany her and a gentleman on a ride."

"She went off with some man? How did she know him?"

"He was a friend, I believe. She listened and asked helpful questions."

Kate had an uncanny way of asking about details a speaker overlooked in his own story. She'd helped Joe see his way clear often enough. If she took time for Tatyana Dorsak, maybe she wasn't as upset with him as he thought. But what friend could she have met? He couldn't imagine anybody.

"We expect my uncle's dollars to be available Monday morning at the hotel's bank branch. You'll be here to accept the transfer at nine, I understand."

"Mr. Winowski, your uncle requested to purchase additional stocks to the value of two hundred and fifty-thousand dollars. My director was very happy." She twisted the end of the royal blue scarf that accented her suit.

Joe almost choked. He'd meticulously shown Ted every detail needed to transfer his money, but he hadn't expected Ted to wire over more without a word to him.

"And your boss, is he coming here to receive such a large sum?"

"No, Mr. Winowski, he is not. He arranges that I accept and sign always. I am directed to transfer money on to him."

Panic echoed in her voice. What was going on? Dorsak's eyes filled with tears, "Do not worry. I will not accept your uncle's money."

To give himself time to assess what she was saying he eased the photo he'd taken from her out of his pocket. "When I came to your room in Warsaw you had pictures beside my papers. I picked this up and I want to return it."

Tatyana Dorsak took the photo from him; "These are the men who trained me for this work. This man, Mr. Majka, is my boss. It is he who calls from Warsaw."

She pointed to the man Skrzycki called Faldo. Marek called him Majka too. Naturally he didn't give them the name he lived under. Joe's heart tightened as she continued, "I wished to record the men who schooled me for this work. I wondered why they considered an untrained person for such responsibility. How could I know if they were honest? I photographed them when they did not see. I kept finger prints and signatures also because in the beginning I was unsure."

She preserved their fingerprints and signatures? Had he heard her right? These men had presumed they were dealing with a fool and she'd fingerprinted them? Why in heavens name was she telling him this? Her eyes filled with tears but she went on.

"Mr. Majka wished to train me. He claimed that my predecessor quit suddenly and I was needed, but I was doubtful. Sometimes the answer to desperate prayer can be the devil's trick, my mother taught me that. Mr. Samil, who works in Ukraine now, said I was a 'can do' woman." She blushed as she repeated their manipulative compliment.

Joe wanted to call Inspector Skrzycki right away but he knew he must hear her out. She clutched at his sleeve, "When first they taught me, all they said I confirmed in the newspapers. I also called a well-known company that sells stock. I see now I didn't know clearly what to ask, but what that man said calmed me. Later, I trusted and they added the internet incentive that your uncle prefers." He patted her hand and prepared to move toward the phones.

"Moments ago an angry guest told me that offer was a scheme and he was sure that none of the money I accepted from investors would buy real stock. When I protested that I had seen the stock—that they were delivered to me—I gave proof to every person who invested. He said they were false— forgeries! He told me to run—he is going to call the police." She'd increased her speed to croak out her story. Then she put her hand to her mouth. "Mr. Winowski, what will I do? I must reach my babies, I must."

Joe led her toward a chair but she said, "No, no, I must go gather my things and flee for my children." The elevator had opened. Joe got in with her. Taking the key from her trembling hand he opened her door and stood back. She ran to the closet and threw a large suitcase on the bed. Clothing flew, until she caught sight of computer boxes.

"What will I do with these?" She flopped down on the bed.

Joe ran a glass of water and brought her a cloth he'd wrung out. Her hair, pulled loose, hung around her face. Her eyes wandered. He said as calmly as he could, "I'm here to help."

She trembled. "I must go to my children. I must go before the police come. Why did I not hear your warning?" Parts of her sentences were in English. Parts in Polish. She began to speak like a child, half to him and half to herself. "I believed I did right. How could this be? My babies need me."

He tried to calm her. His mind raced. "It's all right. I'll help. It will be all right."

"He sends police for me." Tears slid down her cheeks. "Mr. Winowski, please tell them I know nothing." She leapt up, "How can I protect my babies?"

He stood beside her. Where was Kate when he needed her? Joe held Dorsak's hands, "The finger prints and photos you took will prove your innocence. We'll get you through this and back to your little girls."

Her eyes were wild, "I wish harm to no one . . . ."

"I can't pretend to understand a criminal's mind, but . . ."

She interrupted him, "How could my work be criminal? I checked each claim."

Your information was correct, until the Internet deal. Your boss got more greedy so he created the fast hook up idea as an incentive. Majka used you to fund a false company. He hides the money and if you're questioned, you have no correct answers."

"I know nothing but I accepted money. The police will seek me, only me."

"These men knew someone would see through their scheme soon. They put you before them, giving themselves time to change identities. I suspected a swindle and I showed your photograph to the police. It allowed them to locate Majka. He must realize his time is short. You cannot be their first victim. The police watch him now, thanks to you. The fingerprints and signatures, they'll prove you innocent." He spoke slowly and calmly, trying desperately to appease her panic.

She slid her hand behind the lining of her suitcase and extracted a hotel envelope. "Each sample is marked. The second photo is here." Dorsak appeared to regain some sense of herself as she handed him the envelope. "But I accepted money and transferred it to Majka. If he disappears, someone must answer. I was the trusted person."

"Police follow Majka. They will alert the Ukrainians about Samil. With these prints they can stop them. You've identified them and new names won't hide them." He took the photo and waved it in front of her nose.

"You have known? The police know?" She spoke as if in a fog.

He said, "When I saw you with your children, I knew you'd never risk them, so I warned you and I gave police your photo. They promised me you will not go to jail—but you are in no shape to play this out. So now," he backed away from her, giving her a gentle pat. "We must get you out of this hotel quietly. You wash up and complete packing. A small trick will win you time. Have you got anything else that belongs to your firm?"

"I have a credit card for my expenses. Each week I withdraw my earnings in cash at the desk. Majka pays it." She handed the card to him.

Joe used his firm teacher's voice, "Have the girl at the desk charge the room and pay you your normal fee. Then ask her to destroy the card. Place it with the letter of resignation I'll write for you now. They'll only believe you know nothing if you withdraw your earned wages. You must do it."

"I would not steal. I am not such a woman."

"Go wash your face and prepare to leave."

Joe sat at the desk and typed a letter in Polish. It said:

"Mr. Majka,

My child is ill. I must go to her. The hotel holds your computer. It will be turned over when shown your company identity. My expenses are paid. My destroyed credit card is enclosed. The Winowskis wish to purchase stock but I cannot be here for them. I will not return.

If you cannot complete their purchase, I will instruct them to place their order in America.

Tatyana Dorsak."

He'd typed her name. Startled, Dorsak read it twice, then smiled, "Yes, yes, this tells nothing. They have only my former address. I told no one where my children stay. They will not find me. Just these words. Mr. Winowski, you did not spell purchase correctly."

Joe corrected the letter, ran it off, Tatyana signed it, and then he slipped it inside a long hotel envelope, printed "Majka" on the outside and handed it to her. "Give this to the girl at the desk. Send a bellboy to pick up the computer. Then drive your car to the back door where I'll wait with your suitcase and coat. You must move with as little notice as possible."

"I must change my appearance?"

"Drive from here to Krakow and stay in a private home until Monday. It's only two days, but you must use your name to draw all your money from the bank and sell your car. Only after your car is sold can you disguise yourself completely. Assume another name, buy dull clothing and change your hair length and color. Travel by bus through small towns to disappear before you go to your children. Do you understand?"

"They will look for me? They will follow and harm us?"

"They'll forget you if they think you won't testify against them, it's just safer to leave no trail. Change your daughter's names and do not begin your sewing business again until you've checked with Inspector Skrzycki." He gave her the inspector's card. "When you wish to know if all is safe, call him. He is your protector. Now go."

She looked confused. He continued in his firmest voice, "Prepare yourself to behave as a professional. Take this and do what I've told you. Now go!"

She entered the bathroom, washed her face, straightened her hair, gave him the flash of a smile and walked out.

Joe located and printed the names and addresses of others who had invested in the scheme, grabbed her coat and suitcase and reached the staircase just as a bellboy got off the elevator.

Dorsak drove up and jumped out of her car as Joe opened the back door. She tossed her coat in back. He placed her suit case in her trunk, careful of her sewing machine. She threw open her arms, "My gratitude is with you."

"I put you under the protection of John Paul, who cares for all Poles." He tucked her inside and carefully closed her door. Her wheels spun as she sped away.

Joe went inside to a phone booth for privacy. An angry looking, large man banged out of the booth and passed him. Joe entered and used his cell to call Inspector Skrzycki. "Tatyana Dorsak is gone. A guest accused her of swindling him. She panicked and ran. It's over."

Skrzycki knew. "I was just alerted by the Zakopane police. I asked that they give me time to contact you." He didn't try to conceal his disappointment.

"Good, that gives Dorsak time to clear the area." Joe told him that Samil works out of Ukraine and he'd placed Dorsak's copies of both men's prints and signatures in an envelope and left them at the desk for pick up. "I told Dorsak you owed her thanks for this and that she wouldn't be jailed."

"My Warsaw contacts thought Faldo minor, yet they track him. Excellent German monitoring equipment follows him now."

"I instructed Dorsak to empty her savings account, sell her car, and assume a false name. She has your number. I advised her to disappear for several months. She will call you later. I promised you'd tell her when it's safe to resume her identity."

"Good, good—Majka-Faldo's schemes will misfire. A Mafia summit is soon. He will not bring attention to this failure. I will see that Pani Dorsak remains safe."

"I hope you have enough knots in your legal rope to hang those bastards."

"I set myself to turn criminal's dreams to dust. Suspicions will arise against him. He will not know from where his troubles come, only that he has no reward in

Poland." Joe imagined Skrzycki's grin as he spoke. He took a deep breath.

"I'd like to leave now, but my wife went a little crazy on me. I can't leave without her."

"My men watch over her. In the hotel restaurant a gentleman approached her. He suggested a carriage ride up the mountain. My man checked him. He has no record."

"My wife went up the mountain with a man she met at the restaurant?"

"They ride in an exposed carriage with a driver. The man misses his family, and your wife's innocence protects her. I alerted police men along their route and they have spoken with the driver. They won't interfere if she doesn't request assistance."

He didn't say 'trust me', but Joe could hear the echo of his own assurances to Dorsak and his stomach muscles contracted. "Mother of God, I want those thieves in jail."

"We arrest this man or that one, more appear. To know our enemy is best."

"You'll let them go on then? I'm not comfortable with that."

"I'll cause them to say, 'These stupid Poles are hopeless. We make no profits here, we'll go somewhere else.'"

"But they'll swindle people somewhere else. I understand you're trying to operate with nobody getting hurt, but you'll let them begin somewhere else?"

"My men are professional saboteurs. They will never know you helped us."

Joe went back to his room exhausted but he could find no rest. What if Kate got hurt? Why had he left her so upset her brains flew out the window? If anything happened to her
. . . .

# # # # #

By the time Annie knocked on his door, Joe had just begun to collect himself. Marek opened the door for her.

"Hi, Marek. Dad, it's almost six. We're hungry." She looked him over. "Are you okay?"

"Let me wash up and we'll go. Has your mother shown up?"

"No. Why are you two fussing? I thought you were doing good."

"She feels out of place, that's all."

"But she said if you ever felt like taking over K's job it was alright with her."

"I'm not taking his job, so get that out of your head. Why does she have to go crazy when everybody is on my back?"

Annie's mouth turned down. "Yelling at me sure makes you the mature one."

"I'm not going to discuss this with you. Go see Stella. Get moving." That's all he needed, a snotty-nosed kid trying to tell him what an adult was. He stepped into the bathroom to shower.

What, he wondered, was maturity anyway? Acting old all the time? Doing everything other people wanted you to and forgetting yourself? When he was young he'd thought maturity came on a certain day—like graduation, or the day you got out of the army or the day you married. Then he'd thought it was a line you walked over. Well, that was kid's stuff. Maturity was more like the streaks in his hair, some white, others stubbornly dark. Kids imagined adults needed to make the world comfortable for them, but that isn't it either, he thought. Maybe maturity was just acceptance. . . His stomach ached and his heart knotted in his chest. If he fell over dead this minute would anybody care?

He was on the verge of working it out when Ted hollered in his door. "We're hungry, let's go."

Ted, Stella, Annie and Marek piled into the car and Joe headed in the general direction Tatyana Dorsak had described. Nobody remembered which street it was near and Kate carried the card Dorsak had given her. Joe wondered, would she be there?

Annie tried to help, "I think it started with a K and it had a c, a z and a y in it."

"Why can't you pay attention? What else do you have to do?" Joe snapped.

Even if Kate was still mad at him, she'd pretend all was well for the others. Just so long as she showed up, he needed to see her, to know she was all right.

Joe prayed, "John Paul, please look out for my Kate. Don't let my floundering endanger her." But what the hell was she doing going off with a strange guy anyway?

The quest for the restaurant took on a strange significance, as if finding it would earn him the protection of supernatural powers. It took over thirty minutes of winding back and forth, with Annie pouting, but finally he spotted a small sign that said 'Karczma Obrochtowka" and he knew he'd found it

He pulled into a tiny space and they walked down the alley. The wooden door on the basement level was hand-hewn and hung with wrought iron hinges, set into a wall of rocks. Ted said, "Go on, Joe. This is your show."

Joe pushed the heavy wood door open. The waitresses in the candle lit room wore dirndls with bright aprons, their ruddy complexions were those of farm girls. Kate would love this place, Joe thought. He ached to see her.

Joe stepped down to check out a room on the right. A fireplace rose from a hearth cut out of the floor, but Kate wasn't there and he was worried enough to insist on sitting where he had the best view of the entrance. They squeezed into a large benched table set before the kitchen door and he jumped each time the door opened.

A man Joe recognized from the hotel nodded to Joe, then entered the hearth room.

The family ordered Polish comfort food: pierogi, mushroom soup, two portions of turkey and two portions each of chicken, bread, and tea. The meal ended without Kate. The *pierogi* remained. Ted turned to Annie, "Cooperate, leaving food is an insult to hard working people."

"I did my duty as a Girl Scout. If I eat more I'll turn into Miss Piggy."

Ted said, "Poles of good family eat what they order."

Annie ignored him and asked the waitress to wrap the *pierogi* for her mother. Ted began his delayed inquisition on Kate. "What have you done to that girl?" Joe shrugged and reached for the package the waitress had wrapped for them.

Marek asked, "Is the pierogi for Mama?"

Joe's anxiety-anger took over. "Mama doesn't come. No pierogi for Mama."

Annie reacted with the fury of a cub whose mother is attacked. "Oh sure, starve her. Any woman who spends her life catering to a chauvinist like you deserves to starve." She grabbed her coat, scooped up the pierogi and stamped her way to the door.

Joe called after her, "Okay, she can have it, but only if she asks nicely."

Ignoring him, Annie struggled with the door. Suddenly, it gave way, pushed from the other side. Kate stood there, silhouetted in the light like a vision. She turned away and waved to a torch-lit carriage as Joe rushed over. Her cheeks and nose were red. She shook herself as her hair tumbled out of her cap in a cascade of color. Annie threw her arms around her mother with such force they both nearly toppled over.

Kate laughed as she disentangled herself. Annie stepped back just as Joe reached them.

Oblivious to the tension she'd created, Kate said, "It's a long way to turn around. I'll scratch for days from that flea-ridden horse blanket. I almost froze, but what a sight. Did you save me anything?"

Weak kneed, Joe grinned stupidly with relief. He took Kate's arm and they tripped their way back to the table. Joe ordered hot soup as he pulled Kate's mittens off her stiff hands and helped her out of her damp jacket. He saw out of the corner of his eye that Annie had slipped back into her chair and signaled the waitress to bring a plate where she deposited her mother's meal. Joe longed to throw his arms around Kate and have her all to himself.

Just then, the man from the hotel emerged from the side room. He smiled and nodded again. Joe stepped over and asked if he was driving to the hotel, and if he could possibly give Ted and Stella a ride.

Miraculously, he offered to take Annie and Marek too.

They left in a cooperative flurry and he finally had Kate to himself. Could he make things right?

18 – THE POWER OF TRUTH

Joe moved Kate into the cozier earthen fireplace room where iron bars protruded from the hearth. He hooked her coat on a beam and rubbed her hands as she gave out her lovely, full-throated laugh. A couple, with their heads bent together, sat across the small room, oblivious to them.

Finally, she shook her head and ran her fingers through her hair. A lock of her lovely hair fell on her cheek. Joe brushed it away. What had possessed him to risk his Kate? The temptations he'd nurtured were crazy. A merciful God had given him this woman to love; he had to win back her trust.

"Kate, I'm sorry about all this. I give you my word I won't cut you out again."

She faced him, "I thought I cost you your adventures. Realizing you didn't want them threw me. I'll take responsibility for that stupidity, but you're not leveling with me about our obligations, that doesn't go away."

"I know. I know . . . ."

"No, you don't know. I'm on one wave length, you're on another—and they're both fiction. I can't play your dopey house-mate anymore. I'm a smart, responsible, loving, grown woman. It's demeaning to allow myself to be cut out. This has to change."

"You weren't a dope to me."

"Whether you said it to yourself or just got away with treating me like an ignoramus, I played the role. So, when the kids are gone, what will we have left, you and me?"

"Kate, I didn't get a chance to tell you about buying the store, honest to God."

She gave him a penetrating look. "The carriage-ride guy told me he left home because he couldn't meet his wife's expectations. I asked myself, did I put too much on you?"

"I thought my business was for all of us, then the twins got their scholarships, and you seemed relieved when I couldn't get the loan I needed. Suddenly nobody cared but me. First I felt abandoned; then I was ashamed I hadn't seen it coming, all at the same time."

"I've always been there for you, but kids need to go their own way. Then if they return to work with you, you'll have more respect for each other. Any other way is destructive to somebody and I can't be in the middle if you're wrangling all the time. Our bickering has just about worn me out."

"The twins and I don't wrangle."

"You don't because they complain to me about you and I've kept them from open revolt. Not a fun job, worthy of my many talents. If you ever work with our sons again, it must be because you share the dream. Just because you really, really want what you suggest to become our path, doesn't make other adults willing to give up their own choices. You can't keep finding minor changes made by a thoughtful partner a big deal. I won't spend my remaining energy keeping the peace for you."

"I hear you, but Kate, I need you in my life. It's awful out here all alone. My judgment is all off. I resisted their growing up, thinking I was protecting them, and you. We should have talked more. I know you tried, but . . . ," he'd better lighten this up, "I thought it was more efficient if you just shut up and did what I told you. On reflection, I see, that wasn't my best plan." He laughed, she didn't.

"Sure, I'm a minder. That's what I am." Her laugh sounded hollow. "I can't force you to tell me what's going on, Joe, but I can't live without knowing, and I won't."

She'd given up. He heard it in her voice. She said she accepted responsibility for being misled. Now she was figuring out what to do next, and it didn't include him. If he didn't level with her now, he'd never have a chance with her again, ever.

"Kate, I walked into quicksand, then I got too pig-headed to admit it. I figured if everybody depended on me, then I had to make the decisions and worry about what you'd say later." What more could he say? He watched her as if her eating was the most absorbing thing in the world.

She set down her spoon. "You never, pulled our load alone, ever." Anger leapt across her face. He watched as she pushed it down. "But my letting you think you did wasn't honest either. I worked my tail off so things would go well, then you'd find some tiny thread I missed and carry on like Rumpelstiltskin. I should have poured cold water over your head years ago. I deserve better than your critical sniff. I accept some responsibility for this, but I can't stay as part of this craziness." She cut into a potato-filled pierogi. Was she fortifying herself to go it alone?

"I know I was misguided. Just let me tell you what's been going on without interrupting and you can see if I was operating on all burners."

Her eyebrows shot up but she nodded.

"K contacted police to check out Tatyana Dorsak's scam in other hotels."

She stiffened but she kept still.

"When you and I talked about Dorsak's deal I wasn't in touch with him yet, but then Inspector Skrzycki said she'd be arrested if she showed up again and I knew it would upset you if you saw her before that, so I didn't say anything." Kate held her fork mid-air as he rushed through his explanations, ending with, "Skrzycki even checked on the fellow you went up the mountain with and he's clean."

"Well, I figured I'd be safe in an open carriage. The guy only wanted to talk about his wife . . . but it gets really, really cold on the side of a mountain once the sun goes down."

"*Kate*, how could you go off with some homesick guy? Are you crazy?"

"I don't know how I do it myself. People tell me their troubles all the time. Maybe I exude wisdom." Kate shrugged as if simply reporting the facts, but somehow, magically, she let out a genuine laugh. In that shared moment their bond of friendship reconnected. If he was careful, if he didn't presume too much, her habit of turning to him might reassert itself.

"So this guy just spilled his guts to you?"

"That was your fault. He came over after he saw how upset I was with you."

"And he asked you to give me another chance?" He refrained from snorting.

"He said after he lost his job, he left his wife and children. When he found work again he went to get them but they'd disappeared. He said if he ever found them again he'd never let them go. I figured it was that hero complex gone amok again."

He brushed her hair out of her face. "And you helped him figure out how to find them?"

"Well, I'd heard Oprah talk about tracing people. I figured records are similar the world over."

She rolled her eyes and her color rose.

"And he promised he'd try."

"Okay, laugh, but his kids will know he did his best to find them and they need their father. And," she waved her fork in the air for emphasis, "he thanked me."

Their laughter attracted a waitress who Joe waved off. He'd been so critical--and there she sat, decent and true, with a generous and giving spirit and he'd been pining for a woman who knew he'd loved her and hadn't bothered to write him a line, ever.

Joe took her hand, "Today, a man at the hotel accused Dorsak of running a swindle. She panicked and ran and without her, police can't run a sting."

"Thank God she got away. Who knows what might have happened?"

As he explained Inspector Skrzycki's plan to catch Mika-Faldo. Kate's hand responded to his. Then she punched him. "You used Tatyana as a sacrificial lamb, didn't you?"

"You heard me warn her off. Those con men hired her to take the heat off them, but now she's gone and Ted thinks he's investing a couple of hundred thousand-dollars he wired over without a word to me. I could wring his damn neck."

"Why are you surprised? You all operate the same." She used a husky voice to imitate her version of bossy Polish men, "Nobody can tell me what to do. I'll show them who's boss if I have to shoot off my foot to do it." She shook her head. "What fun for the women in their lives."

So far, so good, Joe thought. Kate had taken his justifications well, but the ax that was Gienia was still poised over his head, ready to strike. He had to finish his confessions while she was receptive.

"Kate, there's more. K located Gienia, the girl I lost in Germany for me."

"Gienia, the Polish girl who ran off?" Her green eyes grew large.

"She came back here and married. Her husband owns the shop with the wall hanging you saw."

"How did you . . . ?"

"I had K contact her home town priest. He said they owned a shop in Krakow on the outside of The Ring. I spoke to her there while you were shopping."

She gasped, "You saw her in Krakow and never said a word?"

"I saw her for about three minutes. She told me she owns that shop here in Zakopane. When you walked in I acted stupid because I needed to settle her in my mind before I said anything."

Kate opened her mouth, but he rushed on. "She's married and doing well. It wasn't a big deal, honest to God."

"You only saw her in her shop?" Her eyes watched him.

"I recognized her right away. She was busy then, but she said she'd be here this week. When you walked in there I acted like a little kid. I didn't want the family chirping around me before I figured out my own reaction to her."

After a long moment she said, "I'd probably not want everybody's input if I ran into an old boyfriend. She's part of your history. So, what did you think?"

"I worried she'd be poor and worn out, but she and her husband run five or six stores. She's well off. She didn't mention any children and she looked happy. I was relieved life hadn't treated her badly when I have so much to be grateful for."

"It's good that you saw her then. Now we'd better go tell Ted the sting is off before he falls asleep. He can only take so much in one day."

He'd leveled with her, he'd said it, and she'd been alright with it. His spirits soared as he held out her damp jacket. Outside the cold air slapped at them. Kate stopped to watch the last few torch lit carriages inching their way down the mountain.

He took her arm. "I'll pull down a star for you. Which one do you want?"

"Stars aren't what I need from you."

"Don't turn me in for another model. I'll do better. I'll take care of you."

"I don't need being taken care of. I need to be a partner in our life—and that doesn't mean running your errands." She put her finger on his open lips to go on: "Look, that guy in the sleigh didn't know his wife had resources besides him and obviously she did. Well, I've hidden my input so you'd think you're the one carrying the load and that's stupid. You never asked me to do that. We both need to be more honest and let me tell you, I'm ready to get real, so brace yourself."

"I know you do more than I give you credit for."

"You don't have a clue how competent I am. When I saw you couldn't handle that mortgage I tightened our spending and sold some things. If we moved above that store this summer you'd be on the spot and have more time. Besides, I'd gain time to write. We could rent out or sell the house. There are Muslims moving into Hamtramck who'd love a place like ours."

Joe's eyebrows shot up at that. Kate patted his hand. "I'd been thinking of ways to get you to think you thought that up, but that's more of the same and it hasn't worked well for either

of us. You're going to have to deal with the fact it was my idea.
" She grinned and poked him.

"My God, Kate, you don't want to live above my shop.
You'd hear every tool going." If he'd known she'd sold things
and had cash it would have helped.

"You can fix it up like you did our house. The kids can
stay at your mom's when they're home. She's close. The money
we'd save on upkeep alone should pay for a terrific new
kitchen and bath if the boys help you put it in."

"My God, did you go over there and take
measurements?"

"Absolutely, those boys are thinking of moving their
band to Chicago. They were happy to let me in and keep our
little secret. You've dismissed my input, so I've snuck around.
That's dumb. I need you to swallow your snarl and ask what I
think. You don't have to do what I say, but I'm not accepting
your 'cut-me-off attitude' again, ever. I need to be in on the
decisions that affect my life. We'll get counseling and if we can
both get real I'll stay. If not, I've got other ideas."

He braced his feet in the snow and threw his arms
around her. "We'll do this. But do we really need that
counselor?"

"You've operated like a free agent too long and I don't
ask the right questions. A referee can help me become an active
part of our lives."

He lifted her and her feet left the ground. "Kate, I want
you wherever I am."

She hugged him back. "We can do this, can't we?"

He kissed her. "We can. I'll be so honest you'll tell me to
shut up."

When they'd settled into the car and had the heater on
Kate said, "Tomorrow you go see Gienia while we're in church.
There's a reason she didn't make time for you in Krakow. Ask

her why she never wrote. We're too old for games. She could have contacted you some way. Her callousness hurt more than you."

Joe was amazed at how the conversation had turned. He inched the car carefully ahead so he wouldn't slide in the new snow before he answered her. "I talked to Gienia. We wished each other well. She's married; she has a life that suits her. You're the one for me, no regrets."

"Oh sure, you've dreamed about Gienia for years but you've got me and you're so grateful. Well, you deserved better than she gave you, and so do I."

"But Kate, I had to work to make her smile. Whenever you see me your whole face lights up. Gienia can't touch that." He reached over and brushed her face with his hand.

When they reached the hotel, people milled around the opulent well-lit lobby. The girl at the desk saw him and said, "Mr. Winowski, Tatyana Dorsak wishes me to advise you she is no longer available."

He pretended misunderstanding her. "You mean she went out this evening?"

She whispered, "She's not returning. I cut up her credit card myself. She left her computer here for her director."

Without missing a beat Kate said, "We hoped to complete a business transaction with her Monday morning. Did she make other arrangements?"

The girl glanced over and saw that her coworker was exchanging money. She leaned forward, "Mr. Majka called for Pani Dorsak. I say her things are here. He requested that I read her letter. I read to him her child is ill. He did not sound well then."

At the elevator Joe said, "I'd love to have put Faldo-Majka out of business permanently."

"The men in Tatyana's life let her down. She couldn't risk going to jail for strangers, Joe"

"I wanted her out of it. I'm just sorry those bastards are free, that's all."

"Don't be greedy. Nobody's been hurt and you haven't lost Ted's money."

"Dorsak said Ted wired an extra two hundred-thousand-dollars to add to his original fifty-thousand, to invest with her. He did it yesterday. I can't get over that he didn't say a word to me."

"You're on unsafe ground on trust issues, Joe. Maybe you'd better keep those feelings to yourself." They got in the elevator. "Ted saw you weren't interested in that investment. But you better tell him there's nobody to take his money tonight and let him sleep on it so it doesn't ruin tomorrow."

She pointed to their room. "But go pull yourself together first."

"Let me wash up. I can only go through this once. Do you have aspirin? Never mind, I'd throw it up. Go make sure he's awake. I'll be there in a minute." He went inside and stuck his head under the tub's faucet. He didn't look in the mirror. Tiny drips of water crept under the collar of his shirt. The discomfort helped him gather the courage to face Ted and Stella.

Marek was gone to his own place already and Stella sat up on the bed. Annie was on the cot, a blanket tucked around her knees. Ted came out of the bathroom asking, "What's going on here?"

Kate sat on Annie's bed, "Joe has something he felt you should hear."

Every eye turned toward him. Ted said, "You two getting a divorce?"

"No, no, nothing like that, thank God, but I owe you an explanation. The first time we talked to Tatyana Dorsak I wondered if it was legal to sell stock out of a hotel. I asked K to check it out. Most of Tatyana Dorsak's information was correct, except nobody can put in the infrastructure it takes to get Internet out in the country yet. It's not an incentive for buying stock, and her backer is a fraud."

Kate inserted, "Even I thought it sounded fishy."

"His brokerage firm's fake. That's why I warned her off in Krakow but she misunderstood and came back. I couldn't tell you because you mutter loud protests about things that make you mad. Police wanted to catch them red-handed so that the swindle would end, not just send them elsewhere."

Kate broke in, "So when Tatyana Dorsak showed up and you said you were interested . . . ."

Stella said, "That's awful. That poor girl was so sweet. They must have tricked her."

Ted had a glum, hang-dog expression.

Annie sat up in her bed. "Tatyana isn't a swindler, right?"

"No, they fed her false information so she couldn't direct police to them if somebody caught on. Fortunately, she'd snapped pictures and even got the fingerprints of her bosses. I swiped a photo she'd taken of her bosses when I went to her room in Krakow and K showed it to police. They would have diverted your money and nabbed them tomorrow, Ted, but Dorsak realized they'd set her up and ran back to her children."

Stella said, "Well, thank God she got away."

"But there's no way to get evidence now, so they'll be able to change names and start over. People will get conned before police spot them—and you know how fast tourists zip their wallets. People like them are bad for the entire economy. People hear about them and lose the urge to invest real fast."

Stella said, "So the help Poles need won't come, is that what you're saying?"

Joe threw up his hands. "I thought we could help. Now I feel just stupid."

Ted's face reddened; he looked like he'd explode. Stella patted his arm as he stood beside her. "Joseph, tell us the whole story. Spare nothing."

Joe spoke at length, skipping only his suspicions of Marek. He did relate how the police planned to trick the thieves so the family could get safely home and not lose Ted's money. He ended with the note he'd written for Dorsak and said, "There has to be some transaction to get proof. I kept you in the dark for safety reasons, but I knew you wouldn't want that swindle to go on."

They sat in silence until Ted said, "They have to take your money to go to jail. Stella, you know that from the man who tried to swipe your wallet."

"He put his hand in my purse but I held on till he let go."

Annie smiled, "Isn't that the guy you told us about that you scolded and said that he'd shamed his entire family all the way to the next stop, then people on the bus held him until the police came?"

"They'd have arrested him, but I kept him from taking my wallet so they had no proof."

Ted faced Joe, "So what's so stupid about tricking thieves? Getting robbed costs money. Catching a thief does too. But ten-thousand-dollars, Joseph?"

"What can I say? It's over." Suddenly Joe felt so tired his eyes almost rolled in his head. He patted Ted's back, "Sleep, we can go back to the farm and settle with Leszek tomorrow instead of waiting here for Monday. We'll go from the farm to

Warsaw. We'll rest while Annie sees the sights there. I've had about all I can manage here."

Kate and Joe returned to their room, He kicked the bed. "Now Skrzycki's got no obligation to get Marek's friend Claire out of prison. Mother of God, I can't do anything right."

Kate sat on the edge of the bed. "But won't Faldo send in a replacement? I mean, would he let Ted's money go if he thinks it's only a sick child that's interfered?"

Joe mulled that over as Kate went into the bathroom to get ready for bed. Then, the phone rang and Gienia's voice, husky and intimate said, "Have you forgotten me, Joseph? I stand as I did in our German Pension'. You remember?'"

Joe stammered, "G—Gienia, there's been a crisis. I can't come tonight but I'll drop my family off at church tomorrow and take you for breakfast. Can you get to your shop by nine?" Kate's suggestion that they meet sprang out of his mouth like a full-blown plan.

There was a sharp intake of breath, then her voice came over the line, soft yet urgent, "Oh Joseph, don't disappoint me. I have such an evening planned. I will treat you with imagination. There has never been another like you." Her voice caressed him. If he thought about her now, he was lost.

"I'll drop my family at church and we'll go for breakfast at the hotel on the corner." Why had he said hotel? Seeing her in public, he could handle that, but he wasn't going any place that had beds, for sure. Kate's suggestion could help get Gienia out of his system, but she was a danger to his soul and he knew it.

Joe said, "I can't leave my sick uncle now, but tomorrow I'll come to your shop about nine."

He hadn't been off the phone three minutes when it rang again. This time the hushed voice belonged to the girl at the desk. "Mr. Winowski, Pani Dorsak's director wishes to send a man, Pan Zajac, to claim Pani Dorsak's computer. He is on the phone to speak to you as he prepares to take over her appointments. Do you wish to speak to him?"

Relieved to play the businessman, Joe said, "Yes, please put him on."

After a flurried exchange and a connecting click, a cultured male voice came on the line. "Mr. Winowski? My name is Zajac. I regret the absence of Pani Dorsak. However, I will journey to Zakopane to complete your transaction. We do not wish you to suffer lost opportunity."

Joe said a silent prayer. "My uncle has an appointment for nine-thirty Monday morning and he expects to keep that schedule. I was making other arrangements for investing his money."

"I will meet you and your uncle at the hotel desk Monday at nine-thirty, Mr. Winowski."

"Wonderful," that gave Joe time to wire the extra money Ted had on hand back to the US. "We'll see you by the hotel business office at 9:30 then."

"I will be present."

He sounded very correct, Joe thought. Kate came out and distracted him just as he signed off.

"Kate, you were right. Dorsak's replacement will meet us as scheduled."

"Oh, please don't tell Ted tonight. We all need a good night's sleep."

Now that Kate knew, he could call the inspector from their room. Skrzycki said, "Now your uncle knows the risks, he may refuse to help. If he chooses not to participate, you must say the dollar transfer was delayed and you have only a very small money I will supply for you to show your good faith. I must hope they will not refuse such a small amount. Once they place the wire to transfer those funds, I arrest their innocent lamb. He must spend some time in a Polish jail. It is unfortunate but it must be. Polish papers will trumpet the story. It is guaranteed other hotels will be alerted. This swindle will die. It will take time to construct another, and we will watch closely. To see the back of such men is my dream." On that note they both hung up.

Kate had slid into bed. Joe turned to her, "We're back on. We'll play our parts yet."

But after all that mountain air, she slept. He draped himself around her, consoled beyond reason to feel her warmth and hear her steady breathing beside him.

In the morning Joe intended to announce after breakfast that the sting was back on. Before he could begin Ted said, "Didn't Pani Dorsak give you a number for her firm? If you called to complain she isn't available maybe they'd send somebody."

The anxious expression on Marek's face mirrored Ted and Stella's. He'd gone to their room to leave his small bag while they ate. Ted must have told him about the swindle because he'd paled. How involved had he been, that was the question, Joe thought.

Stella reassured him, "We don't want anybody else cheated by those thieves."

Joe fumbled his roll, "Are you sure you want to play this through?"

Annie cut in, "If we just go home, it doesn't help anybody, does it?"

"Alright then, Dorsak's replacement called me last night. I got huffy and demanded he complete the deal. I've arranged to handle this alone. You don't have to be involved."

"No, no, I want to be in on this. It's something I can do for Poland. But only risk ten thousand, like you said, Joe."

Joe needed their total commitment. He warned, "This man who replaces Tatyana Dorsak will give Ted an official looking certificate. We'll congratulate each other when the fellow says the transaction is complete. We'll act shocked when police rush in, in case his accomplices watch, got that?" Joe looked over his good-hearted amateurs. They nodded to conceal their excitement.

"If anybody wants to play sick, speak up now."

Nobody responded, but Marek looked nervous. If he was part of the scam he'd have to show his colors soon. He only had Sunday to get the word out. Skrzycki had wire taps in place. Police would divert the call if he attempted to warm the swindlers. If Marek didn't call, his innocence would be assured. Either way, Marek wasn't Joe's worry anymore, though he hoped for his innocence he simply couldn't distract himself with good wishes for Marek. Zajac was undoubtedly another innocent, Joe told himself, no need to worry about him either— poor guy.

Joe felt like a high school drama coach before an opening performance, nervous but knowing no matter what, the audience, all relatives of the actors, would be delighted.

19 – A MATTER OF CONSCIENCE

Zakopane's domed church sat on a knoll in town. Mountain men in white felt pants, rib-crushing belts and wide-brimmed black hats strutted uphill to meet their Lord. Their women followed in flowered dirndls covered with large black aprons and huge rosebud-patterned shawls. Kate squeezed Joe's wrist as he dropped his family off.

Joe made *The Sign of The Cross,* and sent up a quick prayer that he could keep his head and his dignity with Gienia. He headed up to his side street parking spot, pulled in, tipped the Pole who watched out for him, and sprinted to the back of Gienia's shop.

Gienia opened the wooden door and stood there in a crisp white lace blouse under her softly pleated gray-flannel suit. She wore the ivory rose he'd given her oh, so long ago. Her dark eyes sparkled.

Kate had suggested he see Gienia. The question was, where? Suddenly awkward he said, "I spotted a little restaurant where we can talk."

Gienia swung her loden cape off a rack, twirling it around herself, matador style. Her suede silver-buckled shoes prompted him to offer his arm for the slippery descent. Inexplicably, they wound up holding hands. Her warmth radiated through their gloves as she looked at him. Again, he was the center of her world. His knees buckled. They laughed, as he recovered himself, pretending he'd stumbled on a slippery spot.

He led her up the steps of an elegant restaurant he'd spotted the day before. A few guests were already eating. The waiter preened as he approached Gienia. He guided them to a linen-covered table on an enclosed porch, overlooking the walker's street. Gienia ordered hard rolls, jam, and black coffee.

"That's exactly what you ordered thirty years ago."

She smiled, "I remain me."

His heart ached with the long-suppressed pain of first love. He'd wondered so many times, were his memories true? Had she been so beautiful? Would she be still?

She was, and she always would be. To Joe, hers was the firm face of a girl. Her figure, even under the boxy jacket and soft skirt folds had drawn the waiter's appreciative eye as she'd twirled her cape onto his arm. She wore no lipstick, but her skin was creamed. She wore Replique, the scent he'd bought her so long ago. Her dark hair, short and wavy, nestled at the back of her neck, framing her face.

"So Joseph, do you live the American dream?"

He spoke of his workshop, his teaching, and finally he pulled out a picture of Kate and their four children gathered before the fireplace he'd installed, to give their home a warm and loving touch.

She smiled as he spoke of carving the carousel horse with Annie.

"And you? Gienia, tell me about you."

"My husband had a small business selling traditional crafts. You instructed me on achieving worker's best efforts, you remember? I convinced him to be generous to workmen as well as officials and we flourished."

"We sat outside a gasthaus and drank Franken wine. You drank mine, I remember." Joe laughed at the memory. "And you listened as I talked about labor in America, as if I was some kind of expert." He touched her hand then drew back.

"I was curious how people with choices behaved." Her smile was sensual, her tone soft. "We have no children so I continue to work with my husband. We nurtured artisans, as you suggested. One master woodcarver lived in our chalet here while carving details. You must see his work. Come by this evening and we will reminisce."

"Will I meet your husband then?"

"He remains in Warsaw. We have an understanding about old friends."

There was no doubt what she offered. Tongue-tied he stammered, "I'll, I'll try." He longed to breathe her in, to lose himself in her. Had he swallowed a magic potion? Joe talked to hide his raising ardor. He described developing his craft and told her about his boys' scholarships in engineering. He said they'd concealed that dream from him until they held it, undeniable, in their hands. Shocked he'd twisted the truth for her sympathy, he felt his color rise.

She followed each word then said, "Do you truly wish to become a director and give others the work you love? Several of my artisans have done so and they have not been satisfied. Beware of what you strive for." She squeezed his fingers gently. Ted had said the same thing but coming from her, Joe heard the ring of truth.

He listened so intently he didn't notice the waving arm, the red figure, bobbing up and down, until Gienia directed his attention to the window. Annie stood beaming at them like a mischievous six year-old. Joe froze, as Gienia waved her inside.

Annie approached their table breathless, "When you didn't pick us up, Mom said you went to meet a friend. Marek took Ted and Stella to that restaurant near the market and Mom and I hot-footed it up here to buy the wall hanging she reserved."

She handed her coat to the waiter, then she extended her hand to Gienia, "Hi, I'm Annie, this man's most marvelous youngest daughter."

"So you are the child I might have had if your father and I had married."

Annie blinked, recognition flooded her face. "You're the girl who ran away? Mom said you were having coffee, but I thought she was putting me on. Am I glad to meet you!"

Gienia laughed, "I am delighted to meet you also. Are you enjoying the land of your forefathers?"

Annie was all dimpled charm as she perched on the edge of her chair and sipped hot chocolate. She asked Gienia about Polish treasures. Her face shone, open and glowing, a vessel waiting to be filled. Joe watched, astounded.

She turned to him, "Why don't you go catch Mom? I'm still really cold."

He arrived on the street in his turtleneck sweater and tweed jacket. Cold air steadied him as he approached Kate, who stood squinting down the street, looking for Annie. She carried a package Joe eased from her arm. "Come join us. Annie, Gienia, and I are having coffee."

Kate nodded, "So, finally we meet." She followed him without another word. The two loves of his life greeted each other with undisguised interest. Kate's skin was taut, pink with cold, her windblown hair hung rich and loose. She looked her best when she graciously asked, "And will we meet your husband?"

"My husband stays in Warsaw while I supervise our distant stores. We do well together. My life is rich but not as I expected." She reached over and patted Joe's hand. "I regret only not saying goodbye to dear Joseph, who was so fine to me. Our parting was too sudden for people so young, don't you think?"

All heads nodded in agreement. It had been too sudden. Yes it had, but things had turned out well for both of them, they all agreed, bobbing their heads in unison.

When Gienia stood to go she did her matador routine, this time flipping the long scarf attached to the top of her cape, up and around her neck. She shook hands with Kate and Annie and kissed Joe on both cheeks.

Then she handed Annie a card for the restaurant by the market; "I invite you all to join me this evening. A marvelous troupe of dancers and musicians come to perform for us. Their vocalist is exceptional. I have reservations for my buyer and myself. There are six in your party, arc there not? I will increase my reservation accordingly."

Inviting the entire family, plus Marek, what could she be thinking? Joe felt himself nodding dumbly as she exited.

Joe paid as Kate and Annie gathered their things. Annie attempted Gienia's coat swing and nearly toppled a table. She shrugged, "That takes practice." Ha, Joe thought, Gienia didn't need practice.

They walked arms-linked downhill to collect Ted and Stella. Annie pointed to the advertisement for that night's entertainment on the restaurant door and announced, "We've been invited by Dad's old friend." Ted said he'd have to go rest up for that. It was early in the day but he'd been pushing himself. Marek offered to show Kate and Annie the World Skiing Championships site. Joe begged off and returned with Ted and Stella to the hotel.

It had all been too much and there was more to come. Exhausted, Joe slept like the dead for an hour. When he woke he walked to the foot of the towering snow-covered mountain that stood unmindful of the plight of the supplicant at its foot. Somehow, the silence of the mountain solaced him.

Annie had taken over when they were together that morning; maybe she'd come across tonight, he thought. What irony that that blessed girl had appeared in his moment of temptation. He'd allowed himself fantasies too realistic to sit across from Gienia with Kate there. He'd have to be careful about tonight's seating.

Joe reentered the hotel to have lunch and prepare for the evening. He set aside an extra blood pressure pill and two aspirin. He thought if men were truly punished for impure thoughts, tonight could well turn into his purgatory. He'd allowed himself the occasion of sin and for that he would pay, he knew, but he accepted all the suffering that might involve. Joe accepted he might well become the butt of family jokes forevermore as part of his penance. "Just let me survive with both my soul and my family intact," he sent his prayer up through John Paul, who he hoped would view him with some sympathy.

# # # # #

That evening Marek brought Kate and Annie to the restaurant. Joe arrived in a taxi with Ted and Stella. The restaurant, decorated for the performance, inspired Annie to ask for her mother's brush to tame her unruly hair. She looked clean cut and fresh in black slacks and her red sweater. Stella had packed a knit dress in her oversized purse for Kate. The women emerged from the ladies' room transformed. Stella wore a black dress and an immense Polish amethyst. Kate wore her navy knit with the brilliant striped-silk jacket she'd bought for Annie for Christmas. Her hair hung rich and loose and her white skin glowed over the vibrant colors accenting her jacket. The ivory rose he'd given his mother, and his mother insisted he give Kate during their first Christmas together, crowned her outfit. Had she noticed Gienia's matching rose pin that morning, or was her choice coincidental?

The walls were made of pine logs. Candles, and the smell of Polish food, took Joe to another era. Annie elbowed him, "Wow, they've dressed this place up with table cloths and the flowered curtains match the bench pads. Pretty fancy for a folk dance."

Joe mouthed to her, "Behave yourself." That earned him a mischievous smile.

Even when addressing his letters to Gienia, he'd deliberately not memorized her married name. He fished in his pocket for her card as the hostess approached them.

Then Gienia was there, elegant in her black leather suit and white-lace blouse. She kissed his cheek, greeted Ted and Stella, and turned her charm on Kate and Annie.

The booths made sitting together impossible. Gienia guided Ted, Stella, and Marek to the second booth where her buyer, Jasiu, stood to greet them. Jasiu was the man who had driven them to the hotel the night before. He seemed as startled by the coincidence as they were. He bowed low in greeting. On seeing him, Joe's anxiety dissipated. This should be a pleasant evening with a friend—and that's what he'd make of it. Gienia had engineered this, he thought, let her carry it off.

The red-checked tablecloth was dotted with wineglasses. Gienia directed Annie to the inside of her bench, and Joe slipped to the inside seat, opposite Annie. Kate sat beside Joe, across from her. Gienia asked Joe to fill their glasses from the carafe'.

Annie looked poised as Joe poured her wine. "Can I propose the toast?" She held up her glass, "Lord, thank you for this chance to gather with family and friends this evening. May we hold this memory dear for all time."

Where, Joe asked himself, did she learn to give a toast? Glasses clinked and he heard Marek speaking Polish and laughing behind him. He glanced back as Ted sipped his wine. Though Ted was a plain man, he appreciated good things. Humor and graciousness reverberated from him as he entertained those at his table. In Polish, Ted expressed a cultured side of himself seldom displayed in English. Joe looked longingly at that carefree table. He'd have to stay sharp, perched above his potential mine field.

Then Gienia said to Annie, "Order what you wish. I owe what I have to the advice your father gave me so many years ago. This is my opportunity to express my thanks. He will accept nothing, so you must help me."

Kate had suggested Joe use their credit card tonight, but when Gienia stated her intention to pay for everything, he felt Kate relax beside him. She probably thought Gienia owed them all that much, but Joe didn't want her to pay. He'd get hold of the waitress later.

Annie said, "Could we order different things, then pass them around like a giant 'S' from their table to ours? I'd like to say I tried everything."

Joe roused himself to intervene, but Gienia seemed delighted. She directed the pink-cheeked waitress, in her rose covered skirt, and white embroidered blouse to record eight different selections. When the dishes arrived Gienia showed each colorfully-arranged dish to Annie before it was placed by its first taster. "You have here: veal, chicken, golabki—I believe you call venison, and pierogi, leg of lamb, trout, and as the English say 'a partridge in a pear tree.' You are correct to taste all. This is unusual variety for Polish people."

The partridge was Annie's to start with. Gienia instructed the waitress to place an order by each person. She announced that each diner had two minutes to cut and taste their main portion and perhaps a side dish. Limited by Gienia's timing, nevertheless they savored each bite.

Gienia rapped on her wineglass twice, signaling their rotation. She passed her plate to Annie, Annie passed hers to Joe, his went to Kate, and the waitress passed Kate's to Ted. As the waitress reached out to take Marek's plate and pass it back to Gienia, completing the S, Marek jumped in surprise, not having picked up on the process. Even the waitress laughed.

Later, eight kinds of cakes and fruit desserts appeared. One had sugar cubes soaked in brandy; it appeared flaming. Again, the group began with tiny bites, oohing and aahing, occasionally attempting not to pass a favorite on—eventually capitulating to boisterous threats based on the obligations enforced by shameless cat calling.

Heads appeared, peeking around corners, then backed off so someone else could look. Joe couldn't actually hear them but their expressive faces said, "Those crazy Americans. They know how to have a good time."

Annie had answered his prayers. Gienia could hardly seduce him with tears of laughter running down her face. Musicians tuned up and high-booted costumed dancers appeared. Male dancers wore baggy red pants tucked in at the ankles and long-sleeved white shirts underneath black vests that almost formed skirts. They were topped off by boxy, red-trimmed black hats. The girls wore hand embroidered blouses above wide skirts topped with lacy-white aprons, their braids coiled over their heads.

Five violinists played mountain songs while the dancers moved with rapid intensity. Gienia was right, Joe thought, the singer had remarkable range. Ted bobbed in his seat as the lead male dancer stomped and twirled in a marathon of physical stamina like the dance they'd seen in "Fiddler on the Roof" years before.

In the next section there were three tables of people in wheel chairs who congratulated the dancers on quick movements and high kicks. Joe became so caught up with their celebratory shouts he let out the blood-curdling holler he usually reserved for polkas. The handicapped group waved to him.

When the dancers stepped back, people began taking the floor. Gienia leaned over and said, "Kate, you won't object if Joseph dances with me?" Kate graciously stood to let him out to take Gienia in his arms.

He'd hoped he'd make it through the night without touching her, but he couldn't refuse. She seemed to float into his arms. Her skin, her smell . . . She was small; his hand fit in the curve of her back. He felt like wrapping himself around her, engulfing her. Then they were moving to the music. He could feel her body against his, graceful, strong and sensuous.

The beat increased and he sped up, twisting his neck from side to side, stamping his feet. She didn't miss a beat. Centrifugal force pulled her from him as they twirled. Dancers made way as they spun past, then Marek was beside them, tapping his shoulder, demanding a turn. Before Gienia could blink, he'd handed her off and turned away. His heart seemed to beat outside his body.

Kate stood, handing Joe a wineglass of water she must have poured from the bottle she carried in her purse. He pushed into the booth and when she sat he touched his head to her shoulder in gratitude for sending Marek to his rescue.

Marek completed the dance and brought a flushed and smiling Gienia back to the table with a gallant bow. She laughed and nodded for Joe to pour another glass of wine from the carafe.

When it was time to head back to the hotel Joe reached for his wallet but Gienia said, "No, no, everything is arranged. If you tip the girl more her father will ask what else she does for money. Please, allow me this simple gesture to right the wrong between us."

Joe protested but Ted poked him in the back, hard. He acquiesced. They thanked her as they all rose to claim their coats.

Then Gienia said to Jasiu, "Deliver the others to the hotel as yesterday and allow Joseph to drive me home, can't you?"

To an open-mouthed family she said, "I have never driven. In communist countries public transportation was good. Now it is more difficult, one of the costs of freedom. Kate, you don't object if Joseph returns me to my little chalet?"

He'd prayed this moment wouldn't come, but how could he expect God to let him squeak by after all the help He'd given free of charge? He knew what to expect from this diminutive woman, but there was no turning back. Now the question was, could he resist her? And did he want to?

Outside, the goodbyes continued, until Joe leaned over to tuck Kate's skirt inside the car door. She touched his hand, "Do you want me to insist on coming?"

"I can handle myself, don't worry." He prayed that was true.

"Well, she's enough to scare anybody. Just remember, I'm waiting, and I care."

Joe kissed her cheek and shut the car door. Jasiu pulled out.

Joe handed Gienia into the Mercedes. She directed him out of town and up a lonely road. He turned in where an arrangement of Antique lanterns shown the way down the drive. The mountain chalet was silhouetted against the mountain. Joe tried to distance himself from her presence by focusing on the stone-covered lower walls and the tiny balcony off the upper window.

Gienia clicked the garage door open and dim lights went on inside the house. Joe found himself inside a spotless stone-walled garage. He exited the car slowly, checking as he walked around the car for the interior garage switch. His heart raced as he opened her door. Kate would have been halfway up the stairs by then, but Gienia took her time. She removed her key from her suede purse, then rose gracefully. She leaned against him, as if they were once more in that German pension where they had first known each other, young, lusty and alive. Their lips met. The surge of his response shocked him.

His heart took on the rhythm of youth. Why not, I'm an adult. Why not, he asked himself?

She laughed as she turned and headed inside. He followed her up the wooden steps into a paneled hallway. A hand-braided rug ran the length of the pine-floored hall; tapestries decorated the walls. Joe glimpsed a breakfast nook with a blue and white checked tablecloth and dried wild flowers in a crockery pot. He drank in details of the place to reassure himself he had control of himself.

He hung his jacket beside hers on a carved coat rack, then she took his hand gently and pulled him into the living room. A dim, antique lamp lit the room. She went to a sideboard and poured vodka from a crystal decanter. He longed to gulp it down and forget all restraints, but he took one burning swallow, then set it aside. Whatever happened here tonight, Joe intended to be a full participant, no excuses.

As Gienia lit a taper and carried it round the room, lighting candle after candle, the room took on an exotic, sensual aura. Joe's head began to swim. He clung to the back of a finely-crafted pine chair as he took in the fairy tale characters adorning her tapestries. Maybe, if he concentrated on details, he thought, his head would clear.

He scrambled to speak. "So, this is where Gienia lives. How many times I tried to picture you at home. I never would have thought this, yet it suits you."

Gienia seemed pleased he appreciated her taste. She said she'd hidden the wood carver in this house when he became too vocal in politics. He'd hand-finished nearly every detail, before he died in a suspicious accident not far away. Her throaty slur told him she'd drunk too much.

To distract her he said, "And when you returned to Poland you didn't go home?"

"Matka has others to help. I sometimes appear without expectation, but I never stay."

Joe shook his head, "Tonight will be a treasured memory for me." He moved toward the door, barely able to navigate out of her magnetized space. He couldn't stay another minute and still leave. He had to remove himself, now.

Her voice, soft and breathless caressed him, "Oh Joseph, I have such an evening planned. We are no longer children. For us, this is a night like no other."

She floated across space and pressed herself against him. He placed his hand on the small of her back. She guided it down the side of her hip, then gently pulled him into the dimly-lit room behind her.

Every fiber in his body responded.

Her back was to him in the dim light as she released his hand and walked to the side of the bed. Her jacket, then her blouse, then her skirt glided to the floor. Burnished wood and white bedding softened the effect as his resolve disintegrated. She slid off her thigh-high stockings and faced him.

With that movement the years fell away. Gienia appeared as she had so long ago. Her arms opened. "I do not wish for you to leave your little wife. I say remember, only remember. Of all the others, not one matches you. Come let us live an unmatched night. I will shake your heart."

"And if I keel over dead, will you to make me presentable?"

Her tone matched his, light yet earnest, "I am quite strong, you know. I would restore your dignity. Your sweet little wife need never guess."

Gienia asked for an hour, a memory. He was an adult; why couldn't he seize this moment? Heat seared his body as he came forward and pressed against her. She slid her hand down his leg, assuring his readiness before yielding to his gentle push onto the plump feather bed.

He unhooked his belt and his pants slid to his ankles before he realized he'd forgotten to remove his shoes. He leaned over to untie them. As he straightened, the lone lamp's dim light shown on the only picture in the room,

The Sacred Heart of Jesus, Crowned With Thorns

His breath caught with such force he choked. He coughed and stamped, giving himself a moment to remember.

What had she been thinking? In the German hotel she'd raged, "That witch put that picture there so we'd remember this night with guilt forever!" This painting, in this room, tonight, was no accident.

He'd thrown himself on his knees before that first *Sacred Heart* and pledged aloud he'd marry this girl and when he'd turned around he'd caught a sharpening of her eyes, a withdrawal he hadn't remembered until this instant. Within two weeks she was gone, lost to him without a word. He hadn't connected the two until this moment. Her smile was broad, her laugh quick, her hand clutched at him as he stumbled back, out of her grasp, tugging at his pants as he jammed his foot back in his shoe.

"I'd said I'd marry you. I'd have gotten you out and we'd have had a family. You knew, yet you ran away without a word, and you never wrote me later."

The look that passed over her face was contemptuous. She didn't have to say she'd never wanted a life of family and children; that she'd never wanted him. He knew it. What she wanted was his guilt and his slavish devotion.

He backed away. Gienia's little joke. If *The Sacred Heart* was a joke, it had reminded him of the mending of Kate's love that had worked on him as he pieced himself together after he'd lost her.

"Kate trusts me, Gienia. And I don't want to give her reason to lose that trust."

Her voice spit at him. "That unimaginative little wife of yours. I can take you where she'll never go. But you know you'll never be the same after a night with me. That's it, isn't it, Joseph?" Her face had contorted. She began to cry, a drunken, abandoned sob.

Mother of God, he thought, she was a force to resist. As he backed away he said, "Gienia, you're too upset. Is there anybody I could call, a friend, a relative? I don't want to leave you alone like this."

"No! Family devours women. Only my husband can ask from me and he is old, so old. You are my youth. No one has loved me like you. Don't you understand?"

He understood no good could come to him from this. She meant harm to his soul. What had he been thinking, he asked himself? Was he so weak his entire value system collapsed? Where was the faith he'd lived by? He shuddered as he turned away.

"I have to go, but seeing you was the highlight of my trip." He couldn't believe he was talking stupid at her.

"So, you fear me. You are right to run from me. Now go. One more moment with me and you would never recover your peace. Never!" She threw a pillow after him.

In the garage he pounded the button and squealing tires propelled him outside, as if the devil nipped at his heels.

# # # # #

The hotel's log cabin café was alight and full of celebrating hotel guests. Joe parked, then he stood behind a bench facing the mountains, highlighted by stars. Lightheaded, he spoke to his Lord from such depth he didn't form words, he simply thanked God for his awakening and asked for mercy.

After a while he sat on a bench, the cold sliced through his slacks. He welcomed the tiny bursts of numbing pain. His ears hurt and his nose tingled as he bowed his bare head and thought. How long he sat there he didn't know, but as he shifted his numbing leg, his father's face appeared before him and slowly, miraculously, Joe's expression relaxed. Peace descended over him like a soft, embracing blanket. The grip Ted's money and Gienia's promise had had on him was broken. He could walk away a man in control of himself. It was humbling to remember the struggle it had been.

Joe didn't know how long he sat, but the movement of a figure coming out of the café to his right tugged at the corner of his vision. The figure was headed toward the brilliantly lit hotel. He watched as it stopped and turned away from the light. It was Kate. She didn't see him until he came up behind her and placed his arms gently around her.

He nuzzled her neck. "I don't know why God saved me for you, but it was a miracle of major proportions. I'd do anything to keep you, Kate, anything."

When she turned to him, tears stood like tiny crystals on her cheeks. "Joe, this isn't about an old Polish girlfriend."

"I know I've been hard on you, but that's over. I know how lucky I am."

"No, you don't. Your hopeful spirit seems to slide away and when it does, you stop being you. I don't know if I can pull you to the surface one more time."

"Look, I struggled my whole life to understand and wipe that sad look off my father's face. Maybe I'd taken on his sadness. I know I've gone off track and you're right, it's not me—not the true me. If I had cancer I'd get help. I'll do whatever it takes to keep you." Twirling her in the light of the hotel windows he sang the words to *Take A Chance On Me* in her ear.

He kissed her neck, her cheeks, her lips. All the feelings he'd rejected earlier rose inside him as he guided her to their room where he whispered, "You're the one I want in my life. You're my everything."

Kate was part of his reawakening, once again, and as he wrapped himself around her and drifted off to sleep he wondered if he'd wake up in the morning. Wasn't he too old to be so blessed?

20 – A SWINDLE MEETS ITS MATCH

Annie woke them to talk about the sting. Joe opened the door and threatened to lock her in the bathroom if she didn't quiet down. Kate laughed as she got out of bed.

"I'll be so cool, Dad. You won't know it's me."

"Oh no, Ted has to be involved, but not you. We're all amateurs here and this is serious business. A wrong look or a slipped word and police won't get what they need to arrest them. We don't want them doing their dirty work on others. You have to stay out of the way, you hear me? Out!"

To her credit, she didn't pout. The Winowskis ate breakfast, then hovered in Hotel Kasparovy's lobby. As 9:00 approached, Joe sent Annie to help Marek pack up the car. He didn't want either of them to witness the humiliation of an innocent Pole.

Ted went to the office to wire the bulk of his money back to Detroit. He came out and looked around like some character out of an old movie, checking the lobby for criminals with quick glances from under his shaggy eyebrows. "There's a policewoman posing as a hotel employee, she'll make sure things go right, real professional."

These dear people, Joe thought, suppressing a smile. He couldn't deny them their fun. Maybe this encounter would be a charade, but it would save others and that was one of Ted's major goals. Zajac, the poor fellow they'd sent to pick up Dorsak's job was probably less aware than she'd been. Joe thought of him with pity in his heart. He was so relieved to be on the right side of his conscience he felt empathy for this man, who was in the wrong place at the wrong time.

Kate touched his sleeve, "Joe, are you okay?"

"I'm thinking that after this, any problem we have at home will seem small, very small."

Just then the girl at the desk waved to them. Zajac had arrived. The Winowskis turned to greet a man about sixty, with a limp, that made his body lurch sideways. He was meticulously dressed, with thick glasses, a neat gray beard and a nervous smile.

He extended his hand to Ted. "Mr. Winowski? I am David Zajac. I represent your broker. You are investing in Poland this morning, I understand."

Ted said, "We were worried we'd have nobody to hand our money to when Pani Dorsak left. We're real glad to see you, Mr. Zajac." He introduced Kate and Stella.

Zajac shook hands all round. "I have papers of purchase for you. When you release funds to my firm I make your ownership official."

"I'll get proof I gave you my money now, won't I?" Ted asked.

"Surely, I furnish stamped certificates. We find foreign investors happier with official documents in their possession."

"And when I want to sell my certificates?" Ted asked, rising to his role.

"You must notarize and mail these certificates to me to transfer to the buyer." Wow, they'd even thought of a way to get proof out of their victim's hand, Joe thought. Brilliant.

The family moved as one into the hotel's banking area. They avoided each other's eyes. Nervous grins crept onto faces, only to disappear at Ted's reproving scowl.

Joe said, "Our entire transfer didn't come through. It will catch up in Warsaw but we have ten-thousand now. Can we use that to get two hook-up orders going?"

Ted broke in, "I want my brother's home hooked up quick. Your agent in Warsaw can complete the purchase, but I want him connected so the family can sell their produce faster than their neighbors."

Zajac hesitated and swallowed hard, "That is unfortunate. However, I see no reason not to proceed. Allow me to call my director."

He turned away. The family stood mesmerized as he dialed. There was a hurried phone conference. Zajac turned back, smiling. "For me this is most interesting. I sell stocks for weeks only, yet my director requests that I travel on to Warsaw to complete your transaction."

Joe felt for the guy. Sure, they'd trust him with the deal. The poor sucker would go to jail for a new suit and couple of weeks in a hotel.

Ted looked genuinely anxious. He handed Zajac a list of addresses where he wanted the hook ups to be made. Joe saw it was pure fiction as Ted chatted on. "Here, I listed the addresses of my relatives and the number of stocks I'll buy after my dollars arrive in Warsaw."

Zajac opened a handsome pigskin briefcase and produced a form. Ted supplied his bank routing number to authorize the transfer and Zajac entered the numbers, then returned the form to Ted for his signature.

"These numbers look right to you?" Ted poked the paper at Joe, signaling him to memorize the numbers. There was no need for that with police electronics working for them, but Joe studied it to please Ted. When he gave his nod of approval, Ted signed.

The policewoman placed it in the fax, then handed the original to Ted. Zajac reached out to take it, "Sir, I am instructed to retain the original and the copy. Your receipt is the stamped document I give you now." He intended to hold onto the proof of transfer, Joe thought.

Ted held tight.

The policewoman said, "It is possible for me to make a second copy."

Confused, Ted held on. Joe stepped forward to prevent a scene, but Stella was faster. She tapped Ted's hand as she pointed to her purse, recalling the pickpocket who got away because he didn't have the evidence on him when the police arrived. Ted released his grip and the woman eased the paper from both men's grip. Another copy appeared. Zajac jumped for the original and the first copy, actually elbowing Ted aside, but Ted had recovered, and he accepted the second copy graciously.

Zajac looked flustered. "They will call as soon as this transaction is recorded. It is but a small wait." He limped around to sit at the desk and busied himself filling in the certificate meant to convince Ted he'd completed a legitimate purchase.

After an awkward wait, the phone rang and the transfer was confirmed. *Matko Boska,* Joe thought, *wouldn't it be shit if Ted's money was gone?* Far-fetched as that was, he broke into a cold sweat. If there was any hitch he knew he'd never hear the end of it. His mouth was dry as he offered up a silent prayer. Ted didn't blink.

Zajac handed Ted two certificates with an official-looking stamp embossed on the bottom. He clicked his heels and shook hands all around saying, "Other American families I spoke to over the last weeks were most happy to discover this possibility."

The innocence of the man touched Joe. They need only check the hotels Zajac had used, contact the Americans who'd stayed there and they'd have their witnesses. He'd hardly completed that thought when Inspector Skrzycki appeared with policemen.

With great flourish, Skrzycki took the certificates from Ted's hand and arrested Zajac, who blustered about demanding an explanation. When he was told he was part of a swindle he said they were mistaken and insisted he be allowed a call to clear things up.

Skrzycki graciously allowed Zajac to phone and Joe saw that he dialed the same number he'd dialed before, that of Majka-Faldo. The moment he said police were questioning him, the person on the other end hung up. He clicked off, maintaining his composure as police escorted him through the lobby, handcuffed. Zajac exited, limping but with his head–high, like an injured gentleman.

Ted kept up his end by collaring a policeman and demanding an explanation. Then everybody, hotel guests included, paraded to the lobby door where a uniformed policeman brought up the rear.

Annie stood outside the door—she shot photographs from her hip as the police led Zajac out to await the police car. Joe stepped forward and took the camera from her.

She whispered, "I can't believe I helped jail that poor man. I felt like hugging him and telling him he'll be okay, you know, Dad?"

Joe did know; he squeezed her arm then followed.

Inspector Skrzycki approached him. "You have played your part well. I understand you wish to return to your family farm. I also must go to the Tarnow area. I would enjoy confirming the return of your uncle's money and thanking him privately. I have business I must attend to now. May I come by the farm later this afternoon?"

Joe told him they planned to leave the farm by 4:00 but he would be delighted to see him if he could get there before that. Just the fact he didn't need to hold Ted's money as evidence was a great relief. Joe stood back when Skzycki's driver pulled up. This scene, of a Pole carted off in handcuffs had to be painful for Marek. Joe walked ahead to greet him as he returned from loading up their Mercedes. Marek's head was down; he looked to the side, avoiding looking at Zajac. He came alongside the police car just as a policeman instructed Zajac to duck his head getting into the car. Zajac gave his habitual polite, "*Dziekuje bardzo.*"

Marek stopped dead in his tracks and whipped around as Zajac disappeared inside the police car. Marek pointed at the police car as it pulled out. "That is Majka. There, it is him. Each time I speak with him he answers me so."

Joe had heard Majka when Marek let him listen in on his phone. Zajac's tone had sounded familiar to him too. Zajac was Majka-Faldo. Joe's own ears confirmed it. They'd flushed out the big boy, disguised as an old man with a limp and a studious manner. He'd truly played his role to a shine.

Zajac-Majka-Faldo believed his disguise was undetected. Well, Joe thought, he had a surprise coming.

Skrzycki's cell phone didn't respond in the mountains so Joe rushed inside to a pay phone and dialed his office in Warsaw. He left word with Skrzycki's assistant, then he instructed Marek not to mention that they'd captured Faldo-Majka when they got to the farm. There was no use getting everybody more excited than they were. He'd leave that surprise for Skrzycki to reveal when he came to the farm later. After all, how many supremely satisfying moments must a police inspector have?

The family regrouped in the sitting area and Ted said to Annie, "Give me a quiet minute so I can calm my heart, please." She bowed to him and walked towards the telephones, bouncing on her toes with excitement.

Ted called after her, "Get on your knees and thank John Paul we came through this good. He stood like a gorilla behind us." Ted turned to Kate, "I ask too much from such a young girl, don't I?"

Kate said, "Young girls thank God for His help every day, Ted. It's just not in a way you'd notice. But it's after ten now. Don't we need to head for the farm?"

He nodded, but still they sat until Annie reappeared beside her mother's chair. She said, "I called Detroit and Mike will pick us up at the airport. He can't wait to see me."

Joe's head snapped back but Kate said, "Don't you dare fuss. She's paid her dues."

Within twenty minutes of the end of the sting they were all in the car. Joe welcomed the drive as he looked up at the snow-capped mountains. The satisfaction he felt over the way they'd flushed out the true criminal salved his shame about the Gienia fiasco. Inspector Skrzycki had Majka-Faldo in custody and the evidence he needed. What a blessed relief, Joe thought, as he pulled out and headed for Leszek's and their final reckoning.

# # # # #

Joe stopped at a neighborhood grocery store that held rows of jars full of fruit, beets and onions. Kate bought bread, butter, tea, salad fixings and a bag of sugar, just in case. They'd carry the kielbasa back to the farm where it came from and enjoy it with the family.

Ted bought *Zywiec,* his favorite Polish beer. Annie selected balloons and ribbons. Would this last visit be a celebration after they confronted Leszek? Joe asked Marek to drive the last distance to the farm so he could collect himself.

The true purpose of the trip was to be the last problem solved, or not. So much had gone right, dare he pray Leszek would make peace with Stasiu? Joe knew he couldn't buy favors from God but he felt, deep down, that a petitioner should offer something of value—because the sacrifice, no matter how unnecessary, made him feel less self-serving.

"Whether my petition to reunite these old men is answered or not, Lord, you've cared for us beyond my wildest dreams. I offer up my own disappointment at myself, and all the agony it caused me in gratitude for all you've done for our entire family, me in particular."

Joe smiled to himself, thinking how pleased Kate would be he was reordering his thinking. Besides, these cousins of his deserved a crack at their own dreams. They'd paid their dues over and over again. Being stymied didn't have to be their birthright. He had time and resources, but history might gobble up the Pole's last good chance if people like him didn't help. Well, he'd do what he could to help pick out good Polish investments, and with Ted's money thrown in, that could be a job worth doing. Amen, he prayed, amen.

# # # # #

They reached the farm by one. Joe squeezed his uncle's arm. This was it; either Ted worked things out between Leszek and Stasiu now, or they'd head home minus that victory.

Marek snailed the car down the muddy lane. It had rained and fields and flowers were in full bloom. The tethered dog barked as confused geese fluttered off the road. A figure appeared at the upper window of the two-story brick house and Piotr appeared outside the log house; he sprinted towards them. Faces appeared, one here and then one there. Piotr and Karolina had stayed on to help harvest after the others left. Only Leszek, his wife, Zosia, their granddaughter, Perky, and Babcia actually lived there.

Piotr said Leszek had gone to see another grandson. When the family realized Leszek was gone, they hustled inside, hitting the doorway in a bunch, tripping and pushing like little kids. Stella's relieved laugh rose over the clamor as she brought up the rear. Karolina set things in order while the men rearranged furniture. Joe sent a boy across the fields to fetch Leszek before he helped Piotr guide Babcia into the dining room to join them.

Marek carried the food they'd bought inside while Stella and Kate helped Zosia and Karolina put the tea on and set the table. Annie and Perky disappeared into one of the back rooms. They all talked at once, mixing Polish and English, creating a comic harmony. Ted told Babcia about the swindle and he didn't miss much, Joe noticed. She listened and muttered, "Bad man. Very bad man."

They basked in the warm atmosphere of their family. For Joe, this was the home of his father. The anger he'd felt for the man, who was always too overwhelmed by the immigrant experience to reach out to him, faded. He acknowledged how painful life became for his father after he'd insisted he must leave this home for adventure.

Annie announced to anybody interested that she'd transfer all the photos she'd taken onto a video and mail them a copy, if they could view it. Piotr jumped up, "From Germany I brought broken American TV and a video player. It works good until the transformer becomes very hot. Then everything stops. I'll show you." In a few minutes he had the equipment assembled.

Fumbling through her backpack for her digital camera's plug, Annie snapped one end in her camera and the other in the TV. Photos flashed in the order she'd taken them from the moment they'd arrived in Warsaw. She had the airport, the hotel, the Jewish girls and their friends. She'd shot pictures of K., Warsaw's Old Town, Marek, Warsaw museums, Dorsak and her little girls and of course Babcia, all the relatives who'd came to the farm, the Pope's church and tucked on the end, Zajac.

Annie clicked through the photos quickly, surprising even herself with all she'd caught. When she flashed on the museums' torn Gregorian chant, she isolated the tear that had been sewn with sinew centuries ago. Ted's elfish sister who shared her log house with the geese announced that she'd mended that parchment and Ted's entire body jiggled at her joke.

Then the head of the fellow who grilled kielbasa by the road replaced Ted's. "Look, Uncle is young again!" Gasps and then laughter followed.

Piotr asked, "Can't you slow down?"

The last shot was of Zajac-Faldo as he bent to enter the police car, a full profile. Joe realized that alone could convict him, but Annie pressed on. After the last three pictures appeared, Annie clicked on six, then nine. She changed heads and bodies, clicking her own head from a picture Kate had snapped, on to one she'd taken of Babcia.

Babcia covered her face to hide tears of laughter, then she shook her finger at Annie. "You are me. You are my American girl!"

When she made the horse kick the fellow wearing the under shirt, grown men cried.

The TV overheated and the show ended. Silence reigned as they savored the moment. When the women set out to make tea Ted asked, "What cash is left?"

Kate said, "I have the dollars you asked me to carry, plus a hundred and fifty of my own."

"How much have the rest of you got beyond the hundred we're each carrying for Fred?" Ted asked.

Ted was going to give away their cash, Joe could feel it coming, but they had a long drive and they'd need money for food and gas. "Here's an extra twenty." Joe had paid out the most in cash, what he had left was in $1.00 bills.

Ted said, "Check all your hiding places. I want to know how much we have, total." He spoke English, but Babcia watched him closely. "I want to pay Marek now. Why should he go back to Warsaw if he'll make business here with Piotr? Besides, he may need to testify against that swindler. We don't want him available as a target for those con men. He'd be safer at Piotr's place." Annie looked to Kate. She probably wanted to slip Marek money herself.

Ted asked Joe, "How much do you think a good used car costs here?" That moved the women. They hustled to hunt down their last zloty. Stella had forty dollars left, Annie two hundred and twenty. Annie lifted her eyebrows.

"Everybody kept slipping me money. I didn't ask."

Ted had almost three hundred-dollars. They each carried $100 for Fred, and they still owed Marek $30 a day for the last three days, and with a hundred-dollar tip for the entire time it was going fast. Ted could replace Fred's money when he got home. Still Joe said, "That won't buy much of a car."

"If Marek put his earnings in it would help," Ted said.

Joe shook his head. "Marek still has to get his girl out of jail."

Stella said. "Couldn't we give dollars when our swindle money is returned?"

"No, God doesn't want me doing that. I'm thinking of importing fertilizer. That takes serious money. They'll need a warehouse and trucks and a good computer system. I'll stake that, but Piotr's business won't fit under that. He needs cash for his set up now."

"When was Piotr forgiven for not repaying Fred?" Joe asked.

Ted didn't blink. "That boy's involved in the politics of his village. He'll run for office; but he needs money to be heard. I saw it in Hamtramck. They'd do okay for a while, then somebody suggests a pension for a man who hasn't contributed much, then the numbers don't work. Everybody has to give value and pay taxes. Only respected men can hold others to the law, especially here, where fooling the tax-man was a way of life. They have to change that thinking for the community to flourish. Piotr swore to me, he would be such a man. That's it, for me."

"If they have the down payment, can't they go to a bank for the rest?" Kate asked.

Ted snorted. "Banks charge over twenty-eight-percent interest here, for starters."

He sent Joe to bring in Marek, Piotr and Karolina. He paid Marek and tipped him. The money formed a stack in his hand. Marek held out his envelope full of tips from Majka-Faldo. "Spy money," he said as he pulled out eight five-dollar bills to give Ted.

Ted said, "You earned it, you keep it." Marek beamed as he folded all his bills up.

Ted gave the remaining cash to Piotr, explaining it was for the car they'd need for the business. "When you make money you still owe young Fred. I expect you to repay him within three years, none of that to the third generation stuff. If anybody in this family wants more dollars from me, you must pay your just debts."

Piotr threw his arms around Ted, then Stella, in gratitude and reassurance.

Stella said, "We think you'll have a good chance once you get going."

Joe glanced out the window and saw a blue Fiat 125 p. pull in the drive. He said, "Marek, go welcome Inspector Skrzycki and bring him upstairs."

Marek hurried out as Joe positioned himself at the door. An arm drew Marek into the back seat and the door closed. Inspector Skrzycki got out without glancing back but the look he threw Joe confirmed his prayer. He'd brought Claire back to Marek.

The Inspector came inside and Joe tried to herd the others too, but they resisted—wanting to see who Marek was talking to. The Inspector offered, "Claire."

Ted barked orders and everybody moved back to the dining room. Joe introduced Skrzycki to Babcia, who greeted him as if he was Pope John Paul. He shook hands all around, kissing the Polish ladies' hands first, then Stella's, then Kate's, and finally Annie's. "You are the young lady who came to connect with our proud people."

Annie blushed, then collected herself enough to respond in Polish.

Finally, Marek appeared in the doorway, his arm around a frail, doe-eyed girl. Claire's long dark hair hung limp, a tired, anxious smile wavered on her delicate face.

Kate walked around the end of the table to hug the cringing girl. "It's all right, don't you worry, everything's all right. Annie, get hot tea and some light food. Claire needs quiet, away from the crowd."

Like ants, the women sprang into action. Stella brought a beautifully arranged plate of bread and kielbasa for the Inspector while Zosia prepared a table in the next room. Bite-sized morsels alongside a steaming pot of tea sailed by on a tray balanced lightly on Annie's arm into the room where they'd taken Claire.

Joe spoke quietly to Skrzycki, "I had almost given up hope we'd see Claire. Thank you for handling the swindle so well and for returning that child."

The muscles moved oddly on Skrzycki's cheek, "I say to you, I strive to keep Poland a land of honor. This story is not yet complete, Mr. Winowski. News leaks will have Majka as more clever than we stupid police. Others will approach him. We photograph where he goes and who he sees. My best man was bored by me. Now he works for him, a man of vision, who does not remain at home today I'm told." He threw back his head and released a full, throaty rumble.

Joe said, "But did you ever imagine you'd catch him red handed? I was stunned when I realized we'd actually lured Majka into the open. It had to be the smell of big money. He went for the bait and it wasn't until he got in the police car and we heard him say 'Thank you' that we knew that was him. When I called your assistant to tell you we'd landed the big guy I was drunk with excitement. I am so grateful for the way you set this up. You got him, and Majka-Faldo's contacts won't ever guess how we fingered him as Zajac. The fingerprints from Dorsak will send him away a good long time."

Skrzycki jerked straight up. "What? Zajac is not Majka-Faldo. No, I would have known. I am professional. I would have seen. No, what you say cannot be."

With a laugh Joe said, "It was the way he dragged his leg, I think. He looked shorter and his hair was gray, he wore a beard and he spoke like a professor. But I heard the clipped way he always said, '*Dziekuje bardzo.*' Marek recognized it before I did, but the minute he said it I knew it was true. I called your assistant to check his fingerprints against those we got from Dorsak and notify you."

"My assistant?" In Warsaw? You told my assistant in Warsaw? No, no, there are mountains, my phone did not function from there to here. I believed Zajac was of no significance. *Matko Boska,* I called from the local police station to authorize Zajac's release in Zakopane."

Ted leaned forward, "Is my money safe to invest for my family?"

Skrzycki stammered, "I, I believed I could prevent Faldo's success. I taped each phone number from Pani Dorsak. I had all that was necessary to retrieve your money." He was gasping as they hung on his every word. "F . . . Faldo arranged all deposits to be forwarded instantly. We had not one moment. I have the Swiss account number but not the password. My man presses the Swiss." Skrzycki was ashen. He couldn't say more. He sat down hard.

Ted slapped his knee and Joe watched as his face flamed red. Reality washed over them all. Joe's chest tightened. The

Swiss don't give out confidential information or turn over assets often. What were their chances? His stomach lurched. "You're telling me Ted's money is gone?"

"It's lost?" Ted turned on Joe. "You lost my ten thousand-dollars?"

"We do everything possible to recover your money," Skrzycki said, "I'm sorry."

Ted said, "I'll follow that bastard to the end of the earth."

"I'm sorry, Ted. I'll do . . . do all I can to replace your money," Joe said.

Ted's face hardened, "You got no way to pay me back. I never should'a listened to you. You know better than anybody, no matter what."

Joe was too overwhelmed to defend himself.

Ted turned to Skrzycki, "Can't you grab that bastard's next deposit?"

"Law prevents me becoming the thief. Yet I use every legal possibility."

Ted exploded, "He pulls this and you do nothing? *Matko Boska*, the bastards win again."

Skrzycki stood. "My men have his fingerprints. He is clever but we know him. When we take him next, disguises will not save him."

Ted's down-turned mouth spoke his disbelief.

Skrzycki stood a moment, visibly collecting himself. "Because of you we have evidence. For that our dear country thanks you. This swindle will stop. The good you did has value beyond dollars. *Stolat!*" He gripped Joe's hands, "You will hear from me." He bolted toward the door. Joe never got to tell him Annie had Zajac's picture. Even if he was disguised it might help. Joe would forward it to him from the hotel.

Stunned with the realization that he, and only he, would carry the burden of this fiasco, Joe walked outside and stood on the softening earth as Skrzycki spun his wheels, whipping mud around, before shooting up the slippery lane.

Marek came up behind Joe and gently put his arm around his shoulder. "Thank you, Uncle. Thank you for my Claire." Joe nodded. That was one task accomplished and he was grateful.

They inspected the Mercedes together. A tire had a bubble from hitting a pothole. Replacing it relieved the tightness around his heart. Upstairs, everyone knew his shame. He felt better standing in the biting wind, then facing those who knew he'd messed up again, out of carelessness, or arrogance, or simple disregard for them—whatever motive they chose to assign him.

Ted was right; he had proceeded when all indicators said stop. His need to pay Ted back would surely affect Kate. His throat tightened as he contemplated stumbling on, with everybody knowing he'd screwed up again. He had no defense; none whatsoever.

Then Annie stood beside him, tugging at his sleeve. She wiggled under his arm and he squeezed her tight. He'd taken this trip to show her what family meant and she had gotten it, despite his blunders.

Tears of gratitude formed in his eyes.

"Way to go Dad, way to go."

"You're talking to me after how I screwed up?"

"You sacrificed that witch for us. I mean, money is replaceable, but you aren't."

"Witch? Gienia's not a witch. How can you say that?"

"What kind of woman tries to take a good man away from people who love him? What kind of a woman does that, Dad?" She demanded an answer.

"Honey, Gienia was my youth. I saw what I needed to see in her, but God saved me for your mother and I'll thank Him for all the days of my life. But Gienia's no witch—she's just incredibly self-serving. She could never have given me a great kid like you."

"Well, anyway, I'm glad you stayed with us. I mean, at your age a lot of men . . . ."

He shushed her. "I feel bad enough about all this already. Can we leave it?"

She pressed Joe's hand, then opened the car door and crawled into the back seat to repack.

Piotr appeared out of nowhere with buckets of water to wash the car. Joe tried to dissuade him and Marek but they said, "We remove all dirt . . . our gift to you."

He joined them, grateful for the activity and their uncritical company.

Annie popped out of the back seat, her arms laden with clothes. "Don't worry, Dad, you won't have to replace these. I have way more than I need, you know?" She hustled inside to give away every stitch of clothing she could spare to Claire.

Joe's head hurt and his stomach jumped, but he still had to deal with Leszek, who hadn't returned yet. They had a schedule to keep. Joe decided he'd drive to Leszek's grandson's farm and bring him back. He climbed the farmhouse steps to prepare the others. When he reentered, he felt the struggle to keep things pleasant hanging in the air. Ted looked disheveled and Stella's slumped posture spelled out her fatigue. For the first time ever Joe looked at Stella and thought *she's an old lady*. He wanted to put his arm around her and help her down the steps. Both their faces sagged from their efforts. It was time to take them home.

Claire stepped into the room and slid her arm through Marek's. Her freshly washed hair hung around her like a veil.

Annie's gift of navy slacks, her red sweater and her cut off red rubber boots she'd brought to wear on the farm did for Claire what the American clothes Joe had given Gienia so many years ago had done for her. She looked so clean cut and vibrant, who could help but try to protect her, he wondered.

Annie might have felt slighted or jealous, but there she stood, bouncing on her toes, thrilled to witness Marek and Claire's reunion. Her generous nature was a credit to Kate, Joe knew. He reached over and touched Kate's arm. She flashed him a smile so warm and genuine he wanted to fold her in his arms right there.

Could he reunite Leszek and Stasiu? Exhausted, he thought, if his penance for courting temptation was enduring one more opportunity to mess up, he'd accept that possibility and plow on.

Besides, what other choice did he have? Inhaling deeply, he braced himself for the great confrontation.

21 – WHAT GOES AROUND, COMES AROUND

Kate tapped Joe's shoulder and whispered, "I just saw Leszek duck behind the old barn. Why don't you go talk to him? He might listen to you better than Ted."

Joe squared his shoulders. The moment had come. "Ask Piotr to get Stasiu over here and then send Ted out. If they self-destruct, its best done out of Babcia's hearing."

It was time for the reckoning. Joe walked down the outside stairway. He approached the agile old man kicking rocks behind the low building his father had once called home. Joe had to keep him out there till Staisu showed up. He touched Leszek's arm. "Uncle, show me where my father grew up."

Leszek led him inside the structure now used for pigs. "This was our home. Our grandparents lived in the log house after our larger home was burned. And we here. How we fit I cannot say, but it was clean and loving always." He turned around. "We brothers slept like spoons together in that corner.

Victor was broad, I was tall and Tadeusz, he was our kitten. Not like today when he is big and I am small." He laughed, "Victor kicked when he slept. I landed on the floor often, very often."

"At the end of the war soldiers torched this house and scarred your land, right?"

"We prayed as the troops moved off. Not all of this house is wood. We used some river stone in the building so fire moved more slowly here. We were able to save enough for our shelter." Leszek waved his hand toward the icon of the Black Virgin painted on the wall. Joe had seen her many places. This crude copy, blackened but not destroyed, moved him deeply. His father had told Joe that he'd gained strength to do his many duties praying before this "Queen of Poland."

Leszek shook his head, "Victor and Ted sent us goods we needed in fabric covered boxes. Stella sewed dollars in the lining of old clothes. Our postman, walked beside his broken-down horse to carry each package he knew would relieve our suffering. Ted and Stella had little to spare in those years, yet they lifted us, on their backs, they lifted us."

Wiping his eyes with the back of his sleeve, Leszek turned on a grinder he'd made out of scrap metal to reduce sugar beets to fodder for pigs. He told Joe that when the communists installed electricity in the 70's he'd fashioned its motor himself. "But Victor, he was a wild boy, he had no love of farm life. We dug beets together and he complained with each bulb. Our father whipped him with his strap and still he muttered." Leszek laughed aloud at the memory.

Relieved to have a shovel to grab, Joe scooped up huge beets, heaving the bulbous plants into the grinder's body, dissipating his own pain to a manageable throb. His father had cut these same lumpy beets amid the vinegar smell of animal dung and he'd described it to Joe when he'd objected to skinning rabbits. He said a boy should give his labor freely to his father. Hearing that Victor himself had protested his own tasks strongly made Joe smile and it comforted him greatly.

Leszek appeared fragile and spent. His conniving, hatched as a kid, had cost his future. And here Joe stood, poised to inflict more pain on him. Joe could barely swallow as he turned toward the old man.

Leszek said, "Victor should have this farm, but Pa couldn't beat the Cavalier from him. Babcia said, 'Let Victor seek his fortune in America.' He sacrificed his home to be treated like an ignorant man in a strange land. Ted tells me Victor felt his mistake from the first day, but it was done. It is good for Babcia to see her wild boy makes for his family a loving home."

His father sacrificed this home for a dream he could never achieve. Joe had always thought six wild boys, himself especially, had triggered his father's sadness.

Leszek moved toward the house. Flustered, Joe asked, "Isn't your old barn on the back of this building?"

Leszek led the way through a scarred wooden door to a room divided into pens. Two immense sows nursed piglets and a boar stood by, still but watchful. Leszek threw ground-sugar beets into their pens. Joe reached around him to unlatch the top of the divided door. The bottom half stayed shut. There was no sign of Ted; he'd have to stall.

"Ted told me how you and Stasiu worked together doing chores on Stasiu's father's farm, then here for your own father. Didn't you keep the horse here?"

Leszek pointed at the corner, "Over there he stood, behind our cow."

"And when you finished your chores you'd flop down on the hay, Ted said that Stasiu stood here, his back to the door. He didn't see Ted return for the hoe to dig carrots because only the top of the door stood open."

The old man squinted, Joe felt him strain to picture the scene. "The heat rose from the manure you shoveled as the horse swished its tail. You said he cooled your face. Stasiu commanded the horse to poop on you and you laughed."

"Yes, many times he cursed me, so many times." Leszek smiled at the memory.

"Ted wished to hear what made you laugh. He squatted down, thinking you told wicked stories, the kind you refused to tell a mama's boy, no matter how he begged."

"We could not say it to Tedeuz. He told Babcia everything, guaranteed."

"He overheard you say you'd write your family that you couldn't send them money."

Leszek's eyes narrowed. A hand waved in protest. He watched Joe, neither acknowledging nor correcting him.

"You said while you saved for Stasiu's ticket you'd write your father that you hadn't enough work to live and save, then you'd send Stasiu immigration papers; and when Stasiu's father threw the covers off one day, his bed would lie empty. No more Stasiu to beat and kick. Stasiu said he would work you through school to be an educated man, the thing your father denied you." Joe paused, dreading driving in the stake, but knowing he had to. "You said the foolish mama's boy could dig cabbage the rest of his life. Ted heard you. He heard. And he told your father. Ted told it, not Staisu!"

"No, no, he heard nothing. Ted could not keep such a secret. He tells this only for Stasiu." The old man trembled.

"He loved you, Leszek, his brother, and you said you would abandon the stupid mama's boy. Hurt silenced him."

Leszek covered his mouth with the back of his hand, staring as if he pictured the scene.

Pity urged Joe to stop, but he could not. "Your father stood over a smoking barrel of drying kielbasa by the side of the house. Ted ran to him and blurted out your plan, but your father waved him away like a fly. Ted never knew, until you read your father's letter out loud, that he wrote Victor to replace you with Ted on your immigration papers."

Leszek stumbled and sat down on a bench beside the wall. Joe took the old man's roughened hand. It was cold and his bright eyes seemed to fade. The muscle on the side of his face twitched. "Leszek, Stasiu is your life's friend, a gift from God. He suffered with you then and he waits to suffer through his last days with you now. Stasiu didn't cause your troubles and Tadeusz bears you no grudge. In the name of our Lord Jesus, accept God's will this change was meant to be— reconnect with Stasiu, Leszek. Please for us all, reconnect with your life's friend."

Leszek's mouth opened and closed without a sound. Was he having a stroke? Joe did the only thing he could think of, he prayed in Polish, "Our Father, Who Art in Heaven . . . ." Suddenly another voice blended with his. The unkempt old man from days before stood over them, but he'd been cleaned up. His hair was no longer matted. He wore a clean sweater. He took Leszek's hand from Joe and continued ". . . as we forgive those who trespass against us . . . ."

Joe felt an intruder on an intimate moment. He walked out into the fragrant farm air as Ted approached. "Don't go in. I repeated the story you told Kate. Leszek listened and Stasiu is with him now. It's over. Now it's time to go home. Say goodbye to your mother, we have to get going."

Ted stood a moment, nodding his head, taking it all in. He clutched Joe's arm. "When I was a boy, they said it takes a month to reach America. But I tell you, Joseph, it takes a lifetime. Only now that my brother is healed is America truly my home."

Joe put his arm around Ted's shoulder and they headed inside. Once again they made their rounds; Ted, then Stella, Joe and then Kate, and finally Annie kissed Babcia.

The fragile woman clung to Annie. "Take me," she begged. "Take me with you."

Annie looked to Joe. What could he say? If Babcia wanted to go with them, how could they refuse? They couldn't actually take her and yet . . . .

Piotr grabbed a lightweight cover, wrapped it around Babcia and lifted her, "Come on, Babcia. We'll go outside to say goodbye. How about that?" Piotr and a beaming Babcia headed for the stairs. Everyone scrambled to clear the way.

This time the kisses were hurried; it was damp and Piotr couldn't hold Babcia long. They reached the car as Leszek and Stasiu came out of the barn arm-in-arm. The old friends scuffled forward. Stasiu smiled shyly at Ted and Ted stepped forward to clutch him in a bear-like grip, thumping on his back in speechless joy, tears streaming.

Babcia's white curls bobbed free from under her flowered babushka as she leaned from Piotr's arms to hug her Ted one last time. Ted stumbled backwards, tear-stained but smiling.

Marek led Ted to the car and gently tucked him inside. As they pulled out Annie stood in the car's open sunroof and snapped pictures. She recorded forever Babcia with Piotr and Karolina, Peppy with Zosia, Marek with Claire and Leszek with Stasiu. When Joe turned onto the farm road, he honked. It was over; they were heading home.

Silence, punctuated by sighs, assailed Joe as he aimed K's car toward Warsaw. Silence was fine with him. He'd done all he could, the best he could. Ted wouldn't forget the loss of his ten-thousand-dollars. Joe's name was emblazoned on that fiasco forever. He might have saved his honor by helping those old boys reunite, but Ted's money was still gone.

Joe shifted and pressed the accelerator. He wanted to turn north before dark. He'd rather die than ask Ted for directions now. How could he have hoped to outsmart professional criminals, he asked himself? And yet, Annie was on his side and Kate hadn't turned on him, so if he got through tomorrow's flight home, he'd live to do what he had to. He simply had to release his dreams and work double-time

To save what really mattered he had to let go. Joe took a deep breath, accepting his loss as part of growing old—or maybe growing up, one more time. He didn't know. All he knew was there was no controlling life. He'd have to take joy where he found it, back off and be grateful for what he had, because if he didn't he'd lose it all. God had given him a second chance and lame and beaten though he was, he intended to use it. He felt grateful and guilty, guilty and grateful, what did it matter? He could go on.

# # # # #

The Winowskis got up and out of Hotel Victoria early the next morning. They'd eaten a light supper and gone to bed. Avoiding catastrophe became their goal.

At the airport, Joe turned over K's Mercedes keys to the rental guy. Ted's credit card covered the rental, plus replacing K's bruised tire. They were so early they made it to the airport's waiting area quickly, once they passed through customs. Nobody else was waiting for their flight yet.

Joe had to hold the family together this one last day. Why, he asked himself, had he become obsessed with making his craft into a business? As things were, he enjoyed every job he took. Between trying to further his father's dreams and the draw of Ted's money, he'd lost his way. He felt like a deep-sea diver finally gasping fresh air. How could he, a grown man who knew what was important, be lured to the brink of disaster by his own self?

The Polish priest had spoken about Peter betraying Christ three times after swearing He could count on him. He'd never hear that sermon again without recalling how close he'd come to betraying his wife, his family, and his God. He had come far too close, too close.

The day was gray. Everybody was exhausted. Annie, who'd given most of her clothes to Claire, wore Kate's green sweater, her own blue jeans and her leather boots. She slumped in her seat. Joe restrained himself from patting her head.

"I called Mike last night and he'll help us chisel out carousel horse shapes and sell them over the Internet as starter projects to fathers who want to work with their kids. I'll start with junior college. I won't take off and leave you high and dry, Dad. We'll work together and repay Uncle Ted his money quick—we'll take the crab right out of his mouth."

Joe couldn't speak. It was like having a child who died come back to life. For that he thanked God, Whom he was otherwise too ashamed to address. He leaned back to rest his mind, counting ceiling tiles.

Stella walked to the waiting-room window for the third time. Ted snapped, "Stella, sit down. You're making me nervous."

Kate jumped up and stood in front of him. "Who do you think you are, disrespecting Stella like that? Can't she even move without your permission?" Ted's body straightened.

"You're acting like Babcia died or Leszek gunned down your family or Joe threw your money out the window," Kate continued. "How dare you talk to the best person in your life like that?"

Ted turned to Joe, "What's she talking' about? What's she doing?"

"Don't you blame me on Joe. I'm talking to you. People have waited on you your entire life. They did in Poland and we do in Detroit. If you sound the tiniest bit crabby everybody hops. And spoiled guy that you are, you expect it, even from God."

Joe started to "Now Kate—" her, but she stilled him with an upraised hand.

"Do you think anybody will care for us like we care for you? And you, who gets constant service, sits here whining like a spoiled baby." She towered over him and he pressed back in the molded chair, "Well, shame on you, I say. Shame on you."

Ted squinted from beneath his shaggy eyebrows. "I know Joe and you been good to me; and I'm not disrespecting Stella."

"No? Well, is there a new refrigerator in Stella's future? I don't think so. You're going to take your one loss out of a million pluses out on Stella and Joe, aren't you?"

Joe watched Stella open her mouth, but she seemed to think better of it too. She adjusted her skirt and sat back. Kate's stance demanded Ted look at her. "Did you pray things would turn out well on this trip?"

He replied with a nodded yes.

"And didn't most of the things you came for turn out better than expected?" Again, he nodded.

"Well, I never heard a six-year-old put out a longer wish-list than the one you gave Joe, but did anybody hear you thank him for the good he accomplished?" Open handed, Kate turned to her audience. They shook their heads, NO! They hadn't heard any thanks.

Ted assumed his basset-hound expression. "He knows, Joe knows. I'm leaving him what's left in America when I die. I don't have to say it."

Joe's head snapped back. You don't have to treat people right if you leave them a little money? What kind of thinking was that? Ted might as well have slapped him.

Kate kept at Ted. "You've had a marvelous trip, now haven't you? So, what's your problem?" She waited, arms crossed, mouth set, demanding an answer.

"You talk like losing ten thousand-dollars is nothing. We worked for that money."

"And we all heard you say to go ahead with the sting so Polish police could squash that scam. That part worked. Plus it got Claire out of jail, a bonus you never even thought of. You got more for your money than you hoped for, didn't you?"

"But he took chances and lost my money. Besides, I still don't know where to put what's left. That's what I'm thinking."

"You brought that money to risk, didn't you? But Joe tried to help and something went wrong, so we all have to suffer your pouting forever. Oh, lucky us. Well, I'm thinking God should zap your ungrateful self with a bolt of lightning, that's what I'm thinking." She'd hexed Ted with his own words and he sat there and took it. A laugh struggled up Joe's throat until Kate turned to him.

"And you, you found out what happened to Gienia. You drove us all over with nothing worse than a bruised tire and the dollars Uncle Ted wanted circulated are circulating. You got Leszek to make up with Stasiu and you got Claire out of jail, not to mention you risked our lives and we're all sitting here in one piece. So why are you counting tiles?"

Put that way, Joe didn't have a ready answer.

Stella's face lit up, "You're right. They shouldn't be carrying on, we've been blessed beyond gold. If they choose to behave like spoiled children they shouldn't affect us." She straightened herself and stood up.

"Kate, didn't the girls who cooked for us talk Leszek into trading two hectares for land by the highway to Tarnow so they could start their own restaurant? Those plots are full of marvelous fruit trees. I was thinking about that drying equipment the engineer from Food-Pro told K about. If they got that going and built a real restaurant, plus living quarters for the cook's family, they could preserve their own fruit, use some and sell the rest at the restaurant; plus they could process their neighbors' fruit. The others could peddle their own specialties through them and make their restaurant a stop worth taking a special trip for, don't you think?"

Stella had formulated a workable plan while the rest of them yapped. She'd done that ever since Joe could remember, but once again he stood before her, amazed.

"Those girls have a mixer, an American refrigerator, two stoves and husbands who can stencil walls," Kate said. "I'll bet they can get people out for a family meal."

Ted glared at her. "Real Poles don't waste money eating out. They'd sit there with spoiling food. Besides, they could use that land to store fertilizer." He slapped his knee decisively, "No, if they want to sell fertilizer I'll go for that. Otherwise, I'll give my money to the Polish church. They know where it's needed." His mouth turned down; he sat straight-backed and fierce eyed, defiant as an obnoxious child.

Joe jumped up. "Are you crazy? Did you slip back into the dark ages?" He struggled not to stutter. "Th-those people have been victimized by anybody who could get at them—tr-treated no better than slaves. And you, you who escaped to America, insult them by overlooking every dream they ever had?" Choking as he struggled to control himself, Joe said, "God didn't bless you with that money to mow over people. They deserve better from you, from me, from the world. If you won't treat them as free people, who will?" Breathless, he couldn't go on.

Ted wasn't out of steam yet. He hollered, "I don't understand. I don't know what to do. I don't get this investment stuff and you're not helping me." Heads in other sections began to turn. He lowered his voice. "The priests have education. Let them figure it out."

"God put you, Tadeusz Winowski, in a position to help and you know it."

"You can't tell me what to do. I don't have to leave you anything."

"Don't. I thought burying you would cost me, so I'm ahead anyway." The laughter of freedom bubbled to Joe's lips as he spoke. That was the truth and when he'd forgotten that he'd forgotten the man he intended to be, his sense of direction exploded around him like sunshine breaking through blinding sleet. The agony of soul he had suffered since the day he heard Ted had money, lifted. "If you want me around, forget the money. You treat me like somebody you know cares about you. If you don't I can get lost real quick." Ted glared back in silence.

"Leave me and my brothers a thousand dollars each so people don't think we did something awful to you," Joe said. "We're good men who've upheld the values you taught us. We deserve acknowledgment for that and that's all we need."

Ted scowled. "So that's all you want from me, a thousand dollars? Well what am I supposed to do with what's left?"

"Send some to Leszek to lend . . . I said lend to those young guys. Let them pay it back and help each other. The old guys can figure it out. They've been enforcers their entire lives. Then look around Hamtramck. Recognize people who did the right thing then got screwed when somebody badmouthed them. Let them know you know they deserved better. You old bucks think if you praise somebody they'll stop doing what's right and that's wrong. You rectify some of those wrongs and I'll stand beside you to your last breath."

Kate stood beside Joe and slipped her arm around him. "You and me too, Pal."

"So you don't want anything from me but a thousand dollars? That's it?" Ted's tone softened.

"I'm blessed with a woman who hasn't stabbed me to death with a dirty fork yet. It's time for me to back her up. Annie says she'll help me pay you back this summer so you won't have anything to holler about. Then I'm celebrating my wife, my kids, and being born in America. I'm shaking the cobwebs out of my head and rethinking my life. That's what's right for me. If you need help, I'll help you too."

Ted's lip protruded. Joe knew by the slump of his shoulders he'd folded.

Out of the silence, Stella said, "My share of that money will get those young women started. Besides, I saw new churches all over Poland. They're doing fine. If you want to donate to churches I'll give the same amount to St. Florian's in Hamtramck. They do good work and our people in Hamtramck need help too."

Kate whispered to Joe, "She who must be obeyed has spoken."

"But how am I going to tell folks why I'm leaving them money?"

Kate patted Ted's slumping shoulder, "You tell us who you think deserves it and Stella and I will write a letter for each one, whether they're in Hamtramck or Poland. We could pass the money out now or do it after you both die. That's up to you. Anyway, whoever you pick will really be surprised."

Annie's eyes had gotten larger as the conversation about Ted's money went on. She said, to nobody in particular,

"Well, I guess I didn't make the cut today."

Ted's head jerked back, "No, no, you're number one. I just didn't say it. We're not forgetting you. You come pick us up, Stella and me, tomorrow morning 10:00 sharp, and $50,000 goes into an account at Huntington Bank in your name; so if we die or get goofy, you've got it. That's for classes only." He waved his finger at her. "No pizzas, and you have to earn the money for your own shoes because you still need to understand where money comes from."

Annie jumped up and kissed Ted on top of his head. "Thank you, Uncle Ted, I'll put every penny you give me to good use. I'll shovel your walk, get you a drink, screw in your light bulbs—anything you dream up I'll do. Just ask me."

Ted grinned. "Well, I sure would like a map of our trip, just the places we went and maybe the countries around us so I can show my friends where we've been without everyplace else getting in the way. Do you think you can do that?"

Annie walked over and picked up an airline magazine with its map. "Let me look at this. I think I can draw what you want." She plopped down to look over the airlines far too busy map.

Nobody knew what to do from then. They all watched Annie as if she was about to pull a cat out of a hat. Joe looked around. Others began to filter into the area. Suddenly, Joe spotted a familiar figure in a white shirt and tie carrying a clip-board walking toward him. It was K. Shocked Joe said, "How did you get in here?

"They didn't want to let me in, but I know the head of security. I lifted an inspector's pass, picked up his clipboard and walked right in. I'll slip it back where I got it when I leave but I wanted to hear first-hand what you think of all you've seen."

Grateful to change the subject, they all talked at once, thanking K for the use of his car and the information he'd gotten for them. K was lonesome and he'd come to chat; and they needed time to digest all that had happened. He was probably the most welcome man standing in Okecie Airport, Joe thought.

K's interest brought out their best. They passed over the lost money and told of Babcia and the cousins, and the heartening experiences they'd each had. As they competed to entertain him, their memories dropped into place. They each Claire they saw hope, tempered with the reality of a long, hard struggle ahead.

"Yes, yes, I see that too. Poles tell me this is their best chance in a hundred-years. They want to be active citizens. Listening is exciting here, even as I watch some of the old commies crawl back into power."

Joe said, "Don't forget, those are the guys with experience. At least the people can insist on a democratic direction."

Ted interrupted, "K. can you let Annie use your clip board? She's working on a map of our trip for me." K handed it over and Annie placed a slip of paper Kate had just handed her and bowed her head to the task; with Kate and Stella to advise her.

K said, "Yesterday a banker explained to me how low interest loans could buy opportunity and discourage recklessness. If you financed a trust fund in your community; you could insist each borrower help another small business get going, like Greenam does in India. It could operate with a support system fostering small businesses, without banking restraints. The old bucks would have to enforce collections, but those old boys are experienced enforcers."

Ted nodded, "Its good we got you to talk to. Stella was thinking about that. Can we call you later?"

"If I'm here I'd be glad to help, but last night I wrote and asked my girl to marry me. I could call, but she's the kind who likes to see contracts in writing."

There was a moment's silence, then the women engulfed him in congratulations, as if his girl had accepted his proposal. Kate sounded so pleased to hear about the coming marriage Joe realized his must not be in as dire straits as he'd thought.

"I'd been holding back thinking what if it doesn't work out? But your family made me realize nobody's perfect. If Winowskis can make things work, I can."

Kate slapped Joe on the back, hard. "You can sure say that about us."

K said, "You're all feisty, but you'll let things go to get along. I figure I can do that."

Stella patted K's arm, "You're Polish. You can get along with anybody."

"I was thinking, would we like the same things? Then you made me see I come from people who aren't easy to live with, but we're loving and we're loyal. So I wrote." He pulled a letter out of his pocket and handed it to Kate. "Would you mail this when you get to Detroit? If it goes on the plane with you it'll get there quicker."

Kate took the letter from him and carefully placed it in the front of her purse. The absurdity of their fussing at each other inspiring anybody to propose marriage stunned Joe.

K turned to him, "If she says yes I'll want to get a month to six weeks off next summer. When you have time off, would you come cover for me during your break? I've got a nice one bedroom apartment and you'd like the people in my office."

Shocked, Joe said, "Your company wouldn't hire me for six weeks."

"I called and asked my boss last night. I told him you taught accounting, did taxes on the side and you speak Polish better than me. They'd do anything to get me to commit to another two years here."

Joe laughed, thinking no way will this happen. "Sure, if your girl agrees to marry you, I'll cover. My wife keeps telling me life should be an adventure."

He turned to wink at Kate, supposing the entire conversation was pie in the sky, but Kate threw her arms around him and started carrying on about writing articles on Poland for Americans. She was treating this far-fetched-fantasy as a promise. Well, if it made talking to each other easier for today, why not go along, he thought?

Annie spoke up, "I've got Uncle Ted's map sketched out. I'll do it neatly when we get home but you two aren't coming back here without me."

Ted reached over and took the map from Annie. He nodded, and smiled as he folded it and put it in his jacket pocket. "This is just what I wanted. I'll hold onto this."

Joe said, "Annie, you'll need to work next summer. And, what about Mike?"

She shrugged. "Oh, I live in America, I'll figure out the money somehow. And, I have to think harder about this lifetime commitment thing, you know."

Joe looked at her in wonder. Ted said, "Ship your equipment here, Joe, and when you come you can teach them to use it right. I'll set you up new and better in that building you bought back home."

By the time they boarded the plane they were all talking. Joe stepped back to watch. If the girl didn't marry K none of this would happen. But today, at this moment, they had something to talk about. They could mend their fences in the name of love. If they never got to Poland again, they'd live, but this unlikely development gave them a positive focus. How many families have found the strength to go on together on the strength of less likely hopes? Wasn't that what faith was about, getting through the bad days with hope in your heart? Joe sent up a prayer of thanks as he stood there fixing this moment in his memory.

In that instant, his family appeared as he'd imagined them when he'd planned the trip. These people he loved stood together, deluded perhaps, but for this magical moment they were united and he knew, he knew in his heart of hearts, the Winowskis were once again ready to face life's challenges—with the help of God, of course.

THE END.

About the Author

I was born in Michigan, the middle child with 4 siblings who urged me to try new things. Michigan State University prepared me to teach military dependents for our Department of Defense Dependent's Schools. I met my husband, Bob Knych, in Germany. We joined forces in work and in life by raising five children, and striving to educate military dependents.

From 1961-1994 we worked for DoDDS, our military dependents' schools overseas. Bob, our children, and I had an opportunity to visit our family's roots. In Ireland we were greeted with warmth and enthusiasm. Though Ireland hadn't modernized at the rate the U.S. had, families had high hopes for their future. We felt good about my extended family.

Bob's relatives were trapped behind the Iron Curtain. As part of a military community we couldn't get visas. Then suddenly, in the early '70's, visas became possible. Bob came back from his first visit with his parents and announced he'd drive Jenny II, Mike, John, and me into Poland during our Christmas break. From 1972-1994 we drove into Poland fifteen times.

In our early visits we saw they were behind times and limited by their government. As the years passed, we witnessed their modernization and increased distance from Russian bureaucrats.

After The Wall dividing Germany from their communist cousins came down Polish cousins stayed with us for months at a time, working for friends who tipped them with goods no longer needed. They gave away or sold those items back home.

Sitting around our table, preparing bright young men to cope with the demands of capitalism was great fun. Friends came over to discuss how to invest and care for their money. As trained mechanics, Bob's cousins bought used cars they drove into Poland, repaired, and sold them for a profit. Or they did until swindlers so polluted the used car business they couldn't sell the last car they'd imported. Though my plot is fiction, I included some of those true experiences to give my novel it's grounding in truth.

We helped those cousins buy washers and dryers during our military draw-down. They connected with Polish truckers who picked through their treasures for payment, so carrying goods back to Poland was a plus for them. When guards decided the American appliances were stolen, they had to bribe them to let them pass. They started a laundromat that failed for lack of hot water. For us, who'd spent our working lives helping others, we were drunk with hopeful ideas. Bob and I retired in 1994. Our adventures were over, yet we'd lived through extraordinary days and had remarkable stories to tell. I had the setting for a novel; I just had to figure out a plot and learn to write.

At the Bread Loaf Writers' Conference in Vermont. William Leaderer, who wrote *The Ugly American* assured me I had strong material for a novel. Meg Files, a Tucson novelist who ran a writers' conference every spring for Pima Community College invited me to take her advanced writers course. I took two classes a year and time and again, people asked questions that helped me redirected my aim.

And so, finally, this novel is ready to reach out to others with curiosity about their own immigrant connections. I hope you enjoyed taking this journey with me.

Carol O'Donnell-Knych